LOOKING DEATH IN THE FACE

Reeve's eyes caught a hump of motion a few yards down the shoreline and he wandered toward a small object draped in scum. It rolled forward and backward with the waves. He bent down and with both hands scooped up a heavy ball in his hands. Dripping with algae, the ball looked like a deeply pitted rock, perhaps a geode of some kind.

A slopping noise sounded behind him. He spun around. There, moving slowly toward him, was a whitish upright figure carrying a sack over its shoulder. An orthong, by the Lord above. Reeve froze, staring. It wore a long belted black coat that glistened in the sun like a chitinous shell. The coat parted in front to show a snowy white hide.

It had no face.

His heart knocked against his chest wall. The creature began loping toward him in great strides that brought it to Reeve quicker than he could have turned and taken even one step to flee. It stood a full head taller than he, and there seemed to be two eyes peering at him from the deep ridges of its face . . . and in the next instant, the creature extruded its one-inch claws and slashed down the front of Reeve's jacket, slicing the material and skimming Reeve's skin in a cut he hardly felt except for the rush of cold air. Reeve staggered backward and fell. . . .

KAY KENYON

RIFT

BANTAM BOOKS

New York Toronto London Sydney Auckland

RIFT

A Bantam Spectra Book / September 1999

SPECTRA and the portrayal of a boxed "s" are trademarks of
Bantam Books, a division of Random House, Inc.

ISBN 0-553-58023-X

Published simultaneously in the United States and Canada

Bantam Books are published by Bantam Books, a division of
Random House, Inc. Its trademark, consisting of the words
"Bantam Books" and the portrayal of a rooster, is Registered in
U.S. Patent and Trademark Office and in other countries. Marca
Registrada. Bantam Books, 1540 Broadway, New York, New York
10036.

PRINTED IN THE UNITED STATES OF AMERICA

WCD   10 9 8 7 6 5 4 3 2 1

For Matthew

ACKNOWLEDGMENTS

Acknowledgments and heartfelt thanks go to:

My husband, Thomas Overcast, for his unflagging support, encouragement, and good humor throughout the journey; to my editor, Anne Lesley Groell, for the fine-tuning and final shaping that made this a better book; to my agent, Donald Maass, for his confidence in me and his enthusiasm for this story; to Dr. J. Michael Brown, Chairman of the University of Washington Geophysics Department, for his review of my manuscript and his marvelous ability to explain geophysics to an English major—he carries no responsibility for the times (few, I hope) when I have taken liberties with strictly possible geology and chemistry; to my long-time friend and physician, Dr. Robert Bettis, for his guidance on physiological effects of high carbon dioxide environments; to Tom Weissmuller for sharing his considerable expertise on hand-to-hand fighting; and finally, to my son Matt Balser of the Redmond, Washington, fire department for advice on my characters' traumatic injuries—which seem to be the price for high adventure.

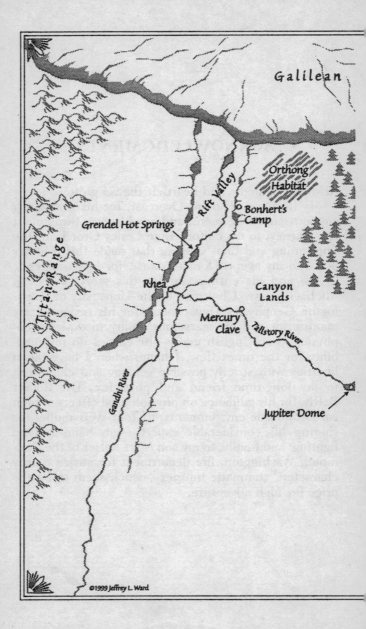

Galilean

Titan Range

Rift Valley

Orthong
Habitat

Bonhert's
Camp

Grendel Hot Springs

Rhea

Canyon
Lands

Mercury
Clave

Tallstory River

Gandhi River

Jupiter Dome

©1999 Jeffrey L. Ward

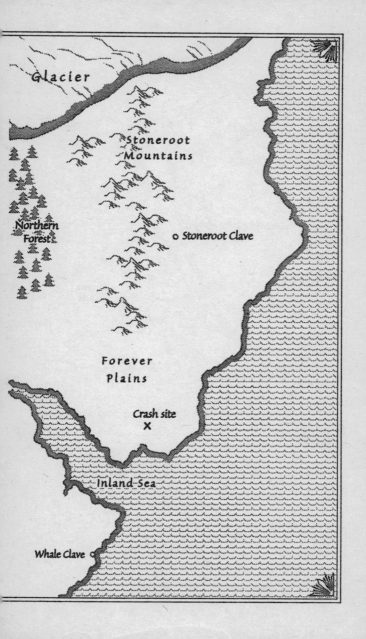

1

COLDWALK

1

Reeve Calder watched from two hundred miles overhead as the planetary winds smeared the ash cloud eastward. In its quiet violence, it was hard to imagine the deafening blast of volcanic debris and the hurtling pyroclastic flows that must have scoured the nearby tundra. From Reeve's vantage point on Station, the eruption was a mere bulge of smoke, unfolding like a silver flower. The landscape it grew upon was a shifting tapestry of reds and greens, the central and contrary hues of Reeve's home world, Lithia, a planet he had never set foot on.

He grabbed the handholds on Station's hull and pulled himself toward the solar array, a favorite perch devoid of Station viewports. Moving slowly to avoid making clunking noises against the hull, he threaded his tether through the clamps as he went, floating free but holding fast. Bad enough if they caught him outside again, unauthorized. Worse yet if they cited him for a coldwalk without mag boots—a fine piece of safety equipment if you didn't mind announcing to the entire crew where you were and what you were doing.

As Station came round to the sun's glare, the flank

of the great wheel lit up, stimulating his visor to darken. In the shadow of the solar array, he settled himself in and turned to face the deeps of space. He recalled the times his father, Cyrus Calder, had taken him on coldwalks and talked of the stars, the known and unknown worlds, and the adventures of the great Voyage On. Someday, his father had always said, they would regain starflight, escaping their Station exile, and find the true home, the home Lithia never could be.

When Reeve was a child, he'd tried to imagine those icy pricks of light being stars like the sun, and tried to believe in the worlds warmed by them. But when the view came planetside and he looked down on Lithia, he thought there would be adventures enough right there. In truth, at twenty-four, he still thought so. Though Lithia had grown treacherous—though its volcanic vents spewed poisons into the atmosphere, though the colony had collapsed—it was at least a familiar peril, unlike the stars, with their abyssal terrors. So Lithia, familiar and yet utterly strange, lured him outside to watch its grand rotations. He would dream of what it might be like to run across a patch of solid ground; to look up at mountaintops and splash through channels of running water; to match wits with the intruder orthong, perhaps infiltrating their chaotic forests to trade; to fight the enclavers, if need be, blasting their assaults of spears with all the technology of Station; and to walk bareheaded under the sun.

But sometimes, when he came back through the air lock, Station security would be waiting for him, exasperated if they were friends, irate if they weren't, but always piling on the demerits and hauling him off to face his father. Taking an unwelcome break from his lab work, Cyrus Calder would sometimes ask, "What were you doing out there, Reeve?" And Reeve would answer, "Watching the stars." It was a desperate lie, told to a father who believed in the stars, whose research was all bent to that end, while his son kept watch on a piece of dirt. Banished to his sleep station, Reeve would fling himself on his bed, miserable for the lie. Sometimes, at times like this, his father's lab assistant, Marie Dussault, would come by to talk—Marie, who believed in letting youngsters find their own path, who gave Reeve planetary colorscapes to adorn his bunk walls and never let her boss berate his son for rising no higher than electrician, third class. It was Marie who spoke for him at disciplinary hearings, her gray hair giving her some authority with Captain Bonhert—though Marie was all for the stars, for the Voyage On, and Bonhert was for reclaiming Lithia. It divided the crew, those separate visions.

Reterraforming, Bonhert's faction said, was all a matter of geoengineering. The geo project could slow the mantle's convection and deep mantle volcanism by dissipating mantle heat. Geo nanotech was the key. Most people clung to this view, decrying Cyrus Calder's crackpot starship idea.

But to Cyrus the majority viewpoint was patently foolish. Lithia had sent humanity packing and unraveled nine hundred years of terraforming in a geologic instant. With a tectonic shrug, she had forced their evacuation to the space station—for the few it could accommodate—and year by year became more inhospitable. And as for geoengineering schemes, Lithia would churn nanotech into slag as easily as it converted iron to sauce in its infernal depths. You could try to battle a planet's tectonic forces, Cyrus always said, but you would lose.

Reeve watched as the great continent of Galileo hove into view, its terran-green Forever Plains veined in blue rivers. And there, cleaving the continent in two, the Rift Valley, that colossal fracture zone of old and new volcanism. Across the land, overlaid in a lacy froth, were the reddish-brown outbreaks of the world's preferred flora. Like a snake preparing to shed its skin, the first cracks revealed the new coat beneath, with its unterran red, its unruly growths daring to thrive where Earth-based grafts had failed.

North of the Rift Valley, a smudge of lavender marked the domain of the orthong. The irregular, spreading patch of purples and blues defined a habitat that, over the sixty years since orthong arrival, had grown to be visible from Station with the naked eye. Station telescopes showed the alien habitat as ropy masses, hexagonal lattices, and walls of faceted protrusions, often in shades of lavender, punctuated by vivid yellow, blue, and white. Wherever they had come from, the orthong had brought their flora with them. And underneath this canopy they themselves remained hidden except in glimpses and what little might be learned from the sporadic radio transmissions of the human enclaves. But radio transmissions were more and more infrequent as the claves drifted into ignorance and savagery. What Station learned of the orthong from claver radio was less than scientific, along the lines of, *If you meet an orthong, kill it before it kills you.* Still, the clavers had seen the orthong, and even traded, guardedly, while Station remained utterly isolated.

He gazed along the slope of the hull to catch a last glimpse of the continent where orthong roamed . . . but a movement on the wheel itself caught his attention. A coldwalker, like himself. In fact, two of them. The helmet had restricted his peripheral vision and now the figures were close enough to notice him. He balled himself up behind the array as tightly as he could, given the suit's bulkiness, and cursed his luck in choosing this exact time to be out-Station. Switching on his receiver, he scanned all channels. For now, they weren't talking. They were twenty feet away, partially eclipsed by the space telescope's primary mirror, but he could still make out, in a flash of sun, BONHERT, G.

on one man's sleeve. And neither of them wore mag boots, either; they were merely tethered, doing their job—whatever it was—quietly.

A rivulet of acid etched into his stomach. Dear Lord, please let them finish in a hurry and *turn in the other direction* for whatever they had to do. For a few minutes more Reeve had the fine advantage of being sunward of them, and therefore hard to spot with his white suit against white hull. But: *Bonhert*. Damn and damn, to get busted by the Captain himself would mean waste collection duty for weeks, or worse. . . .

Bonhert was working out a kink in the other walker's tether, or rather, cutting the tether. But that couldn't be right. No, there it was again, a flash of a small knife—and by the time Reeve's brain stumbled into gear, the tether was floating free and Bonhert was shoving the person off. Reeve's muscles spasmed into action, unfolding him from his crouch, a hopelessly slow movement as the figure glided toward him. There would just be time for him to kick out his line and meet the castaway. He staggered up, and then his face plate was two feet from Tina Valejo's surprised face. He reached out and she flailed to grasp his hand, but she was slipping beyond reach, cord trailing. Reeve kicked off, playing out his tether, but it was too late. She was moving away, with the radio still silent and she mouthing her shouts to him while he shouted back, "I'll get help!" Words that filled his helmet, going nowhere. They'd send the scooter out after her. He turned back to see Bonhert disappearing around the curve of Station.

Reeve was on the com, hailing station ops. "This is Reeve Calder, out-Station; send help, emergency. Over."

A long pause and then, "This had better *not* be Reeve Calder out-Station. What the hell?" It was Brit Nunally, third cousin, and no friend of his.

Reeve blurted out: "Tina Valejo is adrift. She's falling away; get a scooter in lock four. This is an emergency. And yes, sorry, I'm unauthorized out here."

"*Tina Valejo* is unauthorized out there. If you're playing games, Calder, you're fertilizer. We'll feed you to the ponics, hear me?"

"No game—she was pushed off, he tried to kill her, and she's going to be scared shitless, so *hurry*. Please."

A pause. Com crackled to life again. "You are on your way in-Station, Calder. State your nearest lock."

"Lock three, Brit."

"Sir, to you."

Screwing up his face, he made himself parrot: "Sir." And while they were playing soldier on parade, Tina was drifting into the void, and hope to the Lord there were no knife rips in her suit.

"By the way, Calder, who pushed Tina off? Looks like you're the only one out there."

Reeve held back an instant. Could say, *Station captain, that's who.* But he wouldn't. He punched in the command at lock three, looking for Captain Bonhert, who was nowhere in sight. Opening the hatch, he hauled himself into the air lock, sweat lubricating his skin like a sleeve of grease in a piston. After a standard count of five he started to unbuckle the fasteners and ripped off the helmet, just as the panel signaled air pressure and just as the inner hatch swung open. Station guards hauled him into the corridor, making him trip over the suit leggings still clinging around his ankles.

As he fell to his knees, the guards—Kurt Falani and Lin Pao—backed away to let him pull off the suit. At that moment an earsplitting roar screamed down the corridor, and Station shuddered in a way Reeve had never felt before. Alarms clanged. Kurt and Lin Pao dashed away, leaving Reeve on his hands and knees when the second explosion hit. It roared from deep around Station bend, a sickening blast, rippling the corridor under his knees. Screams echoed down main corridor, now filling with black chemical smoke and running crew.

Reeve coughed as the acrid fumes lanced his throat. There were air packs at emergency stations in the corridor, but everyone was vying for them. Reeve scuttled back to the hatch, punching in pressurization commands and trying to hold his breath until the green light flashed. He scrambled into the air lock, pulling the hatch shut. As Station resounded with thudding feet and muffled shouts, he crammed himself back into his space suit, fixed his helmet in place, and opened the inner hatch again, making his way by the bulkhead rail in the direction of his emergency station in electrical systems, one deck down. Pandemonium met him. Up ahead, a crowd was hammering against the fire wall, which must have slammed across the corridor, separating them from Shuttle Bay One. A vicious, shoving melee ensued. Reeve turned back to try the emergency access panel to the lower decks, but as the panel released, fingers of flames leapt through.

Any minute it would get better. Any minute sprinklers would kick in, fans would vent the smoke, crew would *contain* this thing. They'd drilled for these situations. Fire, explosions, orthong raids—they'd drilled for them all. Everyone had their role and backup role. Every system had two backups. Station couldn't fail.

Another explosion quaked the deck. He couldn't hear it, but he felt it, felt Station heave. Rushing now, he headed toward station ops, lights flickering in the corridor. Then they died, and he stared through his visor at utter blackness. Groping at the bulkhead with his gloved hand, he shuffled forward, calling up a mental map of the corridor, counting hatches and servicing panels and bulkhead fittings. He tripped over something. A crew member was down, but there was no time to stop. He plunged on toward ops, thinking they'd need his suit in there. Somebody had to stay conscious, had to *control* this thing. On com, he scanned all channels, saying, "Station command, Reeve Calder here, delta corridor, heading to ops, over." Static answered him, and he shuffled on, fighting off cold dread, intent on not overshooting the door.

And then he was standing in front of the operations center. The door was open—Lord, open—the room lit with the strobing light of bursting electronics and dozens of small electric fires. Abandoned. He swallowed, felt the bile trace a groove down to his gut. He heard his voice cracking: "Reeve Calder here, outside ops. Ops is abandoned. Anybody copy?" Static on all channels. Again: "Calder here, anybody working this mess? Anybody?"

And broken up, barely audible, he heard: *"Get down to Bay Two, Reeve. You have twenty seconds. Haul ass, now!"*

"Marie?"

"Haul!"

He hauled. Stumbling over fallen crew and debris, he raced as fast as the bulky suit allowed, guiding himself with his right hand along the corridor guide rail, scanning all channels, his voice breaking. "Cyrus, Cyrus, this is Reeve, where are you? Get to Bay Two, Dad, they're loading the shuttle at Bay Two. . . ." His mind began tumbling out of control—they were abandoning Station. Lord of Worlds, Station was dying. "Cyrus!" he called, again and again. Where was the bay? He turned in confusion. Then, from behind him, someone was dragging him sideways. He yanked away, struggling—until, in the gloom, he saw emergency lights pulsing, showing BAY TWO, and Marie Dussault was pulling him across the bay to the ramped hatch opening of the shuttle, its running lights sparkling in preflight mode.

The hatch slammed behind them.

"Secure!" Marie shouted.

"Go, go, go!" someone yelled.

But the cabin was nearly empty. Only five people, including him and Marie.

"No!" Reeve shouted. He ripped off his helmet. "There's room for more!"

Dana Hart was next to him, and she swung to face him. "No time! Station's going to blow."

"No!" Reeve threw back, making his way forward to the cockpit.

And in an instant, he was thrown back against the empty flight seats as the shuttle lurched out of Station. A violent pitch of the craft and the sound of wrenching metal registered in every cell of Reeve's body. Behind him someone yelled, "She's breaking up!" And then someone else: "Oh my God. Station . . . Station . . . it's blown to pieces. Lord God."

Reeve turned to Marie, his voice a hoarse plea: "Cyrus . . . is he onboard?"

Beside him, Marie's lined face was ghoulishly white. A long, slow shake of her head confirmed his fears. "No. He didn't make it."

In the gloom of the cabin, someone was sobbing. Overhead, a cabin screen projected the unthinkable: A huge section of Station lay twisted into an odd angle, ejecting smoke and debris. And even as they watched, Station quaked and sundered, separating from the central hub casing. Reeve heard a moan escape from his chest as an incandescent explosion engulfed the hub and remaining structure, obliterating Station and life itself. The flash of Station's demise reflected off a second shuttle, receding fast, downward to Lithia.

Over the speakers came the panicked shout: "We're hit. . . . Secure all gear, we're going into a tumble. . . ."

Reeve buckled in as the shuttle fell into a gut-wrenching yaw. It was all over. This was the end of it. Now they would follow the Station to oblivion. Outside, the hull roared with reentry burn and the craft shuddered endlessly, filling his ears with thunder. He never knew death would be so loud or so welcome.

1

Day one. The smells were all wrong: sulfur, engine oil, humus, and putrefaction. Reeve opened his eyes, peering through a blur at a small, gold disk that at last resolved into focus. A yellow bird perched on its nest, pecking at a bit of meat clutched in its talons. It cocked its head, shifting its weight from one stick-foot to the other. When Reeve tried to move, he found he was pinned down by a metal panel pressing against his legs. Sunlight flooded through a rent in the cabin while the smell of burning fuel threaded its way up his nostrils.

He closed his eyes again to fend off the return of memory. But it was all coming back, it was all true—the roaring descent, his arms shaking as he gripped the seat, a concussive landing, and something glancing off the back of his head. They were down, on planet. And oh God, Station . . .

Something was wrong with that bird. It wasn't sitting in a nest, it was perched on someone's dark brown hair. Dana's, sitting there in front of him. She didn't bother to fend off the creature.

He tried to pull up his knees to leverage the panel

off him. The bird took flight as Reeve heaved the hull
section off and staggered to his feet. Beside him lay
the bodies of his companions. Dana Hart, Marie Dussault, and the three others. Struggling forward to the
cockpit, he found the shattered remains of the cabin
and its occupants. A drift of smoke carried the smell of
burning hull composites and fuel, but the fires were
sputtering out. They'd been down a while. He could
have burned to death. Maybe he should have.

Reeve made his way out the gaping hole in the starboard side of the craft, squinting against the light.

Everywhere, cloaks of green cascaded before him.
The wind rustled millions of leaves. All green, green,
in more shades than seemed possible: bright apple-green, chartreuse, pale yellow-green, deep emerald,
and, in profusion, a lacy moss-green. In the corridors
between the trees, a shadowy blue-green gave way to
distant black.

The shuttle had landed in a swamp. Black water
lapped around tree trunks, glinting here and there
from sun refracted through the festooned moss. The
air smelled brackish and foul. He sat on a tree stump,
boots sunk into the murky water. After a while, he felt
the first sobs come lurching up from his chest.

Eventually, he was able to think again. He stood,
realizing he had to leave the shuttle, and maybe
quickly—enclavers might have seen the craft come
down. He climbed back into the shuttle to hunt for
weapons, but there was nothing, not even a knife.
Then he remembered that the space suit he was still
wearing had a tool pocket. Inside he found a folded
titanium blade bristling with attachments. He stripped
off the suit and substituted a padded flight jacket from
one of the stowage bins, slipping the knife in his
pocket. Rummaging through the bin, he found a field
pack containing a med kit, water purification tabs, and
two breathers. Without taking time to apply a
breather, he combed the rest of the ship for every

breather and food pouch he could find, cramming them into the pack. He'd need the breathers, eventually. He could smell some of the poisons in the air— the sulfur if not the high carbon dioxide—but it was long-term effects he must avoid. For now, he was in a hurry.

He knelt beside Marie's body and reached out to touch her face. *You should have lived, Marie.* Sunlight fell on her hands, and he wished she could have had that instant of sun-on-skin. He brushed aside long wisps of her iron-gray hair.

At his touch, Marie stirred, and whispered something incoherent.

Marie. Lord of Worlds, she was still alive.

Her eyelids fluttered. Blood welled from a gash in her forehead.

"We're down, Marie," he said. "We crashed." Digging into the med kit, he grabbed a bandage and bound it around her head. Then he held her hand until she opened her eyes.

"My arm . . . ," she whispered.

He helped her shift her weight and gently pulled her arm into a normal position. She groaned.

"We've got to get away from the shuttle. Can you walk?"

She struggled to her feet with his help, but slumped against him. He sat her down at the edge of the opening, then jumped out, and scooped her up in his arms. She was heavy, but they had to move out.

He headed for a patch of solid ground and laid her down, propped against a tree.

"Who's alive?" she asked.

"No one. We're the only ones that made it."

She licked her lips, looking stunned. He had to think. What, by the Lord of Worlds, were they going to do? Then, realizing he would never have another chance to grab supplies off the shuttle, he decided to make one more quick trip inside.

Cautioning Marie to remain silent, he made his way back. They'd need more breathers; in this stew of carbon dioxide and sulfur, a breather might last only a few days. As he entered the wreck, the bird swooped past him to settle onto an upended flight seat. Despite his hurry, Reeve kept looking at the bird. He was stuffing another pack with extra breathers and food—and all the while looking at the first live nonhuman creature he had ever seen. The bird's glossy feathers gave way to a speckled down on its underside. It trembled now and then, and on closer inspection looked mottled in an unhealthy way. In the grand collapse of terran populations, perhaps this was all that remained: the ragged, palsied, and infirm.

A moan erupted from the cabin. Reeve swung around. He picked his way around the debris until he found where the sound was coming from. It was Grame Lauterbach, second chief of electronic systems. Not dead. *Reeve, you fool, to make that mistake again.* He did a quick survey and found that Grame had a major chest wound and a badly lacerated right leg. Reeve opened a med kit, thinking to bind Grame's injuries, but what was the point? The man was dying. Grame stirred and tried to speak.

"Don't talk, Grame, it's OK, you'll be OK."

Grame's voice came out thinly: "Reeve?"

"Yes, it's me. You're hurt, Grame. Try not to move."

"OK." Grame closed his eyes, breathing noisily. Reeve left him for a moment to check every other body, carefully this time.

All dead, he was certain.

Eventually Grame opened his eyes again. "Your father," he rasped. "Cyrus. Is he onboard?"

"No." Reeve held the thought at bay, not able to think about it now.

"He should have made it." Little bubbles of blood appeared at the edges of Grame's nose and mouth.

"Yeah."

"Could've seen the *ship*, you see?" Grame appeared to smile, but it might have been a grimace of pain. "Could've seen the stars after all."

He was delirious, Reeve decided. The man was going to die. What should he do? He couldn't move him, but he couldn't stay here, either.

"Reeve."

"Yes. I'm here."

"Listen now, boy."

"I'm listening, Grame."

Grame's watery eyes stared in his general direction. "You got to hurry. Get to Bonhert, save yourself."

"Shh. Just try to rest, Grame."

"No, you can't rest! You got seventy days and a long walk. Get to Bonhert. Then you can go along."

"Go along?"

He reached for Reeve's arm. "To the stars. The stars."

"Just rest, Grame. It'll be OK." God, what could he *do*? Grame was hurt bad, and Reeve knew so damnably little that could help him.

"No, listen, you dumb pup!" Grame's jaw trembled. "Don't think I'm rummy, boy. The ship's coming, the generation ship. We never told folks, but it's on its way. Been coming, all these years." He closed his eyes a moment, stifling a moan. Then: "Bonhert didn't want us to tell. Didn't want the damn Reterraformers to make converts of the new ship's crew . . . persuade them to stay . . . so we kept it secret."

Ship? Reeve bent in closer, concentrating. *Ship, did he say?*

Eyes still closed, Grame's voice came more faintly: "They might want to stay, see? Lots of people are afraid of the stars, Reeve, don't want to drift out there in space. People think, let's stay on Lithia and get her whipped back into shape, but Lithia, she's a goner, Reeve. We—all the science team—we knew we couldn't fix Lithia."

"But the geo project!"

"No, no, just a front. To cover our tracks." A spume of blood gushed from the man's mouth, and he took several desperate breaths. His words came out in a harsh whisper: "Just . . . a front. We were working on Bonhert's scheme. To kill her, so the ship wouldn't stay."

"Kill who?"

"Lithia, you damn fool, Lithia . . ." His voice was so faint now that Reeve had to bend close. Grame's breath was dreadful.

"Kill Lithia?"

"With the mole. It's the only way. So the ship'll take us . . . rid of this hellhole for good. Just never tell . . . the ship's people." His eyes grew bright for a moment. "We got to kill her . . . but, see, they might not think so. So promise . . . you'll never tell."

Reeve opened his mouth to promise, but instead he asked, "Where is Bonhert?"

Grame had slumped over. Reeve bent closer to his face.

"The Rift," Grame whispered. "The Rift . . ."

"Where we were going to set up terraforming?"

Grame nodded. The words came out on his fetid breath: "That's it. . . . Get there, Reeve. . . . Save yourself." He sucked his breath in like he couldn't get enough. He was bleeding to death, and nothing could save him.

The scrawny bird flew to a gash in the top of the shuttle, pausing on the ripped hull, then flying off. Reeve closed his eyes a moment, allowing weariness to enfold him. He heard layer upon layer of sound: the gentle susurration of wind through the nets of hanging moss, the chirping and whistling of a few birds and . . . a distant shout.

Reeve's attention snapped back in an instant. He clambered outside, trying to identify where the noise came from, but the voices filtered in from all sides.

Grame, my God, Grame was still alive. . . . But clavers were closing in. He couldn't carry both Grame and Marie. He began backing up, away from the shuttle, and then turned and ran. Where was Marie, where had he left her? He ran on, splashing through the water, then saw the small hillock of mud and Marie waiting there. He scrambled over to her, shouldering the pack and whispering, "Clavers. We've got to get away from here. Can you walk?"

Lord, he was abandoning Grame. He'd made his decision, an ugly one. Helping Marie to her feet, he used a branch to obscure their footprints as they staggered backward into the shallow water. The voices were clear now, dozens of clavers shouting, but still muffled in the distance. He and Marie set out, away from the shuttle, moving as fast as they could, with Marie leaning on Reeve's arm. The marsh went on and on, trees beyond trees, until in the distance all merged into green-black muck. Slogging on, he searched for any place that could offer shelter or camouflage, but it was all water, moss, and spindly trees.

In another moment the voices rose in excited clamor, announcing that the clavers had found the shuttle. An eerie ululation pierced the swamp, sending a new chill to Reeve's heart. He had never heard a scream like that in all his by-the-book, ordered Station life. Finding a large stump of a tree, he and Marie huddled together, afraid to move. He could see vague movements by the shuttle, but it was impossible to judge numbers through the webs of moss. Then again, whether there were four or forty, it hardly mattered— he and Marie were outmatched in every respect.

It would not be long before they came looking for survivors; for all they might be barbarians, they weren't stupid.

"Marie," Reeve whispered. "We've got to find somewhere to hide." He pulled her along, but slowly, to be as quiet as possible in the water. As they waded onward, the shouting dimmed. Ahead of them, the sun speared through the green maze, creating tunnels of light, wondrous even in this extremity. The glowing chartreuse of leaves, the flash of blue in the water, reflecting planetary sky . . . it was a wonderland. But one devoid of shelter.

Their only hope was a hollowed-out stump, but none were big enough for two. They'd have to separate. He found a stump for Marie, ensconcing her in its crumbling interior and covering her with an insulated blanket from the pack. "Will you be all right?" he asked.

She flashed a crooked grin. "Get lost."

Reaching into the pack, he pulled out a breather. "Use this."

Leaving Marie for now, he set out to find his own bivouac, taking care to remember where he'd left her, and finally choosing a hollow snag, plugging the entry hole with an armload of moss. Leaning against the spongy bark, he felt tiny somethings moving behind his back, but not even that could distract him from the sound of claver screams. He *hoped* they were claver screams. Hoped that Grame was dead. At last the cries tapered off and he fell into a stupefied sleep.

At dusk he was awakened by shouts, and the sounds of clavers sloshing through the water nearby. Flickers of torches created shadows inside his burrow. Afraid to breathe and forced to remain motionless, he closed his eyes and listened to their boisterous calls and occasional maniacal screams. The search went on and on, for what seemed like hours, and ended finally, late that night.

Huddled in his tree stump, frightened and cold but unable to digest the impact of his losses, Reeve Calder closed his eyes and let his mind spin. He listened to the background noise of his brain, and when it finally subsided, he was left with a silent darkness. Through that endless well floated Tina Valejo, her white space suit lit up on one side by the sun, her arms waving as though she could swim her way back home.

2

Nerys slipped out of bed and padded to the doorway without looking back. Jory was asleep, had been for all the hours she'd lain beside him waiting for the moon to set. The only sound in the mud and wattle hogan was the growl of Nerys' stomach. For supper they had sucked the marrow from rabbit bones, and Nerys had given her daughter most of her own portion. Anar must have strength to run tonight.

She crept to Anar's cot behind the curtain and gently touched her shoulder. In the dark, she felt Anar's hand squeeze her own. She was awake, fully dressed, even wearing her boots. Good girl. At twelve, she was old enough to understand what they risked. From her shirt Nerys pulled out the letter and laid it on Anar's pillow. *Jory, I will not forget you. I took only what is mine. Remember that if you catch us.—Nerys.*

Outside, she grabbed the satchel she had hidden behind the hogan and laced on the boots she was carrying. She applied soot to her face and her daughter's, then peered around the hogan for any glimpse of the night watch. Overhead, a rich crop of stars glittered against the black loam of the sky. For the hundredth time Nerys wondered why the sky remained black with so many lamps to brighten it. Such questions had answers, she knew, but they were not for clavers to know. As they watched and listened, Nerys' stomach rumbled again, stiffening her courage for what they had to do. Then Nerys grasped Anar's hand and together they darted across the lane and into the terra patch.

The last of the vines crunched under their feet, brittle stems, all but barren, even in the lush days of the summer. Somewhere nearby a dog barked. Nerys froze in place, sweating.

"It's Pika's mongrel," Anar said.

"Shh."

A chill breeze swept over her, advance guard of the winter. She buttoned her jacket higher and waited for the dog to settle. Even now, if caught, she could still claim they were within the stockade. She would never be trusted again, but they would keep their lives.

After a time they started forward again, running for the cover of successive hogans and finally to the stockade. Pulling back the loose timber she'd dislodged in the early evening, she urged Anar through and then followed.

Now they were renegades. Fair game. She grabbed Anar's hand and sprinted for the woods.

Behind her she'd left the father of her child, three brothers, and her good friend Konsta. She'd left her woven blankets, the meager food of their larder, and all expectation of friendship and mercy from the clave, blood kin or no. Twenty-seven years of her life, now forfeit. She felt no remorse. She had hardened her heart for weeks, preparing for this moment. She had looked at her daughter's wasting frame and determined that Anar would live. Konsta's child had starved to death just before the spring thaw, lending more weight to the adage *Winter eats the children*.

Nerys and Anar picked their way through the twisted avenues between the trees to the meeting place.

A shadow stepped in front of them. Nerys' knife came out of its sheath and she flung Anar behind her.

"Nerys," the voice came.

It was Jory. "Not even a running start?" she snapped at him.

"Nerys." He stood, hands at his sides, weaponless. Was he alone? "Stay," he said.

"Stand back, Jory." Fleetingly, she searched the shadows for any others.

"Leave Anar, at least. Please."

He was alone. She could kill him, had to kill him; she couldn't trust him to remain silent. Damn, that he couldn't have let this *be.*

"Nerys," he pleaded again. "She's my daughter. They'll kill her."

Nerys wasn't sure who he meant by *they.* Their own Whale Clave, foreign claves, or the orthong? Any might do. But she answered: "She'll die if we don't leave. The clave is starving. Or didn't you notice?"

"We'll fish tomorrow. There'll be meat." His voice was desperate. Even he didn't believe it.

Nerys snorted. "We're starving, Jory. And we're leaving."

"You'll starve anyway. They'll slaughter you," he said. "That's how they conquer us, don't you see? By killing the women." His voice broke. "Nerys, don't give them Anar."

He hadn't come to say good-bye, he'd come to stop her. She lunged for him, taking him down and pinning his arms with her knees. Twisting under her, he threw her off, grabbing for her knife arm. They scuffled, but he remained silent, not calling out. For that, she would spare him. She groped for and found a fist-sized rock, swinging it around in an arc and dashing the side of his head. At the blow he fell quiet. She hefted the rock again and brought it down on his head another time, holding back her full strength, but doing the job well enough.

Anar was at her side. "Papa . . . ," she cried.

"Never mind him now!" Nerys found her knife on the ground and grabbed it, then circled her arm around her daughter and broke into a run.

"Is he dead?" Anar gasped as they ran.

"Yes. Dead to us."

Anar began to sob.

Nerys stopped and hugged her daughter. She mustn't cry. The others mustn't see her cry. "Anar, Anar. You must be strong. Your father lives. But now comes the hard part. *We* must live. Whatever else you do from now on, never cry. You understand?"

Anar sniffed and nodded her head. Nerys patted her. She hadn't raised a weakling.

Under cover of the woods they hurried, taking care to step over the fallen trunks of alders and birches, which if they grew too high were prone to collapse. Thus it was said, *Beware of tall trees,* which was also a rebuke to the prideful. Jory was fond of the saying. Nerys was not.

When they found the others, they were all crouched around Hesta, who lay on the ground.

"What happened?" Nerys asked.

"Caught in a snare," Thallia said, inspecting the wound as Hesta whimpered deep in her throat.

Eiko stood up. "Who's this?" she said, knowing full well who stood beside Nerys.

"My daughter."

"We said no children."

"You have no children."

Eiko spat. "No kids to slow us."

"She can run faster than you, and she's a better hunter." Eiko looked to Thallia, but Thallia's attention was on their fallen comrade, whose foot was shattered by a metal trap, the sort that could cripple an orthong or a caribou. Hesta was unlucky this night. Nerys crouched down to put a hand on the woman's shoulder.

"Kill me," Hesta whispered.

Nerys looked up into Thallia's grim face. The wind rustled the overhead branches. Nerys tuned it out and listened for sounds of pursuit.

"Let's go!" Eiko urged.

"*You* want to carry Hesta?" Thallia asked, mocking and deep.

Eiko turned and stalked off, taking up a position at the head of the path.

When the men found Hesta, they would take out

their anger on her. They were deserters, traitors to their human kin. They had gone over to the enemy, the despoilers of Lithia, the orthong predators. It was said human women lusted after the monsters and bore their unspeakable young. Scab-lovers, they were. In the folded ridges of the orthong faces, one could find only eyes. Some said a nose. But no mouths. Tales of the orthong invaders were told around campfires to frighten children. And tales of the fates of collaborators were also told—to frighten the women.

Hesta was frightened now. "Please," she whispered. "Make it fast. Don't ask me again!" She began a soft sobbing.

Thallia looked to Nerys and Nerys nodded briefly. Then Thallia bent down, kissed Hesta on the forehead, and rose. It was clear. Nerys must earn a place for Anar.

"Take Anar up the path," Nerys said.

"Take her yourself," Thallia said, and strode off.

"Follow her," Nerys told her daughter, who obeyed, disappearing into the shadows.

Turning back to Hesta, Nerys said, "We will all join you, Hesta, in the days and years to come. Until then."

"Do it!" Hesta cried. She closed her eyes.

Nerys used her knife, one deep swipe across the throat. A gush of blood warmed her knife hand. With her clean hand, she held Hesta's, waiting with her as she bled into the grass, thinking how badly their journey had begun. Finally she rose to her feet and ran up the path after the others. They needed to put many miles between themselves and their pursuers now, or they would come to envy Hesta's fate.

3

Mitya huddled next to the soaring, translucent wall of the dome, trying to look inconspicuous. Beside him, one of the segmented, carbon-matrix poles soared aloft, forming the skeleton of their refuge. Outside the dome, a toxic white fog pressed in, as it had since their arrival. So far, besides this whiteout, his main impression of Lithia was its smell: the rotten-egg stench of sulfur.

Now that the dome was erected, crew were hauling supply cartons, setting up data stations and air and water filtration systems. They'd partitioned off a clean room, a smaller section of the dome where the quantum processors were housed and where crew assembled the geo cannon for launching the nanotech probe.

Gudrun and Theo passed by carrying a pallet loaded with supplies. In a clatter, a pouch of tools fell onto the hardened resin floor. Mitya jumped up to retrieve it as Gudrun and Theo stood holding the pallet. Stuffing the tools back in the pouch, he carefully returned it to its place.

Gudrun sniffed. "Don't work up a sweat," she said as they trudged on with their burden. Gudrun didn't like him. She'd been among the most vocal in claiming that Mitya snuck onboard the shuttle, stealing Karl Hoeg's place. So that instead of a man who rightfully belonged on the expedition, they'd got a skinny thirteen-year-old boy, more trouble than he was worth. He hadn't meant to force anyone out. He just happened to be near Bay Three when the explosion hit, and his uncle Stepan had marshaled him aboard, though people snarled that there was only room for thirty and they'd best be able-bodied crew. But in the confusion Karl never showed, and Mitya, not even belted in, crouched amid the equipment cartons, holding on to a lithium hydroxide canister bolted to the bulkhead. After the landing, he could barely stretch out his arms again.

At the time of the disaster, the terraforming expedition had already been planned and the shuttles loaded with gear. That was lucky, or they'd have arrived on the surface empty-handed. Of course, it wasn't luck they'd gotten, but disaster. His family was dead: mother and father, his sister, his uncles and aunts and cousins—except for his aunt Lea's first husband, Stepan. The thought of his parents sat in his chest like cold water, numbing him. But it was the same with all the grim-faced crew. Everyone had lost family. Many had lost their own children, and when they looked at him Mitya knew they were thinking: *Why him and not my son?* His only solace came at night when he lay in the dark, and his mind went back home.

Captain Bonhert was Mitya's uncle twice removed, due to his marriage to the sister of Mitya's father's brother's wife. Mitya had been proud of that fact on Station, but it was also true that by now most of Station folks could find a relative by tossing a spitball and seeing who it hit. Besides, the Captain was too busy to notice a twice-removed nephew, and his father had always cautioned him never to presume on the Captain, even if sometimes the Captain smiled and nodded at him in the corridor when they happened to pass.

So there was no consolation from that quarter. During the day he would watch the construction of the dome and the feverish work inside it, staying well at the edge and bristling with energy to *do something*. He'd offered to do hauling or cleanup work, but crew said no, just stay out of the way. Oran was just three years older and did matrix-welding, but Oran was strong as a turbine. Mitya's real yearning was to help with the computer-modeling, even if it was only to sling numbers, but he knew they'd no more let him onto the quantum computer than punch a hole in the dome.

His gaze went again to the whiteout just beyond the dome wall. A small movement caught his attention next to the outside wall. It was a blur, but by scrunching down and lying on his side he saw what looked like an insect, about the size of a baby's fist. It was walking up the slick wall, its ten legs protruding from what looked to be an armored, oblong body. A light bobbed in front of its face. It seemed to take note of Mitya, stopping at eye level with him. Stretching from just in back of its head was a narrow appendage that arced over its face, suspending a point of light right in front of its mouth. Mitya put his palm against the inside wall. The light bug wiggled into a matching position, opposite his hand.

With a small thrill, Mitya realized he was seeing his first planetary creature, and it was Lithian, not Terran, with that Lithian trait of bioluminescence that he'd studied in zoology. And this alien being—old Lithian life—was watching him as though he were a creature in a zoo. Then the insect moved on, fading into the murk.

"Moping, are we?"

His uncle Stepan stood looking down at him. Judging from his heavily quilted jacket and pants, he'd been outside. His breather still clung to his face, outlining an oval from the bridge of his nose to just under his chin.

Mitya stumbled to his feet. "No, sir. Just looking."

"How about helping me at the shuttle?"

Mitya was so surprised it took him a moment to respond. Meanwhile his uncle tossed him a breather.

"Better than moping. You'll find that work can have its reward, boy."

Mitya looked at the breather with some astonishment. "Outside?" His voice broke, as it always did at the worst moments.

"Nothing to it," Stepan said. "Just breathe slowly a few times and don't fight it."

He was talking about the breather. Mitya followed his uncle in the direction of the air lock, his spirits lifting. The dry gel breather had already collapsed into a tangle in his hand, but he shook it out and considered how to put it on.

Turning, Stepan considered his dilemma with amusement. "When in doubt, try the instructions."

"Call for instructions," Mitya said.

The mask responded: "Pull the throat tube forward from the back side and, pressing the liner over nose, mouth, and chin, swallow the tube." Mitya had seen crew apply the masks. He quickly pulled the tube forward, pushing it onto his tongue, and attempted to swallow. He choked instead.

Stepan laughed. "Just relax."

In another moment the gel had spread across his mouth and throat lining, setting up its chemical filters, ten microns thick.

His uncle tossed him a jacket and nodded at the small case on the floor by their feet. It wasn't much for him to carry. Oran was just now plowing through the lock, toting an enormous coil of condensed resin piping. He smirked at Mitya but, glancing at Mitya's officer-uncle, held his tongue.

The compartment wasn't a true air lock. It was fitted with air pumps and vacuums to vent the worst of the dust and undesirable gases carried in by the crew, but it served more as a mudroom and perfunctory cleaning station.

Passing through the outer door, they stood for a moment enveloped in a fog which glowed dully in the midday sun. Visibility was zero to ten feet as the clouds drifted in greater and lesser galleons, trailing remnants of sulfur and gases too exotic to name by smell alone. Mitya's eyes teared up, further blurring his vision. Stepan was gesturing him around the perimeter of the dome, and Mitya followed, the contents of the box clunking in his arms.

The deep mantle plume was nearby, he knew. Here on a jutting finger of high cliff, Captain Bonhert had ordered the dome constructed so as to be flanked on two approaches by the 1,200-foot canyon wall and protected on the rest of the perimeter with a security wire and patrols. Within this safety zone were parked the two shuttles that had carried all their equipment and the forty-five survivors. Attacks from enclavers were always a possibility, but the real enemy was the orthong. Crew said it was an orthong attack that had destroyed Station, orthong who knew that their terraform project was almost ready to go and who would stop them at any cost. The threat of orthong attack had kept the crew on thirteen-hour shifts, around the clock, racing to complete their mission.

Mitya searched the terrain and its clumping mists for any sign of the pale orthong, camouflaged in their natural white hide. Now *there* was alien life Mitya would have liked to see. Twice alien—alien to humans and alien to Lithia. Where had the orthong come from, and what might *that* world be like? Mitya was hungry to know about these beings who, though his enemy, were the only other advanced beings humans had encountered—at least so far as Lithian colonists had ever heard. His uncle had no interest in the orthong except to kill one if he saw it, and the range gun on his webbed belt looked like it could do the job.

They approached the shuttle—a squat, blackened transport perched on landing struts. One side bore a mangled edge where the Station breakup had thrown something hard enough to dent its hull composites. Once in the equipment bay, Stepan explained that they were going to retrieve the main onboard quantum processors to check for damage. Mitya knew the drill: Check equipment, run diagnostics, and then a month later do it again. Station life was about maintenance, though Mitya always dreamed of doing real science instead. Once they got terraforming restarted, that would be his life's work: chemistry, atmospherics . . .

"Open the carton, Mitya," Stepan was saying, his voice husky through the breather. It made Mitya swallow reflexively, thinking of the tube in his windpipe, even if he knew he wasn't likely to feel its microscopic webbing.

Mitya pulled apart the carton flaps and dug inside among the assorted tools.

"Over here." His uncle was kneeling beside the cockpit console housing the processors. "Take out the main bolts and loosen the frame."

Mitya hurried to find the driver before Stepan changed his mind. Inserting the driver onto the bolt head and adjusting for size, Mitya handily slipped out the set of bolts.

Stepan pulled up the assembly, bracing it with a clamp, and began to slide out the main logic nets. Though hard-wrapped against quantum interference, the nets were still surprisingly light.

In truth it was easily done, and Stepan could have managed without him. Mitya waited to see what else was needed, but, after picking up the equipment and tools, they were done. Stepan led the way out of the shuttle, striding off in the wrong direction, away from the dome. Mitya hiked the tool carton up under his arm and followed, feeling his feet press into the spongy mass of the ground. The sensation of walking on a surface that *gave* with every step was an eerie reminder they were on the planet, a fact which otherwise could be doubted, given that they had yet to see the planetary sky or a vista of any sort. After a short walk they stood in front of a cordon that blocked their way.

"Out there," Stepan said, gesturing.

Mitya peered into the haze.

"The valley's out there, Mitya. The Rift Valley."

The words thrilled him. A valley so huge it would take *days* to walk across it . . . and yet it was only a crease on the wider land of the vast continent.

"You remember your geology, boy? Two crustal plates have been moving apart here for thirty million years. The valley must be a spectacular sight on a clear day. Or what passes for a clear day at the Rift."

Mitya squinted, trying to see the other side, the matching cliffs of the western wall, twelve miles away. In his imagination, he could see the fathoms of air and the great well of the valley dropping away before them.

"The plume's down there, somewhere," Mitya said, stating the obvious.

As though he hadn't heard, his uncle said in a softer voice: "Great-great-grandmother Malovich had a homestead in that valley. She grew sorghum and flax, raised ten children, and wrote a family history going back to first landfall. She cultivated orchids for fun. When the vents started smoking, she refused to leave. Said she was too old to start over. Family legend has it that when the fissures pumped out their river of stone, she sat down among her orchids and died along with them."

"Did they ever . . . find her?"

"A hundred feet of lava, boy," his uncle said, turning to him. "She's under a hundred feet of rock. Her and her sorghum and the family albums."

At the dark tone, Mitya stifled his response: *She must have loved it here.* He could imagine the valley full of grass and crops and a farmhouse with a fence around it, and for a moment he thought he knew why his great-great-grandmother sat down and refused to leave.

Stepan had turned back to face the Rift. "We'll have a few surprises for this godforsaken valley," he said. His grim face put an end to the conversation. As they walked back to the dome, Stepan added, "This is a hard time for you, Mitya. No youngster should lose both his parents at once."

That caught Mitya off guard, and he felt the ache of the loss next to his ribs.

"I don't know much about youngsters," Stepan said.

Mitya figured it was Stepan's way of saying he couldn't take him on, couldn't fill in the gap.

"That's OK," he said. He'd never figured Stepan owed him that, but he felt worse for knowing Stepan had considered and passed on it.

As they ducked into the air lock, three crew came in behind them, stamping their feet to dislodge dust and soil and setting the air cycle in motion.

One of the men turned and nodded at Stepan. It was Captain Bonhert. His sandy hair was just tinged with gray at his sideburns, and in the padded jacket his barrel chest and broad shoulders seemed massive. His eyes took in Mitya in an instant, and dismissed him as fast. "Best save the breathers for the adults, Stepan," he muttered as he left the lock. "They'll be needed for real work."

Lieutenant Roarke, by Bonhert's side, threw Mitya a disdainful smile.

Stung, Mitya watched as they disappeared into the dome.

Stepan's hand was on his shoulder, guiding him through the door, watching Bonhert walk off. "Don't worry about it, lad," he said. "Sometimes he thinks we need telling when to blow our noses. He thinks a lot of himself, our Captain."

Mitya disengaged his breather, handing it over and looking around the dome, which now seemed so much smaller than an hour ago, and more foreign.

3

1

Day four. They were being watched, Reeve felt sure. Here in the folded gullies of the grasslands, an enemy could spy on them easily, lying in the grasses or crouching just over the next shallow rise. He and Marie were easy prey, with Marie still recovering from her head injury and Reeve gnawingly hungry. But if clavers were watching, why didn't they strike? Or was it only paranoia brought on by the trek from the swamp and the everlasting pearly-blue sky that stared down at them?

Marie shifted in her sleep, tucked among her blankets. A late-afternoon nap would have been good for her, and kept her from pestering him about his plans, but instead she opened her eyes. Their usual bright blue seemed to take a deeper tincture from the sky.

"Are you leaving now?" she asked.

"I'll be back in two or three hours."

"A brace of quail over your shoulder?"

"A brace of what?"

"Quail. A kind of bird. Gone by now, I suppose."

"Maybe I'll bring back a few claver heads instead." Reeve grinned at the look on her face.

"Don't be a fool."

"Why stop now?"

Marie smirked. "Stubborn, like your father."

Reeve paused. "*Am* I like my father?"

"You have his olive skin, his black hair." She shrugged. "And his stubbornness." As he slapped the dust from his knees and shouldered his pack, she added: "Promise me you'll just hunt animals."

"Clavers *are* animals." He spoke in jest to keep Marie off guard; he didn't need her mothering right now. Handing her the club he'd fashioned from a large branch, he said: "Any of those bugs get near you, defend yourself with this."

"Aye, captain." She gave a mock salute with the arm-length weapon. Her expression turned sour. "I know better than to caution you."

He cracked a smile. "Guard the house. I'll be back before dawn." He turned and set off, not liking to leave her, but without much choice. Unaccustomed to hunger, Reeve's stomach ached and growled in rebellion. If he had to eat animal flesh, he would. He'd seen pictures of cooked flesh, and vids of people eating it. It was better than starvation, and with the food pouches down to a handful, it was turn carnivore or die. Lithia's vegetation was not an option. And the bugs—some kind of hard-shelled millipedes—were too revolting a prospect. He killed them when he encountered them, though, knowing it for a childish reaction to their invasion of his pack. They had devoured most of his food pellets. He had yet to see any Terran creatures except birds, though semiadapted Terran flora still hung on in places, notably the Forever Plains—still green, by the Lord, despite the worst Lithia could do.

In this, the second great biological die-off, the niches once occupied by humans and the imported fauna left great gap—gaps that would remain empty for millions of years. Lithia's creatures had mostly perished in the first die-off, the one driven by terraforming.

He scrambled to the rise, lying flat in the grass, peering out, swallowing reflexively against the minor annoyance of the breather. Even after three days planetside he was still shocked by the view. There was no end to the plains. In every direction to the rim of the planet lay the carpet of undulating grass, a living but somehow desolate plain of green. Through this strange expanse the wind blew hour after hour. It stole the moisture from his face and the thoughts from his head. At night in their tent he heard its breath as he strained to listen past the scuttling of the crabs.

Reeve had learned not to look up. The sky was a blank, colossal emptiness that sometimes made the plains spin around him until he sank to his knees and held on to the grass for support. He gazed into the distance, seeing the cookfires of the clavers. Since they cooked twice a day, it meant they had plenty of food. He hurried on his way, keeping to the gullies when he could, crawling over the ridges when he couldn't.

Behind him, a rock rattled down an incline. Reeve swiveled, scanning the near hillside and down the ravine to the next ridge. But there was only grass bent under the wind. Hunkered down, he scurried over the crest of the hill and set out across the next shallow gully. And the next. He wished Marie hadn't mentioned his father. He didn't need those thoughts at a time like this. Memory was a great sump; it could siphon off your attention faster than the wind took the moisture from your face.

A large, hairy beetle skittered in front of him, another example of Lithia's hospitality to insects. Nearby Reeve saw clustered red bulbs the size of his big toe. He'd found a few of these over the last few days, and kicked at them, sending clouds of brown spores into the air. No doubt these polyps were samples of Lithia peeking out, the old Lithia. In these small, bright knobs was a glimpse of the great Reversion that had not yet claimed the grasslands.

As he paused a moment, he saw the carcass of a dead animal, perhaps a wild dog, lying some thirty yards off in the bottom of the ravine. Maybe dinner was going to be easier than he thought. He hesitated, squinting into the gully. Things looked ordinary enough, but might not be. Might be a ghost hole. You never could tell. Not understanding that pockets of carbon dioxide sometimes collected at low points, clavers thought that ghosts dwelled in some of the valleys, wraiths that kissed the breath from you and claimed you for one of their own. Reeve retreated back up the hillside and hurried on.

Station biologists argued about the exact dynamics of the Reversion, with its complex feedback loops involving volcanism, atmosphere, weather, and chemistry. But the outlines of the process were clear. Lithia's high carbon dioxide atmosphere, always a marginal human environment, was breaking out of its terraform restraints. Carbon dioxide outgasing from volcanism had easily overcome terraforming's prodigious oxygen production, adding minor but unwelcome traces of sulfur and, from deep mantle plumes, chlorine. Always a cold world in its orbit on the edge of the planetary habitable zone, Lithia was saved from an icy fate by its primordial CO_2 greenhouse effect. Moderated by high-salinity oceans that suppressed water evaporation, the greenhouse effect was nevertheless strong and growing stronger, bringing the velvet strangulation of sweeter, warmer days, short on oxygen.

Escalating carbon dioxide and sulfur compounds slowly attacked the lungs of Terran creatures, and acid rain and the erosion of new lava deposits created a biosphere changing faster than many Terran plants could adapt to.

Despite this planetary turmoil, though, the grass-

lands managed, in places, to endure. The claves somehow hung on.

And Bonhert would destroy all this. By some convoluted reasoning—or madness—he would commit an
act of unthinkable destruction. If a dying man's rav-
ings were to be believed. *What had Grame Lauterbach
said . . . seventy days?* Ten weeks and they would sink
the pellet and quake the world apart. And though he
could find the Rift on a map, finding it on the planet
was an entirely different thing. Especially when he had
no clear idea exactly where he was.

He didn't want to believe it—his current predicament was peril enough—but something in Grame's
eyes and the surge in his voice made Reeve uneasy.
That Gabriel Bonhert was capable of it he had no
doubt at all. The man would allow nothing between
himself and his goal, if his iron rule of Station and his
relentless harassment of Cyrus Calder were any measure.

His father openly derided the majority view, main-
taining that Bonhert's scheme to release mantle heat
would boil off the planet's atmosphere. It made more
sense, Cyrus believed, for Station to build a starship,
beginning with the mining of asteroids and complete
restructuring and retooling of Station for the massive
building enterprise. Of course, there was the orthong
ship in high orbit, presumably abandoned and ready
for the taking—except that its automatic defenses had
twice incinerated Station shuttles that dared to approach it. Though the orthong seemed to have no use
for the vessel, they were of no mind to share it, either.

Despite the obstacles, Cyrus believed they must
Voyage On. Many secretly supported this idea, and
Marie openly so. But those who "diverted Station focus," as Bonhert said, gradually lost privileges, and
were passed over for advancement, their researches
chronically underfunded. These political battles were
the subject of many discussions at the family dinner

table until Reeve's mother died; after that he and Cyrus ate alone, mostly in silence.

So the research into habitable planets and starship design were fueled by the relentless energy of one man, Cyrus Calder. And Reeve had no faith in his father's dream. He had wanted to, desperately, but to his shame, Reeve clung to the hope of Lithia. Like many others, he was seduced by the fierce logic that while Lithia was harsh, it was all they had. It was a fact that the generation ship on which the first colonists arrived had found not a single other suitable world—not even a reasonable candidate for terraforming—in 250 years. Nor had the other Terran generation ships of the human diaspora ever reported success, not in the messages that had had time to reach them.

Reeve pushed these thoughts away. No time now to linger on old problems, with new ones clamoring for attention. Like hunger. With the food pouches all but gone, his prospects for a meal were bleak. The luck of the draw had put them down in a swamp surrounded by grasslands. Though he knew little about Terran plants, he knew enough not to eat grass and moss and to avoid the Lithian outgrowths, with their toxins. The insects might be edible—or might not. But by far the safest guide to a proper meal would be the local savages.

As the sun moved toward the horizon, it began cooking up a brilliant sunset, creamy orange with galleries of hot red clouds cooling to purple. He gaped, despite his mission. Finally the show subsided, replaced by the camouflage of dusk. He zeroed in on his target: the campfires of the clavers. Years of practice avoiding detection on coldwalks had given him a sixth sense for stealth. He meant to make good use of that now.

The claver camp lay over the next rise. He crawled up on his belly, peering from the crest. One guard. The barbarians were confident. Looking down from his knoll, he counted fifteen clavers, two of whom were women. Poles or spears spiked the ground here and there, some with curious flat objects crowning them. Over two fires, the clavers were cooking their meals—small chunks of something skewered on sticks. From the smell, he took it for meat—a sickening thought, yet his stomach stirred in response. He would steal flesh if he must, he told himself. But perhaps there was proper food among their baggage. He hunkered down and waited for dark.

The boisterous, hooting behavior he had seen in the marsh was gone, replaced with a more ominous silence. Perhaps intent on their meal, the clavers communicated in grunts and shorthand phrases, sometimes jostling each other with rough camaraderie.

At the head of the draw were their pack animals—huge, stomping horses—and near them, stacks of their supplies, off-loaded for the night. The claver guard made a slow, lazy circuit of the hillcrest; compared with the sensors on Station hull, he represented no challenge. Years of breaking other people's rules had taught Reeve that people usually saw what they expected to see, and since the members of this party were pursuing *him*, they wouldn't expect to *be* pursued.

While he waited, Reeve found himself studying the poles with the flat objects on top. When he recognized what they were, it felt as though he'd been struck in the chest. They were feet. Several of the poles had a severed human foot impaled, sole pointing up. Weak, he turned away. He knew where those feet came from. Damn them to everlasting hell. He didn't let himself think about what else they had done to the bodies of his fellow Stationers, or Grame Lauterbach, poor bastard.

Trembling with rage, he toyed with the idea of stealing those awful poles; his comrades shouldn't have to suffer such outrage. But he wasn't on Station anymore, and the stakes were higher than a dressing-down by the brass. Setting the fantasy aside, he turned his attention to the task at hand: theft and survival. Pulling his jacket around him, he moved off from the ridge, biding his time in the next gully until the night deepened and the fires burned down.

Lithia's moon popped above the ridge. Just a slice of light in the dark sky, it would not threaten his cover of darkness. Waiting for the clavers to bed down, Reeve gazed at the night sky—a vista familiar to him, the only one on the planet that could be. This was the sky as it should look, dark and fractured by star drifts. Seeing this canopy, he longed for Station, his thoughts returning to the moment of destruction, and to what had caused it. Perhaps the orthong vessel had opened fire. But in sixty years the orthong had never initiated an offensive against Station; the orthong remained a shadow threat. Grame Lauterbach said a ship was coming—had this ship fired on them? And could it be true that Captain Bonhert intended to destroy the planet?

We got to kill her, Reeve. Promise you'll never tell. . . .

He sat up, weary of these ruminations. Now that the camp had been silent for an hour or more, he crept closer to spy out the guard's position. After a long while the claver made his pass by Reeve's side of the gully. A predictable monitor, easily avoided.

Reeve made his way to the far side of the defile and approached the horses. Their animal smell was powerful. When they stirred and nickered, Reeve understood they smelled him, too. Moving smoothly and with excruciating slowness, he crept to the pile of claver supplies, passing close enough to the horses to note their enormous haunches and bulging eyes. They were magnificent creatures, far grander than in the vids. Hurriedly pulling out his knife, Reeve slit the ropes binding one of the bundles, revealing coarse strips of a fibrous material. One whiff told him it was dried flesh. He stuffed the strips into his field pack and went on to the next bundle, finding granules of some kind that might be edible. As the horses stomped and grew restless, he crammed his pack to the brim and strapped it closed. Then, thinking about the poles and their terrible adornments, he slit open a few bags with a slash in the shape of an X, so the clavers would know it was no animal that had bettered them. *Stationer, by God.* He began to move off, then turned back. On impulse he pissed on the remaining supply bundles, taking inordinate pleasure in it.

Withdrawing back down the defile, he circled around the next gully and slunk westward across the ridges, putting distance between himself and the camp. After an hour, as dawn lit his path, he ran toward the spot where Marie waited, a week's rations weighing down his back. When he reached their bivouac, Marie was up, having struck the tent. In the first hint of dawn, she looked fragile and pale.

"Going somewhere?" he asked.

She nodded. "Figured we'd be in a hurry this morning. Successful hunt?"

"Yes. But we'll be turning carnivore, I'm afraid." He peered at the crest of the arroyo. "Let's get out of here."

Marie tossed him a food pouch. "Eat something first."

He grinned. In truth, he was hungry enough to chew on his boots. Without taking off his pack, Reeve ripped open the pouch. In his haste, he dropped it, spilling the food nuggets on the ground. Swearing, he knelt in the hardpan soil and scraped together a few spoonfuls of the pellets. He stuffed them into his mouth, ravenous and beyond scruples, crawling to salvage his meal before the bugs descended.

"Reeve!" he heard Marie shout.

As his head came up he found himself facing a

glinting sword. At the other end of the weapon stood a man with a patchy brown beard and bald head. Claver. Though the man's shoulders were covered with a fur pelt, he was thin as a girder. Reeve could take him on, but there were more than one. Another one was sitting astride Marie. The sword edged closer, nudging Reeve's throat.

"Be you a Tallgrass or a Mudder, boyo?" The sword flashed sun into Reeve's eyes. "Eh?" the man prodded.

"I am Reeve." As thin as the claver looked, Reeve judged he was all bone and muscle. Damn, to be caught unawares, to be on his hands and knees weighted down with his own trophy pack!

"A Reeve, he say, Mam," the swordsman said to the other claver. "I say, the liar dies."

"No!" Marie blurted.

The scrawny man eyed Reeve's clothes, especially his boots. "Speak your prayers, boyo." He raised the saber over his head.

Reeve scampered backward, but toppled from the weight of his pack. As he frantically pulled one arm loose from the straps, the claver planted a foot in his ribs and swung the sword back.

"Leave off," came the command.

Another claver stood at Reeve's feet, looking down at him. Her short, ragged hair stood up in spikes all over her head. She was young, maybe seventeen, and filthy. As she kneeled down beside him, her companion slowly lowered his weapon. She peered at Reeve, moving to within inches of his face, her nostrils flaring. Through the mask of dirt on her face, her hazel eyes were her only clear link to humanity. The waif was dressed in rags and fur boots laced with hide thongs, and she smelled of humus. She lifted his lips to inspect his teeth, then probed his clothes, frowning.

"Don't move, boyo," the man warned. Reeve didn't need to be told.

With a grimy finger, the girl traced the breather

around his nose and mouth, drawing her finger along its almost invisible circumference. "This?" she asked.

"A breather."

She looked at him doubtfully.

"Where be your clave, boyo?" the man growled.

A question he didn't want to answer. "Far away."

The sword poked at his chest. "Where?"

Throwing caution aside, Reeve pointed to the sky.

The claver looked up. When he gazed down at Reeve again his face darkened. He twitched the sword until it ripped into the fabric of Reeve's jacket.

The girl lay her palm against the flat of the blade, pushing it away. "He will live," she announced. Standing up, she took note of the swordsman's glare. "Soil eater," she said. Then she turned and walked away.

Under the contemptuous eyes of their captor, Marie helped Reeve to his feet. The man turned his head to one side, as though Reeve were easier to look at with just one eye. A curl of his lip conveyed his assessment of the pair of them. In turn, Reeve surveyed the barbarian who had so effortlessly and ruinously stolen up on them. A little taller than Reeve, and twice as thin, the fellow managed to intimidate with his murderous scowl, black and snaggled teeth, and a sword almost as broad and long as his leg. He stank, even at a distance of several feet. To be bested by the likes of this fellow set Reeve's blood on a rolling boil. Noting the saber, Reeve decided the claver might know how to wield it, and resolved to bide his time before taking the ruffian on.

A sharp whack between his shoulder blades was Reeve's signal to move as the claver herded them down the gully, in the direction the girl had taken. The foul taste of soil lingered in Reeve's mouth, a muddy brine of dirt and saliva which he sucked on for the last shred of his pellet food.

2

By their poles, Loon saw that the Mudders were angry. They had taken feet. She lay on her belly and watched as they argued over which way to go. In the pouch at her waist were some well-chosen rocks. If they started in her direction, she would give a few of them a tap on the head. Clutching her sling, she squinted into the sun setting at the edge of the plains. Loon sucked the mud off her fingers and waited to see what course the hunting party would take.

The lead Mudder was a woman. From her fierce expression, she seemed to be in a hurry—no small wonder, since the Reever said he had made water on their food packs. On *food* packs. The Reever himself must be very fierce, Loon thought, to risk such an insult. The Mudder's hair was braided with odd strips of silver. Some of the Mudders wore jackets like the Reever wore. Wherever he came from, his clave must be very rich. She guessed the Mudders had raided the Reevers and now pursued these two. It might be a feud. Taking feet was a sign of feud.

Spar said the Reevers claimed to be from the Sky Clave. If they were zerters, that would explain why the Mudders took the feet. But after a whole day with the Reevers, and watching them closely, Loon could not believe they were the deserters of the sky wheel. Everyone knew the zerters were fat, and these two were slim. But their captives were strange, to be sure. They could bear no animal meat. Their pack had many oddities. Among these were silver packs containing kernels the Reevers liked to eat. Ah—this was perhaps the silver the Mudder woman bound into her hair.

As Loon watched the Mudders argue, she saw the western horizon bulging with clouds. From this small curdle of gray at the rim of the world, she knew a storm was coming. The Mudders saw it too. They knew they must hurry before rain stole the trail. In the distance, a rare group of six deer bounded across the grassland. Yet the Mudders paid no attention. They must strongly wish to find the Reevers. The group split up, trying three directions, one of which displeased Loon greatly. The woman with silver in her hair set out with four strong men toward the hideaway where Spar waited.

Loon slithered down the hillock and ran along the bottom of the gully, pushing herself to her best speed. She couldn't outrun a horse, but the Mudders would travel slowly even by horse, looking for the trail, difficult to see in the hardpan of the plain. They would look for trampled grass as well—the Reevers stomped grass like buffalo despite Spar's lessons, and, once, a beating. How could they be rich if they knew so little? Far away thunder growled. Loon ran harder, easing into a rhythmic lope, running on rocks whenever she found them, trying to mask her passage. Despite the pursuit of the Mudders, she ran with exuberance. She liked this Reever man, with his good smells and his mud-tinged lips.

Approaching the abandoned farm, she stopped and crept to the top of the rise to check for the Mudders. To her shock, they were just entering the farm gates. As soon as they dismounted, they found the tracks they were looking for. The leader pointed to the barn. That was a mistake.

Sprinting, Loon scampered to the side of the main hogan, flattening herself against it. She trusted that Spar had seen their pursuers, but she worried just the same. An owl flapped above her, disappearing over the roofline. This was the owl that lived in the barn. A bad omen, owls in daylight. It was a thing out of order, a creature out of place. With her heart knocking in her chest, she peered around the corner. In the barnyard, a lone Mudder held the horses, his back to her. She darted for the cellar window, then scrambled through.

Rushing up the cellar stairs to the main floor, she opened the door. And came face-to-face with Spar.

"Mudders!" she hissed.

Spar yanked on the rope and the Reevers—hands bound behind them, and linked together at their necks by a length of rope—stumbled forward.

"Quiet," Spar growled, angry at their heavy-footedness.

They descended the stairs, following Loon into the darkness. In the cramped cellar, she pulled aside a rack of wooden shelves, exposing the escape tunnel. This tunnel-riddled farm had been Loon and Spar's refuge for a week as they'd recovered from their trek across the Forever Plains. Eight large hogans shared the barn; with luck it would take the Mudders a while to search them all. Once inside the tunnel, she pulled the shelving unit back in place and felt for the stack of cut sod to plug the hole from the inside. Spar dubbed this farm Gopher Hole for its maze of tunnels connecting each hogan and leading to escape routes in four directions. Here the homesteaders had hoped to escape the orthong raids. She wondered if orthong had ever come this far south. If they did, that was something more to worry about.

In the tunnel, a fragrant stew of rotting humus, roots, and soil enveloped her. Tantalizing aromas, familiar but without names, threaded into her consciousness while she listened for sounds of pursuit. The old woman was leaning on her companion's arm. They would have to abandon her soon. The woman was so old her hair was half gray. Perhaps this one was half a century old!

"There's a flashlight," the Reever man said. "In my field pack."

"Shut your mouth," Spar said. " 'Less you want to lose your feet."

Loon knew about flashlights. Her father had had one with a feeble spray of light, and he let her turn it on sometimes. She thought she heard voices from above, Mudders calling to each other. She knew how Spar stumbled in the darkness, so she wanted the light. "Show me," Loon said.

Spar opened the Reever's pack, and Loon untied the woman's hands, leading her to it. The woman groped inside, finally pulling forth a palm-sized object. Light flooded around them. Now Loon understood why they called these things *flash*lights. No weak drizzle of light. This was a flash of fire.

"Move," Spar urged. He pushed the prisoners on ahead, shouldering the pack and waiting for Loon to go ahead of him. Then a scream erupted from down-tunnel. The Mudders had found an entrance. Luckily it was not the one Loon and Spar had used, a few feet back.

The old woman switched off the light. That was smart. Loon pushed to the front and grabbed the rope lead, tugging the Reevers along faster. Quickly sorting her options, Loon decided on the long tunnel past the second fork. Unless the Mudders split up, they'd have a good chance to escape. By now Loon was getting to know her pursuers. They scrambled to the fork, where Loon chose the south branch, pulling her prisoners along with her.

A muffled shout came from down-tunnel: "Food thieves!"

At her side, Spar whispered: "Leave the Reevers!"

"No."

"They don't eat soil," he said, repeating the same argument as before. Spar had pointed out from the beginning that the man had been picking food scraps from the ground when they came upon him. Not eating soil.

"No," Loon said again.

They heard, closer now: "Food thieves! We come for payment!" And "That way!" Flickers of light and shadow told of torches around the bend.

They hurried down the tunnel, the Reevers stumbling often on the rough floor. Loon helped the old woman along. "Be quiet," Loon said to her. "Too much noise."

The woman did better for a while, but she was hopelessly clumsy. Behind them came a huffing noise. Someone was running down the long tunnel after them. Up ahead was a speck of light. They ran toward it, finally crawling through a flap of grass onto the open plain. As they emerged from their passage, Spar yanked their prisoners to the side and stood poised, spear raised, at the entrance. Loon grabbed a rock from her pouch, standing back for a good aim.

Overhead, the clouds raced to cover the sky. Their black masses were, for a split second, shot through with lightning, tracing a maze like the one they'd just come from. A ripping crash of thunder followed.

Inside the hole, a Mudder stopped short of the trap. She could clearly see him crouching there, though he thought himself hidden.

"So you wait for us out there, do you?" came the voice. "Give up, and I'll kill you quick."

Spar stood poised with his sword.

"There's four of you, but ten of us," the Mudder lied. "I'll kill you fast." Then he made a mistake. He edged forward to a spot that gave Loon a clear trajectory.

Loon wound up her sling and sent her rock flying to its target. In the next instant the Mudder fell half out of the tunnel, face first. Spar's sword finished him off. Loon crouched to see if others followed him, but he was alone. They dragged his body into the grass and scratched out the grooves where his heels had dug into the ground.

The Reever man stood blinking witlessly at the sky where the thunderheads collected, rumbling loud enough to knock the thoughts out of your head. At an ear-numbing crash, he fell to his knees, covering his ears. Though Spar yanked and yanked on his rope, the man refused to budge.

Through his capture and the flight from the Mudders, the Reever had never shown fear until now. Loon took pity on him. Perhaps he had never seen a storm before, or heard the sky crack open. If he had never seen a Forever Plains storm, he had not truly seen a storm. Loon approached, kneeling beside him. In the gathering dusk, lightning forked again and again over their heads, reflected in his wide eyes. She put her arm around his shoulder and helped him to his feet. He was taller than she was, so she let her arm slide down around his waist.

"Spar, cut the rope," she said. He glowered, but complied. "Hands also."

Slowly, Spar did what she asked. But his face was terrible to look at.

"Now we run," Loon said, urging the man into a walk and then a ragged jog. Behind them came Spar, with the woman in tow.

The rain hit them like a wall. Thunder quaked the land beneath their feet and claimed the sky over their heads. Lightning struck a small tree fifty feet away. Its two halves burned in the rain—another out-of-place thing. Loon began to wonder if Spar was right, that these two brought evil with them. Before they found these Reevers, Loon and Spar had evaded the Tallgrass clavers, had never seen a Mudder, and had stumbled on Gopher Hole, a perfect place to rest from their long journey. Now they were fleeing maddened clavers with a feud to settle, and were exposed in a plains storm with a coward and an invalid for company. Maybe the owl had spoken truly.

When they ran out of breath, they hunted among the rocks of a gully for an overhang to rest under. But there was nothing. Loon raised her face to the rain, letting it drench her. Meanwhile, Spar allowed the man to dig in his pack. From this he pulled a sheet of thin, yellow cloth that the wind whipped about. After a long while the Reever shaped a small hut in the flat of the gully. They all climbed inside except Spar, who refused.

As the night came on, the old woman began to moan. Her companion used small patches on her skin, but if he prayed for her, he kept his prayers to himself. Each time the thunder roared, he winced, but he no longer covered his ears.

Loon rested among their packs, pretending to sleep. Through the slits of her closed eyes she kept watch on the stranger as he tucked papery blankets around the woman and murmured to her. She liked the way he cared for her, as though an old woman mattered. Maybe, in his clave, old women *did* matter. Maybe the shiny circles they wore around nose and mouth were big tech against the bad air, the sickness folk called indigo for its blue shadows around the lips and nails. Maybe big tech let zerters last into the gray years.

Lightning erupted nearby, turning the yellow tent fiery. In that instant the Reever's face looked like it was carved from amber, his eyes like a living being trapped within. Loon thought again of her first glimpse of him, shoving soil in his mouth and swallowing. She knew it was merely the food kernels that he ate. But the memory thrilled her and would not fade.

When she spared his life, he had soil on his breath.

4

1

Day five. Over their tent, the sky shrieked with wind, bellowed with thunder. The noise was stupefying. Reeve lay next to Marie for warmth, shuddering at every crack and boom. He thought he heard rocks exploding, the land ripping, but in truth he knew little about what was going on. He'd read about storms, seen them from Station—but how utterly puny those views were compared with the actual thing. The sky which he had cowered under the last four days, finding its immense emptiness unnerving, had now shown him how benign his first impression was.

The tent walls registered a yellow blot of lightning. Then a primordial roar shattered the world. He huddled in misery, thankful at least for the coming of night so that the filthy girl could not watch him and he eventually might sleep. Amid the disturbing sulfur smell of this world was now added the body odors of three people in a tent who hadn't showered for days, and one who may *never* have showered.

Strange how, amid all his troubles, he could long for something as minor as a shower. And warmth. After days of the cool sun and relentless wind, he'd thought he could never be warm again. Now, with the rain, his chill was profound. Despite their blankets, he feared hypothermia. But there was no time to be sick or weak. To gain strength, he tried eating the dried meat that the claver called Spar favored. It was awful—but as Marie said, they had to learn. Once, the girl had brought him small, bluish berries. Their sweetness was a revelation, but he'd paid dearly for his excess of enthusiasm.

The girl was little more than an animal. She spoke seldom and stared at him as though he was outrageous in some way. And though she was only a teenager, her companion deferred to her, acting like an obsessed bodyguard and demanding similar deference from him and Marie. The creature was even more filthy than the man—especially her fingernails, which were crusted with dirt. The man, in contrast, kept a trim beard and an almost military demeanor. At first Reeve thought he might be able to overpower him, but the fellow's reflexes were fast, and the sword was not just an affectation. It looked like an antique of some sort, with its sheath and belt, but Reeve had seen him spear millipedes with it, in swift feats of casual accuracy. When he cooked them he offered to share with no one, including the girl. Not that Reeve would have accepted—it was repulsive enough to watch him eat. But Marie hadn't eaten anything for a day. He feared her head wound was infected, and it caused him a sharp worry that he might lose her. She was the only one that he knew in all the world.

Beside him, the girl sat bolt upright. In the next instant she had scrambled to the tent opening.

Reeve pushed up on his elbows. "What is it?"

But she was gone, darting out into the storm.

Without taking time to put on his boots, Reeve plunged outside. Wind and rain flew at him out of sheer darkness, with grunts and the clang of metal coming from close by. Mudders, attacking. Squinting, he saw shadows struggling. He spun around, looking for a weapon. A large rock was his only choice. On his hands and knees, he groped blindly for one, grabbed the largest he could hold in one hand, and pivoted, just in time to face the charge of a burly figure. He dove for the knees, smashing the rock into the man's kneecap. His attacker bellowed, bringing a blade within an inch of Reeve's nose.

In a flash of lightning, Reeve caught a glimpse of a long-haired figure crouching, about to push through the tent door where Marie lay helpless. Meanwhile, his attacker had fallen, but now struggled up, staggering. Reeve rolled toward the tent, shouting, "I pissed on your food, claver!"

The figure turned from the tent flap, and behind him he heard a bellow from the man who'd charged him. The one at the tent brought a boot to Reeve's stomach. Reeve clutched the boot with both hands, yanking so hard he thought he'd dislocated a shoulder. But his muscles were charged with steel, and he sent the claver catapulting forward, crashing facedown in the mud. He saw strands of silver roping through the claver's hair. Reeve grabbed on to a hunk of that hair and hauled with all his strength. The claver brought a fist down on his forearm, hard enough to break it in two. Blinded for a moment by pain, he was set upon by someone from behind, who bound his arms to his side in a choking embrace, forcing him to his knees.

The long-haired one crawled toward him, brandishing a short knife. As Reeve struggled uselessly, the claver held the knife between them at eye level. "I'll take your organ while you watch." It was a woman's voice. Behind him, the iron hold on his arms tightened.

Then, with a soft *thunk,* the woman's head left her shoulders. She still knelt before him, blood pumping from the severed neck. Reeve felt himself hoisted to his feet as his assailant backed up. Spar was advancing

on them, holding his weapon in front of him. He
feinted to one side and the other while Reeve was
dragged backward. Then, in a wrenching movement,
Reeve sprawled to the ground in a heap with the claver. He came eye to eye with the girl, Spar's companion, who had crouched behind to trip them. In the
next moment, Spar thrust forward, piercing the claver
through the chest.

The girl rose to her feet, tugging on Spar's hand.
She led him to a spot where a claver lay groaning, in
need of Spar's long steel. It was quickly done.

When Spar returned, he handed Reeve a claver
spear. They waited, poised for more, but they were
alone in the rain, which had softened now to a mere
downpour. When they caught their breath, Spar said,
"Best to leave now, before the Mudders look for their
friends."

Reeve glanced at the tent. "Marie can't travel tonight."

"I wasn't speaking to you, boyo," the man said. He
turned to the girl.

She nodded.

"Leave me my pack," Reeve said. "I earned it."

The man snorted. "You'd be dead three times over,
if it weren't for us."

"I need my pack," Reeve said, moving closer to it.

"Spoils of war, boyo." Spar crouched, ready to fight.

Reeve gripped the spear he'd been given, wondering
if the pack was worth dying for.

"Reeve," a voice came from behind.

Marie was standing outside the tent, dressed in
boots and heavy jacket. "He's right. We can't stay
here."

"But, Marie . . ."

"Get packed," she said, her voice wobbly.

He paused, trying to gauge how far she could go,
then deciding any distance would help, with the rain
to cover their tracks.

They scavenged the bodies for the best weapons. Reeve gave Spar his choice among the handmade daggers and spears.

Affecting not to notice this courtesy, Spar shoved the two best knives into his belt and hoisted the pack on his shoulders.

Reeve locked gazes with him. "I'm not *boyo*. I'm Reeve."

The man produced a mean half smile. "Where you headed, boyo? You got any idea where you goin'?"

Reeve wiped the smelly rain out of his eyes. "The Rift," he said, simply.

Spar snorted, shaking his head. "Now what *rift* might that be?"

When Reeve didn't answer, the claver spat to one side and turned to follow the girl, who had traipsed off.

"What's the girl's name?" Reeve called after him.

Spar threw back: "Call her Mam, or I'll have your head."

Reeve gripped his spear, considering something rash. Slowly, he fought down his anger and, with Marie, set out down the ravine after them. Trudging by Marie's side, he asked, "How are you feeling?"

"Good enough." She glanced at him as they sloshed through rivulets of muddy water. "You would have stayed here with me?" she asked.

By the tone of her voice, Reeve hesitated to answer.

She shook her head. "Your heart is too soft." After a minute she said, "If I fall behind, leave me. Do you hear, Reeve Calder?"

"Would you leave me?"

"Yes."

Her face was hard, but he didn't believe her for one instant.

Reeve took up a position at the rear of the party, apparently trusted now, unbound and with a weapon. He watched as Marie walked bravely on. He wouldn't abandon her, despite her decree. They went back a long way—all his life—and she was his last link with the world as it was Before. The world of Station. The world where he might have reconciled with his father . . . if such a feat was possible. The world where a view of Lithia was a forbidden prize, a lark.

So many times on coldwalks he'd gazed down on Lithia and longed for her adventures. Now, slogging through the rain and mud, he cringed at this foolishness. The real thing was nothing like his fantasies. He supposed that would prove to be true about much else, as well.

2

By the glow of light from the cave entrance, Nerys knew the storm had passed. Raising up on her elbow from her cocoon of blankets, she could see, beyond the blackened cookfire, the wide expanse of mudflats, and in the far distance a scoured horizon.

The others slept except for Anar, whose eyes, still rimmed with sleep, were watching her mother. Nerys put her finger to her lips. She didn't want to wake her companions and shatter the morning's peace. Rising, she grabbed the remains of their rabbit dinner, a carcass still skewered on a stick, and padded to the shelf of rock just outside their cave.

Once this had been a cliff at the edge of the inland sea. Or so the story went. Receding year by year from its former domain, the sea relinquished these banks to the mud lands, with their red clumps of reeds. Beyond the flats, beyond the inland sea, lay rumors, wonders, and legends. They would see some of them, she allowed herself to believe. Perhaps they would find Lithia kinder in the west. There might yet be remnant populations of deer, caribou, or buffalo that had found a means to survive. In this way Nerys and her companions might live freely, never groveling to the orthong.

But no, that was a fantasy. Food might be had, but

their lives would be short. Her father died at thirty of indigo, and her mother at thirty-four. And if tales were true, the orthong would fix their lungs and all else that might afflict them. Old women had been seen among the orthong, it was said, women forced to bear unspeakable litters until their wombs turned to jelly. A shadow passed over her for a moment, to think of the ruthless barter: food in return for the bearing of orthong young. By some lights, it was a harsh trade— to those, perhaps, who had never gone to bed hungry and woke to find no breakfast. Better to starve, the menfolk said. But then *they* had no choice.

Nerys cracked open the rabbit bones and sucked on the marrow. Anar crept to her side, saying nothing, but reaching out a thin hand for a share. Nerys let her daughter finish the largest bones while she gazed at the clouds of birds bursting through the clear morning air.

"May I go down to hunt for clams, Mama?"

Nerys nodded her permission and Anar threw the bone scraps over the cliff.

"Did you think the rest of us need no breakfast?" Eiko's snarl was hard to mistake.

Nerys rose to confront the woman. "There was nothing but bones. No feast, Eiko."

At Eiko's glare, Anar set her mouth, not liking the woman's carping. Then she left the cave, scrambling down the cliffside and scattering nesting birds in white and raucous eruptions.

"Hunters should eat first," Eiko groused, pulling on her boots.

"Hunters need to hunt," Nerys said. "Then we eat." To avoid dealing with Eiko, Nerys turned back to watch the dawn, sparkling orange in the rivulets of seawater, which now at high tide pierced the flats like fingers of fire.

Thallia rose ponderously from her bedroll. Sometimes slow of mornings, the big woman was strong as a boar and as graceful a runner as Nerys had ever seen.

"If our morning bickering is now done, perhaps someone would build a fire." She spoke wearily but with a tinge of humor, softening the tension in the quarters.

Nerys prodded the fire pit for coals and in a few minutes they were warming themselves around the fire. With aching bellies, they quickly turned to talk of the day's hunt. Here in this rookery, a meal of seabird might be had, but the creatures looked to be little more than bone and feather, and were hard to catch. They needed larger prey. Today it would be marsh deer.

Eiko had first spotted the deer at the base of a cliff, just to the south. The arms of the headlands formed a natural pen where they might trap a deer. But it would be hard with only three hunters.

"Anar can help," Nerys said, her voice casual.

Thallia studied the fire, noncommittal.

"This is no child's game," Eiko said. "If she prattles, the deer will flee."

"She knows how to keep silence. You've already taught her to swallow her voice." Nerys didn't bother to hide the bitterness in her voice. Anar spoke seldom, knowing how she drew Eiko's fire.

"Someone had to teach her a child's place."

Thallia nudged the fire with a stick, lighting the tip into flame and shaking it into an ember.

"Already this *child* rises before you of a morning, Eiko," Nerys said, "and is out hunting clams. Perhaps you'll have your breakfast yet."

Thallia blew on the stick, flaring the ember. "I say we take up three watch points in the grass near the alcove and spear a fat buck." She fixed each of them in turn with her steely eyes. "Easier to overlook each other's faults on a full belly, eh?"

Eiko snorted. "Give me a haunch of deer and I'll even kiss the brat."

"Now that would spoil Anar's appetite, Eiko," Nerys said.

At that moment Anar scrambled into the cave, clutching the front of her bulging jacket. "Mama! Look at what I've found." She unbuttoned her coat and out clattered a dozen mollusk shells and sand dollars left by the extreme high tides of the storm. She held one up and turned it before the fire to admire its pearly inner lining.

"A pretty little shell," Eiko said, droll as might be.

"Look, this one has little spines," Anar said.

Nerys patted her daughter's arm. "Take these now, Anar. We must leave for the hunt."

Her daughter settled before the fire to inspect her shells while Eiko grabbed her jacket and spear and stalked from the cave.

Buttoning her jacket, Thallia raised the fur hood over her head. She paused in front of Nerys. "Curb your bile, Nerys." Her face held that neutrality that made her hard to argue with. "You broke the agreement. We said no children. I don't begrudge Anar so far, but you break your word, you make enemies. That's a fair trade."

Nerys kicked at the fire, sending dirt scudding over the flames. "Let the fire burn down, Anar," she said. "We don't need smoke to mark our camp."

"Can I come, Mama?"

"Not this time, sweet one." She nodded at her daughter and followed Thallia down the cliffside.

Eiko was far ahead, striding across an expanse of marsh dotted with tussocks of short, reddish reeds. The reddish clumps of the mudflats were a sullen reminder that they must find meat today.

Red was the color of old Lithia. Her palette was brownish and dark here in the scattered saltwater reeds, knee-high and fluttering in the wind. On higher ground the old hues broke out in blood red, crimson, and dark wine, where centuries-old pods and seeds found new purchase in the changing nursery of Lithia's soils. Sometimes they followed chemical seams in the ground, or sprouted on the rotting mats of Terran meadows. Other times, a blanket of burnt umber would simply wrap around a still-living Terran tree, the two of them living together, yet apart.

But however it erupted, Lithia's red always meant the same thing: poison. Its toxins killed quick or slow, but the end was never in doubt. Nor could the claves raise any red thing at all, including tomatoes, berries, beets, cherries, or apples, lest their red mask Lithia's intrusions.

A briny wind slurred through Nerys' hair as she hurried to catch up with Thallia. Though she put little store in religion, she made a quick prayer for a good kill and prompt departure from these flatlands, so exposed to enemy eyes from the surrounding cliffs. They had seen no evidence of their pursuers for two days, but it wasn't just their own clave they had to evade— any other clave would also draw hasty conclusions from women traveling alone. Hatred of the orthong was reflexive. Their monstrous aspect and viciousness, along with the defection of human women, combined to inspire a virulent hate, tainted with the revulsion of bestiality. Nerys suspected that an even stronger—if unspoken—anger welled from jealousy. Those who ran to the orthong would eat well, and they would live. For that, neither the aliens nor the women could be forgiven.

She scanned the high bluffs. Twisted trees rose in black silhouettes against the rising sun. Nerys reached into her pocket and fingered the hard, vermilion berries she and the others kept in case they had need to choose a quick death.

Ahead, Eiko and Thallia had taken up their posts amid widely separated clumps of weeds some hundred feet from the salt lick alcove. No sign of deer. Nerys hunkered down to wait.

The sun was high before they spotted a group of six does emerging from a path in the headlands. The animals paused at the base a long while, as though reconsidering their venture. Finally they began a dawdling procession toward the alcove.

Nerys couldn't see Thallia and Eiko, but she was sure they were gripping their spears as hard as she.

The plan was for Eiko and Nerys to run forward at each edge of the cove, forcing the deer straight out the middle, where Thallia would be waiting. Eiko would sound the cry, and on that signal Nerys would rise up, forming the left-hand flank. Thallia carried two spears in case her first missed its mark, but her first throw was likely to be her best.

The does were in the gentle arm of the cliff, licking salt. On her right, Nerys saw with dismay that Eiko was stealing forward to a closer patch of weeds; foolish move, but it put her in a better position to block their southern escape, and the deer did not take alarm. Nerys matched her advance, but froze when one of the animals abruptly lifted its head. In an instant, all the does reacted, heads snapping up in spring-loaded readiness.

Eiko charged. It was a bad move, with Nerys still well back of Eiko's position. The deer pivoted in unison from Eiko, and seeing an opening between Nerys and the cliff, they sprang for it, with Nerys' desperate spear throw falling a full twenty feet short. The women gave pursuit, but soon the deer had far outpaced them and disappeared up the defile from which they'd come. Eiko's curses spoke for them all, but the only sound Nerys made was her stomach registering a gurgling reproach.

Panting, they rested for a moment before resuming their run down the beach. Alerted now, the deer would be hard to catch. Still, the women had no choice but to track them.

Eiko had ruined the plan, breaking position, and she needed dressing down, but Thallia's pointed look at Nerys warned her off. They hurried down the beach in silence, Eiko having the grace to be ashamed.

With the deer fled into the headlands, the mudflats stretched barren before them, pimpled with batches of old Lithia and the occasional dusting of birds. For the first time since their escape from the clave, the thought of starvation dipped into Nerys' mind.

Their course led them past their cliff hideaway. Anar was waiting for them.

"Tell your brat to hunt shells," Eiko murmured, pushing ahead. Then she stopped in front of the child.

Nerys hurried forward, afraid that Eiko would take out her anger on the girl. But following Eiko's gaze, she looked down to find a yearling deer bleeding into the sand, dead from Anar's spear.

"It ran straight to me, Mama!" Anar said, still wild-eyed from her exploit.

Nerys laughed out loud as the women stared in amazement. The animal, with her daughter's spear impaled in its gut, was as large as Anar herself. Her joy in Anar's accomplishment was surpassed only by her ravenous hunger. Here was their feast, after all. Even Eiko seemed uncertain whether to laugh or scowl.

Thallia shouldered forward, placing her hand on Anar's shoulder. "Well done, child," she said. "You are our best hunter, this day."

Anar's smile almost lifted off her face.

"Eiko," Nerys said, "give Anar a hand to haul her kill up to the cave, will you?" They shared a long look between them. Eiko broke contact first, bending to her task.

3

Mitya had taken to sleeping under the galley food prep table. There was no privacy to be had except here in the compartment allotted for meal prep, where walls and a door were thought necessary to keep dust out of the dinner. The only other rooms besides the main dome were the Captain's quarters, the toilets, and the clean room for the geo cannon. At night the crew inflated their mats every which way on the dome floor, with officers preferring the perimeter wall, leaving lesser individuals to congregate in the middle. This often left Mitya next to Oran, whose constant hazing inched ever closer to outright meanness.

This morning Mitya deflated his mat and crawled out from under his table just in time to meet Koichi as he ducked through the flap of the galley door. Koichi, a specialist second class in chemical systems, did double duty as galley chief.

"Looking for scraps?" Koichi said, one eyebrow raised.

"No sir," Mitya said. He had learned that taking people's gibes at face value saved him from complicated decisions like how to respond to sarcasm and insults.

Koichi began selecting his breakfast menu, a choice among wet and dry cereal and two kinds of re-meat. As Mitya laid out the bowls, he heard voices on the other side of the galley wall. An argument, from the sound of it.

"She doesn't have the depth, damn it, you know that!"

Another responded: "I've said I need you on the technical end, Stepan. Leave the administration to Cody."

"Administration? We're a damn sight beyond administration! We're stuck in the middle of nowhere and falling behind schedule. At this rate it'll take months!"

"No, it *won't* take months." Now Mitya realized it was the Captain speaking.

"Damn it, Gabriel, we've still got calibration of the model and tests!"

"Stepan, Stepan. I understand that. But *someone* needs to coordinate the science team. We could do worse than Val Cody."

"By rights, it's my job—you know that. It's a bitter thing to report to a woman fifteen years my junior!"

"Don't think of it that way, Stepan, it's—"

"Don't tell me how to think!"

Koichi caught Mitya's eye. "Go check the water gauges," he muttered.

Mitya shuffled toward the door as the Captain responded, "It's temporary, Stepan. When the time comes, I'll be grateful you helped me out on this."

As Mitya emerged into the central dome the two men noticed him and stopped their conversation. As soon as he was headed away, he heard their muffled voices, urgent and spiked with anger.

Over at the input valve for the water purification system, Mitya checked the readouts for contaminants, doing a quick scan for aluminum, methane, bicarbonate acid, iron chlorides, sulfuric acid, selenium, tellurium, and the rest of the caustic brew of the Rift area. All in normal ranges. The filters, awash in a solution of ruthenium disulfide and other purification catalysts, registered within tolerances. It was a make-work task that Mitya was sure they weren't leaving to a thirteen-year-old.

He took the long way back to the galley, passing the clean room. This took up a quarter of the dome, a great wall of translucent resin from floor to ceiling, slightly concave under the sucking pressures of the air filtration fans inside, venting particulates out of the dome. As one of the crew ducked through the door flap, Mitya snatched a quick peek, and was rewarded with a fleeting view of a draped assemblage the size of a shuttle passenger cabin.

"Curious about the cannon, Mitya?"

Mitya swirled to find Captain Bonhert looking down at him with a not-unfriendly look.

"Yes sir."

"Quite a piece of machinery, eh?"

"Yes sir." When the Captain lingered a moment, Mitya asked, "How are we going to get it down into the valley?"

"Good question, Mitya. How would you do it?"

"I'd build it to disassemble in sections, then take it down in the shuttles, piece by piece."

The Captain's broad face cracked sideways into a smile. "Well now, that's exactly what we plan to do. Good thinking, Mitya. Could be you have some of your mother's engineering in you. That so?"

"I hope so, sir." He very much did hope so, for his mother had been a top engineering officer.

"I was thinking, Mitya, perhaps you could lend a hand with something."

"Me, sir?" Voice cracking.

"Our situation is serious, Mitya. We may need to ask everyone to give a hundred and ten percent. Are you up to it?"

"Yes sir! I'm pretty good on computers; I even do a little quantum processing, sir, or anything in math or chemistry."

Captain Bonhert smiled wider still. "Good, good. That's just fine. But are you up for something that might be dangerous?"

"Dangerous? Oh yes, sir, I'm not afraid of danger."

The Captain's smile took on a tinge of irony, an expression Mitya had special antennae for. He realized he sounded like a child. "Whatever you need, Captain," he added, figuring it for something Stepan might say.

"Good. We'll be getting a field unit together this

morning to take readings at the vent. We need a strong back and a man who can follow orders. Can we count on you, Mitya?"

His mood soared. "Yes, sir!" At that moment he would have jumped into the Rift if Captain Bonhert had needed it of him.

"Report to Lieutenant Tsamchoe, then."

As Bonhert turned away, Mitya blurted: "I never meant to horn in on the shuttle, Captain. It was an accident. I was just there and got pushed inside." He'd waited six days to tell somebody that, but he was shocked he'd said it to the Captain himself.

Bonhert regarded Mitya kindly. "I'm glad you're here, Mitya. We need some of your enthusiasm."

That didn't seem likely to Mitya, but he didn't mind hearing it anyway.

"You'll serve me well if you help keep crew spirits up and work hard."

He paused and waited, so Mitya threw in a "Yes, sir."

Bonhert continued: "Anyone with a bad attitude, I'd like to know about that person. You can report directly to me. No matter *who* it is, you talk directly to me. Agreed?"

"Yes, Captain." As Bonhert walked away, Mitya drew a deep breath, filling his lungs with air for what seemed the first time in a week. Then he strode across the dome to the galley.

Koichi looked up at him, raising an eyebrow at his tardiness.

"I won't be able to help you with breakfast today," Mitya said.

"And just why would you think that?" Koichi was pouring boiling water into the cereal pot, and by the look in his eye he'd just as soon pour it on Mitya.

Mitya kept his voice studiously neutral. "Captain has me helping out with a field test in the Rift today."

Koichi looked dead blank at him, maybe gauging whether Mitya would dare such a bald-faced lie.

"Be glad to help you tomorrow, if we're back from the vent." As Koichi stared, Mitya threw him a friendly smile, and ducked out to find Lieutenant Tsamchoe.

As it turned out, a strong back was all Mitya counted for, but he wasn't complaining. Of the fourteen crew packed and ready to descend into the Rift Valley, only five of them carried gear, including him and Oran. The other nine were heavily armed, with both pistols and long, mean-looking automatics. Oran carried a pistol, he noticed. Though they didn't trust Mitya with a gun, nothing could spoil the prospect of this adventure, not even the realization that they'd be lugging everything back out of the Rift today, back up the 1,200-foot escarpment to the dome, lest they leave anything behind for orthong sabotage.

Tenzin Tsamchoe had been into the Rift Valley already, to scout a course to the main volcanic vents, six miles into the valley. It had taken him two days to recover. Today the field expedition had reengineered breathers that made their throats feel like they were full of melted jelly, despite dissolving to microscopic thickness once implanted.

The morning grew brighter through a thin mist, but no warmer for all its brilliance. Heavy jackets and thermal caps promised to keep them warm enough, though Lieutenant Tsamchoe joked they'd walk themselves hot and then have to carry their jackets before long. As the crew set out single file, Mitya waited his turn to descend into the cut in the escarpment. As he watched, the mists thinned to gauze, revealing a wash of azure sky and then the deep valley itself. A stupefying vista lay before him, the red valley fading to purple and brown. There in the distance was a dark bank that Mitya figured must be the matching Rift Valley wall. At this sudden shift in perspective, his stomach dropped down from its tentative perch in his body. The planet seemed to tilt out of alignment.

"By the Lord," someone said. Even Oran was gaping at the view.

It was not possible for anything to be so big and yet contained in one vista. The mists were disappearing below them as though they were soap bubbles popping. Tatters of the valley floor swam into view, deep tubes of vertical space with the black and reds of the valley forming the bottom of the well. The sense of being up very high indeed, and having a long way to fall, was looping through Mitya's mind.

Tsamchoe barked, "Anybody feel sick, look at your feet. Always a good idea to look where you're walking anyway. Let's go."

Oran, just ahead, grinned back at Mitya, "You upchuck on my boots, you'll lick them clean!" It was a disgusting thing to say, especially given the current state of Mitya's stomach, but he said it friendly enough.

They left the plateau and began the descent, scrambling down a cut of black rock that mercifully enclosed them for a distance, screening the view and settling stomachs. Now and then through his breather Mitya detected faint threads of sulfur and chlorine, slightly unnerving and intriguing at the same time. No scrubbed and sanitized environment, this. The planet was a stew of alien smells and untidy geology. And there would be more strangeness: great hard-shelled insects, as big as your arm, Tsamchoe said, and birds in flocks. And crimson plants and maybe lava erupting if they were lucky. Or luckier yet, an orthong.

Mitya's stomach churned as they emerged out of a narrow rock passage and beheld the colossal views of the Rift zone. He didn't *think* it was fear, but rather hoped that the queasiness came from the sense of wall-less distance, which, despite its beauty, did not sit well with his breakfast.

Forty-three miles away was the high fault that had once been close neighbor to the one they now descended. Twenty million years ago, a level plain had existed here. Directly below it lay the great juncture of one of Lithia's crustal plates, and these two pieces were riding the mantle's rocky currents away from each other at the speed of a growing fingernail. As the land stretched, the weak, extended crust allowed magma to rise, bulging slowly into a great hill. Finally the swelling dome split across the top. While the dome continued to rise, a miles-long slice of rock along the crack slipped downward, forming a notch. That was the beginning of the valley.

Over the millennia the valley floor stretched, widening that notch, the floor of which cracked, inviting fountains of magma from deep chambers in the mantle. One of them was the great plume, the one that reached up from the depths, and that the nanotech probes would follow, swimming against the stony current, to begin their dispersal of mantle heat, quieting the engine of the volcanoes, the source of all their troubles.

That plume was a convenient path to the heart of the world. Beginning at the outer boundary of the molten layer of Lithia's core, its upward-creeping rock described a thirty-mile-wide conduit through the mantle until, about sixty miles from the surface, the pressure eased off enough to allow the plastic rock to liquefy, where it ballooned into magma chambers in the crust. This deep mantle plume was also the source of a deadly volatile—chlorine, a taste of the primordial mantle, with its rocky makeup laced with trapped gases. They knew enough to avoid any valley low points, where the chlorine would lie in heavy pools.

Mitya trudged across a tumbled mass of broken rock slumped at the bottom of the cliff. His balance was not the best on an incline, especially carrying fifty pounds on his back; it seemed he was in a semi-controlled state of falling, with rocks shifting under his feet as he plunged downward.

When he reached the valley floor he was sweating and tired, but the team marched on, except for Lieutenant Tsamchoe, who was waiting for him.

"How are you doing, Mitya?"

"Fine, sir. I'm hot, though." He unzipped his jacket, flooding his upper body with a cool influx of valley air.

Tsamchoe fell in step beside him. "You should keep the jacket on, though. I'm not sure what kind of weather we'll have, but the rain around here will tend to be acid, and the sun isn't much better, as pale as you are."

"The rain is *acid*?"

Tsamchoe flashed a broad smile. "A *little* acid. Won't kill you, but might sting. Sulfur trioxide reacts with any precip. The valley here is an extreme environment. Just a few little things to watch out for—nothing we can't handle."

"No sir," Mitya said, adding acid rain to his list of wonders. They were walking through a flat terrain of trees and scrub grass that collected in bowls of soil etched into the rock. The trees looked wrong. From reddish, woody branches rose myriad bumps like marbles stuck to a tube. Not proper trees at all, without leaves, without green. Nothing like the Earth trees of the vids.

"As a last-minute addition to the expedition, you missed my natural history lecture yesterday, when I briefed the team," Tsamchoe was saying. "So here's the recycled version: Nobody drinks the water. When you smell it up close, you won't want to, but no experimenting. Don't touch anything. No collecting. Decontamination will be hard enough without people smuggling in bird feathers and the like.

"The insects are big. No one knows what the size

limit is; they're like Terran crabs and crocodiles in that the older they are, the bigger they are. Don't be thinking shuttle size, be thinking in the range of one meter and less and you'll be about right. They run like hell on a gazillion legs, usually *away* from you, so don't get trigger-happy."

"I don't have a gun," Mitya said, hoping for an instant that that might be an oversight.

"No." Tsamchoe didn't pursue the topic, but finished up with: "This is volcano country. We'll be seeing lots of hot springs, which means there's magma near the surface, and maybe in pipes. Sometimes the flows crust over at the surface so you can't see them, and your foot could break through into a stream." He looked sideways at Mitya, a flicker of a smile playing at the edge of his mouth. "Watch where you step."

"Why don't we use a shuttle, Lieutenant? Are we short on fuel?"

"The shuttles make a lot of noise, Mitya. Draws attention to us." He left unsaid, *Orthong attention.* "We'll use them when the time comes."

Tsamchoe clapped a hand on his shoulder. "Meanwhile, we hike." They walked in silence a few moments, and then Tsamchoe said in a different tone of voice, "I had many long talks with your father, Mitya. He and I worked on the geophysical survey a few years ago. A good man. I'm sure you miss him. If you feel like talking sometime . . . you let me know."

Mitya couldn't depend on his voice just then. He nodded quickly, hoping it wasn't rude. Mercifully Tsamchoe left just as tears started to sprout from Mitya's eyes. He swiped his arm across his eyes and picked up his pace. Behind him were Jess and Theo, bringing up the rear, rifles slung over their shoulders.

Climbing now, they threaded their way among deeply folded ridges. Mitya had been hearing skittering noises ever since they reached the valley floor. Now he came nose-to-nose with the likely source of these scratchings, a many-legged, reddish-brown insect hugging the side of a rock. It was about the size of his boot, shaped like a tube with dozens of overlapping carapaces. He recognized it as a cousin of the visitor he'd had at the dome: A bony strut extruded from behind its head to in front of its mandibles, suspending a glowing point like a tiny lantern.

"Look, Oran," Mitya said to the older boy, who'd passed the creature without seeing it.

Oran turned and clambered back to see the specimen. "Ugly son of a bitch," he said. Then, peering around the rock, Oran said, "Here's another."

Mitya joined Oran at his vantage point, and his heart lurched. There in the next fold of the hillside were hundreds of the creatures, milling in the eroded crack of the hill, making a rustling sound as their shells jostled against each other.

Oran gave Mitya a little shove toward them, grinning. For a split second Mitya wondered how mean Oran might get, but the older boy was already heading back up the path. Theo and Jess, behind them, frowned at their breaking of ranks.

"That's who inherited Lithia," Oran said. "The bugs. Only ones that could adapt fast enough. Them and the plants."

"From what I've seen of the place so far, the bugs can have it," Theo commented.

Mitya wondered if the bugs were collecting in that hillside crack because it contained a slipstream of chlorine gas moving down the ridge . . . in which case the bugs were the least of his worries. He found himself moving a little faster up the slope. From time to time, the air sparkled as the sun reflected off droplets of water and sulfuric acid, forming a shimmering curtain all around them. But step by step as they ascended the hill, the pocket of vapor burned off until, standing at the crest, they looked down at a perfectly round basin several miles wide.

"Volcano," Oran said. "This whole bowl's nothing but a volcano."

Now Mitya could see it, the blue-black curved rim, so far away it didn't register right away as a ring. A small lake formed the center of the bowl while, nearby, mists rose from yellow pockets in the caldera floor and raced along the ground in the breeze.

"The volcano blew out the whole bowl?" Mitya asked nervously.

Jess snorted. "No, it's a pit crater, dummy. It collapsed."

Mitya nodded, as though that answer were more reassuring.

"Close your mouth, or you might catch a flying bug," Oran said. He carried what looked to be an eighty-pound pack, with a bundle of long cylinders strapped to the top of it. Still, he was cheerful despite his burden, and Mitya was glad to take some ribbing of this sort. It helped ground him, here where the view was larger than he was used to, and where the other rim of the crater looked like the end of the world away.

They descended the steep curve of the caldera, zigzagging their way down, their shoes slipping on the slaggy ground, which crumbled at the slightest touch. With this first clear view of the planet's terrain, everyone was staring. Whether or not they felt queasy, their heads were turning, taking in the sweep of the panorama. Drifting carpets of grass and lichens formed an abstract painting in red, purple, and brown, Lithia's signature colors, a result of the evolutionary quirk of old Lithia's biota: Its photosynthetic process reflected red wavelengths, not green.

Up ahead, the expedition had bunched up for a moment. As Mitya joined them, Tsamchoe was pointing out a sputtering waterfall as tall as he was. It erupted from the side of the hill a stone's throw away. "Care to take a quick shower?" Tsamchoe asked the crew.

"Mitya smells like he could use one," Oran ventured, and a few of the team chuckled.

"He'd get clean all right," Tsamchoe said. "That water's boiling."

The crew eyed the sputtering water as they filed past, proof positive that the ground harbored magma not far below.

As midday approached, they stopped for lunch next to the algae-choked end of the central lake. Here flocks of birds—deep yellow creatures—strutted through the shallows on long, stalky legs. The birds' color looked as though it might come from the yellow pigment in the algae, which in turn, Tsamchoe said, fed on soda, a product of magmas high in alkaline carbonates. Dotting the landscape were short mineral spires where steam condensation created lopsided chimneys. Mitya and Oran broke out tubes of re-meat and canteens of purified water and unabashedly gaped. The congregation of bright-plumed birds confirmed Mitya's impression that, on Lithia, animals came in clumps. So they munched on their rations and stared at this place of wonders. It was one way to avoid looking up. Over their heads, the transparent lid of the sky beckoned wickedly for their attention.

He noticed Oran massaging his temples. "Me too," Mitya said.

Oran frowned over at him.

"I have one too," Mitya said. "Headache."

Oran nodded ruefully. "Comes of breathing planet farts."

As Mitya laughed, the near edge of birds rose into the air, flapping their amber wings.

By late afternoon they had climbed the opposite side of the caldera, where the group gathered in a line to view the stupendous main branch of the central Rift Valley. Far in the distance, the Gandhi River pooled into a great lake, flashing in the sun. It lay embedded in a valley floor black with old basaltic lava deposits, which in turn smoked from fumaroles like the cook-fires of giants. Their masks were helpless against the onslaught of acrid fumes.

There was no mistaking their goal. A great line of vents some two miles off belched steam and gases in a gigantic curtain, at the foot of which, red lava pulsed as though from a severed vein.

"Now we make quick work of what we came to do," Tsamchoe said, leading the group into the valley.

Even with a reengineered breather, the fumes made Mitya's throat feel like he'd swallowed bleach. Mitya held the reflector steady for the laser gun, while Theo, having circled around to the other side of the vent system, shot a beam to record the distance. The crew hurried to complete their work as the ground trembled in a series of microearthquakes. Lieutenant Tsamchoe said that was from magma moving through the chambers below ground and cracking adjacent rocks—though if that was supposed to be reassuring, no one felt any calmer.

Some of the fissures in this part of the valley were emitting spatter, forming cinder cones as high as twenty feet. They had passed one of these, and its roar still echoed in Mitya's ears. Tiny shards of volcanic glass had fallen on them and they'd had to pull up their hoods for protection.

But this section of the vent was relatively quiet, except for an unnerving sound of crinkling, as though something very heavy were treading on the broken lava. Oran claimed it was just the sound lava made as it cooled, but Mitya kept looking over his shoulder as he held the reflector. Next to him, stalks of burned trees protruded from the black rocks. Some fifty feet away, a pond of lava was overtopping the roof of a collapsed lava tube. The lieutenant explained that the magma likely to erupt explosively, but would well up slowly; more explosive volcanic activity came from stickier magma, caused by a higher silica content. But even if the vent here got worse, he said, the crew could easily outrun the lava. Nevertheless, the crew kept a watch on it, as they hurried to finish.

One team permanently mounted some equipment at the site to measure ground deformation and give warning of increased volcanic activity. Others took seismic readings to map the magma chamber, a complex configuration of reservoirs, pipes, and conduits on an enormous scale relative to the small visible crack before them. These measurements would be used to program the geo cannon and also to design the superstructure for the cableway used to bring the cannon to bear on its target. Two short towers anchored in solid ground on either side of the fissure would form the braces for the cable system to move a specially designed truck into position over the vent. The truck would carry the geo cannon and keep it stable during firing.

Theo was waving from the other side. With the readings taken, Tsamchoe ordered crew to pack up. By the time they finished, Mitya was drenched in sweat and nervous as a cadet on his first coldwalk.

They hiked out over dunes of rock, the ground quieter now, and more solid-seeming, though Mitya knew that a mile or two below, the great magma chamber still pulsed with red rivers of stone.

5

1

Day eight. They had been heading south for three days, through the rolling, grassy hills. Reeve could have been on a treadmill for all he knew, and crossing the same gully hundreds of times. It was almost easier to believe than that the world held such monstrous spaces, had so little need for frugality that it could roll out these plains forever.

"You said *two* days," Marie groused at Spar. But she set one foot in front of the other and never asked for rest. Marie was on the mend, to Reeve's relief, despite a lingering sallowness to her complexion.

"Depends on if you're runnin' or walkin'," Spar said, without turning around. Despite a persistent, soft cough, the man set a relentless pace. Like all clavers, he'd grown accustomed to the poisons he breathed— poisons that would make him old at thirty, dead at thirty-five. The girl was off somewhere, hunting, exploring, or whatever she did in her long absences from the group. They were headed for the Inland Sea, where Spar said they could raft westward and speed their journey. Mam's journey, that is. The girl was in charge, without a doubt, and Spar was on a mission to follow her to kingdom come, it sometimes seemed. They were both as odd as space wind.

Where were they headed? *Where Lithia tells Mam to go,* came Spar's answer.

And where does Lithia tell Mam to go? *Here and there, by the soil, boyo.*

What does the soil tell her? *Whether she can eat.*

Who is Mam? *Child of Lithia. She'll kill us, by and by, Lithia will. But her own children, she'll give suck. Mother Lithia's good and tired of Earth and all her critters.*

Why does Mam eat soil? *They all eat soil, boyo. It's all that's left.*

Who else eats soil? *The others like her.*

Where are the others like Mam? *Where Lithia tells Mam to go.*

Where's that? *Yonder, by the soil, boyo.*

A few rounds like that and Marie was ready to strangle the fellow, but there was no getting coherence from him, except in some quirky gestalt. It was as though you had to listen for meaning between the words, or blur your eyes to see the shape of his thinking. The girl—Loon was her real name, Marie had discovered—spoke hardly at all, and Reeve suspected she was slightly retarded; thus the genesis of her name. He wasn't sure where she was leading them, except generally westward, which suited Reeve's intention, for the Rift Valley was west of the Forever Plains. Likely it was very far west, perhaps hundreds of miles, and Spar pronounced it was likely farther than what he called a *zerter* could walk, especially ones as frankly stupid as Reeve and as old as Marie.

Spar often frowned as he looked at Marie, squinting his eyes as though trying to pry the truth from her. She was the key piece of evidence that kept Spar from spearing them for the abject liars he seemed to think they were. For Marie was undeniably *old*. Her face, though still attractive, had its share of lines and creases, and her hair was gray as sheet metal, except for a few swirls of dark brown. And if she was *fifty-four*, as she claimed, then she likely had led the pampered life of a zerter, a fat Stationer, where it was known people lived off canned air and the last of the world's medicines and where their lives could go to 120 years. Even the technology in Reeve's pack—the beam of light, filament rope, food pouches, and breathers—could not sway Spar the way Marie's gray head did.

And oddly, it was their possible Stationer origins that Spar seemed to like best about them. He took obvious relish in instructing a high-and-mighty Stationer, and in Spar's estimation Reeve needed teaching about practically everything. It also helped that they shared a common enemy: Spar alluded to his and Loon's journey down from the Stoneroot Mountains, hiding from clavers themselves.

Up ahead, Spar stood on the crest of yet another hill, a scraggly tree of a man, with the field pack a growth on his back like a burl. He turned to Reeve and Marie, pointing out in front of him. They trudged up the slope to join him.

Before them lay a gigantic flatness, a burnished chartreuse plate, edged with distant rumpled hills.

"The Inland Sea, by the Lady," Spar said, gazing out.

In this land of untidy jumbles, the uniform flatness of the terrain seemed an anomaly. As Reeve stared, he noticed a surface disturbance, a slight, rolling swell like the shivers of a mighty green-skinned monster. From Station, portions of the Tethys Ocean were patched with great kingdoms of rampant phytoplankton this very chartreuse color. But up close, the effect was startling.

"I never thought to see a green sea," Marie said in a rare show of wonderment.

"Think this is somethin'?" Spar said. "You ain't seen nothin' yet. Lithia's just tryin' on a new coat." He crouched down, dropping his arms in front of him like an ape, and gazed out at the lime sea. "People used to say Lithia's going through a phase," he said, still staring ahead. "Not a *phase* at all. This here, this is the real Lithia, like she was before Terrans came along and mucked things up, the way they like to do."

"You yourself, Mr. Spar," Marie said, "are a Terran."

He nodded, chewing on the insides of his cheeks. "That's right. I don't deny it. And I'll die like a Terran, no way around that. But it don't blind me to the deeper things, and I like to think I get a glimpse of the Lady's purpose. Now and then."

"What deeper things might those be?" Marie sat a couple yards away, mesmerized by the seascape.

Spar looked sharply over at her, squinting suspiciously. After a moment he said, as though to himself: "See, Lithia's got her own life, same as you or me. What you see on the surface . . . well, that's just the expression on her face, so to speak. You think you're seein' everything on this here hilltop. But underneath you got the live muscle of the Lady herself."

"The Lady?" Marie's raised eyebrow and doubtful voice threw Spar into agitation.

"Yes, the Lady! The planet herself, you damn fool! Solid ground, you think. But nothin's solid. It's all in flux. Terra firma turned to terra deforma. Heh!"

"Basic geology, I would say," Marie commented dryly.

"Geology!" Spar grew agitated. "You and your big tech! You don't understand a thing, old woman. The stony world is alive, I say. And she's turnin' over a new leaf." He nodded a few times, looking at Marie. "You arrived just in time to watch her flex her muscles."

"You have a charming way of seeing the world, Mr. Spar," Marie said with elaborate politeness.

Downslope a few feet sat Loon, arms wrapped about her knees, looking out at the sea. Tired of Spar's mutterings, and wishing to rest from the morning's hike, Reeve joined her.

Loon was marginally cleaner, he noted, than in the first days of their acquaintance. The heavy rain had peeled at least a few layers of grease and dirt from her body. Her hair—what there was of it—proved to be pale blond. One evening Reeve had seen Spar use a dagger to saw off her hair in short, artless clumps. Then she used the side of a blade on Spar's beard, giving the pair the look of chimps grooming each other. But the girl still smelled like a gym, never availing herself of a bath at the streams they encountered.

Her hand was idly scratching in the soil by her side, where her fingers had traced two deep grooves. She held up a pinch of soil to Reeve's lips.

He turned his face away, but she scooted in front of him, hazel eyes intent upon his mouth. "I don't eat dirt," he said, annoyed by her habit of proffering tidbits of dirt, then acting hurt if they weren't accepted.

Unfazed, she poked at his clenched teeth.

"I *said*, no dirt!"

Something hit him hard in the back and he toppled over. Spar stood above him.

"Mind your manners, boyo." His voice was calm, but his foolish, superior attitude needed shaking down.

Reeve sprang to his feet. "Teach the *brat* some manners then! And don't call me boyo." He stepped forward, reaching out to shove Spar in the chest.

Spar snatched his arm, twisting it and forcing Reeve to his knees. Reeve butted his head into Spar's groin, wrenching his own arm in the process but causing Spar to stagger on the slope. Reeve was on top of the fellow in an instant, meaning just to cuff him a time or two, but his swing hit home, square on Spar's jaw.

Despite sitting on Spar with his full weight, he felt himself heaved up and over as Spar leapt from the ground, tossing Reeve downhill, where he rolled, smashing his head into rocks for several full turns. Then Spar was skidding down the hill after him, leaving Reeve one ineffectual, flailing kick before Spar had him by the shoulder, shaking him until his head rang.

Spittle flew from Spar's mouth as he sneered, "I could crack your head like an egg, boyo, and see what comes out besides feathers." His long, skinny hands formed a circlet around Reeve's neck, cinching to the choking point. "Or you could choose the easy way, and say sorry to Mam."

Reeve managed to shove out the words: "Mam's a filthy animal, and crazy too!"

Spar smiled, showing his few good teeth. "Good choice," he said. When the blow came, it knocked Reeve senseless. As Spar stepped off him, he rolled downslope a few turns and couldn't stop himself from tumbling off a ledge of rock. He fell so hard the breath left him. For long moments he lay there, the sun glaring through his closed eyes, his lids popping with light-show squiggles. Before long a huge, hulking shadow fell over him, which finally resolved itself into three figures standing together, one tall, one middling, one short.

"No manners," the tall one said.

"Sky Clave," the short one said.

"Even so, he'll learn a civil tongue."

"You plan to beat him until he eats dirt?" the middling one asked. "What's the mannerly way of saying *No thank you*?"

"Ain't heard *No thank you*," the tall one muttered. "Ain't heard *Thank you*, neither, come to that."

Reeve heard himself moan. He rolled onto his side, pressing the hot side of his face into the grass, spitting out a salty wad of saliva. Marie was next to him, pressing something cold onto his jaw.

"The scarecrow's stronger than he looks," she said.

"He could kill you. So make nice, Reeve. We *need* these people."

"We don't need them. They're crazy; they'll slow us down." *Yonder, by the soil,* indeed. The compass of a half-wit.

"So what's the hurry? You got a hot date?" Her face was coming into focus, her short hair framing her face in a bright back-lit nimbus against the sky.

Got nine weeks left, came the thought. *Then he sinks the pellet. World's end.*

Marie's tone turned earnest: "Listen to me, Reeve. We *do* need them. They know the land, the clavers, the edibles. They can fight, and, sorry to say, all your scrapping on Station never taught you to kill. Until you learn to kill, don't insult the killers."

He hauled himself to a sitting position. Spar and Loon were heading down to the shoreline.

"Whose side are you on? He damned near took my teeth out."

"Lord above, for a fool! It's not about sides, it's about survival."

"Shit." Reeve staggered to his feet. "I can't believe you sometimes, you and your old-woman worries." He stomped off down the hillside, aiming for the shore but avoiding Spar and Loon.

The beach was wide and covered with green slime. His boots made squishing sounds as he strode out across the festering mass of algae, rank in the midday sun. He shouldn't have said *old-woman worries*; that was as rude as he'd been to Marie his whole life. The words had just spewed up from deep in his body where he'd stored a week of grief and fury. Grief for his father, and all they had said to each other over the years—and all they had not said—and grief for all his lifelong companions on Station. The fury was for Bonhert. He breathed deeply, drawing in the putrid air, fanning the coals in his heart. He walked faster, slapping his feet down into the green muck, watching its surface part with gelatinous surges.

He was helpless. On foot in a poisonous land without maps, sidelined by a chance encounter with an addled crusader and his loony-queen. It made a mockery of his vow to stop Bonhert, to expose him for a murderer and traitor. Spar was right—he was just a boyo, now mucking about a rotting shore, stamping his feet.

Turning to face the pulpy water, Reeve gazed out over the Inland Sea, letting the breeze pull some of his anger away. He found himself wondering if perhaps they *could* devise a seaworthy craft and navigate this place. He strolled down the long slope of the beach to the edge of the water. If he remembered his Lithian maps, the Inland Sea jutted into the continent at least five hundred miles from the Tethys Ocean. At its western terminus lay the outfall of the Tallstory River, from whence they might navigate to the Gandhi River, one of the great rivers of the world, cutting down through the Rift Valley. So waterways led him to his goal, or within reach. . . .

His eyes caught a hump of motion a few yards down the shoreline and he wandered toward a small object draped in scum. It rolled forward and backward with the waves. He bent down and with both hands scooped up a heavy ball in his hands. Dripping with algae, the ball looked like a deeply pitted rock, perhaps a geode of some kind.

A slopping noise behind him. He spun around. There, moving slowly toward him was a whitish upright figure, carrying a sack over its shoulder. An orthong, by the Lord above. Reeve froze, staring. It wore a long belted black coat that glistened in the sun like a chitinous shell. The coat parted in front to show a snowy white hide.

It had no face.

His heart knocked against his chest wall. The creature began loping toward him, in great strides that brought it to Reeve quicker than he could have turned and taken even one step to flee. It stood a full head taller than he, and there seemed to be two eyes peering at him from the deep ridges of its face. With supreme irrelevance, Reeve found himself thinking, *It does have a mouth—a tiny vestigial mouth* . . . Then, in the next instant, the creature extruded its one-inch claws and slashed down the front of Reeve's jacket, slicing the material and skimming Reeve's skin in a cut he hardly felt except for the rush of cold air. Reeve staggered backward and fell into the muck.

The creature threw down its sack. Through the net of rope that made up the sack, Reeve saw a few large, perfectly round rocks. The orthong advanced, noiseless except for the slap of its great feet through the algae.

For a moment the creature was distracted, looking over Reeve's head, down the shoreline. Perhaps, he saw the others, Reeve's companions. In that moment's hesitation, Reeve stood, still holding the rock, and offered the geode to the monster.

It was a stupid thing to do. He was the creature's next meal, yet he was giving the orthong a gift. His wits had left him.

They stood unmoving, the orthong and Reeve, for what seemed a long, mind-bending minute. Reeve's arms grew tired, holding the rock out at arm's length, knowing for a certainty that if his arms dropped it would be his last movement. The ridges of the orthong's hide were hard-looking, not the soft folds he'd thought they'd be. Over the back of the creature's elongated hands, a gray discoloration spread and disappeared up the coat sleeve.

The creature was looking over Reeve's shoulder again, its eyes sunk in their sockets like emeralds in snow. Then, slowly, it clutched its giant fingers over the geode and plucked it from Reeve's trembling hands. Finally, with a swift punch, it thumped Reeve in the chest, sending him sprawling onto his back.

When Reeve gathered himself up again the orthong was loping down the beach, its sack riding easily over its shoulder as though it contained oranges and not a bunch of fifteen-pound stones.

More splashing, and then Marie, Spar, and Loon were at his side, staring after the creature. Marie and Loon crouched down to examine Reeve's bleeding chest.

He couldn't speak. The day gleamed preternaturally bright, and the breeze sang with the rich, deep smells of the world. He looked into Loon's eyes. "I'm sorry," he heard himself saying. "For what I said." He turned to look into Marie's worried face. "Sorry," he said again.

Spar reached out a hand and pulled him to his feet.

Reeve felt a sharp stab under his fingernail. Swearing, he yanked out a half-inch splinter of wood.

Spar laughed silently, showing his crooked teeth. He continued lashing the pieces of framing wood together, using a length of salvaged rope.

Reeve sucked on his hurt finger, glaring at the claver.

Shaking his head, Spar said: "Guess they don't teach you how to build rafts up there in the sky, now do they."

That comment needed no response, or not the response that came immediately to mind. Marie was right. No sense killing each other, no matter how the older man goaded him.

They had spent the morning and half of yesterday combing the beach for scraps of washed-up or abandoned refuse that could be used for the raft, and their efforts were hugely successful. The beach was strewn liberally with the castoffs of colonist and colonist-turned-claver civilization; though the rare scraggly trees of the plains offered slim pickings for timber—especially without benefit of an ax—the beach was a storefront of spare parts that might be cobbled together.

They sat on the beach next to a great stack of their gleanings, including sections of half-rotted wooden skiffs, broken sheets of ceramic matrix and scraps of metal, wire, glass, and various broken gadgets that Spar called doodads. They made several hauls, stuffing their finds into the field pack that it was now Reeve's duty to shoulder. In front of them, the frame of a three-square-yard raft was beginning to emerge from the mound of detritus. Loon and Marie, meanwhile, were off foraging for roots and berries, which might have had less to do with cultural gender roles than Spar's desire to keep Reeve under guard himself.

A short way down the beach lay the ruins of a great terraform factory, the first he'd seen on his journey. Its emission stacks were still pointing skyward, but overgrown with an ominous-looking vegetation, glowing ruby red in the sun.

His finger hurt like hell. He examined the fiery path the sliver had drilled under his nail. Add that to the welt on his jaw from Spar's fist and the furrow in his chest from the orthong cut, and his body was becoming a record of mishaps. And he worried about that orthong wound, with infection a distinct possibility. It hadn't been a knife the creature used, but a *claw*. Even liberally doused with antibiotics, the biotics involved might remain unfazed. He pressed his hand against his chest, feeling the throbbing wound under the layers of his clothes.

"Thong gave you a fair nip there, Reeve-boy," Spar said, fashioning a rope knot with alacrity. As Reeve watched him, he noticed that the claver's fingernails near the base were tinged with blue, probably a sign of chronic oxygen deprivation.

"It nearly killed me, I think." In truth, Reeve had expected it to.

Spar nodded, intent on the framing knot. "That was your first life, there, with that thong."

"First life?"

Spar gestured at the stockpile. "Another of the big four-bys, Reeve-boy."

He clambered through the pile, dislodging another framing piece. They had graduated to *Reeve-boy*—a decided improvement—but it still rankled, coming from a mere claver.

"We all got eight lives," Spar continued. "Cats got nine, so figure we humans come in just below cats. Don't be thinking human's something more, Reeve-boy. Humans, why, they thought they were more, and now look." He waved at the pile of scrap. "That's what's left of *human*. That, and the pile of metal yonder." He glanced down the beach at the outpost of bristling, twisted metal. "Thought they'd create a new world from the old. Never occurred to them, old Lithia's just waiting for her chance to bust out." He laughed in his silent way, clearly enjoying his observations on human folly.

"We're not done yet," Reeve countered.

"You got more fight left in you, I can see that." Spar cut a length of rope with his knife and moved to lash the next corner. "Well, you go ahead and fight. You and your big-tech zerter friends, you got fight left, yes sir, after resting up there in your big fancy wheel of fortune."

Reeve set his jaw. "We weren't *resting*. And nothing was fancy. It was repair and jury-rig and fix and worry and reengineer and recycle until even our dead bodies were food for ponics. Everything was breaking all the time. We lived in danger like you can't even imagine!"

Spar had stopped, screwing his mouth into thoughtfulness and gazing at Reeve underneath bushy eyebrows.

"And now it's gone," Reeve went on. "Blown to hell. And everyone's dead." He stood up, shaking. "So much for *fancy*." He glared down at this ignorant claver, with his fantasies of Station life and his preposterous stance of superiority.

They resumed their work in silence. Reeve pitched in as he could, but Spar was done talking for a while except to mutter once, "That was the big flash in the sky that day, then. Your Sky Clave burning up." He nodded to himself, but kept his eyes on his task.

He set Reeve to extracting nails from the salvage, using a notched metal bar that half-worked to pry the metal spikes up.

Over a lunch of jerky and cooked roots left over from last night, Reeve thought again about his orthong encounter. Though a shock at the time, it seemed to have earned him a modicum of respect. "I think the thong would have killed me, except for that round stone I gave it," he said.

Spar narrowed his eyes and moved his head to the side, gazing at Reeve with more of one eye than the other. It was his gesture of skepticism. "Well, that was smart," he said, "for a zerter. Your thongs, they like a pretty rock. Trade for 'em. Only thing they understand except for a sharp sword." He patted his sword, sheathed at his side in its accustomed leather scabbard. "How'd you know to trade him a good rock?"

"He was collecting them. Had a bagful." Reeve worked on chewing the jerky, hard as boot soles. "What do you know of the orthong, Spar?"

"Know?" He spit a wad of saliva to the side for emphasis, one of the disgusting habits that Loon shared. "We don't know the least thing about 'em. Live up north. And they look like humans from a distance. Up close . . . well, you saw up close. Don't often come this far south, I've heard. The bigger the group, the more dangerous. You see a group of, say, twenty . . . kiss your be-hind good-bye, Reeve-boy."

The sun was as warm today as it had been since his arrival. Reeve took off his jacket and examined the deep scratch of the orthong.

"Any group of clavers out travelin', they'll be carrying pretty rocks—the bigger the better, usually. Anything unusual, that's what the thongs like. You meet up with the thongs to trade, and first thing is, they don't talk, so we use sign." Spar brought his hands up in front of him and executed quick, deft movements using fingers, palms, and wrists. "Bet you don't know what I said, now, do you?" He grinned at Reeve and repeated the movements. "I said, *Reeve's got seven lives, Spar's got three.*" He laughed, his hoarse, body-shaking laugh. "Reeve's got seven lives, Spar's got three."

"How'd you learn their language, then?"

"Didn't. Us and the thongs manage our hand sign, but nobody knows their real language. 'Cept maybe the women they steal."

Reeve stopped chewing. "They steal women? Human women?"

"Hell yes, human women! Sex-crazed, they are." Spar stood up, wiping his hands off on his clothes. "Know why? Know why they like our women, Reeve-boy?" He paused for effect. "Because their own women, they look like just what you saw yonder!" He glanced down the beach, shuddering in mock horror. "Ugly! Yes, sir." He laughed at this witticism, and Reeve, thinking of cuddling up to a wrinkled white hide without a proper face, laughed too. They laughed for no good reason, until, looking up, they saw Marie and Loon returning down the beach.

Marie approached them with a wry look on her face. "Share the joke?" she said, putting down her carrying sack.

Spar turned away, wiping the smile off his face and acting busy with the raft.

"Well . . . ," Reeve began.

Marie stood, waiting.

"It wasn't worth laughing about. Pretty crude."

I see, her expression said, eyes flicking over to the claver who just the day before had nearly shoved Reeve's teeth down his throat. But a small smile played at the side of her mouth.

Loon carried two rabbits on a cord of braided leather, more evidence of her prowess with a sling. To his surprise, Reeve found himself looking forward to cooked flesh. As repulsive as the thought was, his stomach had a different leaning. He smiled at Loon as she handed them over. "Thank you. Mam."

She grinned in response. "You skin these," she said, nodding at the carcasses.

Reeve turned to Spar for help in explaining that there was no way he was going to cut the skin off these creatures.

The older man tossed him the Station knife he'd been hoarding. "Reckon you could use that fine zerter knife to do those rabbits," he said.

Marie, watching Reeve, piped up with, "Don't faint on us, Reeve. Give them to me—I've got to learn eventually."

As Marie reached for the brace of rabbits, Loon said, "No. Reeve will."

He stood there holding the rabbits and could easily have just given them to Marie, who was being a sport, but he caught Spar's firm expression and knew it was yet another test of courtesy. By which *courtesy* Spar meant that the dirty creature's every whim was to be satisfied. He looked down at the knife. Lord of Worlds, he didn't even know where to begin. And there would be blood.

Everyone was watching him. Shit almighty. He spun around and stalked off, furious at how Loon could ruin a perfectly good afternoon, same as yesterday with her little eat-my-dirt routine.

He took the rabbits up to a piece of driftwood that

would do for a workbench and made a start with a hunk of fur toward the neck, cursing as blood smeared on the cuff of his shirt. Time was wasting away. While he was learning to skin rabbits his days were ticking off, and they had come south, not west, and if Bonhert and crew were even within a prayer's distance, he was moving *away* from his goal, not toward it. His father would have found this a familiar pattern in his son. That, and not having any goals at all. But he had one now. For the first time in his life, he aimed further than seeing what he could get away with in the midst of Station rules and regs. And still he was showing himself incapable of making decent progress, even in the right *direction*.

Nor was he likely to have any effect on the outcome. He hadn't thought much beyond getting to Bonhert; hadn't thought about how to convince the Captain's followers that he was a murderer—that he planned not terraforming but terrorism. And if Bonhert's people were all in on it . . . then his next steps were as unreadable as orthong sex. He only knew that first he bloody well had to get to the Rift Valley.

The skinning operation was a mess. Meat clung to the pelt, the pelt lay in chunks. Blood everywhere. He stabbed at his task again.

Spar had come up, watching. He shook his head. "What they teach you up there in that Sky Clave? Anything worth knowin'?"

Still doggedly slashing at the carcass, Reeve snapped. "They taught me about electrical systems, astral spectrography, resin-welding, and computer matrices. I also know advanced mathematics and a bunch of literature, history, and the Revised Code of Station, forward and backward."

Spar nodded. "Like I say, anything worth knowin'?"

Reeve let the comment pass by, studying his bloody hands for a few moments. "Why does she bug me like this? Why doesn't she like me?"

Spar picked up the other rabbit and made a quick slice around its neck and around all four legs at the feet. "You got a funny view of *like*, Reeve-boy." He cut down the center of the animal's belly and tugged the skin away from the underside, then made a cut up the legs, pulling the pelt away in quick rips. "She gives you gifts, and you don't much seem grateful."

"A chore like this is a gift?"

Spar paused in his work, narrowing his eyes at Reeve. "Food is always a gift. Used to be in Terran days, if stories are true. Now, when food ain't much around, it's a *precious* gift." In a final, deft slice, Spar had the skin off the rabbit, all in one piece. The tips of his fingers were bloody, but not a spot else clung to him. He glanced at Reeve, keeping his gaze. "This rabbit here, it don't mean a meal for her. She won't touch it." He cleaned his knife in the sand and rose. "I reckon she figured you'd be happy to have rabbit stew. Maybe she's not as smart as I took her for."

Reeve watched Spar walk away with the cleaned carcass, then glanced down at the garbled mass of blood, bone, and butchered meat. Looking more closely, he saw that a thin membrane of fat separated the hide from the muscle. Copying Spar's sawing motion, he pulled the skin, separating it cleanly. He finished the job in short order, thinking hard on whether he really had spent his whole life learning nothing that mattered.

Spar had built a small fire and was boiling roots in a rusty, salvaged pot. He accepted the carcass from Reeve and quickly disposed of the entrails.

"One other thing I can do," Reeve said, as the other three looked up at him from their seats around the fire. Spar affected not to hear, but Reeve continued: "I know how to be invisible."

That got Spar's attention. Cutting the meat into chunks and dropping them in the boiling water, he said, "More big-tech magic?"

"No big tech. But I got a knack for sneaking into places and not being seen. Or heard."

Spar nodded vigorously. "*Now* we're gettin' somewhere."

"I sneaked into the claver camp and stole their food. I stole into places on Station where they couldn't see me, even when they were on the lookout for me. Part of it's moving real slow. And part of it's just a knack I have."

"I can vouch for that," Marie said in a droll tone. "We couldn't keep the boy out of anything. I was for giving him the keys to Station and having done with it, but the brass had too much fun trying to catch him, I guess."

"Brass is?" Loon piped in as she stirred the pot.

"They're the ones in charge," Marie said. "The chief zerters."

Spar's shoulders shook in a laugh. "I can see them brass tryin' to find an invisible boy. Ha! Good on them!"

"Brass," Loon said, "ran off and left us."

"That's right," Spar said. Then in a lower voice he added, "That's why those Mudders took the feet of your friends. For runnin' to the big wheel and leavin' us to starve."

After that, they all watched the stew boil, each lost in private thoughts.

That night, Loon chose to sleep in the open, and Reeve and Marie had the tent to themselves for the first time since landfall.

"Marie," Reeve said, speaking low. "There's something I need to tell you. You awake?"

"Am now." She turned toward him in the dark of the tent.

"I didn't say anything before, because you were sick. But now . . . you should know."

As Reeve struggled to make a beginning, Marie said, "Go on."

"The shuttle crew didn't all die. One person lived. For a while."

"Who?"

"Grame Lauterbach."

He told it then, Grame's dark tale, as close to word-for-word as he could remember. He hated to put this on Marie, hated that it had been put on *him*. It twisted everything and made their trek more desperate than it damn well already was. Before, if they hadn't been able to join their fellow Stationers, they would have died, or lived somehow for as long as they might. But now it was far more than just their lives. It was the very planet, the terrible and grand world itself, that Grame said was to be blasted apart, and everyone with it. And though Lithia was not a home he knew, it *was* his home, in a way he'd known just beneath the surface of consciousness, when, week after week on Station, he'd watched its great orb turning below him. But Marie, maybe Marie saw it as expendable. Maybe she'd take passage on the great ship and never think about a world with mountains and oceans and a scrawny claver like Spar and all his ilk. . . .

She listened in silence, never interrupting. He did wonder what she'd say. It was part of why he had waited to tell her, because though he was as close to Marie as to anyone, he'd never truly told her, not outright, that Lithia was the place that was *real* to him—that despite the Station exile, and despite her and Cyrus' plans to Voyage On and search out new earths, it was Lithia he cared for.

He didn't need her to agree with him that they had to thwart Bonhert. But she deserved to know.

"I'm going to stop him, Marie," he said.

"He's not an easy man to stop."

"He killed Tina Valejo, too. Just pushed her off-Station. Why?"

Marie didn't answer; she had no answers.

From the dark, a theory presented itself. A dark

thought: Maybe Tina was trying to stop him. And if so, there may have been others who wanted to stop him, others he needed to silence.

He spoke the thought, but in a whisper, to weaken its power: "Gabriel Bonhert destroyed Station. By the Lord . . . he killed them all. . . ."

"You're wrong about that." Marie didn't want to believe it; nor did Reeve, for that matter.

He had known Bonhert for a bastard, but to destroy *Station*? Station factions couldn't have prevented him from commandeering a couple shuttles, not if he had his supporters. But for God's sake, why kill every living person they knew?

"He wouldn't have the resolve to blow up Station," came Marie's voice.

"But he has the—*resolve*—to blow up Lithia?"

"That's not the same. He's indifferent to the planet."

But Reeve's mind was curling around that one dark thought. "Even if he didn't have enemies on Station who would try to stop him, he still had to . . . do it. When the ship arrived, what if Stationers told what Bonhert intended? What would the ship think of having a planet whisked from their grasp? Maybe they'd pass on by—a good revenge on Gabriel Bonhert."

"But surely he intended to bring everyone—everyone who knew his plans—on the terraforming mission. They'd all be off-Station. No one left to spill the beans."

"He could never be sure who knew and who didn't. Maybe Tina Valejo wasn't supposed to know; maybe she was one of many." He thought of Tina mouthing her screams, silently, bound for deep space. He thought of his father. . . .

"Bonhert seemed so passionate about reterraforming." Marie's voice was uncertain; she still didn't want to believe it.

"He pretended to believe in it so he could prepare

for a mission down to the planet. My Lord, they must have been hiding their *real* research for years."

"Why would he think the ship would be so keen on staying?" Marie asked. "Reterraforming was a terrible idea; scientifically, it didn't measure up. He could have made his case to the new ship."

Reeve was sick of talking. It was all clear to him. Enough talking. But he said: "Well, maybe he just didn't want to leave it to chance."

A poisonous silence descended. Finally, Reeve whispered: "So he believed in the stars after all. Just like my father."

Marie snapped back, "He's *nothing* like your father. Don't ever say that."

Reeve had thrown aside his blanket and was shoving his feet in his boots. Sleep was impossible now. As he left the tent, he muttered, "I'm going to kill him."

"Yes," he heard Marie say. "I suppose you are. You have to try."

2

When the Stationer collapsed, Spar took over the pole, dipping it to the bottom and pushing the raft forward. The four of them had taken turns at poling. Now there would be only three of them to work. It was Reeve-boy's turn to be sick.

The old woman named Marie called it *mike robes*. But Loon had seen the like before. It was orthong poison, and there was only one cure she knew of once a thong wound turned black. She scanned the hill country around them, looking for the platform trees. The grasses still covered the land, punctuated in these parts by black skeletons of trees, clumped into copses, as though death brought them together for a last comfort. This Loon had seen all their long journey that the small things endured and the big gave up and died. The grasses, the insects, the rabbits—they were as her father described the old world. But this sea, and the tall trees, and the big-game animals—these changed or sickened as Lithia became new.

And now the Reeve-boy was lying on his back, taken ill. Maybe the orthong hadn't spared his life after all. Better if it had killed him on that beach than to let him die the death that puffed you up into a black bag.

Old Marie shaded his face with a cloth as he rested. Her wrinkled but baby-white skin was starting to blister from the sun, giving her a mottled orthong look. Perhaps the lights of the tube they lived in did not darken their skin, and now they were truly like babies, born into this world with no defenses. Still, she hoped the Lady would be kind to them, strangers that they were. It was a thing Loon knew about, being a stranger.

In Stoneroot Clave she had been an outcast. Her father would not let them beat her, but, in secret, the other children pelted her with small stones, calling her Dirt Face and Mud Eater. *Crazy child,* the adults said when she refused to eat, and she took the name they gave her, Loon, because it was one less thing to fight about. Her mother would never have allowed it while she lived, but after Mother was gone, she begged her father to call her Loon, and he relented. But when he said *Loon,* his voice made it beautiful, like a musical note, and his eyes saw into her heart. When it was his turn to die of indigo, he told her she must leave. She was no longer a child, he said, and the clave grew crosser with her as she shunned their meals and thrived. Sometimes to please them, she would eat in their presence, but her vomiting afterward put them in a rage. Even Father couldn't save her from every beating.

At last he extracted her promise to flee the clave. He set fire to their hogan, with himself inside it, and in the commotion of the blaze Loon crawled away into the hills. She hid up in the cliffs, keeping watch on the distant flames. She didn't think they would pursue her, and she was right, but she waited for a few days anyway, hoping for some proof that her absence was noted.

Now Spar was poling through the frothy sea. They steered their course close by the shore where their pole could reach the bottom. Hunks of the stinking suds mounded up onto the front of the raft and, to avoid being buried, one person always worked to free the bow of crud. Marie came forward to relieve Loon of that chore. The old woman was strong and not afraid of work, which was why they kept her. Now that Reeve-boy was sick, Loon waited for Spar to argue for leaving him behind, but he forbore, and this she took for a sign that Spar had warmed to Reeve. She hoped it might be, for she unaccountably liked this boy, and not just for his yellow tent, which was a wonder, but for the things he said, and his bravery with the orthong, and because he was handsome, with his deep brown eyes, the color of good soil.

Freed of the green scum work, Loon crawled back to sit by Reeve. She peered past the white cloths Marie had placed over his wound. Underneath, despite the ointment Marie applied, Loon could see the center of the wound turning purple. Marie's grease was not working.

"Don't touch the bandages," Marie said from up front, adding "Mam," with a glance at Spar.

Loon faced her. The old woman could not tell her what to do. If Loon gave the word, Spar would knock the woman into the water to test how she swam. If she sank, they'd know another thing zerters couldn't do.

Instead, Loon turned away to watch the shore roll by, the scalloped edges of the Forever Plains, all green, with no hint of the splotches of red she searched for.

Up ahead, the sea cleared of gunk. In its choppy mirror, the sky looked broken, with shards of clouds rocking in troughs of blue. Spar poled them with good speed in this new open waterway.

"Blue water," Loon told Reeve-boy.

He opened his eyes. "Thirsty."

She fed him water from the pouch Marie kept putting pellets into to kill the mike robes.

When he slept again, she announced to Spar, "I will swim." Then, as he turned away for modesty's sake, she stripped off her clothes and dove in. As hot as the day was, the water was cold, and her body vibrated with the shock of it. She swam with powerful strokes, in the way her mother had taught her long ago in the lakes of the Stoneroots. Exulting in the press of water all along her body, she dove for the darkness and then curled back up to the sun, with the sense of flying like a bird through the blue.

She felt her legs caressed by sea plants, great ribbons of silk floating in sun-soaked water. She held her breath as long as she could, nosing through the slippery growths, tinged red in their center veins. Rising to the surface, she treaded water. Spar held the raft nearby and waved to her. She waved back, then flipped into the sea again, drilling her body into the depths, reaching for the bottom, and a handful of sand. A fish was slurping its way along the bottom, creating a cloud of debris near its mouth. Ah. Here was a creature that tasted the soil and found it good. Perhaps Loon herself was a sea creature, then, or kin of fishes, since no other creature she ever met would feed on the soil. If so, this creature might know best where to dig her next meal. She rose to the surface, the sand streaming from her fingers.

Just enough for a very small mouthful. She rolled the sand in her mouth, sliding it over her teeth and swallowing, her eyes closed in contentment. It was very salty, as the water was. Concentrating harder, she tasted a flicker of the yellow taste, and the one she thought of as blue. And underneath, a dusting of the good brown taste that her body craved, still faint, but jolting her senses for one sweet moment. She arched her body and kicked into the kelp forest again for another pinch of ecstasy, but the sandy bottom yielded no more. Now and then, however, good tastes flowed past her in the sea current, from the west. She broke the surface, squinting at the gleaming sea that stretched in the right direction.

Exhausted at last, she hauled herself onboard the raft. Spar stood guard by Reeve, gazing outward, and affording her privacy to dress behind him. But as she pulled on her shirt, she saw that their patient was watching her, his eyes narrowed slightly, and craning his neck ever so slightly to peer beyond Spar's legs. She smiled at him. Maybe he was feeling better.

Reeve floated on the sea in the sun. The endless dip and bow of the raft made his stomach feel like it was brimful of green suds, with their smell that could take a strong man down.

He had been sleeping on and off for so long he lost track of the time. And visiting him this last time was Tina Valejo, once more floating past his outstretched hand, within inches of his fingertips. As she reached for him, her other arm sprawled out, pointing to her destination, the constellation Belfire.

When he opened his eyes, the raft was pitching as a sea creature flopped onto the opposite side.

It was Carlise. He didn't remember that Carlise survived the crash, or had even been on the shuttle. Last year on Station she had invited him to her bed a few times, and he thought she'd dismissed him for another, yet here she was, naked. As she stood, her muscular body cascaded water, dripping over her breasts and down her bronze thighs. Her beauty caught at his throat. He hadn't remembered her so small and her hair so short and golden, flecked with sunlight. She smiled at him. And then, to his acute disappointment, she put on her clothes. And when she put on dirty rags he knew it wasn't Carlise at all, and that whoever it was had no intention of straddling him and bringing him some womanly comfort, even if he could have stayed awake long enough to participate. . . .

3

At last the shoreline lost its monotonous grassy ridges and the land began to sprout fields of pinkish boulders. As they poled on, Loon watched the outcroppings grow more massive, giving rise here and there to great flat-topped hills thrust up like furniture for giants. Grasses gave way to a pebbled land of short bushes that looked half green, half gray, as though the color were bleaching out under the sun.

It was in these lands that Loon finally found the platform trees rising from red seams of soil, much as Terran trees would sometimes grow next to streams. They beached the raft and Loon set out on her search. She had seen such seams before, along weathered troughs where rock once flowed like water—a thing she had never seen, but believed because her father had told her of it. Often, as here, the troughs bred bubble eggs, a carpet of tiny air-filled sacs that Loon delighted to walk on. Sometimes they yielded in rude noises to her stomps. In spring, she knew, the bubbles would grow rigid and break, releasing perfumed clouds that drifted many miles. Sometimes a Terran tree or shrub would manage to grow here, but Lithia demanded her due, wrapping the branches and trunks in a garment of her choosing, often in wine-red edging to shades of black. It was odd to see green twigs and leaves protruding. Shuddering to see such wrong-looking mixes, she would hurry past them, averting her eyes.

She spotted the first platform tree just ahead. It

thrust toward the sky, a small copy of the giants sometimes found climbing the west slopes of the Stoneroots. But its bounty would be the same, she hoped.
She scraped the crimson gills from beneath the plates
that wrapped around the trunk, great saucers as large
around as her encircled arms. The gills released a pow-
der, and this she carefully wrapped into a piece of rubbery kelp. The smell of the defile in the sun was a
heady stew. The claves avoided the red scars, where
the perils were not all known. But Loon was attracted
to the fecund smell of decay and growth with its steep
spikes of intriguing tastes. The times she had overin-
dulged in the heady spices, she had been sick for days,
but even the inevitable headaches they engendered
could not keep her from savoring them for the space of
an hour.

Someone was watching her. She brought up her
sling with one hand while reaching for a stone in her
pouch.

It was a mountain lion, a great golden beast staring
at her from the edge of the gully. The creature stood
rigid as a rock carving. Loon loaded her sling and faced
the animal, a short throw away. The lion's sides
swelled in and out as it panted, revealing the sharp ribs
of a starving animal. Loon could see the animal's nose
sniffing hard at her, or perhaps at the unsavory smells
of the gully. Its mangy fur grew in clumps and hung in
spots, ready to fall away. Suddenly, it turned from the
lip of the bank and disappeared.

Curious, Loon scuttled to the brink and watched
the lion retreat, weaving slightly as it departed, moving
onto a flat plain littered with boulders. Out from
prickly bushes two cubs sprang to join their mother,
batting at her great paws as she plodded away. Loon's
hand twitched as her sling reminded her that Spar
would be hungry. She loaded the rock, then stopped.
The lioness had slumped into a patch of shade by a
rock outcropping and, though she and her cubs were

an easy mark, Loon turned away and saved her rock. Following the bank of the red seam, she watched for other prey as she hurried back to the raft.

She returned with a large snake hung around her shoulders, and Spar made short work of roasting it on the beach, creating the meat-smell he so loved. While he and Marie ate, Loon prepared her gill paste, then dabbed it onto Reeve-boy's festering wound.

For all that the Sky Claver had fine clothes and wrapped his food in silver paper and flew down from the great space station, he was no match for orthong claws. He festered and sickened like any world-bound claver. His skin sloughed off in the sun and he would likely starve before he learned to eat the meat of animals. All the tales of the deserters were part true and part false. They did live off canned air, Marie said, and they never starved or died of illness in their clave. But they weren't fat and sleek, as the tales said, and they weren't afraid of their shadows, and they didn't have very much big tech, except for the face-thing that helped them breathe. So they were the same as anyone in most respects, and could die despite their tech, despite her prayers to the Lady Over All that Lithia spare this one named Reeve-boy.

As her turn to pole arrived, she spied Marie wiping away the gill paste from the boy's wound. Loon set the pole down across the raft and approached her. "Leave the salve," Loon told her.

The old woman sighed. "He needs antibiotics, not your vegetable paste." She continued to wipe.

"Leave it."

Marie squinted up at her. "You want him to die?"

"Your grease failed. Time for mine." Loon braced her feet as the raft pitched on the easy crests and troughs of the sea. She felt Spar's shadow behind her, backing her up.

Marie rose to her feet, presenting herself as a barrier to Reeve-boy. "Look," she said. "The wound is infected. I know you mean well, and you've been good to us, but you don't know the first thing about medicine. Don't interfere."

Spar broke in. "How many folk you seen die from orthong cuts, eh?"

"None. And I'm not going to see this one die, either."

"Put her ashore," Loon told Spar. She picked up her pole and went back to work. Foolish old woman, without fear of the black puffing death. She turned the raft toward the beach.

"Mr. Spar," she heard Marie say in an undertone. "This boy . . . is like a son to me. Let me have his care. I'm begging you."

He eyed her a moment before saying, "Maybe we let *him* choose—what you say to that?"

"Him? But he can't think straight. He's sick, damn it!"

Spar leaned in and spoke into her face. "I know he's sick. Dying man. Dying wishes. You got no manners for the dying?"

Marie bit at her lip while Spar bent over the prone figure and nudged him awake. "Reeve-boy. You're dying, you got to know that."

Reeve-boy's eyes were open and blinking from the middle of dark circles. "Orthong killed me, that right?"

"That's the short of it, Reeve-boy. But our women here, they each want to nurse you. Marie, she got her Station magic, and Mam, she got her own medicine. And now you got to choose." He spoke kindly, Loon noted, not like he once would have spoken to the Sky Claver. "It's your death, boy. Choose."

Loon put her pole down and crawled next to him beside Marie.

"Reeve," Marie said. "Without antibiotics you aren't going to make it. Tell them."

"You got to choose," Spar was saying. "Marie or Mam."

Reeve closed his eyes as the raft rocked in the brisk chop.

"You see?" Marie said. "He's delirious."

Spar bent close to Reeve as he moaned. Then he pushed Marie close, and she put her ear by his lips.

After a few moments the old woman sat back up and looked at Loon with a face as flat and calm as that lion in the gully yonder. "He said Loon," she whispered. "Said he wants Loon."

Spar nodded judiciously. "Well, that settles it then."

Marie turned her flat, predatory look in his direction. Loon knew then that Marie was protecting her cub. But like that other lion, she had no way to do so.

Reeve-boy opened his eyes again and reached out for Loon's arm. "Take off your clothes," he said in a hoarse voice.

As Marie sneered, Spar stepped in. "There'll be none of that talk, boyo. Less you mean for *me* to take 'em off." He chuckled. "And I don't mind obliging you, but Marie here, she wouldn't think much of me in the buff. She already had a tough day." Spar looked up at Loon, and she scooted next to Reeve, then opened the packet of her salve.

And from that moment, Reeve-boy began to heal, and they poled on down the inland coast heading west to the Tallstory River, where, Loon believed, the currents brought down nurturing silt from somewhere called home.

4

It was as happy a time as Nerys could remember in her life. The Inland Sea lay smooth before them, with scudding clouds chasing one another in its mirrored surface, while a two-day warm spell buoyed their spirits. Their good luck had begun with the discovery of the skiff. It had been well hidden in bracken near the shore, but the camouflage was no match for Thallia's expert eye. Tarred and caulked with great care, the boat would be a great loss to its owners. Though a lopsided trade, Nerys left her best knife in its place so no claver could call them thieves.

The old maps showed that the Inland Sea stretched six hundred miles from the Tethys Ocean to the Tall-story River, a swift road toward orthong lands. And though Whale Clavers were expert sailors, they would not likely pursue the women this far west, into the bloodlands, where things were red that should be green. Nerys shrugged off thoughts of pursuit, bending with relish into the oars and pulling hard. They were free of those places and those times. Offering satisfying confirmation was the evidence of their full bellies and meat to spare in their packs, thanks to Anar's hunting prowess.

Add to that the fish that Eiko was now pulling up from her trawl line, and they could eat until they were sated. Eiko gutted her king salmon and passed hunks of fish around the boat, even handing off to Anar first. With her exploit Anar had become a member of the group. The girl seemed to recognize her new status, lately taking on a grown-up demeanor, applying herself to needful work: mending Thallia's pack, cleaning the fish, and sharpening their hunting knives. Nerys approved of her conduct, but with a twinge of regret that her childhood was over so soon.

"Look, Anar," Nerys said. They were in sight of the giant terraform factory, the great ruin told of by claver traders. Anar, with slavish attention to duty, looked up for a moment, then went back to gutting fish.

"No, Anar. Look at this thing." The air factories were a rare enough sight that no twelve-year-old should miss it for the sake of a chore.

Pulling close to the beach, they could see the chimneys soaring above the compound of vats, tanks, and turbines. Pipes looped throughout like a nest of resin-hardened snakes. The multi-color-coded components peeked through a carpet of red fur, old Lithian moss that for some reason seemed to like the terrafactory.

"It's pretty," Anar observed.

From the looks on Thallia's and Eiko's faces, it seemed they shared opposite sentiments. Even to Nerys it seemed that the planet had brazenly marked this place as Lithian territory. Not enough that Terrans sickened and died; now Lithia must drape the old wonders in her mantle. Nerys rested on the oars. She'd seen this moss once or twice before. Thick as whale blubber, it sprouted rubbery threads with luminous, bulbous heads to attract insects. When flying insects landed, a fatal glue held their feet fast, allowing the moss to absorb their bodies into the carpet. A chemical factory on a chemical factory, Nerys thought, and said so.

"What is a chemical, Mama?" Anar wiped her hair from her eyes, and strained as though to see the insects with their feet trapped in goo.

"Yes, give us a science lesson, Nerys," Eiko said, with an eyebrow raised at Anar's ignorance.

In truth, Anar *was* ignorant, a little more so than Nerys had been at her age. That was the way of it, she remembered her father saying, that Nerys knew less than she ought, and that every generation lost a little more of science, of crafts, of technical things. The claves had abandoned schooling under the incessant demands of farming, foraging, and hunting. But one thing Nerys' clave still taught was reading. By age seven every child could read, and every family boasted ownership of five or six books, however tattered. Anar and her peers, however, had little interest in books, and her father would not force her to study.

Nerys concentrated on answering Anar's question. "A chemical is a mixture of elements so that you get certain characteristics. Like salt . . . I think."

Anar nodded absently, squinting at the factory while Thallia resumed course. "If we turned on the factories again," her daughter said, "maybe we could make Lithia go back like she was."

"We don't know how to turn them on anymore." It embarrassed her to say so to Anar, to admit her ignorance in the shadow of their ancestors' great feat. "But even if we did know, it wouldn't help. The terrafactories were like peeing in the ocean. In the end, they failed."

"What she's trying to say," Thallia broke in, picking her teeth with a fish bone, "is that Lithia is going back like she was, a thousand years ago. And not a damn thing we can do, chemistry or no chemistry."

Eager to shed the somber mood, Nerys rowed on, and Anar went back to gutting her fish and watching the entrails swirl in the vortices from the oars. Meanwhile, Nerys and the other women kept sharp watch on the shore for any orthong, premature though that search might be. They were many miles, perhaps half a continent, away from the orthong lands in the north. That was fine with Nerys. Let the scabs wait for their chattel; she was in no hurry to glimpse their white hides.

Late in the morning a heavy fog moved in from the east, enveloping them in a woolly curtain. At the oars, Eiko moved them closer to shore, where they might stay on course by following the coast. The slap of the oars and the slur of their boat upon the water were the only sounds for several hours, as their instincts kept the party quiet and they crept along the shallow waters near the beach. Once Nerys called a warning as Eiko rowed them near the mast of a sunken ship, where a great horizontal pole could have rammed Eiko's head, had she not ducked when she did. After that, Eiko pulled out farther, and they kept the shore in view as rips in the fog permitted.

Anar rebraided her mother's brown hair, as she loved to do, forming it into one long plait fastened with deer hide. That done, Nerys settled herself into the bottom of the skiff to rest. Drowsy from their meal of fish and the morning's toil, she dozed. Anar took a turn at the oars, making little progress, but good enough for the whiteout conditions.

A harsh slap of water. Nerys bolted awake. Anar was replacing a loose oar in the gunwale, but Nerys took the oar from her, signaling quiet. She listened.

Again the splash of water, just off their bow. Nerys nudged Thallia, who awoke, drawing her knife.

Then, from the recesses of fog loomed a huge shape. Eight oars could be seen, resting upon the water. And then a giant barque emerged from the fog. Eiko sprang up as Anar screamed and they heard great thunking splashes: the barque's sailors jumping into the water.

Eiko grabbed the other oar from its socket and lunged at the first head to break the surface of the water. The sailor swam out of reach while others grabbed hold of the bow. Thallia's knife caused a yelp at that end, while Nerys' oar made contact with a bearded face lunging for the stern. Next it was Eiko's turn to ward off a starboard swimmer, and then Thallia's at her end. Someone laughed, and in a rage, Nerys knew both that they were hopelessly outnumbered and that the sailors mocked them, taking turns at their forays instead of rushing them all at once.

The looming square sails of the barque snapped in the light wind and its mast creaked as one swimmer called out, "I want the lass in the stern!" Another hooted, "I'll take her there first!" Nerys' heart shrank into a small cold stone, and her hand went to the berries in her pocket. She would slit Anar's throat, by all that was holy, before she would let them ravage the child. They would both die this hour, and by her own hand. Bellowing in grief, she threw her oar at the nearest swimmer and drew her knife.

Too late. The sailors had tired of their play and in the next moment upended the boat, spilling all four of them into the water, and someone with arms like an orthong grabbed her and pulled her down, down, far into the water. Choking, she fought him, but all in slow motion and without effect, having lost her knife. He was drowning her, filling her stomach with bitter water. And then she felt a yank on her arm, and she was floating to the surface, where she broke into daylight. Her fist made contact against a bearded jawbone, and then a whack of a hand against her head drove her nearly senseless.

She felt the clasp of a net around her, as the women were hauled up the deck of the ship, where they tumbled onto hands and knees, coughing and retching amid bass jeers and laughter.

Nerys faced a big leather boot with a silver-capped toe. Finding Anar beside her, she struggled to her feet, meeting her captor eye to eye.

He was a black-skinned man with hair gathered into a tail. Though he was tall and muscular, she longed for one last fair fight. "A game of swords for our lives," she said to him. Meanwhile she searched her pocket, but the berries were gone.

"You had your fight, and lost," he replied in a rich baritone. The other crew stood back from this man, who looked like he might lead them.

"It was two to one—no fair contest unless your men are half the ones I've known."

This drew loud and merry response from the deck, filled with sailors of surpassing ugliness, many bearing hideous scars and heads shaved and tattooed. A breeze pierced Nerys' wet clothes, drawing off her body heat and cooling her heart. She looked for a quick death, for any opening to that silent land where they had been heading, it now seemed, since they'd left their clave.

Thallia stepped forward. "I am the best fighter. Who is yours?"

A woman moved up beside the black man. Her yellow hair was woven into a hundred loose braids. She wore leather top to bottom, bedecked with an array of knives. "What is your clave?" she demanded.

Thallia stood as tall as this giant, and raised her chin, saying, "We are a new clave, in the care of the Lord."

The blond woman sneered. "You are scab-lovers running, and liars as well." She belted Thallia across the head with her fist, but Thallia held her ground.

"Captain Kalid!" someone shouted. "Let's see what we fished up! Less talk, more skin!"

The dark man was apparently the captain. He turned slowly to take in the acclamation greeting this idea, while Nerys held Anar at her side, hugging her fiercely.

"Your berries," she whispered to her daughter.

A ripping sound, and Eiko was struggling as a sailor lunged forward to grab at her shirt.

"Lost, Mama. They're all lost," Anar said in dismay, as though she had the sense to be disappointed.

Kalid turned back to the women, who now stood back to back facing the surrounding crew. "So," he said to his men, "you want a reward for your fishing, do you?" He grinned as his men responded. "Well now. We will see." He turned to the women. "But first, answer. Where are you menfolk?" He spoke with elaborate politeness, putting on a show of power for his men and his captives.

"Dead," Nerys said. "Now, in search of a new clave, we've come from the great ocean—and this is all the welcome our feat earns."

"The ocean, is it?" the blond woman said, clearly disbelieving. "In a rowboat?" Here the men laughed and she strutted for the benefit of her audience.

"And how did your menfolk die?" Kalid asked.

"They starved. There was no food, so they begged us to go," Nerys said. "And without men to slow us down, we came so far in only a week."

The pirates laughed at her wit.

"And now what name shall we give your little clave?" The captain was toying with them, but Thallia answered, "Warship Clave."

The sailors roared at this notion, casting up additional suggestions, such as "Rowboat Clave," and others more salacious.

Kalid laughed and nodded. Then, as the crew quieted, he said: "Here is my command. You six who took a swim may have the women for your pleasure until we dock. I do not reward those who were afraid to fight this battle." He turned to fix the grumbling men with a challenging stare. "Except the girl, whom no jinn would dishonor, without leave of Lord Dante." He flicked his eyes over the unruly men, silencing them. "Take them below, my swimmers. But no savagery. If Dante takes a fancy to one of these warriors we want no scar or ruin to answer for."

The blonde stomped her feet. "They are scabbers!"

Kalid met her eye to eye. "Dante will decide, if you serve him still." He smiled at her with equal mixture of challenge and cheer, until she stalked off.

Their captors led them below, locking Anar in a small hold. The men were hungry for their pleasure, and Nerys submitted for Anar's sake, while she plotted her revenge on each of the stinking beasts in turn.

6

1

Day twelve. The dip and swell of the raft set up a hypnotic rhythm that made it easy for Reeve to remain in a constant reverie. He lay on his side, staring into the fog on which his thoughts took form.

He saw his father amid his data fields and slates in the small room that he and Marie called "the lab," where for twenty-five years he had scanned for candidate planets and revised the working drawings of the great ship. Marie smiled a silent hello amid her printouts, but left the main interaction to father and son. Cyrus looked up at his son as Reeve stood at the lab door: "Reeve," he said, barely glancing up. "Come to lend a hand?" Reeve felt a momentary pang of regret, and wandered in to flip through the ship drawings, endless plans for a gigantic craft that seemed beyond anyone's power to build. "Your children may fly this ship someday," Cyrus said. But having children was far beyond Reeve's span of interest then. "Super," he heard himself say, unconvincingly. Marie faced the flickering screen with an expression akin to devotion. If her screens showed real stars, Reeve might be interested, but astronomy was all about charts and numbers, so even though Marie was sweet, he had no interest in anything in the lab, least of all his father's engineering drawings. "Good-bye, Dad," Reeve said. Cyrus actually looked up then, as though there were a different tone about that good-bye. His bristly eyebrows perched over his eyes, but couldn't hide their hurt. "Run along then, Reeve, run along and do whatever it is you do." Backing away, Reeve said, "I love you, Dad." But his father was already bent over his drawings.

Other times he recalled the Station explosion, the incandescent flowering of the main reactor and the molten spumes lurching away, all in ghastly silence.

Sometimes, in the mists, he saw Tina Valejo, entombed in her glinting white space suit, drifting just out of reach in the fog, and Bonhert cutting the tether and giving her the push that would last ten thousand years. . . .

Spar was leaning over him, lifting Reeve's eyelid with a grimy thumb. "Eyes look like sap welling up in a tree," he heard the man say. And then: "If he dies, how you folks like to get buried?" It was Marie's voice that came then: "I'll burn his remains before I'll let Lithia have him."

At this talk of death and burying, Reeve wrestled himself to consciousness.

Spar's gap-toothed smile greeted him, a tad closer than he wanted. The older man nodded at Reeve, and continued the conversation: "Don't want to bury him, that it?" He sucked on his cheeks, shaking his head. "You folks got to make your peace with Lithia. Stop expectin' her to be somethin' different. She is what she is. It's like bein' married. You can wish your wife was different, but it don't change her, all that wishin'. And it don't help the re-la-tion-ship, neither. Now, you might wonder, what re-la-tion-ship I got with a planet? Eh?"

"Precisely my question," came Marie's sardonic tone.

Reeve interrupted: "Cold," he said. The fog had quite saturated his clothes, and he had begun to shiver.

He felt a jacket draped over him.

Spar continued: "You're like an ant on the bark of a tree, old woman. You got no concept how small and puny you are. That tree's growin' and pumpin' fluid, and makin' leaves and swayin' in the wind, and all you ants can see is the next aphid." His shoulders bounced with his silent laugh.

"Look at the black ant calling the red ant a bug!" came Marie's retort.

Spar turned to Reeve, appealing to him for support. "You like your geo-graphy, Reeve-boy. You like to talk about your mantles and your vents and all that hot rock boilin' around down there. Then that hot rock spits out up here, you get peeved and try to make it go away. Like an ant tryin' to stop the sap from bulgin' out."

"Ants again!" Marie complained.

"OK, never mind ants. But think: Down below, it ain't a pot of boiling rock, boy. It's a world all to itself. We got our mountains up here, but down below, Lithia's got more. Smack in the middle of the big ball of the world, she's got mountains, valleys, con-tin-ents. And not only that, they're upside down! Hangin' like icicles from the ceiling of a cave. Hangin' from the big boundary between mantle and core. You think this great Inland Sea is a wonder? Think of the great sea below. Right this minute, it's washin' up against those anti-mountains, and wearing 'em down. And weather, boy, iron weather. Rainstorms hailing globs of iron, winds blowin', gales stormin'. We could all sink this instant, below the rocky waves. Then we'd be an anti-sea! Anti-raft! Anti. . . ."

"Anti-ants," Marie supplied dryly.

"You got it!" Spar hopped up excitedly. "By the Lady, you finally pickin' it up!"

"Mr. Spar, this is a matter of science, not metaphysics. Those structures you're talking about are naturally occurring features, explainable by science."

"You and your explanations," he grumbled. "That don't change what I'm sayin'."

"Oh, but it does. You're trying to give Lithia . . . a personality. Anthropomorphism in the worst degree."

"Antro-morp-ism? You got a name for somethin', you figure you know all about it."

"It's not just a name, Mr. Spar, it's a concept. For example, those big structures you're talking about, they're reaction products from heat and pressure at the boundary—the boundary between the pure iron of the core and the impure iron mixtures of the mantle. Like rust on that cooking pot we used last night. Over millions of years, it builds up—or builds down, you could say. You're right—it is a grand, inverted landscape. But there's nothing religious about it, I assure you."

"I'm not talkin' about religion!" Spar grew agitated, pacing from one end of the raft to the other, accentuating the lurching of the platform and Reeve's stomach.

Marie would not relent. "Call it what you will."

"You know your problem?" Spar shouted at her. "You got no awe in you."

Marie asked, "What good does awe do?"

Close by, Spar muttered: "You gotta ask that, you beyond help."

In the ensuing silence, Reeve dozed again.

Then Marie was kneeling beside him, offering water. He propped up on one elbow, and decided he was well enough to sit up.

"Feeling better?" she asked.

"Tired of lying here," he said, gulping the water.

"Well, if you're complaining, you're on the road to well." She smiled a flat, no-nonsense smile.

"Where are we? What time is it?"

Marie looked around. "Middle of the sea in the fog. And it's morning."

"We need to hurry, Marie." He'd been sick for two days, and he suspected the others were not pushing as hard as he would have.

"Easy for you to say, sleeping all day." She grinned at him, giving her a ghoulish look amid her peeling skin and pale face.

"Damn it, Marie, we have to *hurry*!"

She nodded. "I know that. I poled all night, rather than have us camp."

Loon was poling now, in deep, easy thrusts like a dancer, pulling up the long metal pipe and slicing it back into the water in a hypnotic rhythm. Reeve flushed, thinking of her emerging from the sea, water slicking over her skin—no fevered vision, but a tangible wonder. Then he thought he must be desperate to want such a creature.

Spar sat on the edge, cleaning his knives and occasionally using the needle end of one to pick his teeth. "So," he said, looking up at Reeve, "not dead after all."

"Six lives left, I guess."

"Nope," Spar replied. "Five."

"How you figure?"

"Well, you said your Sky Clave got blown to bits, so that was one life right there, I figure."

Reeve nodded. "OK, five lives left."

"You not doing too good, Reeve-boy. Even old Spar, he's got three lives to go, and you usin' up yours like there's no tomorrow."

Reeve turned out to gaze at the fog. *No tomorrow.* The old expression had a different edge these days. Throwing modesty aside as the luxury it was, he took a pee off the side of the raft, proud that he could stand by himself.

The fog was beginning to thin in the mid-morning sun. He could make out the near shoreline, where, to his surprise, striated canyon walls shouldered up a hundred feet in streaks of pink and gray. A wash punctuated the cliffs to their port side, forming a pebble beach.

Spar came to stand next to him. "Canyon country, Reeve-boy. Won't be long now we'll be needin' a better boat than this, if we want to do the Tallstory River. No raft's goin' up *that* river."

As they stood gazing out in the presumed direction of the Tallstory, a large ship materialized out of the fog some half mile away. For an instant Reeve thought he was imagining it, but Spar saw it too.

"Beach!" the claver yelled. He jumped to the back of the raft and grabbed the pole from Loon. The women were peering off into the distance, staring at the ship, while Spar was barking out, "Can't outsail 'em; got to try for the shore!" He dipped the pole down and gave a powerful thrust, putting his whole body into it. Loon was gathering their gear up and shoving it into their packs.

"They've seen us," Marie announced.

Reeve swiveled to watch the great oars lift and swoop down into the water.

"Run, run!" Spar shouted. "Leave the pack!" Loon saw the good sense in this as she looked up to see the ship bearing down on them. She jumped into the shallow water with the others and they all splashed to the beach.

Reeve heard Spar's sword clanking out of its scabbard. Marie swooped up the pole that Spar dropped, her face a fury. Reeve clamped on to the pole. "Give it to me." Marie snarled a response, but Reeve yanked it from her. "Run," he said. They all had knives, and Marie could use that if she had to. He turned to watch the ship cast anchor offshore and its occupants dive into the water. They could swim amazingly well, he observed. Adrenaline filled Reeve's muscles with fire.

As the first swimmers rushed onto the beach, Reeve selected his man and swung the pole. His opponent, bald and toothless, tucked his knife in his belt and caught at the pole, grappling with Reeve. Losing this test of arm strength, Reeve thrust his knee into the man's groin. As his assailant doubled over, Reeve chopped his rigid hand down on the man's neck, to no particular effect. On one side he could hear the clang of Spar's sword and the shouts of the ruffians, while before him two men advanced. He drew his knife, lusting to plunge it in at least one belly.

Each of the pirates carried a short sword that put his own knife to shame and gave them a huge advantage. One of them made a feint toward him, then stopped, scowling, as a spurt of blood erupted from his forehead. Collapsing backward, he sprawled on the beach, while his companion pivoted to find the source of the attack, only to receive a hurled rock in his jaw. Loon was at work, bless her. As her rocks hailed down, Reeve found a path to Spar, who was now surrounded, and out of range of Loon's help.

Spar, well bloodied, was fending off five men at once, turning and slicing, ducking and thrusting, moving with graceful economy, his face carved by concentration. The pirates, armed with shorter swords, feinted toward him by turns, waiting for an opening. A larger group of them had gathered at the sea edge, watching with cheers and taunts. Reeve darted in next to Spar, assuming a position covering Spar's backside, and they began defending a shared territory. Spar left Reeve a small segment and carved out four-fifths of the pie for himself and his long sword. The man was breathing hard, but was still steady on his feet.

Within seconds, Reeve took three cuts on his lower arms, though for now the pirates came at him singly. He considered for a moment that he was about to die with five good lives left, an irrelevancy that struck him as bizarre and unworthy of his last thought. As an alternative he shouted, "For Station!" thrusting at his next assailant, a big man with many yellow braids; no, a woman. He checked the swing of her dagger with his smaller one, but overcommitted, receiving a knee in his thigh like a battering ram. As he staggered under the blow, she slapped the face of her blade along the side of his head, sending him to his knees.

The whir of Spar's sword was a split second late as she ducked out of reach. Then she proclaimed, "A quick death for his bravery!"

Still stunned, Reeve looked up for his quick death, but the crowd was ignoring him as Spar crouched in his fighter's stance, bloodied but ready for the next foray.

"Find the rock slingers," someone shouted, and the ruffians ran to scale the cliffs where Loon hid.

Reeve staggered to his feet. He heard himself say, "No one dies! I escaped from the Sky Clave to join you! This man is under my protection!"

The pirates, already in a relaxed mood from the show Spar had put on, laughed at this statement. "Sky Clave!" one of them jeered.

"Yes, Sky Clave! I breathe with Sky Clave lungs," he said, pointing to his breather, "and I bring you gifts of fine rope and flashlights."

The woman held up her hand to quiet her gang. "If you got these things, then I got 'em already. What else you got I don't already have?"

Reeve licked his lips with a tongue as dry as sand. What indeed?

Spar barked out, "This Sky Claver is smart! He knows lectrical systems, astro spectogafy, computer meters, arithmetic, a bunch of literchure, and the despised code, forward and backward."

At this pronouncement, the crowd stood stunned, as though this recitation summarized rare knowledge indeed. Spar nodded loftily. "And you be killin' these folk, you lost your last chance for big tech, and livin' easy like up in the big sky wheel."

Down the beach came a dozen men, with Marie in tow and Loon struggling like a wild animal in the grasp of a man the size of their raft.

One of the pirates had fetched the Sky Clave pack in question and spilled its contents onto the sand. The woman picked up the flashlight and eventually found the "on" button. Its weak beam in the midday sun was less than impressive. Then the pirates were uncoiling the filament rope, which got more approval, but didn't capture the imagination. One of the men pulled open a breather pack, and yanked apart the delicate gel nanoform breather.

"Don't!" Reeve yelled, sick at the waste of the breather. "That's big tech. It can save you from lung disease. Keep you alive twice as long!"

The blond woman snorted at this claim, advancing and looking down at him from a considerable height advantage. "You *were* going to die fast," she said. Then she struck him a hammering blow, sending him to the ground. He heard her say before he passed out, "With lies like you got, I just changed my mind."

When Reeve opened his eyes again it was dark. He woke with a start, remembering his capture, and now afraid for his companions. Where was Marie? He thrust himself up on one elbow and came face-to-face with a black man sitting in a chair next to his pallet.

"Marie . . . ," he croaked.

The man wore a velvet shirt with the sleeves cut out and dark baggy pants tucked into boots with silver tips. As he sucked on a small bone, he regarded Reeve with a seemingly casual curiosity. When Reeve stirred, the man tossed the bone onto a heap of others in the corner. Despite the grease on his face, he was a handsome man, in contrast to his shipmates.

"Glad you woke up," the man said. "I dislike to kill sleeping men."

"My friends?" Reeve asked.

"Alive, for now. Maybe not for long. Depends."

"On what?"

The man sat back in his chair, his feet on Reeve's pallet, leaving the question unanswered. From the size of the boots and their nasty-looking prows, Reeve guessed this pirate had weapon enough if he tried to bolt. While the man regarded him, Reeve took a moment to take in his surroundings. They were in the depths of the ship, in a small room with a bright sun cutting through a lone portal. The place stunk of urine and incense, while the ship pitched in a dreadful rocking motion, sending his stomach into paroxysms.

"I'm told you claim to be of the space station." The man spoke with a deep, modulated voice and good grammar, which made Reeve trust him even less than he would a regular claver. He had a primal contempt for brass, and this was likely the captain of the ship, or close to it. "Some are for cutting you and tossing you to the sharks." He raised an arched eyebrow into a sharp gable over his left eye. "And by that I mean fish, not my men."

Reeve wondered if he was supposed to laugh. He decided not. He rubbed his head, which had gone soft as a cooked egg on one side. His forearms were bandaged, wrapped in clean white cloth. Above, he heard the thudding of feet and the occasional shout of the crew.

"How long have I slept?"

"A full day. You are either sick, like your friends say, or you are a weakling. Perhaps both, I begin to think."

Reeve didn't bother to pursue this line of talk, his mind racing to Marie, Loon, and Spar, and if they'd been harmed. If Spar even lived.

The man reached down and grabbed a bundle by his chair. Slowly, he took off the worn cloth, revealing a black, shiny box. Looking up to be sure he had Reeve's attention, he slowly opened the box, leaving it nested in his lap.

"Nothing," the man said. "Nothing happens."

In the silence, Reeve finally asked, "What's supposed to happen?"

The dark man frowned, watching Reeve with hooded but intense eyes. "You don't know?"

Reeve tried to think of what a box might fail to do upon opening. If it was a toy, a clown might jump up from the box; if it was a computer, a screen might activate in the lid. . . . But this box had an old-fashioned and delicate look, and appeared to be neither for children nor computing.

"It makes music," his captor said. He closed the lid and held it in a delicate grasp. "It used to be a music box."

"Tab might be corroded," Reeve said.

The man's eyebrows furrowed a bit closer, as though straining to meet. "Can a corroded tab be fixed?"

"Sometimes," Reeve said, "you can clean the tab. Or I might be able to replace it with one from my flashlight, if the platforms are compatible. If not, it would take the right tools, but I could rework the program." He reached out his hand and gave the man an inquiring look. The dark man handed over the box.

Reeve sat up and opened the contraption. The inside was lacquered and empty. Turning the box over, he felt for a release latch, but the sides were smooth. "Call for release of the backing," he told the box. From the object came a whirring, a straining to obey.

The pirate cocked his head upon hearing the noise. He leaned in closer to watch.

This wasn't going to be a great dramatic moment. The commands were gluey, the tab was likely ruined, and he was going to have to pull off the backing like an ordinary human. "How old is this thing?" he asked, playing for time.

"You don't ask questions," the man said, nice enough to raise the hairs on Reeve's arms. "You fix the music box, and earn a day's life. My ship. My rules. Yes?"

Reeve nodded quickly. "Yes. Can I take the bottom off the box, and look inside?" If he was dealing with the captain of this vessel, he might just have a chance to earn some favor.

The captain considered his request. "First you take apart the flashlight. Then we'll see."

At the captain's command, Reeve's pack was brought, and he was allowed to plow through its contents. He retrieved the flashlight, then exposed the power panel. "See," Reeve explained, "in here is the miniature board with the smart tabs. The tabs are layered with parallel commands, so each tab contains the full instructions, and the extras act like a power supply and backup computing. If one of these is compatible, I could transplant it to the music box. But that would only be a temporary measure. If you want it to work a long time, I'd need to overhaul the whole system."

The pirate gazed at him a long while, then took the flashlight from him, closed the power panel, and put the light back in the pack. Apparently the test was over, and whether he had passed or failed was completely uncertain. In any case the captain was in no hurry to have his music box fixed.

As the captain carefully wrapped the music box in its length of fine cloth and set it under his chair, Reeve asked: "The girl . . . Is she harmed?"

The captain shrugged. "I gave her to my first mate, but he says she is unhinged, and will have nothing to do with her. You travel with strange companions. Very strange." He watched Reeve for a reaction, so Reeve decided not to give him one.

"Perhaps this is why you are still alive," the man said. He sat with both hands on his knees. "So," he said. "Tell me about the space station, Reeve Calder."

"You know my name?"

The captain shrugged. "The old woman told me."

Reeve had been sensitized to manners by a harsh taskmaster, and he made use of that now. "Will you tell me *your* name, if it's not rude to ask?"

This produced a wide grin from the captain, featuring the best set of teeth Reeve had yet seen on Lithia. "It *is* rude to ask, given that you are a slave and I am your master." He dipped his head in courtly largesse. "However, considering that you are from . . . a foreign land, I will overlook some things. My name is Kalid. And I would know of the great Station." He nodded once at Reeve, by which he knew to start talking.

He began by saying that the Station was in orbit around the planet, and didn't fall to the surface because of the weightlessness of space.

At this, the captain grinned and in a most unfriendly fashion leaned in closer to Reeve. "I am no barbarian, Reeve Calder. I know these things. Tell me something I do not know, and do so quickly."

Reeve sat cross-legged on his cot and tried to marshal his thoughts. So he began. He told of life on Station, its wonders and its routines. How the air filtration system was interconnected with ponics for oxygen, and how the heat exchangers worked to dump off excess heat, and how they synthesized much of their food in the chem lab, and kept to a strict schedule that allowed them to share quarters meant for far fewer. How his bed was the same bed that Geoff Lederhouser shared on second shift, and Amee Ryan on fourth. And the routine that dictated his slot in the gym and in electrical systems and in training labs. He told of how the old-generation ship's order of command had been agreed upon for Station, and the system of officers and crew, and the politics of reterraforming, and how they listened for radio transmissions from the planet, eager—he threw in that part for effect—to hear of their comrades below. He made Captain Bonhert out for a great villain, "descended from the criminals who decided to grab Station for themselves," and told of his father, who had the competing idea of building a craft big enough for everyone, including the clavers, of course. He told of being ashamed of the Station and all it stood for, and that he had escaped, he and his father, and Marie, and that his father had died in the crash of the shuttle. He left out the part about the destruction of Station, figuring it gave him more power to be from a clave that still existed.

All in all, he thought that his mixture of truth and fiction was not too bad, considering he was half goofy from a vicious blow to the head and had to knit up his story as he went along.

After a time, Kalid rose and called for a guard. "Take him to the hold," he commanded, causing Reeve to wonder if he had offended or merely run out of time.

As Reeve was being hauled off, Kalid said, "We will talk again, Stationer. Next time, each lie will cost a finger."

The guard, reeking from sweat and the rancid grease stains on his clothes, hauled Reeve down a narrow passageway to a door barred with a great timber stuck into slots. He opened the door and shoved Reeve inside. When he slammed the door, all light was extinguished except for that allowed in by a small grate near the ceiling. He saw many shadowy figures huddled.

"Reeve!" Marie said. "We're here."

He followed the voice and found Marie, Spar, and Loon, in grim moods. Marie had bound Spar's wounds and he seemed hale enough. Reeve hugged Marie, and nearly hugged Loon, but said instead, "Mam."

"What that pie rat want you for, Reeve?" Spar asked.

Reeve smiled in the darkness, hearing his real name at last from the claver.

He crouched down next to them. "He wanted to hear stories of Station. I told him some." He looked around to discern the other prisoners, careful not to say too much. "Who are you?" he said to the shapes—he counted four—sitting as far from his group as they could all manage.

"Your clave first," the biggest shadow said.

"Stillwater," Spar answered for them. "Up north." Reeve had never heard Spar name his clave, having assumed it was the same as Loon's, the Stoneroot.

One of them spit. "Food for orthong, if you're from the north."

"And your clave?" Spar asked.

"Whale Clave," the big one replied. "Of the great ocean."

"Well, we gonna be Pie Rat Clave from now on," Spar said, "for as long as we last."

One other said bitterly, "Rat Clave it is. You ever been fucked by a rat, you women?"

Marie replied dryly, "Once or twice."

"Well, take it from Eiko, you'll get used to it here."

"A fate better than death, I would imagine," Marie said.

A new voice joined in from the mystery group. "Now, that is a matter of opinion." She seemed to be holding a child next to her, and Reeve hoped that the child was not subject to rat attentions. The woman continued, "What did I hear of this matter of a station?"

Spar started to speak, but Reeve put out a hand to stop him, hoping to get their stories lined up. "Marie and I are from the Sky Clave. The Station in the sky, which looks down on us even now. We escaped, we two along with my father, who was killed in the crash of the shuttle. We came to join a better clave, much good it has done us."

A long silence then as his companions no doubt sorted through this new version of his background, and the newcomers kept their own thoughts. Then one of the strangers said: "So you are a zerter, then." The way she said *zerter* told Reeve what her opinion of him was.

"If that's what you call us. We can't choose our parents." He hadn't meant to say that, and he wondered at himself.

"Easy to blame your parents when they aren't here. And recently *dead*," the woman said contemptuously.

The big woman said, "How'd you get from the big wheel to the ground?"

"An airplane."

Spar interjected: "And you—you're runnin' from your clave, if I guess right?"

"What we are we don't share with *zerters*," the one with the child said. "Or rats either. Right now, I have to think hard about which is worse, zerters or rats. Never thought I'd have to decide." She crawled to the far corner, urging the child with her.

Reeve turned from the hostile group and settled next to Loon, speaking low: "Did they hurt you?"

"They leave me alone," she said.

Evidently their voices were carrying well enough, for the woman in the corner said, "Yes, your women are spared the attentions of the rat men." She didn't bother to hide her bitterness.

"One is too young and one is too old," Reeve said, "thank the Lord."

The woman shot back, "*That* one is not too young; she is of age, the same as us. I'll be sure to remind our rats when they come for us tonight."

In a spurt of anger, Reeve stood up and stalked to her corner. "No," he said, "you won't remind them." He leaned down and grabbed her shirt, hauling her close to his face. "I'll make you wish you'd kept your mouth shut."

In the next moment her fist shot up between his clenched arms and punched him in the cheek. As he faltered backward, she completed her move with a foot in his groin. He drew his knee up just in time to deflect the worst of it, but lost his balance, thudding heavily onto the floor.

Looming over him, she spat, "I should teach you a lesson, zerter."

"Like you taught the rats?" he said, regretting it the instant the words left his mouth.

As she kicked at him, he rolled to grab at her knee, using her momentum to pitch her forward onto her face. Spar and one of the women, a big-boned individual, stepped in to be sure they didn't come at each other again.

"When the wolves ain't around, the rabbits bite each other," Spar said in disgust. "Save your fight, Reeve. This ain't your last stand."

With a long, shaky breath Reeve divested himself of the fury he'd felt a moment before. The woman, after all, was brutalized and desperate. "I'm sorry for what they've done to you," he muttered, and turned away.

From the corner his assailant retorted, "You'll be sorry, all right."

Now that his anger had subsided, Reeve's muscles felt watery. He sank down onto the reeking straw covering the floor and hung his head for a moment, breathing heavily. He heard the woman's breath as well, judging that he had at least one fine advantage in any claver fight: oxygen. However, he was beginning to learn that a fight in earnest seldom lasted long.

The craft pitched and rolled. He guessed it was under full sail, since he couldn't hear the slapping of the oars. Numbly, he wondered if they were heading east or west.

"Are you OK?" Marie had drawn near.

He looked into her face. Her hair was matted with dirt, she had a welt on her cheek from a blow or a fall, and her skin was in tatters from sunburn. She looked like a claver. In two weeks they had regressed from the twenty-fifth century to the seventeenth. They were sick, ignorant, and now prisoners.

"Marie, I am still alive." This was as much as he could say.

"Well, that's something, under the circumstances."

He snorted in response. Touching the bruise on her cheek, he asked: "What's been going on down here?"

She shrugged. "They fed us once. Yesterday they let us collect our waste in a bucket and I took it up on deck to pitch it overboard. They inspected me and decided they don't screw grandmothers. They hauled Loon off somewhere, but I don't think they hurt her. What about you?"

"I must have been unconscious, or maybe I just slept. Their captain grilled me. His name is Kalid. The black one with his hair in a tail."

She nodded. "The one with the boots. He would have killed us except for your claim to be a Stationer. He's a mean son of a bitch."

"What did you tell him?" Reeve asked.

"The truth. Except for . . . Bonhert's plans. Told him Bonhert was trying to reterraform."

"You told him the Station blew up?"

"Yes. Lies are hard to remember."

"Damn." He had her recount all she'd told Kalid. If they aligned their stories, maybe he could yet keep his fingers. Beyond that he hadn't heart to think.

Loon had curled into a ball and appeared to be sleeping, indifferent to the fact that he'd just taken blows for her benefit. But maybe the girl had been roughed up and needed to rest. And, he had to remind himself, she wasn't a *girl*. She was, as the other woman had said, of age. He wondered what had happened between her and the first mate to make him think she was strange.

Many of her ways were bizarre, he admitted. She believed herself on a quest to find her tribe, people like her who ate the soil. Was she in fact deriving nutrients from the dirt in some extreme adaptation, or was she the victim of mental aberration? And what *did* the creature eat? He'd never seen her eat anything but dirt. And she seemed to sample the dirt like a child, exploring the world by putting everything in her mouth. Sometimes she would close her eyes as though savoring the taste. Maybe she was disturbed. Perhaps Lithia's demise was being greeted by many forms of mental illness—dirt-eating probably having a certain logic to individuals who were starving.

His reverie was interrupted by the delivery of a meal, or what might be a meal if Reeve could manage to swallow it. It was a sodden lump of mashed grain, with a faint whiff of spoilage. It was delivered, without utensils, in a pot disturbingly similar to their waste pot. They passed it around, but Reeve could not bear to eat it, despite Marie's admonishments. He fantasized about sucking on bones such as Kalid had—a reward for fixing the music box—and on the strength of that hope, he passed on the gruel.

"You got to get your strength back," Spar said, taking a second handful of paste when the pot came round again. "For our escape, eh?"

Reeve almost said, *You've seen too many vids,* realizing just in time the absurdity of this comment. "Not hungry, Spar," he said instead.

"Picky. You Station-folks, you're real picky about what you'll eat."

"We miss our silver spoons and platters all right," Reeve said.

Spar nodded gaily. "That's right, silver spoons and platters. We got to ask the rats what they can do 'bout this here ugly pot!" He laughed silently, clapping

Reeve on the shoulder. As he chewed on the porridge, he handed the kettle on to the women across the room. Still chewing, he laughed aloud. "Silver spoons and platters!"

Reeve found himself smiling, despite his conviction that Spar was a few neurons short of a network. Looking down at Loon's sleeping form, he asked, "What will Mam eat if they keep us locked up?"

The smile tumbled from Spar's face. "I worry about that myself."

The pounding of feet overhead and angry shouts signified a scuffle between crew. "Maybe they'll kill each other," Reeve muttered.

Marie remarked, "Did you notice they're all strong as oxen and . . . young?"

Thinking back to the gang he'd fought on the beach, Reeve did remember thinking there was something odd about them—tattoos, he thought at the time, but now he realized that it was their youth. Beneath the grime and the scars, not one of them was likely over twenty-five—including Kalid.

After a moment Reeve asked, "How old are you, Spar?"

"Me? Well, I never kept track." He paused as though trying to recall. "Young enough to give the rats a contest, I reckon." He leaned back against the ship bulkhead and closed his eyes. "It's bad luck to count your years, back where I come from."

"Where do you come from?" Reeve thought one clave much like the next, but what he actually knew of the claves would have made a very slim book.

"I told you, Stillwater Clave."

"I thought you and Loon"—here Spar's near eye fluttered open, and Reeve corrected himself—"you and Mam came from the same clave."

"Why'd you think that?" Spar shook his head, closing his eyes again. "No, Mam, she's from Stoneroot—that's a big clave, much bigger than Stillwater." He was quiet a long time, then added: "How we hook up, me and Mam, that your question?"

Now it was. Reeve had never wondered much about either of them. They were clavers; that told much. He never thought of them as his equals, never thought to share his breathers, or much of himself. He noticed a small pang of shame.

"Well sir," Spar went on, "fact is, we got somethin' in common, you and me, Reeve. We both got crunched by orthong." His face tightened with the memory. "I used up two lives that day. The rest of my group . . . well, they must've used all of theirs. Up there in the Stoneroots, you get fogs so thick, it's like the Lady's plucking chickens. And they come on us all at once, twenty or thirty of 'em, and killed us with their shootin' tubes, and some just gutted with their claws."

"Shooting tubes?"

"Yeah, they got little tubes worked into the cuffs of their long coats, and they shoot somethin' out of 'em. Those cuffs glow. By the time you see that, you a dead man. Me, though, I got a claw in my belly, and they left me for dead, which I wasn't. After a day or two I wished I was, though. Then Mam, she come along and doctored my gut wound. And stayed by me. By and by the fever passed and when I could stand again, I knelt in front of her and offered her my sword."

"But why?"

Spar sucked on his teeth. "Ain't you heard of knights of armor? Thought you said you had literchure."

Reeve smirked in the darkness. Always mistaking what clavers knew and what they didn't know. "I heard of it," he said.

"Well, then, you understand. She says she's on her way to find the good soil. And I think, maybe she's got somethin' there. Maybe there's hope for Terran folk, after all. Maybe folks like Mam are lucky enough to be part of somethin' new. You heard of e-vo-lution? Well, it's like that. She's the new Terran. Eats Lithia, so she's got to be somethin' new."

Marie piped in, "Evolution doesn't work that way, Mr. Spar. What are the odds that chance mutation would save us in this circumstance? If Loon is a beneficial mutation, she's probably the only one. There is no grand scheme to produce higher and better. Humanity's a fluke—a temporary one, it would seem."

Spar didn't bother looking at her, but continued talking into the gloom of the ship's hold. "How come you so sure? All your big tech ever got you was patchin' and fixin' your big wheel, and sharin' your beds in shifts. You don't know much, old woman. You just think you do."

Reeve wished Marie could just let Spar talk. What was the point of arguing? "So why didn't you go back to your clave, Spar?"

"Had to follow Mam, is why—ain't you been listening? Besides, why go back? I got only a few years left—though I *ain't* countin'—and best way to spend it is to serve the Lady. I ain't one of Mam's people. I tried that soil-eatin' and it's no good for me, but I can make sure Mam gets where she's goin'. When she finds her people, I can die happy. Die for somethin', instead of for nothin'. So I offered her my sword."

"And what did she say?"

"Why, she put that sharp edge right in her mouth, and bit down. When she gave it back, it had a little of her blood. So I figure we're bound to each other, like as not."

Marie had settled back to rest, murmuring, "Charming, Mr. Spar."

But Reeve was strangely moved. "I never knew all that," he said.

"No, you didn't. Guess you never asked."

2

Koichi snapped a kick high into the air, wearing his black-belt fighting face, calm and yet scary. He pivoted to say to Mitya, "You meet an orthong, you strike at the head. That's the only place a blow will tell." He threw the heel of his foot in the direction of a refrigeration hatch.

Mitya scraped at the burned pot and watched his galley boss practice fighting. He had been sadly mistaken in thinking that the Rift expedition three days ago had advanced him beyond these duties.

"You get one blow," Koichi was saying, punching forward with a rigid hand. "The thongs are fast. One chance, before you're sauce."

Mitya nodded, unimpressed. All the crew learned to fight—part conditioning, part readiness for possible orthong hostilities. No one knew what threat the orthong represented.

He said to Koichi, "If the orthong wanted to fight, I think they'd just blast us from a distance." Clearly they had the technology; their starship, apparently abandoned in orbit around Lithia's moon, was testimony enough to that. "They could blow the whole dome up."

Koichi smiled, shaking his head. "I doubt it. They like to kill up close and personal." An explosive jab with his elbow made short work of another assailant.

"But they kept their distance when they destroyed Station."

"Maybe so. And maybe I'll never get a chance to break an orthong neck." Koichi wiped his face with a galley towel. "What a shame," he muttered, leaving Mitya with the rest of the cleanup.

Mitya scraped at the pot, thinking of the great white beasts and wondering how they'd *known* the Stationers had plans for reterraforming, and how they managed to fire a missile at Station without Station systems giving some warning. Deep in thought, Mitya took no notice of the gradual quieting of the bustle and construction noise from the main room.

Koichi was long gone when Stepan ducked into the galley. "Here you are," he said. "Let's go. Captain's called a meeting." He disappeared again.

When Mitya emerged from the galley he saw that everyone had assembled, taking seats on the floor or standing toward the back.

In front of the crew, Captain Bonhert stood flanked by his chiefs of design, data systems, and geoengineering—Lieutenants Bertram Hess, Liam Roarke, and Val Cody. To the side stood several grim-faced crew, including Gudrun and Koichi. Mitya quickly found a spot and sat cross-legged. Bad news hung in the air like a fog.

"As some of you have heard, hard news came to us this morning," the Captain began. His barrel chest and broad shoulders looked like they bore the weight of that message. "The retrieval shuttle bound for the Titan Mountains has crashed and, I am saddened to report, seven lost their lives. Survivors are Tielsen, Kingrey, and Shinn."

Several among the audience cried out. Mitya stared at those around him. What retrieval shuttle?

"We will be sending the second shuttle to pick up the survivors and continue that critical mission."

Mitya hadn't even known there *was* a shuttle on a mission. What business did they have in the Titan Mountains, hundreds of miles away? He heard someone sobbing quietly.

The Captain went on, "This is a hard loss to bear, so close upon the losses we've already endured. Gudrun and Koichi have lost their spouses, and for them I ask the healing ministrations of the Lord of All Worlds." Lieutenant Roarke put his arm around Gudrun, and everyone stood a moment in respectful silence.

The Captain nodded solemnly at Koichi and Gudrun before continuing: "Our desperate situation does not allow us proper time to grieve as we would wish, however. Crew will continue to work this day, and with redoubled efforts, knowing that our lost comrades would want us to succeed, especially given their sacrifice."

"How did the crash happen?" someone asked from the front row.

"We don't know. If you're thinking orthong attack, that's a distinct possibility. As is a mechanical or pilot malfunction."

A voice from the back: "The ship wasn't in working condition—you knew that!" Someone else growled agreement.

The Captain raised his chin. "What was that?"

Mitya saw Yoo Lee step forward, saying: "The shuttle needed an overhaul. No one took time to do it."

"That's not true," the Captain said. "That shuttle was ready to fly"—he was interrupted by angry protests, but he continued—"and in reasonable working order, given the demands of our schedule."

"Schedule!" A crew member shouted. "Your schedule's killing us!"

A few muttered encouragement while the Captain scanned his audience with a cool stare. When silence resumed, he spoke softly, forcing Mitya to strain to hear him. "This is not *my schedule,* ladies and gentlemen. A ship is arriving, as you all know. When it does, their captain will expect his demands met. That shuttle was needed to retrieve the material the ship needs. The *ship* needs." His voice rose in volume. "If any of you have second thoughts about meeting the *ship's* schedule, you are free to leave. I need no slackers to sabotage our chance for rescue."

Theo, standing next to Mitya, muttered, "Only one who's talked to the ship is you, you bastard."

Mitya was hopelessly confused. What ship? What rescue?

"Nobody's slacking," Yoo Lee said, shouldering forward. "But you send a shuttle out with system glitches, and you're the one jeopardizing the goddamned schedule!"

At this, Lieutenant Hess snapped back, "Those system glitches were—"

But the Captain put out a hand to interrupt him. His voice took on a tone of conciliation. "Those system problems were in noncritical systems. Heating system irregularities. They had nothing to do with the crash. I know it feels better to have someone to blame. If it helps, I freely take responsibility. If I had a full complement of crew and we weren't in extreme emergency, you're right, that shuttle wouldn't have flown. I've done my best to juggle our priorities, and if I've failed to control everything, you can rightly blame me."

Mitya turned to Theo and whispered, "What ship is he talking about?"

Theo looked startled to see Mitya, though they'd been sitting side by side since the beginning of the meeting. He frowned, then said, "Ask the Captain."

"Is there a ship from Earth?" Mitya asked, jumping to the only conclusion he could.

"Not exactly," Theo said, turning away.

Mitya looked around for Stepan. Meanwhile the argument continued. ". . . chain of command," the Captain was saying, "the same as on Station. We are operating under RCS 12.181, 'Reconnaissance Party,' in which the party leader—in this case myself—has somewhat more authority than under ordinary circumstances. I do share decisions with senior officers, as Lieutenants Hess, Cody, and Roarke will attest." After a pause he continued, "We will soon inevitably be under new leadership. We will all take our places in a different organization than we have known before. I look forward to that day, I assure you. But until that time, I ask for your continued support, no matter what tests the Lord may put before us."

With that, he departed back into his quarters, pausing a moment to speak with Koichi and Gudrun and offering a passing comment to Lieutenant Cody.

Cody made her way toward Mitya then as the rest of the crew dispersed, some of them resuming work and others talking in knots and embracing each other for comfort.

She looked down at Mitya. Cody was a tall, angular woman, with a sympathetic demeanor, which emboldened Mitya to blurt out, "What's going on, Lieutenant? What ship are they talking about?"

Cody looked at him, crumpling her lips in thought. "There is a ship coming, Mitya. It diverted its journey to come by for us."

"Why didn't we hear about it?"

"You *are* hearing about it."

"No, but why not on-Station? Did everyone know except me? I don't think my father knew, I don't—"

Cody interrupted. "I'm sure you must have questions. We'll get to them later. Can you just hold your questions for a while?"

Her tone was patronizing. He wasn't a child. Of course he could wait. "But . . . ," he said.

Cody smiled at him, raising an eyebrow.

"But does this mean we aren't going to stay? To terraform?" He was just exploding with questions.

Cody put more starch in her voice. "You hold that question, Mitya. For later." Someone else was waiting to talk to her and Mitya was left alone with the others, who avoided his eyes and made a wide berth around him.

They knew. They all knew about a ship, except for him. He saw Oran standing in a group of techs, their voices subdued. Even Oran knew. Mitya's cheeks burned with embarrassment and anger. Keeping a lookout for Uncle Stepan, he slunk over to his refuge near the east strut of the dome and watched as several crew, led by Lieutenant Tsamchoe, put gear together for the rescue party. When he saw that Stepan was among them, he jumped up and strode over to his uncle, waiting near the group until he caught Stepan's eye.

His uncle's face was closed and he gave no sign of seeing Mitya, but Mitya waited there, a silent demand he hoped Stepan would answer. Finally his uncle shouldered a pack over his heavy jacket and approached him.

"A piece of advice," Stepan said, as several others in the rescue party looked at them with interest. "Be careful about jumping to conclusions. Especially be careful about voicing those opinions. Crew is watching you to see if you're one of us or not. I've fought for you, Mitya. Don't disappoint me."

"Lieutenant," Mitya said. "Aren't we here to terraform, then?"

Stepan sighed. "Ask Oran if you can't wait until I get back." He leaned in with a fierce scowl on his face. "But you keep your opinions to yourself. No one is going to listen to a thirteen-year-old. No one cares what your opinions are. You're either with us or against us. You understand me?" He fixed Mitya with an impaling gaze.

Mitya's outrage faltered under his uncle's glare.

"That little trip to the valley? That was my doing, boy. Bonhert owes our family some respect, and you deserve a chance to prove yourself. But some of the crew don't like you, and if you screw up, if you act mad or doubtful, your life isn't worth a damn." Stepan adjusted his pack straps and took a deep breath. "Wipe that stricken look off your face. Keep your face a blank if you can't do any better."

As Mitya obeyed, Stepan relented a notch, saying: "When I get back, I'll answer any questions you still have. Privately. Meanwhile, you figure out how much your opinions are worth. If you still have opinions after you hear our plans, well, you just take a long walk in the fog, boy. If you're here when I get back, I'll know you've made up your mind." He put a firm hand on Mitya's shoulder, and without another word he rejoined the mission crew assembling in front of the air lock.

Mitya struggled to keep his face *blank,* as Stepan said. But his emotions were boiling, and he'd never been much good at hiding what he felt. Some of the mission crew were looking up at him from their checklists. He smoothed out his face the best he could, nodding at them. *Your life isn't worth a damn. You act mad, your life isn't worth a damn.* He wandered over to his spot at the dome edge. Sitting down, he practiced a blank face. *You still got opinions, just take a long walk in the fog, boy.* How could he have opinions when he didn't even know what was happening? All he knew was that there was a ship. *Not exactly from Earth.* Maybe from some colony planet. But if there was a colony planet, why would they be coming to Lithia?

Someone walking by glanced over at him, sizing him up. He wondered if it looked sulky, sitting here all by himself. He went over to the galley, thinking to find useful work, but to his surprise Koichi was there, practicing his fighting moves. He was batting at thin air, swirling to meet another attack from behind, oblivious to Mitya—dancing through a fight routine after hearing that his wife was killed. From the look of Koichi's face, he was far, far away.

Mitya left him, heading over to the water filtration meter in the shadows next to the looming wall of the clean room, where he pretended to check the gauges. Then, suddenly overcome with fatigue, he crawled behind the electric generator and rolled into a ball, covering his face with his arms.

It was dark when he crawled out, having slept the afternoon away. He strolled into the main dome, where pockets of crew were still on task under the harsh lights hanging from the main dome struts. Lieutenant Hess turned when one of the crew nudged him, pointing at Mitya.

Hess set out in his direction while Mitya considered an alibi for where he'd been: *Not moping, sir, just don't feel well.* . . . But before he'd thought through an answer, Hess was saying, "Captain wants to see you."

"The Captain?"

"Yes, the Captain." He nodded at the Captain's quarters, and Mitya mumbled his *yes, sir* and walked slowly in that direction, wondering if he was in trouble. And, if he was, why the Captain was dealing with it.

Captain Bonhert was seated at a small desk cluttered with touchboards and slates. Two data fields shared a large, curved screen forming a half circle around his desk. Mitya was surprised to see that the Captain had the luxury of a padded swivel chair. The rest of the room contained a cot and a makeshift sink with a stack of towels. Towels. Mitya always knew the brass lived better than others, but this was luxury indeed, compared with crew sleeping on mats in the dome and sharing a communal head with cycled pulp sheets for drying hands.

The Captain swung around and nodded at Mitya.

"Sir," Mitya thought to say when the Captain didn't speak.

The Captain gestured to the bunk, and Mitya perched on the edge of it, his stomach in a slow churn. Whatever else happened, he wasn't going to think about his parents, and what his parents would have thought of all of this. What his dad would have done, to learn that a ship was coming and nobody knew.

Captain Bonhert rubbed his eyes and drew his hand down the stubble of his beard. The man was tired. No doubt the Captain hadn't slept the afternoon away, but had been in the thick of it for many hours now. His large shoulders slumped a little from his usual military posture, and his graying sideburns gave him a look of wisdom and fatherly patience. Mitya hoped he was wise. He'd always believed the Captain was wise. . . .

"Mitya, thank you for coming. I wanted to speak to you earlier, but as you see, we've had pressing business."

Mitya swallowed, his throat so sticky it almost closed shut. "Yes, sir," he squeaked.

"Sometimes we can't do the things we want to. Sometimes we have to choose the lesser of two evils." He seemed distracted, almost as though he was speaking to himself. But his attention snapped back to Mitya, and Mitya sensed he was to respond.

"Yes, sir," he said.

"Now, Mitya, I'm going to share with you a dilemma. Do you know what a dilemma is?"

He thought he did. "It's when you have to choose, but you don't want to."

The Captain raised his eyebrow and cocked his head slightly. "Exactly so. You have to choose and you don't want to. You're a bright lad. Stepan's told me that you have ability, and I see what he means." He rose, looking down on Mitya as though taking a new measure of him. Then, from a standing position, he coded a sequence into the touchboard. A view of the planet in cross-section filled the screen, layered into the familiar pattern of core, upper and lower mantle, and crust.

"Come here, Mitya." He gestured Mitya into the upholstered chair and touched the board again, bringing the schematic to life. Complex mantle convection currents flowed, and a moon-sized molten core spun slightly faster than its housing. From the patterns, Mitya could tell the representation was color-coded for heat. In one spot, dark blue subducting crustal plates created a cool sink that fell mantleward and collected at the boundary between upper and lower mantle, then crashed through the boundary like an avalanche.

"Where are we in this grand scheme of the planet's makeup?" the Captain asked.

Mitya pointed to the fine line of dark blue crust. "We're here, sir."

The Captain leaned in and punched in another code. With the core-mantle boundary at the bottom of the screen, a needle-slim tube could be seen, beginning at the boundary and threading its way to the surface: the hot-spot plume under the valley, under their very camp. In this close-up view, some surface features of the crust appeared, such as the ridged profile of the Titan Mountains, and there, a shallow notch representing the Rift Valley.

Bonhert pointed to the tip of the plume. "This is what's feeding the vents in that valley out there, Mitya. And the planet's got more plumes like this one." His face darkened. "The whole churning sphere is feeding volcanism. That's what we're up against. The whole damn machine."

Mitya was looking up at the Captain, knowing what was coming. He tried to stiffen his face.

"The nanotech geoform project, Mitya . . . It was deeply flawed. It could never succeed."

In the ensuing silence, Mitya remembered Stepan's cautions, so he asked as casually as he could, "You changed your mind then? That it could save us?"

"Yes. When another possibility presented itself."

The Captain left a lot of silences, and somebody had to fill them. "The ship," Mitya said.

"Yes, Mitya, the ship." He walked over to the bunk and sat down, leaving Mitya in the Captain's chair, which made Mitya extremely uncomfortable. He rose, but the Captain waved him to sit back down, as though where people sat was the least of his worries. "They contacted us a year ago. They'd been homing in on enclaver radio transmissions, and found us, probably decades ago. They don't tell us all they know, believe me." This he said with some heat, and Mitya realized there was a lot more to the situation than he was likely to be told. "But they did . . . express *interest* in Lithia. As a potential colony planet. We told them the situation here, that it was a poor choice, that it was a better option to stop by to pick up survivors and continue their journey in search of a decent home world. We did ask for rescue, in return for specific fuel resources they needed. The ship agreed, with the proviso that they would look over the Reversion process themselves and judge how serious it was, with a view to colonizing Lithia if they thought it could be brought under control."

"Whose ship is it? From Earth? Somebody said it wasn't."

"Well now, that's an important question. What is this ship doing here?"

It wasn't exactly what Mitya asked, but he'd settle for the answer to this new question.

The Captain went on: "This Terran ship has been traveling for eight hundred years, Mitya, a generation ship. In all their travel they've found nothing habitable—not even a prospect for terraforming. They've had bad luck, but in some respects their fortunes have been better than ours. Their ship was launched four hundred years after our mother ship, with superior technology. Their ability to survey for planets is leagues ahead of what Cyrus Calder used. They'll find a planet eventually, I'm convinced they will. In any case, it's our only hope."

"People on Station didn't know about this?" Mitya found that the question just couldn't be suppressed.

The Captain frowned quickly. "Some did. I shared the information with my lieutenants, the ones I felt had the most maturity. Because you see, Mitya, there was a catch. The ship agreed to rescue, all right—to rescue a hundred of us." He snorted at this pitiful offer. "They didn't have *room,* they said, for all of us.

They're overpopulated, resource problems. . . . that sort of thing. So you see, I had a dilemma."

He flicked his eyes up to Mitya, to see if he was following. Mitya nodded. He was—and almost wished he weren't.

"The dilemma was how to choose one hundred survivors. The pressures on Station were already overwhelming, what with Cyrus Calder's cockamamie starship schemes and the devotion of other factions to the prospects of reterraforming. I knew some of our people would have trouble letting go of the hopes we'd had for generations, to reclaim Lithia. I myself used to support reterraforming. When the ship contacted us, all that changed.

"How to choose one hundred survivors," he went on. "Can you imagine the upheaval it would have caused to try to choose who could go?" Captain Bonhert looked long at Mitya, until that weighty thought had time to sink in. Actually, to Mitya, it seemed a lottery system might work, or—

But the Captain continued: "The dilemma was compounded because some of my officers felt that we were placing everyone at risk, that none of us would make it. Because the ship would choose to stay, and that would doom us all."

"But if they have new technology, maybe they *could* reterraform." This seemed like a terrific idea to Mitya, but the Captain's face betrayed another viewpoint.

"No, Mitya. Nothing like that is in their power. You see, it's thinking like yours that sets the fools to hoping for the impossible." He stood up and began pacing, while Mitya absorbed the sting of the criticism. Here was the Captain making him out to be a fool. But wasn't it so that they might at last find a way to fix Lithia?

"Someday, yes, Mitya, humanity will have the galaxy at its fingertips. It will harness the power of suns, calm the seething mantles of planets, travel faster than the speed of light and command the universe like gods. But for now we have limits. That ship has limits. Never doubt it." He stopped pacing and looked down at Mitya, perched in the great chair. "Here's what we are capable of doing. Here's what we *are* doing: We are building a cannon, all right. Not to implant nanotech, but to put an end to ship's hopes for this place. We will blast the planet out of existence. We will trade the damned ship its uranium ores, and in exchange they will take our crew onboard. If the orthong attack hadn't occurred when it did, we would have taken a full one hundred, not just the forty-five in this dome. And we will, by the Lord of Worlds, be rid of this hellhole forever." The Captain was staring at the screen, with its representation of the deep magma plume. He continued in barely a whisper: "I'm not going to rot on this sulfurous heap of slag for the rest of my life. Not when the stars beckon. Not on your life."

Hearing this, a chill lurched over Mitya's arms, as though it *was* on his life.

The Captain was gazing down at him. He was supposed to say something, but he was struck dumb. The Captain was not quite everything he'd thought, not quite the wise man he'd imagined.

"You're not one of those fools that wants to play God with this planet, are you?"

But what was Captain doing if not destroying like the Lord of Worlds could destroy? Mitya wondered. Then Stepan's voice came clearly to mind: *Your life's not worth a damn, if you have opinions.* And Mitya said, "No, I'm not one of those."

Captain Bonhert was looking at him with an assessing gaze. "Good. I know I can count on you to pitch in. You work with Lieutenant Cody if you have any more questions. She'll fill in the details." He waited long enough that Mitya realized he was dismissed. He jumped up from the chair and faced the Captain.

He felt more reckless, suddenly. It didn't matter so

much what the Captain thought of him. "Sir, won't the ship be mad if we decide *for* them? About Lithia?"

The Captain said wearily, "We're not *telling* them, boy. What we will tell them is that the nanotech project went awry. Anyway, nothing they can do about it, if they want their ore. You don't need to do any thinking, Mitya. You leave that up to me."

He was surprised the Captain told him that part, but then why wouldn't he? Everyone else in this dome knew.

As Mitya turned to go, the Captain's voice stopped him. "Just one more thing, Mitya."

He turned to face the Captain.

He was looking at Mitya with a friendly but flat expression. "You haven't been reporting to me, the way we agreed."

Reporting? Oh. Their conversation before the expedition to the Rift. Mitya had hardly thought about that. And anyway, he didn't have anything to report.

"You remember our agreement? You would do the work of regular crew, and in return, you'd keep me personally apprised of any trouble?"

"Yes sir, I remember, only there hasn't been any trouble, not that I've noticed."

"Well, you pay attention, Mitya. You *notice*, from now on." His voice mellowed. "This isn't a minor assignment, lad. Can I count on you?"

Feeling hot and dizzy, Mitya squeaked out, "Yes sir." Then, in a better voice, the voice of someone without opinions, he said, "You can count on me, sir." And the lie felt awful, as awful as everything else on this day had been.

"Good lad."

Mitya stumbled out of the cabin, his mind a kaleidoscope of half thoughts. There were questions the Captain hadn't answered. Like, if the ship stayed to reterraform, and if it didn't work, then in later years they could leave. But on a second's contemplation,

Mitya realized he *had* heard the answer: *I'm not going to rot on this sulfurous heap of slag for the rest of my life. Not when the stars beckon. Not on your life.* And then an even nastier question floated to the top of his mind, one he had forgotten to ask. *If the orthong hadn't blown up Station, how were you going to choose the one hundred?*

It seemed the orthong had conveniently solved the Captain's dilemma. And, Mitya knew, the Captain didn't like dilemmas.

<hr>

3

Kalid gouged out another cut from the small block of wood. The knife flicked with quick, needle-sharp incisions. They sat in the same places as yesterday: Reeve on the straw bed, Kalid leaning back in his chair, feet up, careless of the fact that Reeve could lunge at him and topple him in a hurry. His captor seemed content to whittle in silence, perhaps making some point about the knife, and fingers. The man's own fingers were edged in blue, the mark of a claver as surely as the coughing.

After many minutes, Kalid finally spoke. "It's not often I have leisure to sculpt." He swung his feet off the pallet to the floor, examining the palm-sized carving now taking shape as a female form. His eyes snapped up to capture Reeve's. "But I've had my leisure. Now, as it happens, I'm in a hurry." He tucked the carving into his vest pocket and wiped the blade on his pants, rather more elaborately than was necessary. "We will have, unfortunately, no time for detours. You'll give me truthful answers to my questions." He smiled. "Strive for believability, Reeve Calder."

Something about that smile made Reeve smile too, though Kalid's smile was in no way friendly. It seemed instead to say, *We understand each other, and that is good.*

The barque was making fast headway under full sail, piercing the low chop of the waters with a rhythmic slap and dip. West, Reeve knew, from the reports of those emptying the slop buckets. They were headed west, by the grace of the Lord of Worlds. Whatever awaited him among these outlaws, he was at least in some measure still making progress. It was little enough to hold on to, but it put him in a mood to smile back at Kalid.

Kalid nodded, once, knife resting on his thigh. This man savored subtlety, apparently, over torture. Reeve resolved to withhold nothing except for what he had learned from Grame Lauterbach.

"To begin," Kalid said, "I would know by what transport you arrived among us."

Reeve hesitated. "Do you mean at the Inland Sea or . . . from Station?"

His voice came with a deep musicality. "Station."

"A shuttle. We came on an airplane we call a shuttle."

"Where is this shuttle now?"

It was dismaying to think how easily he might give the wrong answer, while trying to be truthful. Despite Kalid's veneer of courtesy, Reeve didn't doubt the captain could be ruthless. He responded: "We crashed in an area unfamiliar to us. It was a thick swamp about three days' walk from the sea. We were on the raft for two days. So by that reckoning, it might be about seventy miles from here."

While he spoke the other man regarded him with calm intensity. His nostrils flared slightly as though smelling for the truth. "What was your rank among your crew?"

"I was . . . that is, on Station I was an electrician. I worked on electrical systems. It was an unimportant job. My father was a chief, of sorts, an officer. My mother died in a Station accident when I was young. I was still trying to figure out what I wanted to do with my life."

Kalid probed his teeth with his tongue. "What does one do with one's life?"

Reeve tried to process this question. The knife turned in Kalid's grasp now and then, scraping against his pants with a soft static. "I could choose to learn science better. I could choose to help my father. Or I could do the easy work, like electrical."

"You could rise among your people, or remain lazy." When Reeve hesitated at this summation, Kalid raised an eyebrow almost imperceptibly.

Reeve hurried to answer: "Yes. That's how my father saw it."

A knowing smirk tugged at Kalid's lips. "And why did your Station send a shuttle to our world?"

"I was afraid to tell you yesterday. But it's true, the Station was destroyed. We escaped."

Now Kalid leaned forward. "Yesterday you were afraid to tell me the truth. And now are you still afraid to tell me the truth?"

One thing Reeve was learning: Clavers didn't like lies. Why these ruffians should be so scrupulous, he didn't know, but he was already in trouble about the few lies he'd told so far. He went on: "If you saw the light in the sky, you have evidence I'm telling the truth now. The Station exploded. We were at war among ourselves. One group tried to force us down to the planet, to get the old domes working again, to terraform—to make Lithia like it was."

"I know what *terraform* is, Reeve Calder. I am not entirely uneducated, although I do not know electrical systems." He enunciated *electrical systems* carefully, and got it right.

"No offense. We know little of your ways, being strangers here."

Slowly, Kalid moved back, resuming his position, his silver-tipped boots pointing at Reeve's nose. "So you might say. But you've been among us long enough to learn something. You are not a child, seeking what to do with your life. In our world, a man your age is in his full power, and soon to decline. Understand this, Reeve Calder. When my lord questions you, do not act the fool. We might think you are looking down on us, and you don't want to look down on Lord Dante. He is proud, and notices a slight."

Reeve was soaked in sweat. It was a fine line to walk between talking above this claver, and talking beneath him. "I thank you for your advice. I've often been in trouble for saying the wrong thing."

Kalid put the knife in a sheath at his belt. "Here is what I would know: How many soldiers have come among us, and in how many shuttles?"

"I'm not sure of the number. On my own shuttle, only Marie and I survived. I know at least one other shuttle also escaped. We had four shuttles total. The other one might be at the Rift Valley, one crew member told me."

"And what Rift Valley is that?"

"The great valley to the west. But I don't know if they made it. We barely escaped the explosion, and our shuttle was damaged. Theirs may have been also."

"A shuttle can carry how many?"

"Forty at the most."

"With what weapons?"

"The shuttles carry no weapons. But the crew have guns and maybe explosives. Other weapons might be fashioned, if they put their minds to it. But I believe their intention is to defend themselves and concentrate on terraforming."

"And can you yourself fashion weapons?"

"I have no experience in such things. It takes big . . . it takes the right technology. But I have some knowledge, and with the right parts I might come up with something." Perhaps they would hesitate to throw a fashioner of weapons to the sharks. As Kalid mulled this over, Reeve slipped in his own question: "What will your Lord Dante do with us?"

"You are weak and would make a poor servant of my lord. He may hang you for a zerter. Your Spar is an oddity. This may amuse my lord, and he may be allowed to die fighting. The old woman offers no amusement. And the Loon creature is wrong in the head and may be traded." He shrugged. "But it is impudent to guess what my lord will do. And seldom successful."

He stood, taking a few steps over to built-in drawers in the bulkhead, drawing forth the music box in its clean but tattered cloth. "It would amuse me if you could make the box sing again."

Kalid called for the backpack, which arrived in the grasp of a very large individual of surly demeanor. "You will have to persuade my man Bunyan which tools in your pack might be needed. He will be watching you to be sure you proceed in good faith."

Reeve looked up into the guard's face, wondering if the man understood what it meant to *proceed in good faith*, or if the ape would kill him at the first opportunity. After Kalid left, Reeve carefully began removing the bottom plate of the music box. As he worked, clamor from the deck resounded in the semidark hole where he worked. Soon the creaking and crash of the oars shook the bulkheads, and Bunyan peered out the high portal of the cabin at the goings-on.

Sometime later Reeve replaced the panel and wrapped the box in its cloth. Substituting the flashlight's power assembly had no effect, and without the right tools he couldn't assess the state of the memory tab. Shivering in the breeze from the open portal, he thought about Kalid's intimation that one must be either amusing or useful. He looked down on the bundle containing the broken music box. He would much rather fix things than *amuse* people, but in this, as in so much more, he was apparently to have little choice. Under Bunyan's scornful gaze, he carefully placed the bundle down on the cot, bitter at his failure and the vanishing possibility of a reward.

Instead of returning to the brig, however, Reeve was led up to the deck, where the other prisoners were already assembled against one side of the railing, staring out at a bubble in the sea.

In the distance a giant dome rose from the waters. A jagged maw defined a collapsed section toward one side, like a jigsaw puzzle with one piece missing. Boats thronged around this edifice, hugging its sides, some with sails like their barque, but most barges, rafts, and canoes. The sea bristled with activity near and far, laden boats heading to and from the dome.

"Trading center?" Reeve asked Bunyan.

Bunyan smiled, showing teeth the size of walnuts. "Not for you" was his answer.

From below deck, the grunts of crew bearing down on the oars could be heard in rhythmic pulses. The great paddles, zooming upward toward the sun, became mirror-bright before falling in unison below his vision.

"Where are we? Where is the Tallstory River from here?" Not expecting the brute to answer, he was surprised to hear Bunyan say:

"Yonder." He nodded toward the dome, presumably to some point beyond it. "Atlantis commands the sea and the river here. As it now commands you."

Visions of slavery and barbarity sprang to Reeve's mind; he hoped he was wrong. Turning from the panorama of this so-called Atlantis, Reeve saw the huddle of the claver women, sticking together, disdaining to mingle with Spar and Loon. The one he'd fought with—Nerys, she was called—swept her gaze across him with undisguised contempt. Some distance away, Spar squinted into the sun, eyeing the dome with the disgust he had formerly reserved for Reeve. Marie stood at the deck railing, also mesmerized by the dome. Loon, however, was watching *him*. He approached her.

"This is . . . ?" she asked, cocking her head at the dome.

"One of the old master domes for terraforming. This one was called the Jupiter Dome, if I remember my history."

She dipped her forefinger into a splash of water on the rail, then sucked the finger in what seemed a childish gesture, but one he knew was something else entirely. "Spicy-sweet," she said.

"Sweet?"

She nodded, turning to view the dome with new interest. "The good brown taste." She glanced back at him, smiling an infectious and joyful grin, sharing with him whatever happiness this observation brought her.

Reeve put his hand on her far shoulder, and she stepped closer to him, allowing his arm to rest on her back. He wasn't sure how this had happened, that he was now holding her in the circle of his arm as they watched their fate approach, but she felt warm at his side and that was enough at this moment. Spar, observing them, pursed his lips, no doubt refraining with difficulty from commenting on Reeve's presumption.

Kalid stood at the prow, one leg braced on the gunwale and his hand resting on his knee, leaning into the wind and seeming to tow the ship behind him as he sped onward. While the bow smashed through the waves, Kalid rode the heaving deck as though bolted in place, a man at home in a way Reeve had not felt since that last coldwalk on Station.

As the barque drew near to the dome, they began to tilt their heads upward to view the great loft of the structure, several hundred feet high. With its slightly blue color, it looked for a moment like a partially submerged Earth sinking into a galactic deluge. Reeve wondered if any of the founding colonists had ever had that thought, or if, in their optimism, the dome was a jewel in the crown of the colony's achievement. Indeed, the latticework of hexagonal supports lent a cut-diamond look to the construct—save for the gash in its side, from which a long pier stretched out. Alongside this dock boats moored next to stacks of trade goods. Darkness filled the opening, cutting off a further view.

Other boats were now swarming alongside their ship. The sloop just starboard of them was piled high with junk—great heaps of rusted metal, sheets of fiberfuse and arcane machine parts. Atop the mound of refuse rode cages of animals, including game birds. In the prow, a buffalo stood resolutely, its fur glistening with sea spray, two of its legs chained to rings in the deck. This boat and others began jockeying for slips at the pier, but if they thought to compete with Kalid, they were soon disappointed, for he ignored the pier and headed straight for the mouth of the dome, the holdfast of Dante.

4

Nerys refused to betray fear or dismay as they approached the dome. Clearly the rats had herded their prisoners on deck to behold the mighty stronghold and cower before it, crushing their spirits before commanding their bodies in slavery. Though only the tiniest victory, she kept her face strictly neutral. Meanwhile she surveyed everything hungrily, searching for any handhold to pull herself up. Every collection of humans had its stairway to power. Here in this warren of rats would be the lead rat and the top attendants; if there was a way to rise among them, she would find that way, for Anar's sake.

On Eiko's face she saw a slave mentality already crouching amid her slack features. Thallia was stalwart as ever, but her eyes, sunk to small black beads, betrayed her grim assessment of their future. To Nerys, however, if one looked beyond the sheer size of the place and the multitude of slaves and traders, one could see the small details that might offer advantage.

The stronghold was well situated for defense. Located far offshore, the dome afforded its lookouts a view for miles in every direction. At the nearest shore, a gap in the cliffs formed a narrow wash that would pinch an invading force into columns. The exterior of the structure looked intact except for a collapsed section just large enough to stage a fast counterattack against an approach by water.

Despite these defensive advantages, though, the place looked less preoccupied with war than trade. Beside a long dock, dories and rafts surged three and four abreast to off-load their wares. As the rat ship passed these vessels, Nerys surveyed the chaotic variety of trade goods: machinery, lengths of pipe and timber, industrial drums, rolls of wire, canisters, and the occasional piece of furniture, some common and others grand.

She pulled Anar closer as the child trembled in the cold breeze. "Never forget, Anar, that I love you." The child looked up at her as though hearing a far-off voice that she struggled to recognize.

The shouts of traders and dock leaders arose in a clatter of voices as the rats and the subrats haggled over price. Sometimes the price was people, Nerys saw, as a man in a canoe led a bound woman into his boat and paddled away.

Now the mouth of the dome rose above the rat ship, and the shadow of its gullet fell over the deck.

Lights bloomed from tall sticks along the interior wharf. They weren't torches, but clean-burning lights, hissing gently as though fueled by some source in the stick. In the ghostly light a bewildering interior landscape emerged. The rat ship had snugged up to the dock next to a giant tank half the size of the ship. From this rounded mass sprouted parallel tubes that turned in unison and dove into a cylinder that soared hundreds of feet above their heads. In the shadows behind the tank were coiled ducts and metal casings and strangely fashioned chambers. Remnants of bright-colored paint defined each drum and pipe, as though the builder of this place had striven for beauty amid utility.

Then the oaf named Bunyan shoved her in the back, and Nerys staggered forward with her daughter, down a plank hastily laid from pier to deck. The Stationer called Reeve preceded her. At his side walked the old woman, who had already lived twice as long as the common claver, yet breathed freely, with no trace of bluing. Her companion was a foul-tempered fellow indeed, for all his trappings of superiority. The smear of clear jelly around his mouth might be evidence of his mastery over the indigo death, Nerys mused, but couldn't protect him from the rats.

So much for big tech.

There was a time when Nerys would have been eager to speak with one who had lived in the sky amid all the learning of the old days. No time for such things now. It was always the way, that learning came last. *Save your breath,* the claves said. By which they meant don't bother with something unless it's building, fishing, toiling.

From behind her, Thallia mumbled, "They are slavers, Nerys. You saw?"

"I won't be a slave," Nerys answered.

"Nor I."

Eiko muttered, "If your brat had not been asleep at the oars . . ."

Nerys chose to ignore Eiko as she watched the securing of the ship with ropes and the hauling of trade goods in both directions down the broad wooden causeway. When all the prisoners had debarked, Bunyan ordered them into single file and led them toward the deeper shadows. The jungle of machines pressed in on them from every side as they entered the domain of the rats. Above them, the arched ceiling strained the sunlight to a pale glazing.

----------------------------- 5 -----------------------------

Marie and Reeve sat on the floor sharing a meal of smoked fish, the remains of Bunyan's meal. Lord Dante would soon interview them, they'd been told, a prospect first fraught with anxiety, and later boredom. At the dock Loon and Spar and the others had been led in another direction, despite Reeve's pleas to keep them all together. Why it should matter, Reeve was unsure, but he did take some comfort in their presence. Now, awaiting their interview, he and Marie dozed, leaning against each other. After several hours, Kalid joined them, freshly showered from the look of him, and richly dressed in a bright vest and clean trousers tucked into his boots.

Kalid nodded to Bunyan, who grinned in obvious pleasure. "Who would have thought the zerters so meek?" Kalid said, scanning his prisoners.

"Dull as stumps," Bunyan agreed, to Reeve's great annoyance.

At that, a commotion issued from down the hall, and Reeve saw the great doors open. He sucked the last of the fish oil off his fingers and stood up with Marie as a guard approached them, beckoning Kalid to follow. The back of the guard's bald head was traced with an intricate design, almost familiar. When Reeve drew closer, he saw that it was two words, wrought as a design: marco polo. Marie noticed it too, and shrugged at Reeve. From behind them, Reeve heard Kalid say, "Only the truth, Reeve Calder, or you will shame my training."

As they entered the room, their attention was arrested by a man standing immediately before them, arms crossed in front of him and looking down at them from a height of over seven feet. He was dressed in a long flowered coat without sleeves, beneath which he wore a bloused shirt tucked into brocaded pants. Suspended around his neck was a medallion the size of his considerable fist. His head, though shaven, had been tattooed in great detail, giving him the appearance of having blue hair. Beneath the layered clothes, a powerful body bulged.

Kalid bowed before the man, and Reeve followed suit, while Marie stood stock-still.

Dante—for it could be no other—looked at her with skepticism. "Some who live with the orthong," he said as though to himself, "grow old as this one. Perhaps she has escaped from the scabs." His voice boomed effortlessly in the large chamber around them.

"It is possible, my lord," Kalid said. Attendants stirred around Dante and Kalid, giving Reeve and Marie wide berth. All were bald except for Kalid and the women, one of whom was also very tall and dressed in an elaborate gown out of some eighteenth-century drama. Beneath a towering headdress her frazzled black hair stuck out in every direction, as though she had dressed in a hurry. But she was the most beautiful woman Reeve had ever seen, with sculpted ebony features and full lips tending toward violet.

Dante moved closer and examined them each in turn, not touching them, but squinting at their faces.

Though Reeve guessed his age to be almost thirty, the man's face was a great ovoid, curiously lacking in planes or lines. His light brown eyes were flecked with gold, as though something had recently exploded there. Dante's full lower lip protruded as he scrutinized their breathers. "Curious," he said.

The room was tucked up against the edge of the dome, its steeply slanting wall forming a sort of pavilion over a great carved desk and chair, behind which Dante now took a seat. A feather pen stood upright in an inkwell, and papers cluttered the surface. "So you have come to invade Atlantis," he said.

Kalid raised an eyebrow at Reeve, and Reeve stuttered, "No . . . no, we . . ." Words failed him. He must be careful about what he said.

"No?" Dante boomed.

Reeve shook his head. "No."

Then Dante shouted out loud. It was several seconds before the startled Reeve realized the man was laughing. "No!" he bellowed as though at a great joke. The room erupted in the laughter of his lieutenants. He became quite serious. "*No* is the right answer, Stationer!"

He waved his hand at his officers, settling back in his chair. "Tell me something interesting, *Stationer*. Of your great sky wheel, for instance."

Reeve groped for something impressive. "Gravity," he said. "We produce our own gravity. So we don't float in the air, but walk on the floors, as you do."

When a crumple appeared in Dante's forehead, Reeve glanced quickly at Kalid, who gave him a tiny shake of the head.

"So you walk as real men, on the floor," Dante said. "Now *that* is a wonder." The woman in the headdress walked to his side, resting her hand on his shoulder. She smirked in derision, but it couldn't alter her exotic beauty—which was marred a moment later when she cleared her throat, producing an ugly, scraping cough.

"We create our food in bottles. We fly in airplanes." If he wanted wonder, Reeve knew, he must think of things that would sound wonderful to a barbarian.

Unimpressed, Dante absently rubbed his cheek against the arm of his gowned attendant.

"We—," Reeve began, but Dante interrupted.

"Kalid tells me your airplane broke, that it killed those who sat inside it. Is this true?"

"Yes."

"So you die as we do, walk as we do, and have no meat on your plates, but suck your food from bottles," Dante summarized in derision.

Marie stepped forward. "On-Station," she said, "the air was pure, the food plentiful." Dante's attention flickered into focus for a moment. Marie continued, "We could live forever."

Dante narrowed his eyes, cradling his chin in a large, pale hand. "You look like you're dying."

"The sun burns our skin a little. I may be ugly, but I'm happy."

Laughter erupted from the leader, a barking sound like a struck drum.

"And"—here Marie fixed the tall woman with a piercing glance—"I do not cough, though I am over fifty years old."

Dante looked up quickly at his attendant, as though afraid of her reaction. "Careful what you say to Isis, old woman."

Marie lowered her eyes in deference. But she had made her point. The beauty named Isis was all attention now.

"Prove that you are over fifty," Dante said. "You *could* just be ugly . . . or diseased."

Marie smiled, accepting the insult with grace. "My skin is wrinkled, but I can walk long distances—if you do not starve me," she said. At this boldness, Dante leaned forward, as though surprised to be addressed with candor.

"I am past my monthly bleeding, and can have sex without getting children. I still have my wits, and can count backward from one hundred by sevens." Dante raised an eyebrow, as though this were of particular significance.

Marie continued: "I know fifty years' worth of big tech, and I know how to talk to a great leader without wasting his time." This last she said with a dismissive gesture at Reeve.

"By God," Dante said, rising to his feet. "This woman is fifty!"

A soft, lisping voice interrupted him. Isis spoke: "You cannot have children?"

"No, thank the Lord," Marie said, with no small irony.

Isis' face lit up in a stunning smile, which Marie matched, while the men in the room looked from one to the other in bemusement.

"Enough of babies and bleeding!" Dante pronounced. He strode to an elaborately carved side table heaped with rolls of paper. He gathered up a handful and waved them at Reeve and Marie. "Do you read?" he bellowed. "Everyone says they can read! But do they read these? My captains bring me readers from the ends of the world, but what do they read?" He turned a fierce scowl on Reeve, the scowl deepening when Reeve didn't answer. He swung toward Marie, his face questioning. When Marie remained silent, he went on: "Words!"

As his tone and volume veered into a rant, Dante's attendants shifted uncomfortably—all except Kalid, whose ironic smile seemed nailed in place.

"I'll tell you what words are worth!" He stabbed a finger at the sloping back wall, and a servant rushed to pull on a rope and tackle. When the curtain had been raised, there appeared, through the semitranslucent walls, three cylinders swaying outside the dome.

"Now, tell me if you can read!" In his excitement a dry cough racked him for a moment. When he recovered, he strode forward with an armload of rolled papers, thrusting them at Marie.

She unrolled one and scanned it. Reeve drew near, looking over the unfurled engineering drawing. The paper was stained and yellowed, and almost illegible. He thought he and Marie would have a hard time guessing its use, if this was their assignment.

But Marie knew her engineering, and said, "The dome."

By Dante's pleased expression, Reeve knew she'd

guessed right. It was then that Reeve focused once more on the shapes suspended outside the dome walls. He couldn't know for sure, but suddenly he was almost certain they were bodies, hanging from a beam.

Suppressing his revulsion, he grabbed for some of the papers, vying with Marie to name the drawings and their features. "Condensing turbine," Marie said. And: "Flow meter, heat exchanger, exhaust conduit."

Dante grew animated. "Conduit!" he repeated, looking in triumph at his lieutenants.

"Air handler, circulation pump, generator," Marie continued, followed by Dante's echo: "Cir-cula-tion pump, gener-ator!"

Rifling through another sheaf, Reeve found something he knew very well: an electrical diagram. "Coils!" he blurted out. "Armature, voltage, magnetic field!" It was an industrial-sized induction meter. If the batch of papers related to each other, it might be a piece of equipment in the dome.

Dante now turned his attention to Reeve. "What do you know of hyp-notic fields?"

"I know about electricity. I can read these."

"E-lec-tri-city!" Dante shouted. His lieutenants repeated the word, *Lec-tricity, lec-tricity,* while Isis, losing interest, slumped into Dante's chair and picked at her teeth—a startling gesture from one done up like a queen.

The horrid trio of lumps outside and the mad shouting of Dante had combined to make Reeve disoriented and dizzy. He leaned on a nearby chair, bringing a look of alarm to Dante's face. The man called for refreshments for his readers. At this, the momentum was lost, and Dante and his thieves turned their attentions to setting up a table and chairs.

Meanwhile, Kalid approached the two prisoners, grinning. "You are in favor today, Reeve Calder."

"And tomorrow?"

Kalid shrugged. "*A new day, a new Dante*, we some-times say."

Reeve smiled as Kalid rejoined his lord at the table, where servants were bringing trays of food and great pitchers of wine. While Dante and his attendants fell upon the meal with gusto, forgetting their readers for the moment, Marie and Reeve settled themselves on the floor, studying the drawings. They appeared to be industrial designs, many if not all related to terraforming. "What does he want from us?" Reeve whispered to Marie.

"Whatever it is, we're going to give it to him," she replied, the chill in her voice belying the pert smile she directed at Dante.

He waved at her from his table, ordering an attendant to bring them food. A great tray arrived, piled high. They picked their way through masses of rotting fruit to find a few edible pieces.

Dante shouted at them, "Eat!" For now Dante was clearly of a mind to feed them, not hang them, a mood Reeve suspected was subject to instant change.

He and Marie were coaxed to the table, where the entourage was making short work of a roasted half pig, eating with their hands and gulping wine. Gobs of grease trickled onto the velvet of Isis' gown, which at this closer view appeared badly stained.

"Now we feast!" proclaimed Dante. "Time enough later to start the engines!"

Isis looked up, managing to lisp even with her mouth full of food: "Fixth the dome home?"

"Yes, my queen," Dante replied with great tenderness. "So we can live forever."

Marie glanced at Reeve, her expression frozen in place. At her urging, and with a sinking heart, he joined her as she raised her glass to toast Lord Dante.

·   ·   ·   ·   ·

In the exact center of the dome a great throng had gathered. Raised faces strained to see Lord Dante atop the tank, a gigantic drum at least a hundred feet high, with a flattened top the size of a small gym. Reeve and his companions stood alongside Dante and Isis as the pair received the cheers of their followers. Between Kalid and Bunyan stood the Whale Clave women, on the opposite side of the drum. On catwalks and scaffolding at two levels above the floor, Dante's people crowded, some cheering, some silently observing with the demeanor of slaves.

"My jinn!" Dante cried out, holding his arms in front of him and stalking the perimeter of the drum. Reeve hoped he might topple by misstep.

"You will welcome my exalted visitors among you!" bellowed Dante, his voice echoing through the metal labyrinth of the machinery. He gestured for Spar to be brought to the edge next to him. "This one," he said, gesturing at Spar, "will be known as Quixote!"

"Quixote, Quixote!" the crowd thundered.

He nodded at Marie and she stepped forward, standing next to Spar. "She shall be Medea!"

"Medea!" came the response from below.

Reeve's turn was next, as he stepped to Dante's side. "Spaceman!" Dante proclaimed.

A roar of laughter. "Spaceman go home!" someone shouted.

At this Dante frowned, holding up his hands for silence. "No! This *is* his home. The dome home!"

"Dome home," came the echo from many throats.

Dante turned to Loon. As the guard shoved her forward, Dante edged away from her slightly, as though he did not want to accidentally touch her. She approached the edge of the drum and gazed out at the dome, her nose twitching, as though she was actually thinking about smells, even at a time like this.

Dante shrugged. "Loon!" he pronounced.

"Loony!" someone called, eliciting laughter all around.

"What they ask, you shall do!" Dante said, in deep oratory style. "Whoever harms them dies. Whoever offends them dies. Whoever . . ." Here he paused, and grinned boyishly. "Ah well, you get the picture!" The crowd, warming to their king's performance, laughed heartily.

Dante turned to Kalid. "Now the others."

Kalid brought the Whale Clave group forward, the three women and the child, hands behind backs.

"These four love the orthong," Dante told his jinn. A strong murmur moved like a wave below. "They fled their clave to give body and loyalty to the invader!" He raised his arms in supplication. "What is the punishment for such?"

"The fire," someone growled from below.

"The rope," another suggested.

And another: "Toss them down!"

The big woman raised her chin defiantly, while the one with the child pulled her daughter closer, her face wild.

Pacing back and forth along the edge, Dante received these suggestions. Then he turned to Kalid. "What says my captain of ships?"

Kalid shrugged. "I care not, my lord." He added: "But let the young one live. She is a child, no traitor."

Great boos greeted this notion. And the shout came: "Traitors breed traitors!"

Acclamation erupted from the throng. Dante strutted upon his ramparts until the shouting died down. He leaned close to Kalid and said in a genial manner, "They wish for blood, Kalid. What can one do?"

Reeve stepped forward. "Lord Dante . . ." In his mind, he saw the bodies swaying from the [ ] side Dante's room. Kalid frowned at this [ ] and Dante swung to glare at him. "Lord [ ]" went on, "I ask for their lives."

A peeved expression bloomed on the great lord. Beneath them, the crowd growled its discontent. Dante said in an undertone, "Bother." As the jinn grew unruly, he snarled, "Ask for something else, Spaceman."

Kalid walked over to Reeve, a thin smile tightening his face. "You make my lord look ungenerous, Reeve Calder."

Reeve bit into his cheeks and gazed past Kalid at Dante.

Then Dante's face brightened. He turned to his jinn. "My exalted visitor has asked a favor." He turned to Reeve, his face sliding into a scowl. "I grant *one* favor." Facing the crowd again, he said: "We want no traitors in our midst! But I will release one woman in a boat, to fend for herself." He turned back to Reeve. "That is my *one* favor."

Kalid whispered harshly, "Take it, and be grateful!" At Reeve's hesitation, Kalid snarled, "Another moment, and you will fly from this tower."

Reeve bowed toward Dante, saying in as steady a voice as he could muster, "Thank you, my lord." He stared down at the rusted metal cap of the great drum, trying to think.

"So then?" Dante's voice came.

Kalid nudged him. Dante was speaking to him.

"So then?"

Reeve frowned in confusion.

"Choose."

It was at this moment that Reeve realized the import of this word. He opened his mouth to protest and met Kalid's fierce stare. *Choose?* Despite the clear warning on Kalid's face, Reeve said, "I can't."

"Choose Anar!" Nerys shrieked.

Dante waited, along with the horde below, in deepening silence.

The ghastly decision would be forced on him. He ...ced at Marie, who raised an eyebrow as if to say, ...ourself in this one, now get yourself out.* Sweat threaded down his sides as he waited for inspiration. By rights, he knew, he should choose the child, but she wouldn't survive, cast adrift alone. He guessed her to be eleven years old, no more.

Dante sighed noisily and gestured to his men, who lined the women and the girl up on the very edge of the drum.

"Wait!" Reeve shouted.

Dante turned to face Reeve.

"The mother," Reeve whispered. "I choose the mother."

Nerys howled. "No! My daughter! By the Lord, she is only a babe!"

Reeve met her eyes. They were chaotic and black. He had to break his gaze, and looked down at the floor, whispering again, "The mother." Then, looking up at Kalid, he said with venom, "Take her away, now."

Kalid strode forward and grabbed Nerys, as another guard grabbed the child from her arms. The woman struggled fiercely, planting her feet firmly as she came even with Reeve. "Please," she whimpered. "Lord above us, choose Anar!"

Reeve's voice rasped out, "She'll die left on her own. This was not my doing, by the Lord of Worlds!"

Assisted by two guards, Kalid dragged the woman off. Her screams could be heard all the way down the ladder, and longer, as they took her away. Far in the distance he heard her cry out: "May you be damned in hell, Reeve Calder! Damned in hell!"

Reeve shuddered, hearing her curse, feeling the truth of it. The shudder visited him again as Dante lifted his hand, then chopped it down through the air before him.

Amid the tumultuous roar of the jinn, th[...] firmly grasped each of the three victim[...] though they were sacks of trade goods, [...] from the edge of the platform, where t[...] from view.

7

1

Day fifteen. A touch on Reeve's shoulder startled him to wakefulness. By the light of the guttering candles at his bedside, he saw that it was Loon.

He slept in a great bed so high off the floor that he had needed a box to climb into it. Loon stood on that box, reaching over to trace her finger down the side of his face. Her short yellow hair stuck out on every side in a glowing corona around her face, and she wore a green velvet riding habit, pulled from the jinn's storehouse of costumes.

"Loon?" He raised up on one elbow and tried to shake off sleep.

She put her finger in her mouth and sucked on it in her habitual way, with a casual eroticism that succeeded in waking him thoroughly.

"Loon?" At his second query, she backed down from the bed and receded into the darkness of the great room.

"Spar is unhappy," her voice came.

"His wounds? Is he sick?" Having slept in his clothes, he sat up, swinging his feet over the bed rail.

He admitted to himself that he would forsake sleep if Loon were to share his bed, but that he'd rather save minor issues for the morning. The horror of the day's events had chased his thoughts late into the night, and he couldn't have slept long. But as he had noticed before, Loon seemed indifferent to times of day.

A large spider was crawling down the canopy of the bed. Reeve swatted at it, reflecting anew that he disliked sleeping in the jinn's grimy and sumptuous bedding. In fact, the covers stank of sweat and grease and had hardened in places, from spills of one sort or another.

Loon was pulling on his hand. He relented, hopping to the floor and following her. As he passed the enormous gilded mirror leaning down from one wall, he saw the two of them pass, Loon dressed in her fine riding habit and he in his regulation Stationer jumpsuit. The flickering light registered their passing like an old vid in which an unwashed young man with a patchy beard followed a beautiful young woman into a world of dark, tattered elegance. His growth of beard made him look older. As Kalid had said, in this world, people matured quickly. Here, a twenty-four-year-old was at his peak, a ruler of jinn. And soon to decline. . . .

The guard at his door followed them, but made no comment on their night foray. Perhaps he remembered that he who offended them would die. Or perhaps the jinn were curious about what he might do.

Now that he was up in the middle of the night, Reeve accepted Loon's lack of explanation and simply followed her. Gas lamps lighted their way among the industrial innards of the dome. It made Reeve uneasy to think of the barbarians running pipe for gas, and he could only hope their skills were up to the task. At the least, the jinn had devised a primitive gas process, perhaps a remnant system of the dome's old terraform functions.

Once leaving the edge of the dome, where quarters were fashioned against the angle of the wall, they quickly found themselves walking a metal grid among the inert machinery of the dome. They passed great tanks and cylinders and gigantic mains punctuated by meters. The Jupiter Dome had been one of the first colonial habitats, serving not only terraforming, but providing a refuge during the first years of settlement, when the colonists had needed shelter from Lithia's poisons. This dome was one of the largest of Lithia's many chemical recycling plants, pulling carbon dioxide out of the air, transforming it, and trapping it as calcium carbonate while changing Lithia's seawater into basic elements and pumping improved mixes into the air through the outflow stacks, long since rusted and toppled.

Loon climbed a ladder into darkness. "Up," she said.

Reeve began climbing. After several minutes, he was still climbing, his body prickly hot from sweat. As he continued upward he guessed they were scaling a distilling column, one of the towering cylinders that inhabited the center of the dome. Behind him, Reeve could hear the ring of the metal ladder as his guard followed.

At the top, the ceiling of the dome was within a jump, the fretted metal skeleton forming a madman's jungle gym. The cooing of pigeons told who ruled these heights.

In the gloom, Reeve could make out Spar's form, facing outward. Loon settled in by the claver's side.

Grasping the railing, Reeve sat on Spar's other side, letting his feet dangle. "Can't sleep?"

"Slept."

"You're luckier than me, then."

They gazed into the black rafters for a while. "Your mate's got a mean streak, all right," Spar said.

"Mate?" Spar could always find a way to annoy

him, never mind he'd just given up a good night's rest and climbed a thousand steps into thin air to help him.

Spar snorted. "He seem to like you, Reeve-boy. Give us all fancy beds to sleep in, and got people bowin' to me, left and right. All for your big tech."

"You're the one brought big tech into this, there on the beach. We could've all been happily dead without my big tech!"

"Well, what you gonna do for these rats? Give 'em all breathers so they can swarm over the world?"

"Reeve's good air," Loon piped in, thoughtfully.

He sighed. He hadn't thought that far. Lord of Worlds, he *couldn't* think. Two women and a child had just been hurled from a height like this one. Any one of whom he could have saved . . . which *didn't* make him a murderer, but which felt like the worst thing he'd ever done. And among all the ghastly things he'd ever seen, it ranked high, right up there with Tina Valejo. . . .

Reeve looked behind to see if the guard was within hearing distance. Testing the limits of his exalted-visitor status, he barked, "Wait for us at the bottom." Soon he heard the retreating slaps of the man's feet against the ladder rungs.

"I don't even know what they *want* me to do," he admitted. "I can't make breathers, not even close. I can't start this machinery again. I don't know how." It would take a specialized crew years to do the diagnostics and rebuild . . . all far beyond either Reeve's knowledge, or Marie's.

"You can't figure out what they're after?" Spar turned to gaze at him, and there was no need to see his face in the darkness to figure out his expression. "Close up the big hole in his house. Fix the air high and mightiness don't have to cough."

Spar's and Loon's shapes were just separating from the blackness as a dull glow in the doorway heralded the coming of dawn.

"What do you want me to do?" Reeve asked.

"Do what you like. I ain't your boss." A sulky quiet claimed them for a moment.

In high pique, Reeve scrambled to his feet. "What's your big problem, Spar? You want to come out and say it, or you just want to bellyache?" When Spar remained silent, Reeve turned to go.

"Lost," he heard Loon say.

He swirled back to face her. "What the hell is *lost*?" If she wanted to communicate, let her damn well string a few words together.

"Spar's sword." She rose, facing him. "Lost."

"Damn it, Loon, we *all* lost our weapons." He waited for Spar to react to his use of her name, but, perhaps as a result of his funk, he didn't even budge. Reeve went on, "We're prisoners; don't you get it?"

"You find sword," she replied in her infuriating, single-minded way.

Lord of Worlds. "Did you ask the jinn yourself?"

Spar answered: "They scurried to find it all right, but came back a few minutes later. Said it's lost." He slapped the empty scabbard at his side. "Hard to protect Mam when I got no sword."

"We'll get you another sword, then." What was he bothering with this for? He needed to be rested for the morning so he could outwit mad Dante. Lord of the galumphing galaxies, how did he let himself get roped into this craziness?

Spar bestirred himself, getting to his feet in a world-weary fashion. "You think one sword's as good as another, don't you?"

At this, Reeve started back down the stairs. "Yes." He'd had enough.

After a few yards, he heard them clambering after him. Spar's voice came from far away, like a ghost: "Trouble with you sky-wheelers, you think everythin' ___mes easy. Swords, air, worlds, ships, you name it. So ___ got value."

"Shut up, Spar."

"You big-tech fellas, you think *thinking* is so important. You got all your big ideas. But you got nothin' to hold on to. No world, no things."

Reeve picked up his pace, slapping his hands around the rungs and trying to get away from Spar's voice. Around him, the coiled pipes and water stains of the cylinder hove into view as the dome bloomed around them, a giant bubble of slow light.

Spar droned on, just above him. "You figure people can live up in their big brains. People don't need ordinary *things* when they got those big brains. But old Lithia's gonna show you that her stuff matters. Yes, sir, she's gonna show you."

Addled, the man was. Off on a tangent, and no way to escape it. "Well, I'm sure we'll both get a dose of Lithia's revenge," Reeve hurled up at him.

Spar cackled. "No doubt, no doubt! And no doubt you're glad I had my sword when we hammered on the rats that day! And if it was another sword?"

Reeve stumbled onto the floor of the dome at last, trembling with anger and ready to punch Spar when he reached the bottom.

In the next moment Spar was down, saying, "If it was another sword, you'd be dead by now, boyo! That sword kept us alive from the Stoneroots to the Inland Sea. And it's gonna get us up the Tallstory River, by the Lady!"

Reeve's fist was bunched and ready, and then it was unbunched and dangling at his side.

Loon jumped off the last rung and waited by the tank.

The Tallstory River. That was the way to his goal. Forget the crazy claver, and just try to keep the mind. And this crazy claver had indeed saved several times. So if the sword gave his arm passion, then he'd find the damnable logic. Forget trying to figure Spar out and Marie were his only allies, and if they were a ragtag group, it was a lot better than going it alone.

Kalid emerged from the shadows.

Nodding at him, Reeve said, "Can you assign some crew to find Spar's sword? It has sentimental value. I'd appreciate it."

Kalid shrugged. "Likely traded by now. We'll get him another."

"He needs the old one."

The group held an uneasy silence. Then Kalid bowed. "As you wish." He nodded at the guard accompanying him.

Spar shook his head. "I better come along. You folks don't know a good sword from a pipe wrench."

Watching Spar and the guard march off together, Kalid said, "You rise early, Spaceman."

"Couldn't sleep."

"Forget the Whale Clavers. It was their fate."

A flicker of annoyance prompted Reeve to say: "No one is fated to be murdered."

"You've not been long among us if you think that," Kalid said. He gestured down the metal-grated pathway. "I've come to show you our fortress. Dante would have you study the machines." He looked slyly at Reeve. "So you may fix them."

"It's a tall order."

Kalid nodded. "So it is. But the queen will die, else."

Leading the way into the rusted maze, Kalid said, "Already her lips are tinged with the indigo. My lord fears for her." As though reminded of the poisons they all endured, he coughed, low in his throat.

A scuffle from above drew Reeve's attention. Looking up, he saw a flash of green: Loon was scrambling along on top of a great vat next to them. Then she jumped onto a catwalk several feet away, spanning the distance in an effortless leap. She seemed healthier than any of them, but he'd asked her to wear a breather anyway, as he'd asked Spar. When they both refused, it was something of a relief. His supply was running low.

"She has no fear of heights," observed Kalid. "I could use such a one on my masted ships." He walked on, saying, "You would not mind? If the girl served Kalid?"

Reeve minded. Did not, in fact, care for the innuendo. "She serves the Spaceman," he said, carelessly. One did not gain the respect of a man like Kalid by being timid.

Kalid laughed. His boots clanged on the grating, echoing from the metalworks. "You grow bold, Spaceman. It was not long ago you would have lost fingers for such a remark."

"Well, I have my fingers. And Loon."

"For now." As ever, his tone was genial. But walking behind, Reeve could not see his face.

2

Loon peered down on the two figures, crouched around a small hump of metal with dials and many pipes. They talked endlessly of engines and big-tech workings.

Her attention was focused on foraging for breakfast. Up here, atop a large metal vat, the soil was undisturbed. Pigeon matter had fallen from the ceiling, while the top of the machine supplied flakes of paint and rust. She sampled all but the very recent pigeon dirt and the paint, finding a snack here and there, enough to stave off hunger. It was a wonder to her that such a place held soil. Soil, she realized, could be made up of decay and death and droppings, and was the child of everything around it. So here in the great bubble in the sea, she didn't look for the good taste. She could wait.

Lying on top of the machine, she looked

the two men. The dark one was frowning, as though he didn't believe Reeve.

". . . forming water droplets," Reeve was saying. "It forms water when it encounters the cold metal. Like steam, when you boil water, it condenses on something cooler nearby, and forms drops of water."

They went on with their talk of big tech. Kalid would know about things such as chemical re-cyc-lers and de-salin-ation. He was keen to learn but reluctant to be taught by Reeve. For Loon's part, she loved to hear Reeve talk, for in big-tech things he showed the grace of a deer in its woods.

"Dis-till-a-tion," Kalid was saying. "I have heard of this."

"Right, distillation. You can separate substances according to their volatility. The distillate is carried off by those pipes there." He looked up, and seeing Loon, waved at her.

She waved back, liking his attention. Standing, she jumped onto an exposed pipe and shinnied down to his level.

"Be careful, would you, Loon?"

She grinned. After everything they had been through, he now thought sliding down a pole was dangerous? But no one since her father had urged her to be careful, and she took this for a kindness. She grasped his hand. At this, a color rose to Reeve's face, and the dark man's lips tugged into a tiny smile.

Kalid asked, "Where did you learn to climb, my Loon?"

"Trees of the Stoneroots."

"They must be tall trees, to teach you so well. You are graceful indeed."

She smiled in response. At the slight stiffening in Reeve's hand, she looked at him. He seemed uncomfortable. There was anger between the two men, but they pretended they did not feel it. Very odd.

The space where they stood was like a high, small

room, its walls formed by towering machines. Through this space the colorful jinn would thread their way now and then, carrying things, endless streams of junk, large and small. From deeper in the gut of the dome came the continual sounds of feet, collecting items to trade for other items, making heaps of belongings here and there. It was so different from the clave, where there were few things, and each useful.

The men were talking of dis-till-a-tion again. Loon put her hand to Reeve's mouth, stopping him from talking.

Kalid laughed. "She is bored with these matters," he said.

She shook her head. Not bored; she just liked to touch his lips.

"Perhaps she is uncomfortable with all this talk of things so foreign to her," Kalid suggested. "Perhaps it makes her wonder, what good is all her life's knowledge when she does not know *distillation*? Perhaps it makes her feel . . . uneducated."

It hadn't occurred to her to feel that way. But she cocked her head, thinking about it for a moment. No, it was not how she felt. But—ah! It was how *Kalid* felt.

"She should understand," Reeve said, "that there are many things I don't know which she knows."

"But things of value?" Kalid asked.

"Things that keep one alive. Things that are more useful than chemical processes. I envy her knowledge, and I feel inadequate before her."

After a pause, Kalid said: "That was a courteous thing to say."

Reeve looked frankly at the other man. "I meant it."

Kalid turned his large smile on Loon. "So, what would you have us discuss?"

Loon thought for a moment. She pointed upward.

"The dome?" Kalid asked. "The sky?"

She nodded. "Tell about the sky."

"What would you know?" Kalid asked.

"The ship," Loon responded.

A startled expression flitted across Reeve's face. "Ship?" He looked so closely at her she almost backed up.

"The great ship."

"I have it!" announced Kalid. "The colony ship. Of long ago." At this, Loon nodded vigorously.

Reeve's features softened. "What about it, Loon?" "Where is?"

"Oh." He shrugged. "It was destroyed by meteors. Hundreds of years ago. It was—in orbit around the planet. After it was damaged, it tumbled down, to the sea."

"No ship." Loon sighed. "No ship to take Spar back to Earth." Sometimes she had dared to wish Spar a long life in a place that could feed him well, but it was not to be.

As though on command, Spar appeared on the catwalk above them. He held a long, slim object aloft, and his voice rang with vigor: "Snatched from the grasp of a filthy trader!" he proclaimed. "We're back on track, Reeve-boy!"

------------------- 3 -------------------

There were flat pink sands interrupted here and there with rock monoliths. There was the wind rushing from nowhere to nowhere, passing through her. There was sun and heat, dark and cold, and sometimes, a gnawing in her belly that she quieted by eating small insects. She walked on, a pair of eyes moving through a stark landscape.

From the path of the sun as it traced the day from dawn to dusk, Nerys knew she was traveling north, but she had forgotten why. Perhaps this was what all things did—the monoliths, the insects, the ripples of sand. All traveled north until desiccating and merging.

In her backpack she carried a small blanket and

come. Through this crimson world the road stretched, a spill of cooked blackberries. She followed it. When night came, she found an outcropping of rocks to settle among, and slept within moments.

At first light Nerys found herself staring at a dead campfire. Digging among the ashes with a stick, she found some warmth. Then she found a footprint. She stared. It could have been the footprint of a big man, but no man would venture here without boots. She crouched down for a closer look. Very large and broad, with an opposable toe. Putting her hand in the indentation, she filled up a third of its span. Other footprints told more of the story. A human wearing lug-soled boots traveled with this creature. They had slept here as recently as last night.

The footprints led northwest, departing from the road. Finding the bike little use on the sands, she abandoned it and set out on foot, noticing from the tracks that the human was weak, resting often.

When, late in the day, she saw a large rock outcropping, she approached it quietly. If the human was tired or injured, here would make a fine camping spot. Climbing the boulders, she inched forward to peer down into a crater-shaped declivity.

In the little hollow, someone was digging a very deep hole. The digger paused, wiping hand across forehead. It was a woman, her hair in reddish braids.

The orthong was seated on a rock, watching the digger. Its long, dark coat bore a dull sheen in the sun, and its head, hands, and feet were white.

The woman disappeared into the hole. When she emerged, she held something in her hands. Placing it on the edge of the hole, she clambered out, then picked up the object and approached the creature. Next to the orthong, the woman seemed the size of a child. She held out the object, a small tray, and the orthong placed its hand in the tray, handing it back after a few moments. It made a motion with its right arm and hand, signing something to her.

Nerys' lip curled. The lazy giant had made the woman dig a hole for water. Even orthong needed water, apparently, absorbing it through their hands, perhaps.

The woman went back for water four more times, while the creature sat impassively, accepting the water offering. When it was done, the woman drank, long and quickly. So, the beast had made her wait, as well.

After a time, the woman went behind some bushes to relieve herself. When she returned, she brought branches and began to build a fire. As the sun dropped below the horizon, Nerys began to envy the warmth of that fire, but for now the rock still gave off some stored heat. The orthong finally bestirred itself, rising from its seat and approaching the woman. It handed her something. Reaching up for it, the woman ripped apart the wrapping and was soon stuffing the contents into her mouth. Again the beast spoke to her, with darting movements of its lower arm and fingers. At this, the woman looked up directly to where Nerys hid.

Nerys flattened herself against the boulder. When she dared to look again, the woman was standing at the bottom of the rock outcropping.

"Do you seek refuge of the orthong?" the woman asked, looking up at her.

Nerys struggled to a sitting position. The orthong paid no attention to her.

"Do you seek refuge?" she asked again.

"Hungry," Nerys said.

The woman smirked. "My lord says you may come down."

Nerys slowly rose. Night was coming on, and she longed for the fire and food. Standing before the woman, she saw her thin face and wispy red hair, and wondered that the orthong bothered with her, as sickly as she looked. "What clave?" Nerys asked.

"We don't speak of claves now. But my name is Galen." The effort of speaking brought on a fit of coughing. Regaining herself, the woman asked: "Do you sign?"

"A little."

"Then don't try, until you master it. I'll speak for you." She led the way toward the creature, sitting on a rock.

In the breeze Nerys shivered. The orthong had a great, long face, the famous white skin registering slight overtones of gray and yellow. A mere slit where the mouth should have been, almost lost in the skin ridges. Eyes of moss green. No nose. The skin looked tough and corrugated, like a walnut skin. She looked quickly down at the hands, checking for claws. There was always argument in the clave about whether the thong could retract their claws. She could tell them, if she ever saw them again, that the orthong indeed could.

Galen said something in sign, and the creature responded. She began signing again, but Nerys snatched her wrist. "Speak as you sign. Tell me what you say."

Galen jerked her wrist free. "You do not touch me. *Never* touch an orthong."

Nerys smiled at this admonition. No doubt this woman, already far gone with indigo, was full of cautions, of how to live, how to serve. But life did not greatly matter anymore to Nerys. This, she realized with a small shock, gave her the first real power she had ever known.

The woman spoke as she signed to the orthong, "This human comes for teaching, my lord."

"How do you know what I'm here for?"

Galen snorted. "The same as me. You want the same as me." She looked at Nerys stonily. "Don't you?" When Nerys didn't reply, the woman nodded toward the hole. "You can start by bringing Bitamalar a drink of water." She handed her the tray.

"What game is this?" Nerys whispered.

Galen smirked. "It's called Learning Your Place. You don't have to play."

At this fair pronouncement, Nerys took the tray and walked over to the well, its bottom covered with a few inches of muddy water. She retrieved the water. Crossing the distance to the orthong, she contrived to stumble, slopping almost all the water out of the tray. She heard Galen cluck her tongue in reproach. Continuing, Nerys handed the orthong the little drink that remained.

The creature did not move for a few moments.

From deeply recessed eyes came an unblinking, green stare. Nerys held that gaze. Then, ignoring the tray, the orthong walked past her to the spot where the water had spilled. Its foot covered the spill. When it removed its foot, the sand beneath it was dry.

That night as the fire burned down, Bitamalar, as Galen referred to the creature, came over twice more, bestowing food packets on the woman, which she devoured alone. The lesson was not lost on Nerys, that food is power. And perhaps the lesson was not lost on the orthong, that food is not all that matters.

8

1

Day sixteen. Dante's entourage crowded around a small mound of machinery painted bright yellow. Isis wore an enormous dress roped with peeling fake pearls. From her headdress trailed a length of black lace which fluttered each time she coughed. Kalid and Marie stood by as Reeve held forth on the wonders of the dome machinery, half truth, half fabrication.

"This device," Dante said, indicating the squat yellow machine labeled SWANWICK COMPRESSOR.

"This is a compressor," Reeve said, as Marie rolled her eyes.

"Yes, yes, compressor, we can read," Dante said with impatience. Speaking loudly for the benefit of the small crowd, he continued, "And a compressor works in such a manner as?" He smiled at his followers, showing off the Spaceman, his latest acquisition.

Reeve knew that Dante liked him to use industrial words to impress his jinn. He obliged. "Air is drawn in at the casing by a rotating impeller that's driven by an electric motor. This one has four impellers to deliver very high-pressure air out the other end."

"Im-pellers, yes," Dante said. His doughy features

brightened as he said, "Im-pellers will bring us good air under high pressure." The jinn clapped at this conclusion, as though it were an accomplished fact, not a vain hope. But as a hedge against failure, both Dante and Isis now wore breathers. It had been an ugly introductory lesson to the breathers, with Isis gagging and Dante alternating between rage and tears as he struggled with the simple dexterity and patience needed to apply one. When Dante was in a better mood, Reeve and Marie had managed to convince him that *they* must wear the breathers too, or their service to Dante would be short.

Meanwhile the supply of breathers was rapidly dwindling, with the appliance's useful life proving to be about five days, a defect that could be fixed if Reeve had the tools and the skills, which he did not.

Dante waved at Reeve to continue.

"This one probably uses mated lobed impellers. They revolve in opposite directions, driven by meshed gear wheels."

Marie mumbled, "You don't know if this one is lobed." She smiled at Dante, who bowed deeply. Still smiling, she muttered to Reeve, "Don't promise more than you can deliver."

"Methed gear wheelth," Isis lisped as she absently pawed through a tray of jewelry held by an attendant. These attendants appeared regularly, bearing new platters of trinkets. If Isis chose a trinket, she bestowed a coin on the servant. On closer view, Reeve saw that these coins were plastic game coins, perhaps legal tender of the realm, or perhaps only mementos of the queen's favor.

They had been at this tour for over an hour, and Dante's courtiers were growing bored. When the one called Pinocchio yawned hugely, Dante frowned, pushing out his lower lip.

Observing his lord grow distressed, Kalid spoke up:

"My lord, a ship has just now arrived, fully laden. It may amuse to watch its treasures unload."

At that moment Spar and Loon appeared at the back of the crowd, which now parted as they were escorted forward by Bunyan.

"Quixote," Dante said. He bowed with a flourish, revealing the inked curls of his head tattoos. This bow was followed by the dip of the entire entourage. Only Isis never bowed, it being a close thing whether with all her hair and headdress she'd be able to raise her head again. "And Princess Loon," Dante added.

Spar nodded in military fashion, while Loon cocked her head at all the bowing and scraping.

In the pause, Kalid repeated, "The ship, my lord?"

Startled, Dante swirled on his captain. "Ship? Ship? Am I deaf?" Here he appealed to his jinn, who laughed uneasily.

"Thip?" chirped Isis.

"Ships arrive every hour! Who is amused by such a thing? You may keep your ships, Kalid; we have larger matters before us!" He waved his hand to encompass the towering machinery crowding in from every side. "My Spaceman must tour his laboratory! Medea must catalogue the dome holes!"

"Dome hothes," Isis said. She shook her head sadly, pouting her violet lips.

Kalid bowed his acquiescence, his face carefully neutral.

"But we tire of compress-ors and un-peelers for now," Dante said. "Dante will present his own wonders to the Spaceman." In his best oratorical manner, he intoned: "We will tour the dungeons of Atlantis!" He flicked his wrist at Pinocchio, adding, "You have no science in you. Take your useless friends and beat it."

Led by Isis, the entourage shuffled away.

"I should attend my ships, Lord Dante," Kalid said, moving off.

"You work too hard, Kalid! Show us the dungeons and the ships be damned."

At this, Kalid led the way, followed by Dante, Reeve, Spar, Marie, and Loon. They snaked through the ribbons of pipes and great vats until Kalid stopped them and, bending down, lifted first one, then the other of two large metal doors set into the floor. A gust of air carried a fetid stench from below. Selecting a torch from a stack, Kalid lit it, fumbling with a tiny lighter. He and his torch disappeared into the hole, down a set of steps, with the others following.

Loon held back.

"What is it?" Reeve asked. She had been teaching him some sign language, and now she used two signs he knew: <Bad smells,> she said with her hands. Her nostrils flared, as though the smells were not entirely unwelcome.

"Stay here then," Reeve told her. But when he turned to go, she followed him into the recess.

They were in an underwater chamber. The flame illuminated nothing but their faces for now, but Reeve could hear the steady drip of water nearby, and, in the distance, the sounds of gurgling pipes. The place reeked of human waste.

As Kalid lit a torch on the wall, a voice called, "A light! Yonder, yonder!"

Another voice joined in. "Valences, chemical bonds, isomers!" And another, farther in the distance: "Refraction. Also, diffraction! The blue color of the sky due to scattering of sunlight with short wavelengths of blue!"

"Quiet!" Kalid roared.

Spar mumbled next to Reeve, "No prison. This here's where they keep their crazy folk."

"Show us Madame Curie," Dante urged.

The torchlight was directed to the first cell, where a face appeared between the bars. A mass of wiry hair surrounded a woman's face, so grimy her features were obscured. "My lord!" she breathed. "Did you bring my mail?" Her voice was plaintive, childlike.

Dante moved closer. "Did you fix my dome home?"

She cast her eyes down, shaking her head.

"Then you shall have no mail!" Dante bellowed. "They say Madame Curie knew science. But all she knew was radio-ogy!"

"Radio-ogy," she giggled. Then her voice came deep and sane: "Or was it radiology, Lord Dante?"

He cocked his head, as though considering. "I forget, actually. But in any case, you failed." Gesturing for Kalid to lead on, he said to the group, "These are all my readers."

"The punishment for failure is steep," Marie observed.

"Not punishment! They're fed and clothed until we need them, when the dome engines start up again. These will be your helpers, Medea. My jinn are ignorant. But these are scientists!"

"Socrates," Kalid announced at the next cell.

An emaciated man with a very long beard lay in the corner.

"Old man!" Dante snapped.

From the corner, the man whispered: "On the other hand, the whole fusion process, it could be reengineered! Take a while, of course, and I'd need my laboratory. . . ."

"You *had* a laboratory," Dante said with some kindness. "Remember?"

"No," the prisoner said, as though speaking to himself, "it was just a big, broken terraform dome."

Dante's expression froze for a moment, and Reeve watched for a reaction to this insolence. But Dante only shrugged and moved on, saying, "That was harsh. A *big, broken terraform dome.*" He sighed. "Socrates has let his failure make him bitter."

Reeve didn't want to see any more. Dante's cruelty was revolting. He tried to get Kalid's attention, to appeal to him, but Kalid avoided looking at him, his face carefully neutral.

"The smell, my lord," Marie said, putting her hand to her nose.

Dante looked peeved. "Yes, it stinks down here. Quite right, Medea. Perceptive, as always."

Marie bowed.

"To the end then, Kalid! Show them my monsters!"

They trooped past cell after cell, passing thin arms reaching out. The inmates' imprecations were all laced with fragments of science. Loon placed her hand in Reeve's, and they followed Kalid as he lit another torch along the wall and proceeded past a spate of empty cells. They sloshed through water standing in puddles which glared from the torchlight, as though below them were yet other levels—the levels of hell, perhaps, as in the real Dante's story.

They stopped in front of a cell, larger than the others, while Dante turned to face them, his eyes glittering in the flickering torchlight. "Here, my exalted visitors, is my humble servant, Pimarinun."

Spar was the first to recognize what lay within, and his sword came swiftly from its sheath.

"Lord of Worlds," Marie said. She stepped forward, pressing her face between the bars of the cage.

"Careful," Spar said. "This here's a thong."

"I can see what it is," she said, unmoving.

Reeve peered into the gloom of the cell. There sat one of the white aliens, immobile. The scar on Reeve's chest flushed tight for a moment, remembering his first encounter with a creature like this.

It sat on the floor, though a bed lay within. One foot was drawn in close, so that its knee was crooked in front of its chest. Past this knee the creature watched them carefully. It wore a tattered black coat, but nothing else, and its great feet protruded from the garment, the hide yellowish and tinged with gray streaks. One ankle bore an iron ring sprouting a chain that bound the creature to the wall.

"Keep your sword, Quixote," Dante said. "We have taken its claws." He nodded at Kalid, who produced a key from his pocket and opened the cell door.

Dante was the first to enter the cage. He waved the others through, laughing at their hesitation. "I have said, Pimarinun is my servant. Have it speak to us, Kalid."

Kalid signed for a moment, and they waited for the creature to move, but it remained immobile. The orthong had no nose, but it possessed a small lateral indentation—where its mouth would be if it were human—from which issued the sound of labored breathing. At last its fingers—four of them, Reeve noted—made an answer.

"It greets you, Lord Dante," Kalid said.

Spar snorted, apparently interpreting the signing otherwise.

Kalid shot a warning look at Spar, and proceeded to interpret: "What would the great lord learn from him today?"

"Ask him how he is feeling. He looks sick."

Kalid signed and the creature responded with a bare motion of two fingers. "He says he feels nothing."

"Well, then, he is in no pain. Good. What would my visitors know from this thong?"

"Who are the orthong?" Marie put forward.

Kalid signed her question, but the orthong did not respond.

<Why are you an enemy to humans?> Reeve asked in halting sign.

Just then Loon darted forward and put her hand on the creature's face, near its mouth. Spar lunged for her and dragged her back as she sucked on her finger. The orthong sprang to its feet in a surprising show of agility, prompting Dante to flinch into the opposite corner. In an instant everyone had moved well away from the prisoner. Kalid brought the torch down to keep it between them and the orthong.

It stood even taller than Dante, but its limbs were thinner than the creature Reeve had confronted on the beach, and it stood swaying in place, as though the effort of standing had sapped its strength.

"Best that we leave, my lord," Kalid said, leading Dante out of the cell. He clanged the door shut, locking it.

As the orthong moved as close to the door as its chain would allow, it signed something at them, but Dante was marshaling his tour again. "Tomorrow we will question it further. When it is . . . feeling better. Bring it more food," he ordered Kalid as he proceeded onward into the dome's underbelly.

Spar hung back with Reeve, muttering, "That thong's ugly *and* rude."

"What did it say?"

Spar hucked a wad of spit to the floor. "It said, 'Bring me this woman.'"

Reeve whispered, "As though we would!"

Spar nodded. "Like I told you. Sex-starved." He patted the sword at his side. "I'll bring him somethin', all right!"

Reeve followed along, his heart oppressed. Of all the pathetic creatures buried in this place, the orthong called Pimarinun bothered him the most. An orthong had spared his life once—had given him a scar to bear, but no worse a scar than a human or two had given him. He found himself thinking that he would come back and speak to this Pimarinun, and the thought gave him some comfort.

Dante stood before another of his cages, talking with Marie.

"Deformed," she was saying. She peered in.

Joining her, Reeve tried to see what stood just beyond the bars, but in the gloom he saw at first only a man's pale face. With a scrape of chained feet, the prisoner came nearer. Reeve heard a low whistling sound in a one-two rhythm, supposing it to be very labored breathing. Something rippled on the neck of the man. As he breathed, gill-like structures fluttered there.

"Lord of Worlds," whispered Marie. "What is this affliction?"

Dante laughed. "No affliction! He's proud of that neck of his! Tell them, Kalid."

"Their strangeness is their religion, Medea," Kalid replied. "They are Somaformers, of the Mercury Clave. All this clave are monsters."

The creature's voice sounded like it rustled through straw: "Transformation is the burden of living creatures. . . . We are the Somaformers. You will become one of us. . . ." The prisoner appeared normal except for the neck—and the intensity of his gaze, as though he were buoyed by a desperate evangelism.

"So!" boomed Dante. "Have you such wonders in the great sky clave?" He looked from Marie to Reeve. "Well, Spaceman?"

Reeve bowed. "No, Lord Dante. Your dungeon is more terrible than any sky claver could imagine."

"Excellent!"

"But the smell, my lord," Marie said, looking shaky.

Dante lifted her hand and kissed it. Straightening, he announced: "Enough for today! Tomorrow we can visit again."

They filed past the prisoners once more, Spar keeping Loon well away from the orthong's cage.

Back in the lighted world of the upper dome, Reeve breathed deeply, but the gloom of the depths remained with him.

As the group dispersed, Reeve caught Kalid's eye, and Kalid moved closer to him. "My lord has little mercy. I trust your fate will be better than theirs." He glanced in the direction of the dungeon.

Reeve wasn't so sure this was Kalid's hope. Kalid

made a dangerous enemy, and Reeve meant to win him over if he could. "I have something to show you," Reeve said.

Kalid gestured him onward, and Reeve made his way back to his quarters. From under his bed he withdrew a small parcel that Kalid obviously recognized.

"I asked Bunyan to fetch this for me. If you are displeased, punish me, not him."

Kalid opened the wrappings. Inside lay the black lacquered box. He looked at Reeve, eyes narrowing.

"I found the right tools," Reeve said.

After a long moment, Kalid gently raised the lid. A simple tune like a child's song issued forth, in perfect fidelity. A smile began at the corner of Kalid's mouth, then overtook his face.

Reeve said, "A favorite song?"

"Yes." After a moment he said, "My thanks. It is a welcome gift." Wrapping the box again, he bowed and turned to go.

"Not a gift," Reeve said, plunging onward with his plan.

Kalid stopped and turned back. "No?"

"I was hoping for something in return."

"And what can I possibly offer my lord's exalted visitor?"

"Something I need to learn." As Kalid waited, Reeve swallowed hard, and said: "I need to learn to fight. To kill a man."

In the dull glow of the room's gaslight, Kalid's face was all in shadow. "This is easy. To kill a man."

"Maybe it is for you. But I've never killed anyone. Will you teach me?"

Kalid considered Reeve for a long moment. "I'll come for you in the morning. We'll see if you are as soft as you look."

2

Mitya was scraping pots when a commotion outside the galley signaled that the off-loading of the shuttle had begun. Koichi looked up from his preparation of Captain Bonhert's preferred lunch of re-egg omelette. His hand gripped the frying pan handle without a potholder, as though he would use the hot pan for a cudgel if anybody spoke to him at that moment.

Through the galley door, Mitya glimpsed the crew bringing in the uranium casks for safe storage inside the dome. Under Uncle Stepan's command, the second shuttle had buried the dead, picked up the survivors, and flown on to the Custler Ridge processing plant deep in the Titan Mountains, in the hopes that its treasures had survived looting and the containment casks had held true. Now Stepan had accomplished what the first shuttle had failed to do: retrieval of the ores, the fuel that was their coin of trade with the great ship. But many, including Koichi, held Bonhert responsible for the deaths, though outright accusations had subsided into quiet grudges.

Koichi pulled his apron over his head and began folding it into a neat pile. When the folded material could be folded no more, he set it down on the edge of the counter and walked to the door like one asleep, disappearing into the dome.

Mitya took that for permission to leave as well. He knew better than to tag along with Koichi, whose grief sucked everything into its wake. Mitya was alone, more than ever before. Not just a stowaway intruder, he was now a traitor, in his heart at least. After his interview with Captain Bonhert, it had taken him about three minutes to figure out that everyone in this dome except him was an outlaw, a terrorist. They had sabotaged Station to save themselves—to be among the one hundred offered berths on the great ship. They were monsters, and he hated them—even Stepan. He was utterly alone, walled off by his own emotions. And at all costs, he knew, he must never let on.

Crew was coming through the air lock, bearing the long canisters, two men on each canister. Each four-foot titanium cask held an internal slug of exceptionally rich, unprocessed uranium ore. They carried them to the far side of the dome and set them on end, and when seven canisters had been unloaded the men went back for more. Everyone stared at the containers, the size of children's coffins, but with housing to last the ages. Each contained cargo more precious than seven human lives. One by one the containers came through the air lock.

Oran stepped up next to him. "Your new quarters are right next to that hot stuff," he said. "Give it a day or two, we'll need sun visors to look at you."

Mitya grinned. "I dare *you* to sleep next to them."

"Yeah, I need a good tan."

Bonhert had come out of his room and was scowling at the silent crowd gathered around the canisters. "This is the price of our bail, our rescue," he said. "Though we paid a heavy price for the ore, Lord help us."

To Mitya's surprise, Oran whispered, "*You* didn't pay a damn thing."

As Bonhert urged them back to work and the group dispersed, Oran went on: "None of that crew needed to die. We had hull damage that affected the fuel lines—it was scheduled for work."

"If you knew, why didn't you say something?"

Oran snorted. "Lots of people knew! Cody knew. Captain knew." He made full eye contact with Mitya. "Guess they were willing to suffer the consequences. Willing for *us* to."

Mitya allowed himself to shake his head in disgust. He did feel some solidarity with Oran, and was relieved that someone had the sense to criticize the Captain.

"Don't you boys have work to do?"

They turned around to find Bonhert standing there. Mitya felt a pang of dismay arc through him. How much had he heard?

"Yes, sir," Oran replied in unison with Mitya.

As they peeled off in their separate directions, Bonhert called after Mitya, "Walk with me, lad." Mitya could only comply as Bonhert strolled over to the ore casks, running his hand along the smooth side of one of them in a slow caress. He turned to Mitya, smiling. "Make you nervous?"

"Sir?"

"The radioactivity?"

From the Captain's demeanor, Mitya thought he hadn't heard them grumbling. Bonhert was in an affable mood, and Mitya strove to cover his own feelings. "Yes, sir, a little." In truth, Mitya hadn't given the ore a second thought, thinking Bonhert more dangerous than the canisters.

"Needn't be, Mitya. The ore is shielded with lead housing. You can get more radiation from a short walk outside."

Watching Bonhert as he talked, Mitya was aware again of what a physically powerful man he was. He had four inches more of height than Mitya and was maybe eighty pounds heavier. His broad chest and chunky upper arms suggested that the man could squeeze someone senseless with a hug.

"We need to look in the right direction when we're watching for threats," Bonhert said.

In the silence, Mitya threw out a *yes, sir*. More silence. Familiar now. This was the Captain's way of prying words out of you. Mitya acted dumb, though he figured he knew what was coming.

"So then, lad, have you anything to report?"

Everybody hates you was what he thought of saying. *I hate you.* But, "No, sir; everyone's behind you, sir," he offered.

The scowl on Bonhert's face told him how far that was going to get him. "Now, son, I'm sure you think that's what I want to hear. But understand this—my best lieutenants are those that are willing to tell me what I *don't* want to hear. You see?"

Mitya nodded. "You don't want yes-men. You want the truth." He hated himself.

Bonhert smiled, shaking his head. "By the Lord, you're no dummy! That's just it, Mitya, I want the truth. Even if it's a hard truth." He nodded his encouragement. "Go ahead then."

The inside of Mitya's mouth was dried glue. He tried to swallow and couldn't.

At his hesitation the smiling face on the larger man transformed first into neutral, and then into annoyance. "Mitya. I know that you hear things. People don't perceive you as . . . fully grown-up. They let their guard down, I'm sure of it."

Mitya touched one of the cylinders. It was covered in condensation, and his finger started a drop of water down the side like the sweat pouring out of his armpits. When the drop hit bottom, Mitya said, "Oran," his voice a hoarse croak.

"Go on."

Mitya cleared his throat. "Oran said you knew the shuttle fuel system needed work." He looked up at Bonhert, who edged slightly closer. Mitya felt pinned between the big man and the cask behind him. Bonhert's eyes demanded more. "He says it's no skin off your nose if people died."

"That's what he says, does he?" The Captain's voice was low and measured.

"Yes."

Bonhert nodded. "And?"

Mitya pleaded for release with his eyes. Bonhert continued to stand in front of him.

"And he says you'll let us pay for your mistakes."

Mitya was so sick of himself that he thought he would lose his breakfast. He was a miserable coward.

After a couple of moments Bonhert's hand was on his shoulder. "I know that was hard for you, Mitya. You did the right thing. The brave thing. Believe me." After a moment's pause, Bonhert clapped him on the shoulder, then left him there, surrounded by the silver tubes that he wished would leak and strike him dead.

No one wanted to sleep near the canisters. Therefore, despite the feverish pace of work on the cannon, crew halted their labors for a rancorous discussion of whether the ore could be safeguarded from the orthong outside the dome. In the end Lieutenant Cody convinced them that the modules needed the highest security, inside. Then the meeting deteriorated into assigning sleeping slots on the floor. To Mitya's dismay, Cody intervened for him, assigning him to sleep near the officers' quarters. Afterward, Cody wouldn't hear of changing the assignment, though the last thing Mitya wanted was special privileges that others would resent. Oran started calling him the "Captain's boy," a term that struck closer to home than Oran could know. Worse, Uncle Stepan started avoiding him, and in their few contacts regarded Mitya with cool detachment.

Every night after the officers retired he would take his pallet and carry it over to the canisters, sleeping there like a mouse on a bed of nails. No one stopped him, but he imagined that he noticed a difference in how the crew treated him. Once, Oran even donned a pair of sun visors, pretending that Mitya hurt his eyes.

That horseplay stopped for good, however, when the Captain assigned Oran to take Mitya's place on kitchen duty.

3

Kalid and Reeve stood before a high wall of fiber-fuse suspended from the dome roof some seventy feet above. As they walked alongside the wall, it puffed out toward them like a great sail filled with wind. In places the material had torn, and through these fluted passages, the breeze piped in a low-throated moan.

"That was the keening I heard at night," Reeve said.

"The wall has a voice," Kalid said. "Some say it's the voice of our fled ancestors, grieving over their lost dome. But it's only the wind whistling through rips in the Red Wall."

"Red Wall?" Reeve looked at the wide expanse of brown fiber-fuse.

"You will see." Kalid ducked through a large rent in the fabric.

They entered a murky cavern, barely illumined from a splotchy section of dome wall. A wisp of sulfur met Reeve, along with a fecund aroma both like and unlike the ponics module of Station.

Here in this section the metal workings were nowhere to be seen, but in front of them was what appeared to be a park bench festooned with cobwebs. As Reeve's eyes adjusted, he saw a circular construct about six feet wide, in the center of which stood statues of Greek goddesses bearing pots that they tilted into a now empty pool.

"This was the fountain of Dome Park. The ancestors came here to relax and watch the maidens poor water."

Rather than water, the pool supported a small ecology of Lithiaform plants, the latest growth an arterial blood red, the bottommost a rust brown.

"So these are the plants of old Lithia," Reeve said, peering at the alien-looking growths.

"Yes," Kalid said. "And these." He gestured back at the wall itself.

The fabric wall rippled. It was covered top to bottom in a red beardlike growth, an embankment of thick crimson polyps, sagging in places from the weight of long clumps.

The effect was like looking up into the frothing underside of a gigantic wave. Reeve stepped back for a better view. "What happened to this place?"

Kalid smiled. "I thought you might know." When Reeve remained silent he continued, "Lithia likes this section of the dome. For whatever reason, these growths don't venture past this point. So my lord had a curtain hung, that we might avoid looking at it."

"Maybe it feeds on some spill here—some waste product."

"Limestone," Kalid said in answer. "They stored powdery kinds of limestone here." He nodded at vats anchoring the far corners of the cavern.

Reeve knew something of the carbon dioxide–trapping processes of the old colony. Apparently the calcium carbonate, with its slow leak of carbon dioxide, attracted the polyps.

Kalid urged him on. "Come." They made their way into the gloom until they stood in a small clearing.

"Here they played an ancient game with fence and rackets." Kalid removed his jacket and cast it over a metal post standing devoid of its net. They faced each other. "So, Spaceman. You want to learn the killing art. Should I fear you then, when you've learned to kill with your bare hands?" His face blended into the permanent shadow of the region around him, darkened by large masses hugging the dome wall, likely more Lithiaform growths.

"You and I are friends, I hope," Reeve said. "You spared my life—and fingers." He grinned.

"Among the jinn, *friend* is not a word we use lightly, Spaceman." Kalid made a beckoning gesture. "Attack me." He seemed very relaxed for a man about to be assaulted, an attitude that needed some adjustment.

Reeve charged, butting Kalid with his head and fists, planning to knock the man to the floor and land on top of him. But a blow to Reeve's exposed neck sent him to his knees. In the next moment, Kalid had him in a neck-lock. As Reeve struggled, he managed to angle his throat into the space next to Kalid's bent elbow, but he was soon snugged close by a locked grip.

"First lesson: Never lead with your head." Kalid tightened the vise.

"Enough," Reeve sputtered.

Kalid released him. "So, that is one way to kill a man. Tighten your grip until he can't breathe." Standing up, Kalid beckoned him with his hands. "Again."

Reeve surged forward to grab Kalid, managing to get a fistful of shirt and receiving a sharp blow to his hands in return. As Reeve stepped back to evade another blow, they circled each other, feinting and jabbing.

"Don't grab in a fight," Kalid said. "If you are close enough to grab, hit instead."

Kalid was too relaxed. The man's cocky attitude might be an advantage, Reeve thought. Seeing an opening on Kalid's left, he moved in with a kick to the groin, which was blocked out of nowhere by Kalid's knee. Kalid was grinning now. As Reeve lunged, Kalid moved in to grab his chin, causing a wrenching twist to his neck that sent Reeve staggering.

"That is the second way to kill a man." He beckoned Reeve forward, demonstrating. "Push the chin one way with your hand, grab the hair and yank in the opposite direction." He snapped his fingers. "Dead."

Reeve nodded, filing the move away for future reference. "What else?"

"Size up your opponent before attacking. Begin with small blows to the hands and arms; see what response you draw. The better the fighter, the more cautiously you must fight. Don't give it your all."

"You're saying hold back?"

"Calm your fire. Be dispassionate. And watch for your opening to do real damage."

"Sounds like a slapping contest."

Kalid's mouth crumpled into an ironic smile. "If you can break my hand you can win a fight with me. Likely my hands are the only thing you will get close to."

As Reeve charged, Kalid swung to one side, sweeping Reeve's foot out from under him, sending him once again to the floor.

Reeve felt his head jerk back for a moment, then Kalid sprang off him. "Dead again," he pronounced. Reeve lay staring at Kalid's silver-tipped boots. His face appeared there for a moment, stretched into a rounded mound of pink flesh. Then, pulling himself to his feet, he faced his opponent once more.

After Reeve had taken several more falls, his initial goodwill was wearing thin. Kalid's ready smile needed knocking off. Reeve was never the biggest fighter on Station, but he had a reputation for scrappiness, and no one had ever trounced him quite as thoroughly as this. The idea of winning Kalid over by becoming his humble student was beginning to reveal its shortcomings. Reeve's right cheek was swelling from a particularly harsh blow and his left arm felt like it had been wrenched from its socket.

"Enough for one day, perhaps?" Kalid asked.

"Yeah." Reeve turned to go. "Enough." Then he spun on his heel and aimed a solid kick at Kalid's groin, connecting. Kalid stumbled and fell into a roll, moving back onto his feet and crouching in a fighting stance.

"Better, Spaceman."

They circled each other, with Kalid deflecting some of Reeve's blows, but not all. Still, the man was hardly panting with exertion—unlike Reeve, who was quickly tiring. Kalid moved in, pummeling him, using what seemed like every part of his body as a weapon: elbows, knees, fists, in quick succession. As they closed, Kalid spoke through gritted teeth. "Who is your enemy, if not me?" He broke away and lunged in again to yank at Reeve's ear. "If it is my Lord Dante, then it is me, truly."

"I am Lord Dante's guest, not his enemy," Reeve said. He managed to say this while looking into Kalid's eyes, though he would rather not have lied to his face. Reeve resolved to bring Kalid down at least once, and hurled himself against the man so hard he thought they would both crash to the floor. Instead he found himself sprawled alone on the hard court surface.

Kalid stood above him. "What is in your heart when you fight? Fire or ice?" He held out a hand and pulled Reeve to his feet.

Panting, Reeve looked at his adversary. "That's easy. Fire."

Kalid nodded. "That's why you are easy to topple." Kalid feinted toward him. "You show me your next move in your eyes." In a snap kick, Kalid's foot brushed Reeve's chest. "You must be cold. Watch your opponent. He'll show you his belly, in time. Then kill him." He tipped Reeve over with a slice of his foot and a tug on his arm. Reeve looked up to find Kalid's boot on his neck. "Dead again." Helping him up to his feet, Kalid said, "Next time we will fight with knives."

They sat for a time drinking from a flask of beer. Reeve's bruised skin was starting to blur into a blessed fog. After a time he said, "His name is Gabriel Bonhert."

"Your enemy." Kalid wiped his face with a kerchief. "The one who put the fire in your belly."

"Fire." He thought of the flowering explosion of Station. "Yes."

As though Kalid saw the same vision, he asked, "He did not die then, with the rest of your clave?"

"No. He didn't die. Yet."

"It's a strong fire, to carry so far." They sat side by side, gazing into the abandoned dome section. Kalid passed the flask of beer to him and Reeve took a long pull.

"Gabriel Bonhert killed Tina Valejo."

Kalid looked at him, cocking his head.

"And then he killed the rest."

"The rest?"

"The rest of my people." Reeve screwed the cap on the flask and set it aside. It was either that or drink to oblivion.

Kalid nodded, slowly. "Where is this man with the name of an angel?"

The question bumped him out of his spiral for a moment. Angel?

There was a sound behind them. They turned to find Loon standing silently, watching them. Today she was dressed in a pale blue jumpsuit that glistened with a pearlescent sheen. Fine red leather boots hugged her feet to her calves. She had combed her hair straight back off her face, highlighting her cheekbones. Her beauty stirred him.

Loon was serious today. She put her hand on Reeve's face, touching his bruises.

"Kalid is teaching me to fight."

Kalid rose to his feet and bowed, saying, "Until next time, Spaceman." His eyes flicked to Loon, and he smiled at them before turning and departing through the rent in the red wall.

Loon put her hand in Reeve's and they strolled together down the metal paths of the dome. Every now and then she would slip into a crawl space, as though she heard or smelled something worth pursuing. He had begun watching Loon with some of Spar's odd deference, half-believing, or half-convincing himself, that Loon followed a trail of meaning invisible to others. *Yonder, by the soil.* It was a trail that she could not or would not describe, but she pursued it with sure-footedness and what looked like simple trust. This gave her a certain inevitability and definition so lacking in himself. Here in this altered world, he had need to construct himself, piece by piece. He wasn't sure what the end product would be.

They emerged into the glaring daylight of the great dock, where Reeve once again felt the loss of comforting walls. Dante's tattoo-headed jinn conducted trade all down the wharf, in a din of haggling, bartering, and outright argument. To Reeve, it seemed that the jinn merely exchanged one pile of junk for another, but they executed their trades with enthusiasm, and their suppliers departed the dock with canoe and barge piled with booty. Here were the remains of civilization relegated to scrap and musty treasure, dug from the rubble of the colonies. It was both pathetic and ingenious, a testimony to the clavers' ability to thrive even on such leavings.

A crisp breeze swept off the Inland Sea. Winter was coming, he remembered, whatever that would mean on this world of weather and storms. He and Loon strolled hand in hand to the very end of the dock, where they stood looking up toward the mouth of the Tallstory. Reeve sat on an antique trunk with Loon crouched beside him. For a while she pointed at objects and things in the landscape, giving Reeve the hand signs for them and correcting his attempts to mimic her. When they tired of sign practice, she spoke: "No family," she said, looking out.

"Who is your family, Loon?"

"Dead," she answered. "Like Reeve's."

He turned away from her, into the breeze.

"You are sad?" she asked, turning to search his face.

"Yes." Reeve put his arm around her shoulder. "But I'm glad I'm here. It's strange to be happy and unhappy at the same time." He hadn't known he was happy until this moment, and he wasn't sure why he was, but his heart seemed to fill with the wind off the water. He was alive; he was here, on Lithia, the place of dreams and tall stories.

She was watching his face intently. Amid the commotion of the dock, they were alone. He drew her face toward him, very slowly, allowing her time to draw away. She didn't. He kissed her lightly, and the taste of her filled him with longing.

He felt a violent jerk at his shoulder. In an instant he was flat on his back on the dock, looking up at Spar.

"Stand up, boyo," Spar growled. He unbuckled his scabbard and waited.

"Come on, Spar. Leave it be." Reeve was in no mood for another fight, one that might be in earnest.

A savage kick in the side was Spar's answer.

Reeve sprang to his feet, anger surging. "Time for you to learn some Station manners, claver." Then, remembering Kalid's lesson, he circled around the older man, feinting a couple times.

"Ain't scared, are ya?" Spar's snaggle-grin was hard. "Or you like those easy pickin's'?" he said, glancing at Loon.

"Do not fight," she said, alarmed.

Spar shook his head. "Got to. Boy's got himself a big dose of bad manners." Spar struck out, missing as Reeve evaded, then staggering as Reeve jabbed at his knee with a kick.

Jinn had started to walk toward the fight, leaving the two combatants a rectangle at the end of the pier. "Quixote!" someone cried.

Spar landed a slap on Reeve's head, reminding Reeve to fend off hands, but Spar jabbed fast, connecting with a flurry of blows. A shout went up as Reeve recovered and circled around Spar once more. As Spar threw a long punch, Reeve intercepted the swing, sweeping it aside and slicing a fist up to Spar's chin, driving it home with a satisfying crunch. As Spar crashed backward, Reeve leapt on him, but not before Spar's feet came up to vault Reeve over him and into the water.

He felt the wind go out of him as he belly-flopped onto the hard blue surface of the sea. When he got his wits he saw a line of jinn roaring with laughter and pointing at him as he flailed. Gulping saltwater, he found himself sinking more the harder he thrashed. Then someone splashed into the water beside him and a jinn was grabbing him under the armpits and dragging him to the dock.

Once pulled, puking and flopping, onto dry land, he struggled for breath, only to find himself slammed down on his back with Spar's knee on his chest.

The old fool grinned, his teeth alternately yellow, brown, and missing. "Stay away from Mam, I say."

Reeve glared up at Spar, wanting to pound him, but helpless under his knee. Coughing and spitting, Reeve said, "Let her choose. Or do you think she's not as smart as you've always said?"

Spar cocked his head to one side, eyeballing him with his left eye, and raised his fist to smack Reeve. But he let his hand fall when Loon came to stand by his side. He didn't give her a chance to speak. With a sneer, he eased off of Reeve and looked from one to the other of them, finally grabbing his sword and scabbard and stalking off.

Now aching in every joint of his body, Reeve watched Spar retreating down the pier. "Talk to him, Loon. Tell him . . . you like me. If you do."

"He protects me," she responded.

"Yes. But is that what you want?"

She didn't answer, but pulled a long coat from a pile on the wharf and draped it around Reeve's shoulders as he shivered in the breeze. The jinn with a proprietary interest in the coat nodded a begrudging permission.

All Reeve wanted now was a warm bath and a moment's peace. But it was not to be. They heard a commotion from inside the dome as they approached the entrance. Distant shouts, and then a bellowing, "Spaceman!" It could be only one man.

Making their way toward the noise, they came upon an assembly of jinn, milling well back from Dante, who stood bellowing like a stuck bull. Isis stood by him calmly, as though she had seen such displays before.

"Only a guilty man flees! Only a coward runs from jinn justice!" Spittle flew from his mouth and his sequined cape billowed out behind him as he paced before his entourage. When he spied the two of them he cried, "So! You still obey a summons from Dante?"

Reeve bowed low. "What would you have, my lord?"

Standing beside Dante, Kalid smirked at this obsequiousness. But when in the dome, one learned to grovel.

"I would have the murderer!" Dante shrieked. "Do you mock me?"

"Who has been murdered?" Reeve asked.

"My guest!" roared Dante.

"Who would dare to harm a guest of Dante?" asked Marie, who stood at Dante's side.

"Who indeed," Dante said, his voice now menacingly soft. "Perhaps one who thinks himself above our rules. Who breaks the rules."

Isis cocked her head in amazement. "Breakth the ruleth?"

"Who is dead?" Reeve asked.

"Pimarinun!" thundered Dante. "Pimarinun is dead!" He swirled and dove into the crowd, grabbing a man by his collar and hauling his face close. "And where were my guards? Asleep? Whoring?"

The man stammered his denial, and Dante thrust him back toward his companions, rushing to another. "You will find the man who did this!" When the jinn stared at him in terror, Dante shrieked, "Find him!" He shoved the jinn savagely backward and swirled to face his attendants. "Find him. All of you!"

At this the group dispersed, jinn on the run in all directions.

Dante turned to Kalid, ignoring Reeve for the moment. "He was killed by a blow to the head, Kalid. Who would have thought the monster could be killed in such a way?" Dante touched the back of his head near the base of his skull. "Right here. The murderer struck him right here." He looked at Kalid, his face collapsing into dismay. "My thong is dead, Kalid."

"Then we shall catch you another monster," Kalid replied.

Dante brightened. "We shall?"

"Yes, my lord." He bowed.

"Well then," Dante sniffed. He frowned at Reeve. "But the murderer does not go free."

"No, my lord."

Still in a pout, Dante repeated, "Murderers do not go free."

Unless their name is Dante, Reeve thought.

The rant having left him, and devoid now of his large audience, Dante turned mild. "The Spaceman is too weak to kill an orthong," he muttered. "The blow was struck hard." He looked back at Reeve suspiciously. "I hope he is up to our journey."

"Journey?" Kalid asked with no small surprise.

Marie caught Reeve's eye and smiled a quick, knowing smile.

"Yes, my captain of ships." He threw his arms wide, and his voice became triumphant. "A great journey. To trade for the science of the dome."

"And where is such science, my lord?"

Dante turned a stunning smile on Marie. "The Rift, Kalid. The Rift!" He clapped the astonished man on the shoulder. "Medea has revealed how we may find readers aplenty."

Reeve turned to look at Marie in confusion, and she made her way toward him, saying, "I told Lord Dante

that you and I had our limits, but that Captain
Bonhert could fix the dome home."

Dante nodded at this summation, then turned to
Kalid. "Come, we have preparations to make!" He
linked arms with Isis and set off toward his apartments. Kalid followed.

Reeve looked at Marie, stupefied.

"We'll use one of Dante's big ships, Reeve," she
said; then, pausing for effect: "We'll all travel to the
Rift. Together."

It took him a moment to process what Marie by
ingenuity and bravado had accomplished: the reversal
of their fortunes. A ship would take them to the Rift,
in the company of armed men. To the Rift. He looked
at Marie with undisguised awe.

She smiled in a self-deprecating manner, saying,
"It'll be a great improvement on the raft, don't you
think?"

<hr />

4

They had been traveling north for a week, finally leaving behind the high desert and entering a land of dying
trees. At first stunted and sparse, the remains of the
great northern forest soon compacted into a true bone-
yard of conifers.

As Nerys stepped onto a fallen trunk, her foot collapsed into the interior of the tree, releasing a small
cloud of dust. Their orthong guide easily strode over
the downed tree trunks but moved slowly, allowing the
women to keep up without too much strain. Galen,
weakened by indigo and incessant coughing, was no
match for Nerys' robust build and health. The two
women remained cool to one another, despite Galen's
attempts to pry into Nerys' past. When it came out
that Nerys had lost her daughter, Galen remarked bitterly that they had all lost loved ones, which Nerys let
pass, thinking, *But not in the way I lost my Anar. Not*

that way. The thought was never far from her as she rolled it round and round to make up a skein of hate reserved for the Stationer whose choice had poisoned her heart.

Galen had been acquired by Bitamalar just two weeks prior to Nerys, and attempted to lord it over the newcomer, parceling out tidbits of information about the orthong when it suited her, though Nerys doubted Bitamalar revealed much to Galen. Nerys learned that the creature was male, as were most wandering orthong, and that his purpose had been to scout for women like themselves as well as precious rocks and stones. Indeed he did carry a sack of rocks, bearing it with apparent ease. Galen carried her own backpack, filled with the needs of her journey, which included many warm clothes that Bitamalar ordered her to share with Nerys. Frost had covered the ground the last two mornings.

Galen claimed that the sudden cold was the wind off the high glacier not too far north, and Nerys thought it might be so, from what geography she knew.

Perhaps it was the same glacial winds, Nerys reflected, that allowed the dead and dying trees here to resist rotting, though they seemed to have succumbed to drought, so brittle were their needles, twigs, and bark. Nerys hadn't known that such a place existed, this vast wasteland of toppled trees. Perhaps a volcanic eruption had blasted the trees flat; yet no ash lay on the ground, nor any sign of fire. Even so, the undulating valleys bore a gray shroud pierced by the bones of an occasional upright tree. Without Bitamalar's handouts, this land would have meant sure starvation, devoid as it was of animals and even bugs. It was just as well. The desolation reflected Nerys' grief in a way she found oddly satisfying. She stepped over the corpses of the forest with a peace she could not have felt in a more vibrant world.

Every noon and evening Bitamalar doled out their

meals, retrieving from his sack packets of dried meat and seemingly endless coils of dry, gelatinous rope that tasted of nuts and honey. They sat together in a parody of a family meal and he fed them, a piece at a time, seeming to take pleasure in their feeding, watching them chew and swallow and urging choice morsels on Galen, and sometimes on Nerys if she had been good. But he did not help them in other ways. As the nights grew colder, he watched as they struggled to fashion a lean-to against the wind. And twice he ordered them to dig for water. He never asked Nerys to bring him a drink, a forbearance that surprised her but did little to allay her hunch that he could be vicious should she defy him openly. That he could easily hurt her was obvious from his size, and was vividly demonstrated early in their journey when he spied a white hare, outrunning it and slaughtering it with his hands before bringing it back for the women. At Bitamalar's indulgence, Nerys and Galen had immediately built a fire to cook this rare meal of fresh meat, a kindness which Galen took as having some significance of friendship.

At times during their trek through the broken forest, Nerys considered wandering off and waiting to die in the lee of some great, warm stump. It would free her of the annoying Galen, and the certain slavery still to come. Then she could truly mourn for Anar, abandoning herself to the tears that lay buried inside her body, and which, once tapped, would carry her away. Her thoughts of her daughter were carried in a separate place, like a sled tethered on a rope and pulled behind her; in this way she kept her daughter, but not too close, allowing her to tolerate each new day. It was easier to conjure Reeve Calder's face, allowing anger to fuel her limbs.

So, in this state of suspended life, she allowed herself to be led by Bitamalar. Once, as they topped the rise of a hill, they found that they could see the Stoneroot Mountains far in the distance to the east. The mountains were so tall, it was said, that even in summer they had snow on them. This was a wonder Nerys would have liked to see, but their journey was northwest into orthong country.

To pass the time, Nerys practiced orthong sign with Galen. Nerys considered their orthong guide to be little more than a dumb beast. He was no more sentient than a bear or a dog, a judgment that suited her dark mood. But soon they would be among many orthong, beings who Nerys realized were likely to be far more civilized than her own people. They had come from the stars, it was said. They had weapons such as clavers could never fashion. Once among the orthong, she would have need of sign. What she would do with the orthong language, she wasn't sure, but surely knowing was better than not knowing—a principle that had always seemed obvious to Nerys, if not to her clave. Galen was an inadequate teacher. Her vocabulary consisted of the practical stuff of trade and servitude, such as *How much?* and *How many?* and *What would my lord have?*

Galen's demeanor with Bitamalar was by turns cowed and familiar. She took to hanging around the creature and talking at him, trying to engage him in conversation. But her obsequiousness was never far from the surface. He seldom responded to her, though he seemed to tolerate her overtures. When he grew impatient with Galen's chattiness he made a sign with his two hands shielding his stomach, which Galen interpreted as *Enough talking,* and Nerys as *You make me sick.*

Soon the forest began to fill with slowly drifting particles. The white bits clung to their clothes and clumped in the twiggy upper reaches of the ravaged trees.

In another day or two it became clear what the particles were. The forest was slumping into complete desiccation. The needles of the trees fell at a touch, and even the larger branches sloughed away in crumbling husks. Nerys and Galen wrapped scarves around their lower faces to keep from breathing the laden air. As they walked, they crunched tree shells and grass remnants under their feet, and the ruined plants gave way before their boots. The cremated particles coalesced into dust balls, which streamed through the landscape, collecting in drifts against tree stumps. To Nerys it looked as though the world were drying up and blowing away. As a new course of coughing and hacking overtook Galen, Nerys wondered if this desolation was the fate of the entire northern forest. This was the first colonial forestation project, and its domination of the northern Galilean continent was among the great successes of terraforming, soon pumping oxygen into the atmosphere in far greater amounts than the giant domes. Now, this powdered land made Nerys fear for what Lithia had become.

As they continued northward, the drifts grew in height, and at times they found themselves wading through a puffy gray froth. Once, when Nerys stepped into a drift, her boot tore away the upper layer, revealing a startling gash of red beneath. Peering into the tear, she saw dried bubbles of Lithiaform crimson, already starting to reclaim what the conifers had so recently lost.

One morning when they awoke, a stiff breeze had cleared the air of its haze. Nerys and Galen found they could breathe freely for the first time in days. A short march from camp revealed a wide valley extending to distant hills. Filling the center of this valley was an enormous mass that Nerys would have called a forest, except that its shapes and colors were both repetitious and bizarre. A lavender outer perimeter looked to be plated, while peeking out in seams were extrusions of yellow and orange. From this distance she could make no sense of it, could not determine whether it had been constructed or was growing naturally.

Bitamalar turned to the women and stood silently gazing at them.

"What now?" Galen asked Nerys.

But it was all too clear to Nerys what this pause in their journey meant.

"If you want to leave," Nerys told her, "now's the time."

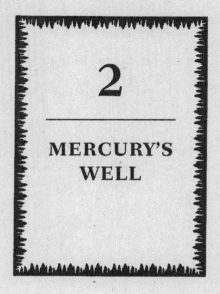

2

MERCURY'S WELL

9

1

Day twenty-two. As they set out from the Jupiter Dome, Dante was in high spirits, strutting the deck in full regalia with Isis on his arm. He had the good sense to let Kalid direct the crew as they clambered aloft, adjusting the sails on the two looming masts. The *Cleopatra* was the best in Kalid's fleet, a sleek ship that tacked up the Tallstory River, moving against the current with patient ease. Whatever else the jinn lacked in knowledge, their seamanship was deft, and their shipbuilding bestowed a spartan beauty on the vessel.

In a small pavilion set up by the foremast, Dante's entourage gathered to carry on their usual gaming and feasting. Reeve and his companions were expected to attend him, which they managed with good grace. Except Spar, who disdained to mix with the "rats." He sat on a chest at the edge of the tent, often leaning on his sword hilt, staring out at the shore.

Marie, a great favorite of both the queen and Dante, was at Isis' side, delighting the younger woman with stories of Station life, bringing a flush of pleasure to her face, which Dante loved to see. Still, her cough was terrible, and in full daylight Reeve could clearly see the "touch of indigo" that marred her complexion. But despite her state of health, the queen was tranquil—or, more likely, simply exhausted. Certainly, she showed little interest in her husband's schemes, perhaps having grown weary of them long ago, even as Dante brayed about how "King Gabriel" would fix the dome home and seal it forever against the harsh breath of Lithia. To this end, the holds were bursting with trade goods, items that Marie and Reeve had personally selected as having value to the sky clave leader. In reality, the cargo was ludicrous: lengths of rusted pipe and sheets of aluminum, hopelessly antique pieces of machinery, and costumes such as Dante and Isis wore, including some precious gems and finely wrought jewelry. Nothing less germane to Bonhert's true purposes could have been imagined, but it all fed Dante's delusions of his status as a ruler equal to the sky clave king. From Marie, Dante learned many personal details of Captain Bonhert, the better to conduct the trading when the time arrived. This line of conversation always set Reeve to wondering how they would manage to divest themselves of the jinn, but that problem was still many miles away.

Once past the mouth of the Tallstory, with its barrier of chaotic currents, Kalid joined Reeve at the rail to gaze out at the high desert vista in the distance.

"I hope we can continue our lessons, if your ship duties don't prevent us," Reeve said. His forearms still smarted from the sharp wooden practice knives of his second lesson, but he knew he must press on.

Kalid's eyebrow arced. "You would take your falls in front of Dante's court?"

In truth, he didn't relish the idea, but he nodded. Out of the corner of his eye, he noted that Loon was climbing the aft mast, and that the crew was indulging her. She was dressed once more in her claver trousers and shirt and her claver fur boots, but looking better, somehow, in leather and fur.

Kalid, still gazing outward, said: "Perhaps we can trade lessons."

"Lessons in what?"

"Science."

"That could be a lot of lessons."

"The same could be said for your fighting skills."

It stung, but Reeve had to smile, knowing it for the truth.

"I know a little of science," Kalid said. "I have read. But I would know more."

"Well, I am the least of Station scientists."

"That may be. But we start with smaller goals." Reeve nodded, and Kalid went on: "If we had not been in such a hurry to leave, I would have opened the body of the orthong to learn of its organs."

"My people know nothing of the orthong," Reeve said. He checked on Loon again, finding her in the crow's nest next to a jinn twice her size. She waved at Reeve, and he returned the gesture, conscious of Spar's disapproving stare.

"I would also have learned to operate the transmitter better," Kalid was saying.

"Transmitter?"

"Radio transmitter. It is hard to hear, sometimes. It needed repairs beyond what we could do. But it was possible to reach other claves, and learn of their doings. I talked with our close trading claves, especially, but I was more interested in those far beyond. Their customs and their affairs."

A radio transmitter. He'd never thought of it. Reeve wondered what else the dome contained that he might have used. But even if he'd been able to contact his fellow Stationers, what was the point when they were likely all accomplices? Yet Bonhert always had enemies. And though he would not have knowingly given them a place on his shuttle, sometimes a man doesn't know his enemy. It was this thought that Reeve clung to, hoping to find allies at the Rift.

"What I know, I will be glad to share," Reeve said. "Tonight we can start with chemistry."

Kalid beamed. "Chemistry, yes. I would learn of com-pounds and mol-e-cules." He slapped the rail with his hand. "Mol-e-cules and more!"

"Yes. Molecules and more." The darker thoughts of Bonhert gave way to the great adventure before them, the sunny salt spray, and the pleasure of a moment of friendship.

The next day, a squall drove Dante's retinue below-decks, where crowding and boredom led Dante to order the wine casks tapped, which soon led to brawling and then stupor. Isis pouted when the churning of the ship sent Marie to her bed. Then several of Dante's concubines, each a drop-dead beauty, displayed their dancing talents to a retinue too drunk to notice. Dante urged Reeve to take one of his women to bed, an offer that stunned the jinn. Their surprise deepened when Reeve refused, tempted but thinking he'd not yet fallen to that level. So as not to offend, he pleaded a queasy stomach from the pitching of the ship—not far from the truth. Dante concluded that the Spaceman needed a physician, and brought forward a filthy jinn doctor. Opening an ancient black suitcase, Dante's medic produced various vials of congealed pills, laying them on parts of Reeve's body in a solemn rite of healing. When at last the fellow left, Reeve fell into a nauseous sleep.

Once during the night he thought he saw Dante hovering over him, peering closely.

"Did Quixote kill my orthong? Tell the truth, Spaceman!" he whispered. "For the insult to Princess Loon?"

Reeve, muzzy-headed from sleep, could only say, "He did not. I swear it."

"Someone must pay, though," he heard Dante say.

He thought he heard his door close, and Reeve slept again. By morning, bright autumn blue reclaimed the skies, with Dante holding forth under his pavilion once more, and Marie attending despite the yellow cast to her skin.

The canyon country had now become a high and rocky passage through which the Tallstory flowed swiftly, forcing them to break out the oars at times to make any progress. With their vision cut off from any wider prospects, it seemed their craft was aimed into the heart of the rocky planet, where the cliffs towered ever higher. Once, a great cave appeared halfway up the starboard canyon wall, drawing every eye to its gaping orifice, as though Lithia's trolls might be seen within, forbidding or blessing their passage. Spar nodded at the cave as if it were the eye of the Lady herself, and whether she condemned or approved them Reeve was not about to ask. Spar dipped his head at Reeve, one of the few exchanges they'd had since their fight. Reeve smiled in return, not hoping for a Spar smile, and not getting one.

As the days passed in this stone tunnel, Reeve joined Kalid in his cabin for tentative science lessons, aware that he must teach cautiously, allowing Kalid to set the pace and not fan their rivalry. Kalid was an apt learner, his memory suited to the regularity and logic of physics and chemistry; but he had only rudimentary math, and Reeve scrambled in his role as teacher. Still, Kalid took great pleasure in learning, often keeping Reeve up late into the night.

His fighting lessons, however, showed no reciprocal restraint, and Kalid gave Reeve sound thrashings, to the delight of the crew and courtier alike. But Reeve learned to kill a man with his bare hands, with a stick, and with a knife.

Meanwhile, Loon quickly assumed complete freedom of the ship, including climbing the masts and into the rigging, drawing deference from the jinn, who took great stock in her open eating of soil. They could observe this when, the ship at anchor, she swam to shore. Reeve noticed that small offerings of food and trinkets appeared regularly outside her cabin door, and just as regularly disappeared. Perhaps Loon took such offerings as her due, or perhaps she just disliked the mess outside her door. Whether owing to Spar or a spontaneous assumption, the crew began to refer to Loon as "daughter of Lithia," and the notion seemed to give them the same comfort it afforded Spar—that Lithia's malice was tempered with a slim but redeeming streak of mercy.

The only one who remained aloof from Loon's spell was Marie, ever antagonistic to glosses of science and superstitious spins on reality. "Lithia's daughter!" she groused one day. Turning to Isis, but speaking for the benefit of Reeve and Spar, she said, "How many *daughters* have you seen, or *sons*? If she's the first, it would take hundreds of thousands of years for her progeny to establish themselves. Humans will be long gone before that, I assure you."

"You got a harsh view of evo-lution," Spar mumbled from the sidelines.

"Evolution plays no favorites, Mr. Spar. Not even for humans."

"Playth no favorith," Isis repeated, coughing up a small clot of mucus.

That night, a brisk wind sent Dante and crew belowdecks for warmth. Reeve remained on deck, pretending to scan the canyon walls but hoping for a chance to talk to Loon. This time of evening was her time to swim, and she was soon over the side, dressed only in her shirt. When she finally returned, she seemed oblivious to Reeve's watching her, but sucked on her fingers—a gesture that Reeve tried to see as dirt-tasting, but which had become intensely erotic. The shirt hugged her as the moonlight sculpted her body in silver highlights. Meanwhile, lounging against the opposite rail, Spar pretended to watch the water.

Reeve finally turned away and descended into the hold, where, without words, he took Dante's smallest concubine, Joti, by the hand and led her to his cabin. He closed the door behind her. Her hair was drawn back into a golden braid, which he unfastened, releasing it around her shoulders. Her face betrayed no distaste, but to salve his conscience, he asked her if she would share his bed. In answer, she removed her clothes; as Dante's slave, she could have given no other answer. Partly in shame, partly in relief, he led Joti to the bed and bent over her hungrily. By the light of a small candle he saw her body in flickers, and it became Loon's, and he became part of her, again and again.

As they lay side by side, Reeve held her and savored the lift and roll of the ship and the peacefulness of this trough of his passion. Then he heard a click. His door had become unlatched. It might have been the rocking of the ship, but then he saw that a hand held it open a few inches. It stayed thus for a long time, as Reeve stared at this intrusion. For a moment he caught a glimpse of a yellow nimbus of hair around the watcher's face. With a shock, he realized it was Loon, and his desire peaked again. He ran his hand down Joti's body, pinching her gently and signaling her for her attentions. He rose to meet her mouth and abandoned himself to her ministrations, lost in a haze of desire that for a while swept aside his confusion about Loon and why she watched, and why he couldn't have her and why it mattered.

A long while later the door gently closed and Reeve, spent and depressed, sent Joti away. Pulling on his clothes, he went to the door and peered into the narrow passageway. It was deserted. But there on the threshold was a small pile of stones, still gleaming wet from the river.

·   ·   ·

A raging sunset ended their seventh day on the Tall-story River. The startling intensity of the display brought every jinn to a standstill, gaping, their faces tinged in crimson. Striping the fiery swath, a few cirrus clouds glimmered gold, then cooled to orange as the sun fell away.

By the next morning it was clear that the reason for the glorious sunset was a major volcanic eruption. Already, a curtain of ash covered half the sky and winds were fast spreading this veil to the horizon. The jinn assumed it was volcanic, and there was little reason to doubt them. They had seen skies like these before, and had suffered weeks of dark and cold from the worst of them.

By mid-morning, the ash cloud eclipsed the sun and everyone's spirits. Dante ordered pipes and dancing, but few jinn gathered to watch and the effort at merriment dwindled. In the afternoon, flakes of ash began to descend. Isis, despite her breather, began coughing so hard that Dante ordered the entire entourage belowdecks to attend her. Kalid was tasked with making all possible haste to the confluence of the Gandhi River, where a northward course would take them, Marie assured him, to King Gabriel's camp.

Actually finding the camp was a problem that she and Reeve discussed often. Poring over Kalid's maps, they thought they could pinpoint the site of the proposed geo nanotech project, but whether or not Bonhert would use that location for his altered plans they couldn't know. In the end, Marie and Reeve were prepared to escape Dante and conduct their own search for Bonhert's group. However, the matter of Spar and Loon was a point of contention between them. Marie argued for leaving them behind, while Reeve solidly refused. But as the day turned black as dusk, more pressing questions plagued them, such as whether their breathers would withstand this new on-slaught, and how long their supply of them would last.

Despite the ominous skies, Reeve felt a grim confidence about his mission. They had finally begun to make good time on their journey, traveling under the best security they could hope for. To be in the midst of such an adventure on the planet itself, with their fortunes as Dante's prisoners so recently reversed, filled him with a strange joy.

By sunset, with another neon show in the west, Kalid and Reeve leaned against the ship rail once again, joined this time by Spar. The ship swayed at anchor; Loon swam off the port side; from below, Isis could be heard barking like a walrus.

"I have seen the like before," Kalid said. "It will pass, like the others."

There hadn't been a question in Reeve's mind that it might not pass, but now the thought stopped him. "Does this look different from the others?" Several times Reeve had seen planet-enveloping ash clouds from Station, but he had no way to compare the two perspectives.

Kalid pursed his lips. "It is vast, this time."

Spar nodded. "This is what Lithia looks like, when she coughs." He seemed to take somewhat less delight in Lithia's revenge than usual.

"In the Dark Days," Kalid began, "when Mount Woden blew, the skies went black for a year, or so they say."

"Yeah, crops went down, all at once," Spar said. "Then your granddaddies, Reeve, they got so scared they wet their pants."

"*Your* ancestors too, Spar!"

Spar shot a wad of spit off the ship's side. "Zerters were no kin of mine."

"Nor mine," Kalid said, firmly establishing Reeve's sole claim to zerter lineage.

"That was a long time ago. When do we forget the sins of our fathers?"

Kalid smiled, an unpleasant grin. "I'll tell you a story, Spaceman."

On the shore, Loon had crouched to pick something up. Into her mouth it went, as though she were a toddler. Reeve watched her, and Spar seemed to stand guard over his watching.

"There lived once," Kalid said, "a woman named Willa Achebe. This was in the Dark Days, at the beginning. She had one child, and like women do with one babe, she put all her hopes on this child. She was the wife of an important man, and when night came to stay for a year, they had plenty of food. Her son was eight years old. Her husband was unfaithful."

As they watched the sunset burn itself out, Kalid continued: "The husband was a scientist at the great lab-oratories, where his lover also worked, and all the conspirators who planned to steal the Station. On the day of the taking of Station, he sent Willa on an errand. When she returned, he had taken the child. She rushed to where the rockets took flight, along with everyone else who knew by then what the scientists had done. But when she got to the place, it was too late. She cried at the skies to bring the ships back. Then she found one of her child's toys, a music box. Inside, the child had cut off a lock of his hair, the only part of himself he had known how to give her.

"Willa never spoke again, but let the music box speak for her, opening it when the need came to speak. And in time, it is said, the music box began singing, and became her voice, saying whatever was needful. Since then, the box has been handed down from mother to son as a sign of devotion. And a warning against betrayal."

"Now that is a hard tale," Spar said.

They all watched Loon as she dove into the water for her return swim.

A long silence ensued. Reeve wasn't sure why Kalid had told him the story, but it didn't seem prudent to pursue the topic. Reeve was descended from zerters, Kalid from those they had wronged. He could not much blame Kalid for wishing to remember the very thing that Reeve wished to forget, but it was a strange irony that the zerter had fixed the music box that sang out against him.

As Kalid took his leave of them to pay his respects to Isis, Loon clambered up the anchor rope, scrambling back onto the deck.

Reeve spoke softly for Spar's ears only. "Why do you come between Loon and me, Spar? Because I'm a zerter? That old hate?" Spar picked at his teeth, not answering. "Or because she's some kind of goddess in your way of thinking, and no man's good enough for her?"

"You think too much." Spar turned back to watch the waves chop up against the ship's hull.

Reeve could hear another lecture coming. Whatever he was, he was wrong, from Spar's point of view. Wrong clave, wrong culture, wrong skills, wrong philosophy. Now he would learn what else was wrong with him.

And sure enough: "You don't need to get all bolloxed up, Reeve-boy. That Station Clave, they got funny ideas about edu-cation. Teach you to count the stars and eat from tubes, and don't teach you 'bout people."

Now that was unfair. Psychology and sociology were things he'd studied, yet here was a claver who could hardly read telling him he didn't know anything about people. Reeve took a calming breath, determined to avoid reacting to whatever Spar might say.

The older man went on: "Mam's special. She ain't your jinn sex slave."

This outrageous remark deserved a response, and he spat out: "That what you think I want her for, just sex?"

Spar turned toward him enough to fix him with one hawk eye before turning back to his river watch.

Reeve struggled for the right words, struggled to control his outrage.

In this silence came Spar's words, softer now. "I swore to protect her, and on my sword, see? That means, from Tallgrass clavers, from jinn, and from you, if you mean to have her body and not love what she is."

"And what is she, then?"

Spar nodded to himself. "She's a miracle. Now maybe we're all miracles. Could be it's a miracle any of us got lives left at all. But to me, she's a daughter. That's who she is."

Reeve's anger fled, a fire collapsing. It was as simple as that, then, a question of whether Reeve loved Loon. . . . And *did* he? In truth, he didn't know. To his shame, he hadn't asked himself, hoping for simple sex and thinking that liking Loon was good enough. But he could see Spar's point: Here, on this world, with this young woman, it wasn't enough, not by a long shot. He wasn't sure why, but Spar was right. Even if Loon wanted him, it wasn't right to take her casually. Damn his luck.

"So it's not because I'm a zerter." He had to respond somehow, and for now this was all he could think of to say.

Spar grinned his gap-toothed smile. "That's bad, all right. Zerter's real bad. But not much you can do 'bout that, I figure."

Then a thought occurred to Reeve, and he blurted it out. "Well, I don't have a clave anymore, Spar. Technically, I can't be from a clave that doesn't exist, can I?"

Spar turned to face him, scowling in concentration. "Sometimes I got to admit your head's not *all* stuffed with hay." They shared the moment's revelation. "You thinkin' you need a new clave, then?"

"Maybe I do."

Spar glanced away, screwing his lips into thinking mode. "Well, we got to take this under ad-visement." He leaned against the rail once more, mumbling, "Man's got to have a clave."

2

As the jinn ferried everyone to the burial site, Loon gave up her position in the boat in favor of swimming to the shore. She spent every possible moment in the water, diving for the rich brown sediments at the bottom, the strong, intoxicating taste that spiked the blue soup of the Tallstory. Gone were the shouting salt flavors that masked her nourishment. Pull away the salt, and the good soil was here, in little swirls and pockets. They were headed in the right direction, ah yes! Up the Tallstory, somewhere up the Tallstory—that was where she could eat at last.

She could hardly feed enough. At first, gulping down fistfuls of sand, she made herself sick. Now, more cautious, she snacked, pacing herself. She took one last pinch of soil and swam to shore, hurrying down the beach to join the funeral procession.

The jinn looked at Loon from the corners of their eyes as she joined the group. These jinn put gifts in front of her door, but why? They feared to touch her, or to look her in the eyes, and yet brought gifts. Spar said they were paying respects. But it was another wall around her. Always, people put her on the other side of a wall, whether with jeers or respect. Everyone except Reeve of the Sky Clave.

Isis was dead. The sad queen had choked during the night, after a coughing fit that no one could fix. The ship had rung with Dante's bellows as he raged against the doctor and the queen's attendants for failing to cure her. His screams were terrible. Finally the ship had grown quiet, and no one dared to stir. Perhaps the breather had killed her. Loon had watched how Isis gagged to swallow it, how she feared it each time she had to change to a new one. But Dante made her do it, because he loved her so much, and thought it would save her. So it is sometimes that love will kill you, Loon thought, if by love is meant that someone thinks he knows what is good for you.

Ash snowed down from a dark sky, covering their heads and shoulders with gray dust. Through this warm snow they carried Isis on a bier long enough to lay her out in her accustomed headdress. Along the shore they walked, four jinn on a side, making their way toward the side canyon, where a path led up to the burial site. Dante walked in front, leading the way, stripped to the waist—leaving behind his fine clothes, as befitted one who mourned.

Loon stepped in line with Reeve, who draped his jacket over her shoulders. It stirred her to think that its warmth had just come from Reeve's body, that body that demanded so much of his slave lover at night. She had wondered if Sky Clavers bedded each other like ordinary people, and now she knew. She was learning how like—and how unlike—her clavers they were. She stuck out her tongue, wanting to taste a flake of ash, but it was the same as ever, dusty gruel.

The grave was very long. They lowered the queen into the earth, all wrapped in a fine velvet cape. Three brass-trimmed trunks were brought up from the shore. From these chests, the jinn drew forth many fine things, arranging them around the body: a cup studded with jewels, sparkling necklaces, science books, gowns, and a mirror with two sides that made you big or small. Dante himself stepped into her grave to lay two magnificent headdresses at her side, as though she might have them without reaching too far.

Tears streamed down his face. Among the many wonders Loon had seen on her long journey was this man who could fling a child from a great height and yet love a woman and cry at her grave.

Many jinn were also crying, and even the old woman, Marie, dabbed at her eyes with a cloth. Loon thought a funeral was a very fine thing, where people showed how much they loved someone. She would have liked to have seen her father buried, to cry like Dante and not care who saw. She wondered who was crying because they really minded that Isis was dead, and who was crying so that Dante would notice.

Marie approached the grave and, glancing at Lord Dante for permission, knelt to place a breather among Isis' burial gifts. Then they filled in the grave with soil, shoveling the leftover soil into the now empty trunks, which they carried away, lest anyone see there had been digging here. They sprinkled rocks and twigs over the grave, and upon a tiny branch of a willow bough Dante set his largest ring.

On the way back to the ship, in the cold, ash wind, it struck Loon that in just two days the joy had fled from their journey, and now no one would dance on board the ship as the beautiful women had danced. She would have given much to see more dancing. The people of her clave never danced, and Dante's dancers had set her heart racing, even more than the sight of Reeve taking his pleasure with the woman he preferred to herself.

3

Bitamalar walked purposefully into the orthong jungle, without a glance backward. Clearly, Nerys and Galen could follow or not, and for a moment Nerys doubted that she would. Their domain was vast and strange, an assault to the eyes. Once inside, who knew what aspects of her life she could still control? It gave her pause, but at last she hurried after Galen, who was already growing dim on the lavender path.

The outer stockade was many yards thick, composed of rows of what looked like stacked bubbles looming thirty feet or more. As she and Galen passed through this outer region, she saw something stirring within the giant bubbles. Beyond the lavender bubble walls came a hedge of yellow stalks the thickness of her legs, each with a spray of rubbery tendrils forming a topnot. The yellow forms lined the pathway, blocking any view to the side. Yellow gave way to blue forms, and white, establishing a succession of evenly colored patches.

If the orthong thought their forest beautiful, then how they must despise the flora of the outside world, so much more subdued and irregular. But perhaps this region was cultivated to some purpose, and a wild region would be found deeper within.

They emerged into a small clearing where four orthong stood or kneeled among looping coils of dark blue. These forms might be anything: crops or weeds or artwork or unimaginable machinery. Nerys hesitated to touch anything. She would learn these mysteries, in time, she supposed. The orthong turned to watch the procession, their faces betraying nothing she could decipher. One of them curled its hand in a speaking gesture, to which Bitamalar responded with the merest of finger movements.

Bitamalar led them onward through tunnels of vegetative matter. The forms seldom penetrated into neighboring patches, but maintained boundaries of form and color. Nerys stared at the bands and surges of growth until she grew weary of their strangeness. At times the contour of the valley floor took them uphill or down, but most often their path took them around hills. Some of the hills contained bermed dwellings, with transparent walls, permitting a brief view of orthong inside.

When at last they emerged into a great plaza, its openness soothed Nerys' ragged nerves. Beside her, Galen whispered, "Look up, Nerys." The clearing was more open to the sky than the outer settlement, and

Nerys saw that the sky had turned very dark, tinged in red. Never one for portents, Nerys answered, "It's a dust storm likely." But Galen kept looking up, a single line furrowing between her eyes. Within the plaza, many orthong went about their errands or gathered in small groups, some turning to watch the strangers pass. The plaza was framed by low, bermed enclosures, larger than those they'd seen before now. Like the region through which they'd just come, the berms formed blocks of colors, this time in shades of blues and grays.

The cloth of orthong dress had a polished look, like the burnished shell of an insect. Two styles predominated. One was a belted, sleeveless tunic. The hides of some who wore this were silvered in the exposed arms and legs. Others wore a very long, belted coat over a tunic. The long sleeves of the coats bore the ominous cuffs that clavers had come to fear. No orthong wore shoes, and Nerys had seen why. She spied one very small orthong, a juvenile she guessed, holding on to an adult's belt for what might have been reassurance. Several orthong moved together to form a white wall, masking her view of the young one. She didn't know if any of the orthong she saw were female, there being only slight differences so far in their sizes and their clothing. As they left the clearing, Nerys looked back to try to glimpse the juvenile again, but the white wall remained intact. Good enough to bear the pups, are we, but not to look at them? Nerys allowed herself a little sneer, judging that they couldn't be very good at reading human expressions—no more than she could read theirs.

They passed into a side channel, where the habitat forms grew more sparsely and where groups of orthong could be glimpsed, standing quite still or sitting among the outcroppings. They might be resting, arguing, or praying, Nerys thought, not even attempting to guess which was most likely.

Nowhere they had penetrated so far showed any evidence of paving, flooring, or bridging. Everything simply sprang from the ground in outbursts at once impressive and inelegant. If this was their civilization, Nerys thought, the orthong must be awed by the great colonist cities, still magnificent even in ruin. *We were once great,* she mused. *We would have held a place like this in low regard, all piecemeal and garish.* But if the orthong habitat was crude, it still dominated, imposing its will, along with its insistent colors. Amid all of this, who would remember human things?

They continued their walk for a quarter of an hour, until Nerys was startled by a familiar sound penetrating the forest. It grew louder until they entered yet another clearing where, as they paused at its edge, human voices greeted them. Framed by bermed constructs, the center courtyard held perhaps fifty human women. They sat in chairs or recliners, laughing and talking, some weaving or drawing, a few fixing each other's hair, one or two writing in tablets. All of them were pregnant.

All she could see was mound after mound of swollen belly. Soon she would be one of these faceless, ripe females, filled with a wrinkled white pup. Beside her, Galen moaned in dismay.

A woman separated herself from her group of companions and approached them. "I am Haval," she said, smiling but looking them over. Without waiting for their names, she signed to Bitamalar, too quick to follow. Bitamalar said to Galen, <This woman will teach you.> With that, he abruptly left, choosing another path from among several that radiated out from the clearing. Haval, Nerys noted with some relief, had a flat belly. In fact, a few others did as well, upon closer scrutiny of the group.

Haval beckoned them to follow her. If she wasn't going to wait to learn their names, Nerys was not about to offer it for nothing. "I'm hungry," she said instead.

"Well," Haval responded. "You would be."

The women of this human oasis watched Nerys and Galen with frankly appraising stares, some smiling, others merely rude. It was like entering any cohesive group where you are a stranger, Nerys thought, with everyone sizing everyone else up, and wondering what might change for good or ill. In her turn, Nerys assessed those she passed, drawing her own conclusions of who was a player and who sat on the sidelines.

Haval brought them to a shallow run of stairs in front of one of the shelters—if that was what they were. They paused at the bottom, looking out at the courtyard, where the other women soon withdrew their attention from the newcomers and returned to their pursuits.

"I'm sure all this is very strange to you," Haval said. "We all felt that way, when we first got here." She was a large woman, with a big-boned friendly face.

"Actually, how I feel is tired," Nerys said. "And hungry."

Haval turned to Galen, "And you?"

"Do they hurt you?" Galen blurted.

"Do we look hurt?"

"No," Galen said. "But when they . . . if they . . . And bearing, does it hurt?"

"Lots of questions. You'll find that the place will become known to you little by little. There's no point in hearing it all at once. But no, it doesn't hurt." She smiled indulgently at Galen, who looked abashed.

"And the food?" Nerys asked.

Haval turned to face Nerys, and her voice took on an edge. "Food is received from our orthong teachers. I have none. You will be fed."

In the awkward silence that followed, Galen rushed in with: "I'm Galen, and her name is Nerys. We've both lost our children. Nerys is from Whale Clave, and I come from Two Rivers Clave."

"Galen," Nerys interrupted, "You don't speak for me. You don't speak of my daughter. Ever. We traveled together for three weeks. I would gladly have had other company."

"We all have hard tales," Haval said. "Some of us share them, some of us don't. But you *don't* bring divisions among us. We all miss our claves and families, but we try for what happiness we can find." She turned to climb the stairs, saying, "Sometimes it's not much."

"But you can leave, if you want?" Galen asked.

Haval turned back, with a smirk. "Leave now, I suggest, before you get used to the meals."

"What do you eat?" Galen said. "And when?"

"We eat whatever we want," Haval answered. She led the way up the stairs. "Come."

They entered the bermed construct at the head of the stairs. It had no door, but gaped open like a cave, with half of the large room enclosed by the hillside. Farther back, a corridor led within. Light from the opening flooded this outer room, revealing a bench along the perimeter piled with pillows. The latter were stitched with flowers, stars, and patterns of the human world. A large table commanded the center of the room, surrounded by pillows for sitting.

"We gather here, sometimes, to do our work or drink tea," Haval explained. "They let us make tea."

"How generous," Nerys remarked.

Ignoring this, Haval led the way into the hillside. In this underground area, a transparent ceiling admitted a dim light, augmented with lighting sconces that may have used elec-tricity, or other big tech. The corridor changed shape and direction, as though following a river path or seam of dirt. In a wider portion of the corridor they came upon an area with many side rooms.

"You may choose to have your own room," Haval

said, "or share with another. If you have no liking for women partners, you will not be pressured, but you will not criticize. Clear?" Such things were not often tolerated in the claves, but Nerys had heard of women partners, and from the conduct of the claver men, she didn't wonder that some women turned to each other, especially in this alien place.

"I would have my own room," Galen said.

"As you like. Choose an empty one; get some rest. Later, your lords will come for you." She looked with amusement at Galen's expression. "Just to bring you a meal. Don't worry." She turned to go, then turned back. "Also, don't touch an orthong unless asked. Never. They can kill you with one swipe of a hand. They're usually patient, especially with newcomers. But not always."

In the growing dusk Haval led Nerys down a path from the women's compound. Edging the path were luminous, coiled ropes, lighting their way through what Haval called the outfold. It was full dark by the time they got to their destination, the dwelling of the "lord" to whom Nerys was assigned. It was grander than the women's berm, its front face looming high into the outfold around it.

"Lord Salidifor is important," Haval said. "You're lucky."

"Why?" Nerys asked.

"None of us can figure it out. You're the newest, but the orthong do as they will."

"No, I mean why is it lucky?"

Haval turned a wry smile on Nerys. "You'll soon lose that attitude, my friend. Use it on me if you think you can get by with it. Use it with an orthong, and you'll quickly learn to curb your tongue. You can tell if they're unhappy because the claws come out. Most freewomen don't need to be told to have some respect—but in your case I guess we start with the basics."

Nerys raised her eyebrow. "You call yourself *free-women*?"

Haval laughed, shaking her head. "Good luck, Nerys of Whale Clave. You're going to need it." With that, she headed back into the maze.

The courtyard was deserted. Nerys walked up the broad stairs leading to the lord's dwelling and entered as she had been told to. The whole front wall of the place was open. As in the women's quarters, the entry room was partially surrounded by a seating bench, but here the center of the room was empty. She stood upon a white floor with dark lines tracing hexagons. From the inner rooms, brighter light beckoned her forward. Lord Salidifor would feed her, Haval said. She hoped it would be a decent meal, or at least that there would be plenty of it.

Here again were the irregular rooms and corridors with undulating walls, pushed out into rocklike extrusions or sunk into hollows in an apparently random fashion. The walls were covered with soft textures of what might have been cloth or even moss, while a narrow strip of clear ceiling still glowed dully from what remained of the daylight. Several orthong busied themselves inside the dwelling, cleaning and straightening, perhaps. They took little notice of Nerys as she proceeded farther into the dwelling, as Haval had instructed. She came to a great room with a domed, translucent ceiling where she found an orthong waiting for her in a hooded chair. He gestured her to a matching chair opposite him, across a small table.

As she sat, the back of her chair rose and bent slightly over her, mirroring the other chair.

With a shiver of revulsion, she looked at the creature's face, what there was of it. Her days with Bitamalar helped her to adjust to the sight. A streak of silver on his large hands disappeared up the sleeves of his coat—devoid of its armed cuffs, she noted. The white hide with its gnarled ridges made him look as though he were carved from alabaster stone. Badly. On the table was a large rock, olive in color, and glistening as though rubbed in oil.

He gestured to her, and it took her twice to read it. <You are Nerys.> She had never seen her name done in sign. It was two downward slashes punctuated by an end finger—they did not look like proper thumbs—stretching out. She was pleased with the gesture, which seemed to say, *Push down so hard, and no further.*

She copied it. <Nerys>

Then he offered his name. <Salidifor,> he signed, a word she only recognized because Haval had prepared her. Then, slowly, the creature signed, <Are you content with your dwelling?>

<I don't know. I slept there a while.> They were alone in the room. Stupidly—Nerys felt it was foolish—she looked for a bed. The idea of sex with this creature was alarming. But so far the only furniture she had discerned in the dim room were the wall benches and these two chairs with the table.

<What would you like for your dwelling to be content?>

I will never be content. Never again. <Nothing. Thank you.>

Salidifor looked up to watch another orthong enter the room carrying a tray. There could be no doubt what that tray bore. As the server placed it in front of Nerys, a tantalizing aroma met her nostrils. In an ample bowl, bits of meat floated in a gravy with vegetables. No watery stew, this. Sometimes in lean weeks, Nerys had stretched a soup out for days, until, at the last, only a cloudy liquid remained, or as the claves said, "water that couldn't remember a potato." This bowl would have fed her whole family twice.

As the server left, Salidifor said, <You may take this.>

Nerys wondered if he meant she could take the tray and leave. But Haval had said they would "share a meal," so Nerys picked up a spoon, hard as bone, and sipped at the broth. It was so delicious her mouth hurt. There were very complex spices, some familiar. The meat was venison. Its only flaw was that it was not piping hot, but rather barely warm. She chewed a morsel, and then, following her resolve, she did a very hard thing: She placed the spoon down again.

<I seek instruction,> she said, glancing at his face and then away, careful not to be too forward.

The orthong looked at her spoon, lying there. Then at her. <What is lacking?>

<I speak poorly.>

<The breeders will teach you.>

She looked down at her soup, hoping it was a gesture of deferral. <The humans speak poorly.> Damn if she would use a term like *breeders*.

The orthong became very still, watching her from glacial eyes.

Her fingers itched to pick up the spoon, but she forced herself to wait.

Finally Salidifor said, <Enough talking. You may eat.>

Judging it best to defer somewhat, she took another spoonful of the stew, chewing it a long while to get the most out of it. The orthong cooks were remarkable—especially for beings who couldn't sip from their own cooking pots. She put the spoon down again. <Why do the rooms have no flat walls?>

He looked at the undulating walls around them as though seeing them afresh. Finally he said, <The . . .>—here he used a word she didn't know—<followed the rocks of the deep soil.>

So the white chief *would* answer questions. Good. Not that he gave up much information. To reward him, she ate half the remaining stew. Then she asked, <Why?> She placed the spoon again on the tray, looking at him pointedly.

<It pleases us. It is . . .> Again, an unknown word. She attempted to copy that word.

After a pause, he repeated it. To Nerys' dismay, a glitter in his hand revealed a quarter inch of claw on several fingers.

She bent over her stew and devoured the rest of it.

When the servant had cleared her place and departed, Salidifor stood.

He must have stood over seven feet tall. In one step he was behind her chair. The hood retracted, leaving a chill on her back. Salidifor grabbed a hank of her hair, which fell off from a quick slice of his claws. Meeting his eyes, Nerys trembled as she suppressed an angry retort. She sat rigidly until, gripping the swath of hair, he signed: <Good night, Nerys.>

She rose as slowly as her dignity could muster. <Good night, Salidifor,> she signed. <The food was very nice, but a little cold.>

Then, she turned and left.

4

It seemed to Mitya that his position had considerably worsened since the first days in the dome. Then, people had disliked him for a stowaway. Now they suspected he was a traitor. Crew avoided him, figuring his new status with the Captain had somehow come at Oran's expense. With no real work to do, Mitya felt the snubbing all the more, and found to his surprise that he missed the galley, and even Koichi's gruff discipline.

Instead of working, he slept. If he didn't sleep well at night—and he seldom did—he napped during the day, seeking out a hidden spot behind the water tank, where the cool darkness left him in blessed isolation.

There he would lull himself to sleep thinking of the starship.

Soon they would board the craft in successive cargo hauls, taking a few people and a few canisters up to the ship at a time, to be sure no one was left behind. It thrilled him to think of his turn to board the great vessel. It was the *Quo Vadis*, a new class of generation ship with tech and luxuries undreamed of when the Stationers set out from Earth. With three habitat spheres, it provided a variety of climates and simulated geography, urban nodes, quarters for thousands of inhabitants, a major industrial plant, and, Mitya was sure, its own mysteries. Sometimes, lying behind the water tank, he pretended he was onboard the great ship, in his private cabin, gazing out at the stars.

It was during one of these reveries that he heard angry voices approaching. Peering under the tank, he saw two pairs of boots. He recognized the voices— Stepan and Bonhert, going at it again. For all that Stepan had warned Mitya to keep his head down, it seemed that his uncle had no fear for his own safety.

". . . any further, people are going to crack," Stepan was saying.

"We're all tired. It's the damned truth." Captain Bonhert spoke in a harsh whisper, making him hard to hear.

"But three weeks! We can't shave three weeks off the schedule—it's impossible!"

"Stepan. I agree with you. It doesn't seem possible. But what can I do? We've got enough ash coming down to choke a turbine! No one expected a major eruption, and the breathers are running out. We've got five weeks left, on the outside. The *outside*."

"Our people are working the filter problem!"

"I *know* that. We'll coax things along as best we can, Stepan, but we're in the direct path of the airstream. Have you looked outside lately? It's a Lordly blizzard!"

Stepan swore. "I've got people who're making basic mistakes just from lack of sleep."

"Maybe you need to lower your standards."

"My *standards* aren't the problem. Some crew think it's gone too far, especially posting guards at the shuttle."

"Who thinks so?"

A pause. "Never mind that. I just don't want you jeopardizing the mission because you've got some wild hair up your ass about an orthong raid!"

"It's not that." Bonhert shuffled closer to Stepan.

"What? Not the orthong?"

"Listen, keep your mouth shut about this, you hear?" A pause. "We've got more trouble than orthong."

"What could be more trouble? Clavers?"

"Yes. Led by someone I think you know." After a significant pause, Bonhert said: "Calder."

"What the hell are you talking about? Cyrus made it down? In one of the shuttles?"

"No, not Cyrus. The boy. Reeve."

A snort of derision. "*Reeve?* Now that's a real threat!"

"Maybe. But he's got a small army of hoodlums with him, and they're bent on taking apart our dome, strut by strut. Maybe they're stupid, but they could do damage."

"How do you *know* this?" Stepan sounded more than a little skeptical.

Someone walked up to the two of them, mumbling a question. Bonhert answered the crewman, and then he and Stepan began walking away, with Bonhert saying, "Radio transmission. They left the mouth of the Tallstory two weeks ago, headed our way. In a *sailing* ship, if you can imagine it . . ."

Their voices were fading as they moved off.

". . . a bunch of barbarians?" Stepan asked incredulously.

"No, no . . . could hardly hear for all the . . ."

Mitya strained for more, but they were gone.

Oran landed a punch to the side of Mitya's face. If Mitya hadn't ducked, his face would have caved in, he figured. Outside the galley, the larger boy stood over him, an apron tied around his thick waist. "Come on, you gunk-head."

Mitya flew at him, propelled by a fury he didn't know he could muster. Oran's fists came up. Mitya didn't care but ran at him, getting in one good blow before he found himself in a heap against the galley wall.

"How'd you like a cast-iron pot for a hat?" Oran asked, bunching his hands at his sides.

"It'll look a lot better on *you*," Mitya spat.

Oran grinned. "Let's try it out." He dashed into the galley, returning with a pot dripping with cooked gruel. As Oran lifted the gigantic kettle over his massive shoulders, Mitya had time to think that this was going to be a bad way to die—after surviving the Station explosion, to die now with a pot on his head—but then crew came running, pulling Oran back.

Lieutenant Cody strode up with Tenzin Tsamchoe. Tsamchoe took Oran by the ear and shagged him into the galley while Cody helped Mitya up to his feet. "What's this about?" the lieutenant snarled.

From the galley, Oran shouted, "He's an-ass licker, the little cheat!"

Mitya glared at Cody. "He got the job *I* should have had. Everybody knows *galley slave* is my job." A week ago he would never have dared use this tone of voice with an officer. Now he didn't care; in fact, he hoped that Cody would punish him.

She surveyed the gathered crew, many not bothering to hide their contempt of Mitya. And perhaps of

Cody. "OK, show's over," she said. "Unless anybody else wants to beat up on a youngster?"

"Line forms on the left," somebody said from the back. Snickers. But the gathering began to disperse.

Across the dome, Mitya saw Bonhert and Stepan emerge from Bonhert's quarters, watching them. The side of Mitya's head felt like a water balloon. He would have liked to land one solid punch on Oran, except Cody had his elbow in a firm hold.

"You should know better than to rattle Oran."

"I didn't rattle him! He's got *my* job. A kid job!" He tried yanking his elbow away, but she held on. "If you don't want me to have any friends, you're doing a great job." From the expression on Cody's face, he knew he'd gone too far. Mustn't say everything he felt.

"And why would we not want you to have friends, Mitya?"

He scrambled for a more neutral stance. "Maybe you think we're not working hard enough. Goofing off together. I don't know."

Cody fixed him with a hard smile. "You think we've got time to worry about your social life?"

Mitya decided it was time to hang his head in shame. "No, sir."

Stepan joined them. As Cody passed custody of the boy over to his uncle, she said: "He thinks he should be back on galley duty. Maybe we should give him his wish."

Stepan watched her retreat back across the dome before muttering, "Got yourself into a pickle, don't you?" They walked away from the galley, strolling as Mitya tried to get his temper under control. Hammering noises erupted from the clean room, where work on the geo cannon proceeded at breakneck speed.

"You got a bunch of pressure from Bonhert to squeal on me," Stepan said, "so I figure you tattled something on Oran." Before Mitya could figure out what to say, Stepan held up his hand to silence him.

"It's OK. Maybe that was the best you could do. But now Bonhert has you cut off from everybody, doesn't he? You beginning to see how the man operates?" He caught Mitya's eye with a fierce stare.

"Yes, sir."

"You want to redeem yourself, Mitya?" They stopped dead center of the dome. The glow of daylight lit up a light suspension of ash in the air, despite the fans and filters.

"To who?"

Stepan smirked. "Politics got you spinning? That's all right, boy. I know you can't be going over to Bonhert. We're still family, you and I. Aren't we?"

Mitya looked at Stepan and nodded. He hoped that was true.

"Well, then. Bonhert has need of you to work the modeling." He noted Mitya's look of surprise. "Just little stuff. Data maintenance, cleanup. Maybe sling numbers for the calibrations. With crew lost and others assigned to security, we're short, and that's a fact. Comes at a bad time, this ash-fall. We're pushing up the schedule, and everybody's working double shifts."

"I'd rather work the galley."

Stepan sighed. "I know you would, right now. But your feud with Oran is kid stuff, Mitya. You've got a chance to be our man inside Bonhert's gang. He controls the information flow. There're things going on he doesn't tell people. So you tell me." He smiled at Mitya's stricken look. "You're not a child anymore, Mitya. We're fighting for our lives, and we don't trust Bonhert to be in charge. If you feel the same way, join us."

Despite his better judgment Mitya blurted out: "Did you help blow up the Station? Because if you did, I'm not helping you." He felt his eyes grow hot.

"No, Mitya! Most of us had no idea he'd go that far. We thought we'd come down here to set up a false terraforming mission and the Station folk would fend for themselves. Still harsh, but we never would have slaughtered them!" He cast a venom-filled glance at Bonhert's quarters. "That was Bonhert's doing, and that's why crew hates him."

Mitya wanted to believe him. And because he was so weary of lies, he *decided* to believe him. "Then I'll help you," he said.

Stepan nodded, once. "I'll be feeding you some things you can tattle to Bonhert. Don't seek me out, but let me find you when it's safe to talk. Act like the Captain's your hero. That's what he'd expect. It's his Achilles' heel."

He snapped his gaze back to Mitya.

"Yes, sir."

"Report to Lieutenant Roarke, and he'll tell you your new modeling duties." He turned abruptly and walked away. All part of the act. Mitya acted like he'd just had a lecture and headed to the computer banks, thinking maybe he was going to be a real member of the crew at last, even if it was mutinous crew.

5

"Loon!" the sailor cried out.

From the canyon walls, the echo came: "Loo, Loo, Loooon." White birds, startled by the voices, lifted from cliff perches in swarms, cawing and screeching.

The *Cleopatra* tacked up the great river against a brisk wind. The towering canyon walls formed a respite against the relentless ashen sky, here in the upper reaches of the Tallstory River where even Kalid had never ventured. A few jinn gathered at the rails to coax echoes from the rocky folds.

"Princess Loon!"

". . . cess, cess, Loo, oon!" came the ghostly cry.

A thudding up the stairs from the cabins, and Loon appeared in the doorway, wide-eyed. She stumbled forward to the center of the deck, spinning around as her name floated from every side. She looked like a small animal on high alert.

At her expression of alarm, Reeve hurried forward. "The jinn call your name. And it echoes back." He took her by the hand, leading her to the rail. He thought she was frightened by the echoes, but when he looked at her he saw tears collecting on her eyelashes.

"What is it, Loon?"

"My people," she said. "Not calling me?"

Reeve felt a keen stab of helplessness. "No," he whispered. Then, to his surprise, he added: "Not yet."

She looked up at him with childish trust, as though he had just promised her something. And had he? Before he could think of what to say, she retreated belowdecks, leaving the sailors to their game of echoes.

It had been three days since Isis' funeral, and Dante had just this morning come on deck for the first time, his entourage trickling after him, taking clues from their king as to the prevailing mood. It was, more than ever, a ragtag group, their costumes bedraggled and tawdry, their pallid faces rendered even more faded by the gray light.

One of the courtiers took up the chant of "Isis, Isis," but the name didn't resound like Loon's, and the effort fell flat. Miffed by this failure, Dante ordered his minions to swab the decks, a spectacle of great amusement to Kalid's sailors. The moment of levity caught on, and even Dante laughed at the sight of his fops on their hands and knees with buckets and rags.

"One week, I figure."

Reeve turned to find Marie standing next to him. Her face had finally shed its awful peeling, and a healthy sun- and windburn brought a flush of color to her skin.

"One week?"

"To the Rift Valley. With good winds. Westerlies will

go better with us once we're headed north up the Gandhi."

"I suppose." Reeve gazed out at the cliffs, dented here and there with nooks, crannies, and a few great caves.

"There a problem?" she asked. Marie was the only one among them who seemed impervious to the somber mood brought on by Isis' death and the dark skies. He attributed her constancy to the wisdom of age. Marie was always Marie, unflappable, steady, and contained.

"*Yes*, there's a problem." His annoyance surprised him. "These people have become our friends, Marie. Doesn't that bother you?"

One eyebrow arched. "*These people* made us captives, slaughter with the ease of leopards, and keep dungeons of scientists. They'd kill us in an instant if we tried to go our own way. Some friends."

Her tone infuriated him. "Lord of Worlds, Marie! There's Dante, but then there's Kalid. And Isis. Didn't her death bother you? We dragged her out here on this farce of a mission, and she died."

"She was a dead woman anyway."

He stared at her. "And what about Kalid?"

"He's a killer, same as the rest. Charming, I grant you. But charm doesn't buy much in this world."

"This world! Exactly. This is their world, Marie. How would we be in their place? Without Station, we'd be exactly like them!"

She sighed in exasperation. "Yes, and without fur, the lion would be a pig! What's the point, here, Reeve? You want to tell these folks we lied about fixing the dome? Tell them King Gabriel isn't interested in a gang of barbarians, but thanks for the ride?"

Reeve looked around to see who might be close enough to listen. A nearby jinn noticed their sharp words, but went back hastily to his scrubbing.

"I don't know," he said miserably. "I just never betrayed anyone before."

"Well, you're young."

He caught her eye for a moment, then stared out at the damn pink canyon walls.

She continued: "Don't be asking to bring Kalid along, if that's what you're thinking. Take Spar and Loon if you insist, but I draw the line at Dante's chief thug!"

With the story of Willa Achebe hanging on, the name *deserter* seemed apt indeed. If he wasn't born a zerter then he would soon become one in earnest. Worse, he would betray a new group of friends in order to betray the remnant of his clave. If a shuttleful of murderers could be considered a clave.

"Marie," he said at last. "Tell me about my father."

Her hand covered his on the rail. She looked out, summoning her thoughts. "Cyrus was an idealist. He gave his life over to the dream of Voyaging On, every minute of his waking life, despite the mockery."

"Why didn't Bonhert support him, if he really thought terraforming wouldn't work?"

"I don't know. Your father had a dogged faith that we could build a starship. I believed that as well, but I had some doubts about finding a home. We never found another decent planet, in all our astronomical surveys. That's what his enemies ridiculed, and maybe it's what kept Bonhert from going over to your father's side. But Cyrus kept on searching to the end."

"I never much understood all that." His voice sounded thin and reedy, even to himself. "I just missed him."

"For some people, Reeve, their work is everything. They don't have time for other people's feelings. Try not to hate him."

"Hate him?" Reeve frowned. "I don't hate him."

She patted his hand. "No, of course you don't."

A bird lighted on the ship rail nearby. Its wings and

feet were tipped in red, as though it had walked through a pool of blood. After a moment he asked: "Were we selfish, do you think, to keep Station for ourselves?" He knew what she would say. Practical Marie.

"I guess everybody has to decide when it's right to be selfish and when it isn't. It's a dilemma."

"Like whether to abandon this ship and its crew?"

As the bird took flight and soared skyward, she squinted up at the sun, a faded blossom of light poised above the canyon. "No. This one's clear as day."

Reeve lay awake that night thinking about Station, about Cyrus and Marie. The ship rocked at anchor, and the noises of the crew sleeping in the next cabin reminded him of being in his cubicle at home, amid the cozy, tubular corridors and the sounds of a hundred people above you, below you, and on every side. Could it be that just three weeks ago he had suited up and crept out on the Station hull to spy on Lithia? How could everything change so utterly, so fast? It was like a giant fist had crushed through his life, inverting it, leaving everything opposite to what it was.

He closed his eyes again, listening to the creaks and muffled groans of the ship. By now Tina Valejo was dead, just a husk cartwheeling through the dark—face plate glinting now and then from a stray photon of light. It helped that she was dead. It was her being *alive* that had disturbed him.

Finally Reeve cursed and sat up in bed. It was the middle of the night. He thrust his feet into his boots and grabbed an overcoat from the peg on the door.

His door flew open, nearly hitting him. Loon stood there, panting. "The echoes are coming," she said.

As he stood, frowning in confusion, she repeated, "They are coming."

Taking the stairs two at a time, he burst onto the

deck, startling the night watch. He spun, looking for something amiss. Nearby, a rock cascaded down the canyon wall.

One of the jinn guards strode to the rail and looked out at the moonless night. A slither of rock and sand sounded from another direction. When Reeve squinted in that direction, he discerned shapes on the rock face, slinking down.

Reeve was at the guard's side in an instant. "Attack. Alert everyone, quietly!"

"Where?" the jinn said, surly.

He grabbed the man by the collar. "Call your men, silently! Run!" He shoved him backward, and the man raced to the foredeck.

Reeve was down the stairs, banging on doors. "Attack!" he called. Kalid burst into the corridor from his cabin. "Down from the cliffs!" Reeve spat out. "Clavers!"

Kalid raced for the bridge, sending Reeve to rouse Dante. Reeve flew to Spar's cabin and met him at his door, finding Spar already buckling his sword belt. "Where is Mam?" Spar asked.

"Awake. That direction." He nodded to the foot of the stairs, then sped off to get Marie. Shaking her awake, he cried, "We're under attack. Get up!" As she struggled into her clothes, he said, "Any weapons in here?"

"Dante," she said. "Dante keeps knives."

Together they ran for Dante's quarters. His door was already thrown open and Dante was bellowing in rage. He pushed past his guards and Reeve, carrying a sword nearly as big as he was. His attendants cowered near a bulkhead as sounds of fighting erupted on deck. Marie and Reeve found the cache of swords and armed themselves as best they could, then followed a stream of jinn up to the deck.

The fury of the fight met them as soon as they stepped outside. Marie ducked as a man with a head like a tree bole swiped a sword at them. Reeve was forced back down the stairs, crashing into jinn just coming up. The press of bodies finally brought him back to the head of the stairs, where two attackers thrust their swords at him.

Howls of wounded and dying jinn filled the air. Someone engaged one of the swordsmen from behind, evening the odds for Reeve, who burst through from the hold, followed by a dozen jinn. Many black shapes jostled and danced in the dark. Close by, he caught a glimpse of a demon with one long arm and one short. The creature thrust forward with his long arm, skewering his opponent. The enemy were pouring over the rails, screaming with a mixture of rage and glee.

Reeve was exchanging blows with a woman whose sword flew at him as though under some machine power. He hacked at her, a killing blow—then watched in horror as she sank to the deck, spouting blood. *I killed her*, he thought, and turned to kill again.

He found himself facing Spar. They soon found better targets and battled three invaders back to the rail, with Reeve forgetting everything he'd learned from Kalid, and barely holding his own. Blood flew like spittle through the air, greasing the deck. Dante's roars made his the only single discernible voice. *Loon*, Reeve kept thinking. *Loon*.

The man with the huge head was backing him toward the aft mast. Reeve's heart raced at the sight of this apparition with bulges for a cranium. Behind the creature, Reeve saw Kalid fighting like one possessed, roaring orders to his men, who rallied to his side. Kalid glimpsed him and shouted, "No fire, Spaceman! Kill with ice!"

Reeve saw that his opponent was full of fire, rushing him. Reeve dodged as the man lunged past him, tripping but knocking the sword out of Reeve's hand on the way down. Savagely, Reeve kicked the preposterous head, following it up with a booted toe in the man's kidneys. Beyond his fallen opponent, he spied Loon beset by two attackers. Desperate, Reeve wove through the melee to reach her even as they carried her to the rail and muscled her over it. A flash of a small knife riveted his attention as someone lunged at him. Reeve had lost his sword, but managed to slam the attacker against the mast by grabbing his forearm and yanking with his full strength. The man's head struck the mast with force, and as he dropped his knife, Reeve snatched it from the deck.

Now armed, Reeve rushed to the rail, where Loon had disappeared. Then the world blanked out as, from behind, a cloth was slipped over his head and crushing arms came around him, hoisting him off his feet. He felt himself lifted up and grabbed from below, despite his wildly kicking legs. He landed in a boat next to the ship, where a daunting thud on his back pushed his face painfully into the wooden slats. Working the hood off his face as the boat jostled and rocked, he found himself among several prisoners, anonymous in their hooded state. Amid the slap of oars, he called out for Loon until a claver sat on his back, driving the breath from him.

He heard Spar cursing in the back of the boat, and the cry of someone wounded. At last the oaf on top of him left his perch, and Reeve rolled onto his back. The waters glittered, reflecting fires in many small boats and shedding an infernal light on the battle for the great ship. From the decks, its crew still repelled attackers, casting them into the glowing river and turning to meet the next wave.

But the *Cleopatra* was under way. Its great sails had unfurled and took the wind into them with a smack. What clavers still clung to the ship's sides were beaten back by a rally from Dante's jinn. From the crow's nest someone was shooting flares at the smaller boats, searing the air with crackling arcs. Though he would not have wished the *Cleopatra* defeat, Reeve was bitter to see it pull away, leaving him behind.

"Reeeeeeve!" He heard his name called in the distance, once, twice. It was Marie. He thought he saw her leaning out over the ship's rail.

The ship was under way. In the brimstone light, Reeve saw Dante standing at the back of the ship. His booming voice carried plainly: "Farewell! Farewell!" He waved wildly as the ship detached itself from the invaders' boats. As the great ship sliced through the flotsam of battle, Dante's jubilant voice came from the middle of the river: "Die bravely, my friends! With style!"

For many minutes afterward, as the dinghy jostled on the waves, he could hear the distant echoes of Marie's plaintive calls, jumbling his name: "Ree, Ree, eeeeeeeeve!"

10

1

Day thirty-seven. The face peering down at Reeve seemed normal enough. Slightly wedge-shaped, the young man's face was preceded by a very prominent nose, accentuated by close-cropped hair.

"I really hope you're comfortable." His captor peered down at him with apparent concern. When Reeve didn't answer, the young man tugged at the ropes, testing them, and then slightly loosened the one holding Reeve's left wrist. "Have to tie you up right now." He bent close and said in a conspiratorial manner, "This part doesn't last long, though, so don't worry!"

Reeve struggled to move, but the ropes held him flat to the cave floor. During the night, Reeve and the other prisoners had called to each other, figuring out that they were in separate, open cubbyholes carved into rock, with Loon next to Reeve and Spar four cells down. The six jinn prisoners were comprised of five sailors and a courtier of Dante's.

"One of your people died last night. Sorry. He had an intestinal wound that Brecca couldn't repair. His name was Zuni, and we gave him a good burial. You sailors put up such a fight! Well, people always do. They're afraid of us, because of . . . how we look." He sprang up and fetched a small thermos. "Thirsty?"

Reeve nodded, and the fellow held up his head so that he could drink. No harm in drinking what they offered. They could kill him anytime they liked, and poison was just as good as any other death. His thoughts were of Loon in the next cell, and of the *Cleopatra,* sailing toward its destination, *his* destination.

"I'm Dooley. You?" He screwed the cap on the burnished metal thermos and waited expectantly. "Don't feel like talking yet. I understand!" He looked with concern at Reeve's spread-eagled form. "I can loosen these a little."

As he worked the ropes one at a time, Reeve could hear his labored breathing, as though he had asthma or an advanced case of indigo. Remembering the cold night just passed, Reeve looked enviously at the man's quilted jacket and fur boots.

"The others say you're the leader, so you'll get top-notch inturning." He cocked his head impishly. "What's inturning? That's the first thing people ask. Well, inturning is the first stage in your apprenticeship. Then you go—if you have talent—to assistant-ship, and on from there." He sighed. "It's mostly grudge work, I'll admit that. But everybody has to start somewhere. You can't be too proud if you mean to work for Brecca. Take Gregor, for instance. Please take Gregor!" Here he laughed, a squeaky titter of enjoyment that snapped off when he glanced down the corridor. "Even Gregor started as an inturn, flat on the floor, all roped up just like you! We start everyone the same—very democratic—and then each rises as high as his talents. I would have risen further, but my offering wasn't accepted. It's no shame. Most of us stay assistants. But someone like you, you'll probably reform grandly! Brecca will try a bold theme with you."

His eyes filmed over with emotion. "I envy you—not because you'll be important, but because you're at the very beginning, the start of your transformation."

Reeve looked away, toward the cave wall. Punching this fellow in the nose was his foremost thought. But that was as impossible as tearing loose his bonds or reaching the Rift in time.

A noise down the corridor caught Dooley's attention. He darted to the den opening. "They're getting ready. But we still have some time." He scampered back to sit at Reeve's side. "You want to talk yet?" He licked his lips and waited, eyes darting. "I guess not. I don't blame you. I talk too much—it's part of my offering. Along with the lungs." He took a deep breath, creating a deep, fluted sound. "The lungs are layered, like parallel filters. Take up half my chest. The talking-too-much part is just extra." He nodded. "Annoying, isn't it? Don't worry. It won't hurt my feelings."

He turned once more to check out the long corridor that Reeve and the others had been herded down last night. "I'd better hurry. Let's start at the beginning." He began to talk, in rote style:

"We are the Somaformers. We offer ourselves—test subjects—to transform the human colony. Transformation is the way of new life, the survival of the fittest, according to Saint Darwin. Who is fit, only the Labs can say. As subjects of the Pool, we offer ourselves in humility, reforming for the greater glory of the Labs and the resurrection of humanity. Outside the Pool we are monsters. We are the Mercury Clave, the children—stealers, the scab-lovers. These names cannot hurt us! This too is a sacrifice, that everyone names us and yet no one can name us.

"We are the Somaformers. We offer ourselves—test subjects—to transform the human colony. Transformation is the burden of living creatures. The rocky world transforms without volition. Humanity transforms as an act of devotion. We do penance for the sin

of terraforming, that betrayal of the world as Deity
made it, for which we now accept our punishment.
Where there is pain, we endure. Where there is defor-
mity, we are grateful. Where there is failure, we accept. Where there is success, we exult. We are the
Somaformers. You will become one of us. You will
transform."

His eyes shone with emotion. "Beautiful, isn't it?"

Reeve yanked at his ropes in frustration. Then, taking a breath to calm himself, he asked, "Who is
Brecca?"

This provoked a startled reaction from Dooley. He
scuttled closer to his prisoner. "That's it! No sense
sulking now, is there?" He cleared his throat, reciting:
"Brecca is the Ministrator, Chief Operating Vizier, the
COZ. She ministrates the Lab, the resurrection of—"

"No, Dooley. Who *is* she?" He turned to look
Dooley in the eyes. "In plain language."

Crestfallen, Dooley hesitated. "Well, I should recite
the convocation. . . ." Then, looking at the expression
on Reeve's face, he sighed. "OK. Plain language.
Brecca is . . . the holy representative of Deity on the
world. She keeps all the secrets and science publica-
tions and the computers. She is the Holy Gengineer,
Chief Scientist, the Ministrator." At Reeve's glare, he
took a deep rippling breath, flattening his mouth in
concentration. "OK. Brecca is . . . the one who'll reform all you inturns. The Lab assistants will do the
analysis, but Brecca has to approve all transgenic
plans. She may even do you herself, if you're blessed.
She's fierce, Brecca is; you'll see! Life and death—
she's got both. She's got your life, she's got your death.
She controls all the pairings. Last year she did the
codes on my future mate, and now we're base pairs.

"But Gregor, the Successor, tried to snip us off, be-
cause he doesn't like me and Lillie, especially together.
You'll meet Gregor. He's the one that never smiles.
He's got all the Somas afraid of him because he can

make or break your career, put you on some backwater sacrifice and advance his friends to the cutting edge. But Brecca relies on him, and puts him through advanced degrees so the Pool will survive. Otherwise, after Brecca goes, we'd end up just like you." He winced at his own words. "No offense. But look at you. Utterly undifferentiated, completely maladapted. And your breather doesn't fool us, either. It's a device, not blessed by the body. If they hadn't already seen the breather, I'd have dumped it for you. It'll get Gregor off on a tangent, I bet." His eyes snapped up in anxiety. "Here they come. Good luck. You'll do just fine."

"Dooley?"

"Yes?"

"You folks use genetic engineering to turn yourself into freaks?"

Dooley's face turned slack-jawed. "Shhhh!" He scuttled back to Reeve's side, fidgeting. "Don't say anything like that to Brecca, or you're a dead man!" He shook his head sadly. "I take responsibility for this; I'm a lousy teacher."

"No, Dooley, you were brilliant."

"I was?"

"It's just that we disagree. In science, that's a good thing."

A crowd was heading toward them down the passageway.

"Shhhh!" Dooley enjoined him, prancing in nervousness, finger to lips.

A shuffling of many feet told Reeve that people were approaching. Despite the ineffectual Dooley, Reeve's stomach tightened in fear. He was to be a lab rat, an experiment. And so were Loon and Spar. He heard singing, a sonorous, liturgical chant.

"Loon," Reeve called out. As she answered him, her voice was a saving counterpoint to the dooming song that approached. "I love you," he said, surprising himself. *Take me*, he wanted to say to the Somaformers.

Let her be; release her in the company of the scrawny warrior. Take me.

Marie was on her way to Bonhert's camp. It was on her shoulders now, saving the world. In some ways, it was a relief to give this mission to someone else. Marie made a better hero: smart, unsentimental, tough. She wouldn't be haunted by the memory of the fight on the ship, wouldn't be thinking about people that fell to her sword. . . .

Past Dooley's shoulder, Reeve could see a procession of deformed humanity dressed in white gowns. They passed his view in syncopated step, some tall, some short, some limping. One had limbs so thin he looked like a sapling tree. Another had a bubble protruding in place of a mouth. Yet another had a chest too large for her frame, housing, perhaps, the future lungs of Lithia. At last the white robes gave way to mere white shirts or jackets over quilted pants, but under those jackets bulged humps where none should have been.

They had passed him by. Down the corridor the sounds of a scuffle, and the curses of a jinn. After a moment, the procession approached Reeve's cubbyhole again, led by an imposing woman of lush dimensions. Her ample chest was adorned with medallions, covering an enormous white gown that flowed around her like a tent. Circled around her head was a long braid of gray hair, making her surely the oldest claver Reeve had yet seen.

At her side was an ordinary-looking man with a flat white hat, from which hung a tassel. This individual turned to regard Reeve with a piercing stare.

"Gregor," Dooley whispered. "That's Gregor!"

Behind Gregor shuffled one of the jinn, bound in heavy ropes and sneering at his fate, whatever it might be. As a resounding clang of a door announced the procession's departure, silence reclaimed the network of caves. Until Dooley began again.

"It's not fair. I thought they'd take you first." He shook his head. "I should have helped him. I try to give some instruction so they can make a good impression. And not be so scared." He sighed.

"Don't worry about that fellow," Reeve said. "It takes more than a white parade to scare a jinn." He settled back onto the floor, his neck weary.

"A jinn?" Dooley sat next to Reeve, cradling his knees with his arms.

"Some of your prisoners are members of the Atlantis Clave. They call themselves jinn."

Dooley plugged his ears with his fingers. "Da da da, da da da da. Don't want to heeeear!"

Reeve fixed him with an ironic stare. "Sure you do."

The fingers came out of his ears. "OK, Atlantis Clave—where is it, and how many people live there? Quickly, before I start talking again."

"Atlantis Clave is at the mouth of the river, on the Inland Sea. Got thousands of members. All going to come looking for us, mad as hell."

Dooley shrugged. "That's all right. That's what the Labs were built for. Assault!"

"How so, Dooley?"

"Because that's what they were built for, to look like dumb caves! The First Scientists built these Labs in secret, so mundane people wouldn't pillage them. Back then, it was forbidden to transform humans, against the law of the land. But in the Dark Days, in the first hundred years, the fore-scientists knew that only Somaforming could save us. So they built the Labs deep in the canyon rock, and hid them, and we've kept the faith, all these generations. Each generation raises up the next generation of scientists to carry on the transformation."

"Doesn't look like you've gotten very far." Reeve thought of the fantastic variations on the human theme, some painful-looking.

Dooley scrunched up his face. "That's not the point. It isn't necessary to succeed. Just to try."

"Dooley, do you ever listen to yourself?"

A slow, sad shake of the head. "I don't think Gregor is going to like you."

"How's he going to like wearing that stupid hat around his neck?"

From behind them came a gravelly voice. "He would not be amused."

Dooley scrambled backward as fast as he could to get out of the shadow of the white-coated man with the funny hat.

"Untie him," Gregor ordered Dooley. "Here's a creature badly in need of reforming."

2

Nerys emerged from her room, groggy with sleep. By the slant of light from the ceiling, she knew the morning was well along. Odel was just heading down the passageway, securing her long gray hair at the back of her neck with a clasp.

Odel smiled as Nerys caught up. "I'm an old woman. What's your excuse for sleeping late?"

They all wondered what she did, coming home late each night from Salidifor's compound.

"No reason to rise early without work to do." She kept her tone friendly; Odel seemed accepting of her, and it was a surprising comfort.

They walked into the tea room, as the women called the front area. Here they gathered for talk and tea, especially in the cool mornings when the heat of the berms was most welcome. As Haval and several others glanced up, conversation ceased. Nerys was getting used to this cool reception. In a friendly overture, Galen patted the cushion next to her and Nerys sat down, reaching for the shiny pot of tea and a palm-sized cup. Before long the women would scurry into the outfold to share breakfast with their lords at their respective habitations. For now, though, there was excruciating human conversation.

"Luce has gone to bring forth her pup," Odel said. This, everyone knew. Luce was fairly bursting with her pregnancy, and was looking forward to having it done with. "We should do something special for her when they bring her back."

"A bath and a massage," Haval suggested. She looked at Luce's partner, Callie.

Callie grinned. She could hardly wait to have Luce back in sensual trim again.

"Last night," Mave piped up, "Himirinan brought me a dish of custard laced with nutmeg."

Haval moaned. "My favorite. Your lord seems to be coming around." *Coming around* was the term the women had for a lord's becoming more personal with one of them.

"I was almost asleep. But I didn't turn it down!"

Pila, the youngest of the group, said: "It took them forever to learn how to make custard. It used to taste like glue."

Mave went on: "He even told me that his work involved patrolling the eastern perimeter. So that fits in with the idea that they work the defenses in quadrants. Since he reports to Salidifor, that would make Salidifor the eastern chief."

At the mention of Nerys' lord, the conversation trickled away. They hadn't forgiven her for snatching up an orthong of consequence.

Nerys took her tea and went out to sit on the steps. The morning mist had cooked up a spicy, aromatic stew in the outfold, and she breathed in deeply, thinking of Anar, and how Anar would have delighted in this place of mysteries. Up in the swaying second story of outfold on a narrow, suspended bridge, orthong pups could sometimes be seen scampering and playing, a secure upper layer where they apparently roamed with impunity, oblivious to the women in their compound below.

Anar would have loved to see such a sight, and to hear how the outfold sang with birds in the mornings. Massing in the columnar growths the women called trees, the birds pecked at unseen delicacies. Perhaps, Nerys mused, the orthong engineered delights to attract birds as they did to attract human women.

Since coming to the orthong habitation ten days ago, Nerys had tasted foods that she had known only in stories and myths. How the orthong acquired and prepared this food, the women had yet to discover. But they brought the women rich cream soups, cuts of tender meat, berry compotes, vegetables simmered in gravy, crusty breads, salted butters, and fruits called melons, grapes, tangerines, and pears. Once when Salidifor urged her to eat a bowl of red strawberries, for a moment she thought he meant to poison her. Though the crimson bauble was achingly pleasurable, Nerys stopped after tasting just one. If he wanted her to eat, he would have to first teach her something. She put her spoon down on the mat, signaling her demand. Eventually she finished all the strawberries, but it was very late before she got home that night.

Odel came outside to sit with her. "Want some company?" Seeing Nerys nod, she settled onto the step, elbows on knees, and gazed out on the orthong forest. "Sorry about that nonsense back there," she said. "It'll get better once they get to know you."

"Sometimes the more people know me, the less they like me."

Odel laughed. "Well, you can make waves. But some of us enjoy the shaking up. We're too set in our ways." She looked sideways at Nerys. "Do you suppose the thongs planned this? Put you in number two position just to test us?"

Nerys' position of number two woman in the compound came from Salidifor's being second in rank to

Haval's lord, Simeranan. Though Lord Simeranan had recently died, his status still clung to Haval. Nerys had assumed that the orthong couldn't care less about the women's hierarchy, but it was an intriguing thought.

The older woman cocked her head. "Maybe they're studying our reactions to this little upset in the routine."

"So they secretly watch us?"

"Maybe not spying, but perhaps noting our reactions in the larger sense. Don't you suppose they're curious about us?"

Nerys wondered. She scanned the jumbled outfold that stopped just short of their courtyard, looking for orthong, perhaps camouflaged. Who knew whether the orthong hides might change color in this place? Who knew much of anything about the orthong?

"Seems to me we'd do better to learn about *them*. We have more to lose by ignorance than they do. They're already in charge."

Odel inhaled the fragrant wisps of her hot tea. "We're always learning about them."

By pooling information with women from other compounds, they estimated there were at least four hundred other human women in the forest, which stretched for at least ten miles east to west and in places filled out to three miles wide. The women lived in groups of thirty or so, and were free to walk and visit between berms, but not to change berms, a thing that could inconvenience their orthong lords. Clear of outfold growths, the paths through this place were sometimes edged with high-growth walls, effectively blocking intrusion. Behind these walls might be anything the orthong wished to hide, and if women had penetrated these areas, they weren't talking openly about it.

Though unnaturally colorful, the outfold was apparently composed of cultivated plants, but since orthong didn't ingest food, its exact function wasn't understood. Climate control was the best current guess. For its latitude, the outfold was relatively warm, despite being close to the Galilean glacier—a location the orthong liked, it was rumored, because the retreating ice sheet left rocks behind that they prized. When the women asked their lords about these kinds of things, the answers were often unintelligible, and many tea talks revolved around trying to decipher the answers.

Orthong females—usually distinguished by their sleeveless apparel—were often seen in the public compounds and occasionally in the outfold, but they never interacted with the human women. The freewomen argued whether their female orthongs' status was high or low. Most guessed high, since they were rumored to participate at the top level of the orthong hierarchy. The orthong lords preferred that the freewomen call the orthong females *weavers*, a term the orthong had selected when they'd observed the human women with their looms.

Tempering the imperious nature of the orthong males were their frequent gifts of food and queries after the women's happiness; some lords were known to be exceptionally solicitous, sometimes visiting the women's berms to bring a food delicacy.

Yet none of this had a sexual motivation. The women were incubators, receiving what were assumed to be fertilized embryos from their respective lords. The procedure was quick and impersonal. A woman reported to a berm off the central plaza and, as she lay on a platform, an orthong performed the operation with help of a device that arched over her belly. The woman felt a sharp thud on her skin, and it was over. So much for Galen's lurid imaginings. Then it was up to the orthong lord to look after the woman's welfare for the two months of gestation. Every woman was expected to bear three pups a year, but a lord could impose less, if the woman wanted to rest. Most didn't. They had known when they came what the deal was, and those who had courted starvation before entering the outfold counted it handsome payment. And they could look forward to nonbearing years as well. Women of Odel's age were retired from bearing, yet they ate as well as anyone.

Young Pila came out to the steps with the pot of tea and poured out another cup for Nerys. As second woman in the berm, Nerys had certain privileges, but she would rather have had a friend or two than her tea poured. "Join us, Pila," she said. Pila looked back at the others, still chatting around the table, then shrugged and sat down.

She patted her stomach. "Soon." She smiled half-heartedly.

Odel put her arm around the girl, barely seventeen years old. Pila's yellow braids hung like old washrags down her back, giving her a tomboy look.

"He's going to be a great lord," Pila said.

Nerys clamped her mouth down, trying to be nice. Pila was young, after all.

"I think he'll be a leader, because he kicks like someone who wants to be noticed!"

"Oh, they all kick," Odel said.

"Not like my baby, they don't."

Nerys couldn't help it. *"Baby?"*

Pila's face crumpled. "Did I say baby? I didn't mean baby. Pup." She looked in consternation at the other two women. "Honestly." At the women's stony silence, Pila fled down the stairs in tears.

Nerys went after her. "It's all right, Pila. Who cares what we call them?"

"No! I'm supposed to say pup, I know that. It's just that—I don't like to think that way."

Nerys smiled. "Then don't But be ready when people frown at you. It's the price you pay for breaking the rules. Usually, I find it's worth it."

Pila was looking behind Nerys. "Haval wants you."

At the edge of the compound, an orthong stood,

talking to Haval. Nerys was learning to distinguish one orthong from another by the subtle hints of gray streaking on hands and head. This one, by the flush of silver circling his neck like a collar, was Mave's lord, Hamirinan.

"Are you all right?" Nerys helped Pila to sit on the bottom step. She looked like a child, despite the protruding belly.

"You better go," Pila said.

The other women were standing as Hamirinan made his way toward the stairs where Pila and Nerys were. The women clapped as he came by, in one of their revolting customs. He carried a packet of food, which, by its fragrance, was venison stew. As he came closer the women stepped back to give him room, but Nerys misjudged, and found herself close enough to him that he brushed her arm as he went by.

In an instant, he swung around, and with his free hand he slapped her on the collarbone so hard she sprawled into the courtyard. She hit her tailbone painfully and would have cried out, but the wind had gone out of her. As she tried to move a stab of pain warned her to be still.

The orthong turned with something like nonchalance and continued up the stairs, amid the frozen women. When he disappeared into the berm, Pila ran to her. Nerys' collarbone hurt so badly she had to pant. Between breaths she considered how to kill this orthong. They said the place to kill them was on the back of the neck.

Odel and Pila helped her to her feet, where she came face-to-face with Haval.

"When an orthong comes to the compound, you stand with me to greet him. And you get out of his way when he walks."

Callie and Galen were smirking in a cluster of their friends. When Nerys fixed them with her gaze, they turned away, but someone laughed. In a rage, Nerys shook off Odel's and Pila's hands. The exertion brought her to her knees.

Haval crouched down beside her, opening Nerys' shirt to inspect the injury. "Your collarbone may be broken." She rose, telling Odel and Pila to help Nerys inside.

"He touched *me*. I didn't touch him," Nerys whispered through her gritted teeth as they helped her to climb the stairs.

"When this starts hurting like hell, I hope that comforts you." Haval stomped up the stairs ahead of them, while Nerys took the steps one at a time.

3

The caves were a labyrinth, but just as Dooley had said, they were a subterfuge. A neatly chiseled boulder rolled aside before Gregor's voiced command, and Reeve saw through the opening to a vast, tiled atrium flooded with light.

The Somaform guards, engineered large, tugged on his ropes, and the group proceeded into the great room. Behind them, Reeve could hear Dooley's whispered mutterings, talking to himself if no one else would listen.

The chamber rose three stories, with exposed hallways at the second and third levels, revealing long rows of doors to what Reeve figured might be Somaform quarters. Hanging from ceiling cables were huge placards displaying images of especially grotesque human mutations. Beneath this mobile of oddities were the oddities themselves, Dooley's transformed humanity, theme and variation. A shriek of laughter momentarily halted Gregor as a small boy chased a ball to the man's feet. The youngster looked up, and with hands protruding directly from his shoulders, dipped sideways and grabbed the ball, rushing merrily away. From the upper floors, people leaned on the railing, gazing out on the atrium or gesturing and talking. It all seemed normal enough, except for the diverse morphology.

Gregor paid none of them any attention and, hat tassels swaying, strode up a broad, curving staircase to the second level, where tall double doors opened at their approach.

Only Gregor and Reeve entered. Gregor bowed before the woman who commanded the center of the room. Behind her was a simple desk, almost hidden from view by the breadth of her hips. This could only be Brecca. She no longer wore the white robe, but a huge purple jumper hanging to the floor and a glittering yellow shirt underneath. With the many necklaces bristling around her throat and earrings that cascaded to her shoulders, she made a jingling noise when she moved. Bright red lips and blue eye shadow defined her features under a mound of gray hair. All in all, the impression was stupefying.

Gregor intoned, "Behold Brecca, Ministrator, Vizier, and Final Sign-Off."

As tall as Reeve, Brecca looked at him with mean and beady eyes. "Bow," she said, in a voice as smooth and mellow as Reeve had ever heard. "It's expected."

He did so.

"Good." She spread her arms apart, rattling her bracelets, saying with a world-weary boredom, "Welcome, my son, to the Labs." Then, dropping her voice a mean octave, she said: "Now, on your life, tell me if you are from the sky wheel. You probably can't imagine what we do to liars around here." She raised her penciled eyebrows. "Or maybe you can."

"I'm Reeve Calder, son of Cyrus Calder, of the Station Clave."

She smiled. "You can drop the clave shit around here, son."

Gregor delicately cleared his throat.

"Clean up my language, that it, Greggy?" She sighed hugely. "You'd think a woman in my position could do any damn thing she wanted, wouldn't you?" She shook her head. "Greggy—I mean the Successor here—is responsible for making sure that we keep the proper forms. And I thank him for that." She smiled a pert and awful smile in Gregor's direction. "If it weren't for him, I'd be a disgraceful mess."

Changing tone with alarming speed, she snarled, "OK, Reeve Calder, talk."

Gregor faced him. His squarish face had a few lines, marking him for middle age. His irises, Reeve noticed for the first time, were so light as to appear colorless. As they locked gazes, Reeve had the odd sensation of looking through the eyes to some point beyond. "Bear in mind," Gregor said, "that we have debriefed several jinn sailors, and we will be disappointed at discrepancies in your stories."

Reeve talked. He was getting used to telling his tale by now, how Station had blown apart, the crash of his shuttle, his journey to rejoin his fellow Stationers. He embellished the strength of the jinn, playing that feeble card for all it was worth. He toyed with the idea of revealing Bonhert's plan, thinking that the Somaformers might be persuaded to help him, then discarded the notion. Why should they believe yet another desperate prisoner, eager for release? Of Loon, he said nothing.

When he had finished, Brecca shrugged. "Well, Gregor," she said. "What do you think?"

"Like any claver, he must do penance. It is the way of the Pool."

"Why do I bother asking?" she said, rolling her eyes at the ceiling. Then her eyes narrowed. "Maybe Reeve Calder could rise rather rapidly through the hierarchy. He's got some science, probably make a fine gengineer. We could always use more *real* scientists, don't you agree, Gregor?"

Gregor's chin moved as he struggled to speak. Finally he said, "As you say, Ministrator."

"As I *say*. And as you connive, isn't that right?" Then she straightened and cheerfully plunged on. "How would you like a peek at our Labs, Reeve Calder?" She waved off Gregor's objections. "Before I give you to Gregor, that is." She smiled sweetly at the smaller man and, sweeping across to Reeve, took him by the elbow and led him to an inner door. "Leave us, Gregor. I'm sure you have more important work than to show a mere inturn around." With that, she led Reeve away.

Brecca escorted him into a long corridor flanked by doors. The walls and floors shone with cleanliness and sterility, reminding him of home. For the first time since his crash landing, he was in a place with regularity, neatness, and warm, artificial light. The memory produced an ache in his throat. For a moment he imagined his father emerging from one of the doors, clipboard in hand, nodding at Reeve. But this wasn't home, only a mirror-image world, picking up a few mutations along the way.

The Somaform leader turned to him, arms akimbo. "Tell me about protein folding."

"That has to do with genetics, doesn't it? I don't know much about—your specialty."

"All righty," she said with elaborate patience. "You don't know much. Tell me something you *do* know about it. Surely the space station held on to some science?"

Reeve swallowed. "Of course. Functional genomics was a course I took. Determining interactions among genes for polygenic traits." He searched his brain for something more to say, but he had truthfully slept through most of that course. "Modifying our genome to . . . do what you've done here . . . is beyond Station science. We never pursued it. It was illegal, for one thing. I can tell you about simple stuff—morphogenetic protein, homeobox complexes, DNA—"

"Good boy," she interrupted. "Yeah, you gotta be a

Stationer. This way." Brecca was holding open the first door. He followed her, ropes trailing on the floor.

They stood in a large room where a portion of the ceiling was raised, enclosing a screen. A flickering display artfully contrived to look like a skylight showed out onto a sunlit forest canopy. Beneath it was a desk and a great chair, created for one of Brecca's bulk.

"My office." She sank into her chair and waved Reeve into another, smaller one. Closing her eyes, she let out a long, slow breath. With one hand she slipped off her earrings, slinging them onto the desk. Next came the necklaces, in a clatter. "You have no idea how tiresome all this is. If anyone ever offers you the job of God, turn it down. Pay's lousy." Her voice carried effortlessly, even when she muttered, with the tones of one who might have been a singer. Raising her face, she basked in the apparent sunshine from the skylight. She had attractive features for a woman who must have been over sixty years old.

She gazed upward at the treetops. "I can imagine what you must think of all this. The Holy Gengineer stuff."

Reeve let that pass for now. There was plenty he thought about it, foremost how not to be gengineered—a term he could readily deduce, given the circumstances.

"You're really from the space station, huh?"

He nodded.

Shaking her head in wry amusement, she opened a drawer and took out a small square packet, and held it out to him. "Cigarette?"

He stared at the object as the top sprang open to reveal several small white tubes.

She put the end of one in her mouth and slapped the pockets of her jumper, finally finding a packet of matches. She smoked the tube. Reeve watched in fascination as she sucked in and blew out smoke.

A fan kicked in, whisking the smoke away. "One of

the few vices Gregor allows me." She held up her hand. "I know, I know, bad for the lungs. You have to understand, my lungs have been done three—or is it four?—times. So the lung argument doesn't get far with me. I don't smoke in front of the Somas. Might burn a hole in my goddamn white robes." She blew smoke viciously out of the side of her mouth, looking like a great purple dragon.

Reeve allowed himself to smile at this.

Brecca grinned. Then she let out a great peal of laughter that gushed up from her ample chest. "Absurd, isn't it? Here sits the mighty representative of Deity in the world, sneaking a cigarette and resting her weary ass." The laughter trickled away, and she smoked her cigarette with profound contentment.

After a time she said, "We've got to leave your ropes on, Reeve. For appearances."

He nodded as graciously as he could. "Tell me about this place . . . Brecca. Can I call you Brecca?"

She stubbed the cigarette out in a small round tray. "Oh, please do." She had a way of speaking that was drenched in irony, at times taking on a singsong condescending tone as though she were speaking to children. It softened around Reeve, ratcheted up around Gregor.

"And you don't need to play coy. You think I'm a monster, right? Human experimentation, all gone awry. I may even be mad, you're thinking. She could erupt in an instant, like the Red Queen in *Alice in Wonderland*!" She regarded him with a deadpan stare. "And you'll be thinking of the *ethical* question, of course." She reached for another cigarette, rolling it between her fingers in sensual appreciation. "Ethics. Yes, a nice tidy topic for graduate seminars." Lighting the cigarette, she spoke between her teeth: "How long you figure you're gonna last on the surface once your breather wears out? Don't strain your brain. Thirty years. That's how long the clavers have got. A short, brutish life. And getting shorter all the time."

"I can see why you'd want to try," Reeve decided to say.

"But how come we've got so many . . . *odd people*? Is that your question?"

"OK, yes."

She smiled a sarcastic, stagy grin. "They *want it*, that's why. Hell, they vie for creative looks. We've got to work overtime just to think up some of these body plans! See, if you haven't figured it out yet, this is a religion. It has its own internal logic, completely opaque to an outsider. Why do Catholics kneel and take a little piece of bread in their mouths? It's a long story, right?" She drew on the cigarette, blowing a puff of smoke in the direction of her ceiling fan.

Reeve was still stuck a few sentences back. "They *want* these deformities?" The thought shook him more than his assumption that they were coerced.

"Righto, they want 'em. Seen those pictures in the great hall? They're proud of their *offerings*, as they call them. They want to resurrect humanity on the planet—humans *are* doomed down here, if you didn't notice—so they figure the worse they look, the more daring my experiment must have been. See, subtlety doesn't work with the great unwashed masses. They want clarity. A statement, if you will." She dropped the sarcasm for a moment, saying softly, "And meanwhile, I am trying my best to find an adaptation. Some of the . . . more pleasant Somaformers actually have a chance of living a few years longer." Her eyes flicked up at him, with a bitter edge to them. "You're not so naive to think that one geneticist working with five hundred-year-old equipment is going to make rapid progress, are you?"

"No. So you're alone, then?"

"Yup. The last one. The last scientist. Shit, sounds like a bad story title."

"I thought you had assistants."

"Yeah, I got 'em. Worthless, half-educated techies. And Gregor is the best of them, so you see how far we've slipped. Can you imagine how hard it's been to do research, and keep up on the atmospheric and biome transformations on the surface, and repair the Lab defenses and systems, all the while carrying out a decent education program?"

Reeve could imagine. It had been exactly the same on Station. He nodded.

"Add to that, we've got processions and rituals and the goddamned pretense that all this has to do with Deity and our original sin of terraforming." She glared at him momentarily. "*You* try being a sixty-three-year-old glamour girl doing a show a day."

She sighed. "Look. I'm an old woman, doing what I can in the corner of the world I got stuck in. I'm a colossal failure. But when I'm gone Gregor takes my place, the spineless panderer. And, of course, he never grasped the science, not solidly. For him it's about power and prestige. Saving humanity, that's just window dressing. So when I'm gone, window dressing is all that's left." Her voice became eerily quiet. "If you think it's monstrous *now*, just wait."

"Why did you teach them enough to do such harm?" He regretted saying it the instant it came out. He rather liked this Brecca, but he knew he shouldn't presume on her forbearance.

Brecca gazed at the unlit cigarette in her hand, slowly working it back and forth between her thumb and forefinger. "I'm not sure how it all happened. It just . . . evolved—you see? It happened so slowly, I didn't even notice."

He kept his silence a long while.

Finally she said: "My parents taught me science, and when they were gone, I taught others, and the scientists tolerated the religious stuff because it provided experimental subjects. Then, suddenly, the scientists were . . . gone. They had died out. The science was small, the religion was big." She put the cigarette back in the box, and sat limply holding the container. "I tried running away once. Gregor came after me. We never talk about it, but he has me watched all the time." She smiled a stony smile at Reeve. "You wonder why I let it all hang out around Gregor? Because he already knows what I am: a complete sham, both as priestess and scientist. Yeah, Greggy knows me all right. We're close, in our own sick way. Like a juvenile animal will cling to its parent even if the adult turns on it. That's how important it is to be known."

She perked up, hands on knees. "Well! That was fun. Talk therapy. How much do I owe you?"

Reeve spoke quietly. "Let us go, Brecca."

She rose to her feet, slowly and gracefully, smoothing her jumper. "I'm *watched*, Reeve. Don't you understand? I'm a prisoner here. I can't help you, much as I'd like to." She touched a screen on her desk and called for the guards. "We'll go easy on you," she told him. "No morphological deformities, no health impairments. I can't promise it for all your friends. I'll have to fight Gregor over each genetic plan."

Reeve stood to face her. "Save the girl," he said, "and the thin guy named Spar."

Brecca only shook her head.

"Then put us together. We want to be together."

"I'll do what I can. But don't get your hopes up."

When the guards came, he asked, "How long do we have?"

She had turned away by now, activating the computer screen, which sprang to life in a half circle around her desk. It filled with mathematical equations and diagrams. "A few days." She turned around then, gripping something small in her hand. "Hold him," she said.

As the guards immobilized Reeve, she advanced on

him and drew a small blood sample with a retracting needle. She held the ampule up to the light, gazing at the glimmering red contents. "This is how we begin," she said, lost in the wonder of blood secrets.

4

Captain Bonhert's face was icy blue in the reflection from the display, as several of the modeling team gathered around Lieutenant Roarke's data screen to watch the first simulation. Bonhert waved Mitya over to join them.

Mitya left the station where he'd been assigned to cross-check the calibrations on the geotherm, the planet's interior heat gradient as a function of depth. He had to compare actual readings they'd already taken at the Rift with the output of the model, to check for discrepancies. The science team had worked these numbers many times already, but Mitya ran different progressions to hunt for anomalies. He supposed it was make-work, but he wouldn't have passed by a chance to work on the processors, however menial his task.

As Mitya joined the group, Bonhert nodded at him, then turned his attention to the screen. "Take us through the sequence," he told Roarke.

The lieutenant paused to organize his thoughts. "This is a composite simulation of some of the features the probe will have to negotiate on its way down. We've seen most of these features in our scans at one time or another, and I put them all in to see how our mole handles a few obstacles."

On the screen appeared a broadly layered and minutely detailed cross-section of the globe. Color-enhanced for chemical makeup, heat, rocky structure, and magnetic lines, the display possessed an intricate beauty, like a profoundly complex agate cloven in half. As Roarke zeroed in on the great plume, Mitya saw an inverted V berthed at the planet's core-mantle boundary and crawling upward to break surface at the Rift Valley. On its way the plume penetrated the vast, solid lower mantle and the more shallow upper mantle, where at last it thrust into a region of partially molten rock, and then into the rigid lithosphere, a journey of two thousand miles.

Though the plume was their best path to the interior, it was only a hundred degrees hotter than the surrounding mantle rock. Like the rest of the mantle, it was hot enough to be molten, but enormous pressure kept it solid. Over geologic time it flowed—with the approximate viscosity of glass, which over hundreds of years can respond to the force of gravity, much like the windowpanes of medieval churches on ancient Earth were seen to be slightly thicker at the bottom than the top. The mole, a heat-borer, would use this slightly hotter corridor, generating enough heat at the front end to deform the rocks in its path, while the mantle pressure closed in the tunnel behind it. Station had spent a generation developing the industrial capability to process carbon nanotube for the reterraforming moles. Now that ultimate material would form a new kind of probe, would house a new payload.

Val Cody leaned in to point out a swirl in the outer core, just beneath the plume's origination. "We've factored in the effects of this magnetic flux bundle. This one is rolling around like a tornado down there. We've also got the cooling effects of the subducting continental crust, plus the heat—that's five degrees for every hundred yards we go down."

"At fifty miles," Roarke said, "we reach the melting point of rock, so you can imagine what the rest of the trip is going to do to our probe. Anyway, it's all factored in."

Mitya ventured, "If the heat increases that fast, the core must be hotter than a star."

Bonhert patted him on the shoulder, an intensely annoying habit that brought Mitya's jaw together in a vise. "No, radioactivity thins out the farther down you go, so that means less heat," Bonhert said. "Or, less from that source anyway." He smiled indulgently. "If the core were that hot, we wouldn't be standing on solid ground, boy."

Mitya flushed and resolved to shut up.

Roarke continued. "If we focus in"—here he selected a small section near the core-mantle boundary and enlarged it—"we can see that there are some reaction products built up on the boundary. Our bullet isn't going to get that far, I wouldn't think. But if it does, it's going to meet up with a mountain taller than Woden—hanging upside down from the boundary." He grinned and shook his head. "If it doesn't detonate before then, that'll be its last chance. Once in the core, it's at melting point." He looked up at Bonhert and shrugged. "Sometimes I'm sorry we're going to blast the place apart. Scientifically, the interior's an amazing place."

Silence reigned for a moment. "Losing your nerve, Roarke?" Bonhert's voice was friendly enough, but every eye was on Lieutenant Roarke.

He blinked, as though just waking up. "No sir." He looked from face to face. "Ka-boom. Let 'er rip." He smiled uncertainly.

After a few last adjustments in the program, Roarke launched the simulated mole. Under the initial firing from the geo cannon, and sustained by its onboard thrusters, the mole plunged, its course marked by an arrow as it slowly threaded its way into the skin of the planet. They estimated that at 340 miles the outer shell and thrusters would be either melted or otherwise inoperable. The simulation would tell whether it would get that far, and whether the explosion would do enough damage. It would be a several-hours wait to know the results.

Bonhert watched a few more minutes, his eyes milky blue, like snowmelt.

Mitya turned away, sickened by the little white arrow and what it represented—what it *would* represent in just five weeks' time. He faced the hulking form of the geo cannon occupying the center of the room. Its bulging cylindrical mass of some six tons was shrouded in a white tarp, making it look even more sinister than when crew had been crawling all over it, putting the final touches on its external housing. To get this monster to the fissure would take three shuttle trips, and hours of reassembling once transported. But for now, it was finished. One mole was ready, and two more were being assembled. They'd fire three shots—three chances to kill Lithia.

Bonhert's voice came from behind him. "We've worked like dogs to get this far, ladies and gentlemen. It's a great accomplishment. We're not done yet by any means, but we have, by the Lord of Worlds, begun our first full-model run to test our enterprise. Our goal, my friends, is in view. Nothing can stop us now."

One of the techs motioned from the doorway to the main dome. Bonhert nodded. "Crew is assembling in the main room. I have a treat in store." As he gestured them to proceed him to the assembly, Mitya stepped to his side.

"Sir," Mitya said, voice lowered.

"What is it, Mitya?"

"Something I heard, sir."

Bonhert watched as the rest of the science team left the clean room. "Well?"

In his nervousness, Mitya's voice broke, but he said, "Someone's been coming in here late at night. Into this room. Some of the crew saw it. But it's just a rumor; I don't know if it's true, or if I should repeat it." He tried to look confused and worried.

"Someone comes here?"

"The guards allow it."

"Who is he?"

"She."

"Well, she then—who is it?"

"Lieutenant Cody, sir." He looked up at the Captain. "Probably it's nothing. But you asked me to tell you things like that. I hope I haven't got her in trouble."

There was a longish pause as Bonhert's high forehead wrinkled as if thoughts were churning behind it. Mitya hoped he'd lose plenty of sleep over this tidbit, one suggested by Stepan.

"Have I, sir?"

"Hmm?"

"Got her in trouble? Because it's probably just a rumor."

One of the techs was watching from the doorway. He caught Bonhert's eye.

"You don't say anything about this to anyone but me, you understand, Mitya?"

"Yes, sir. I'm sorry, sir."

Bonhert, for the first time since Mitya had known him, looked a little lost. Mitya almost pitied him. If Val Cody was against him, Bonhert had lost his biggest ally, perhaps even a friend. He turned to go, then turned back to Mitya. "I . . . appreciate it, Mitya. Good lad."

In the main room, crew had gathered in a semicircle in front of the Captain. They were a bedraggled group—wan, greasy-haired, and rumpled. They had been pressing hard for a week, cleaning vents and filtration systems, repairing equipment and welding the superstructure that would help position the geo cannon over the fissure. A group of them had been on duty all night guarding the shuttle. They stood now, leaning on rifles, watching Bonhert with wary eyes. Some, like Koichi and Tenzin Tsamchoe, looked at him with a less charitable stare. Mitya took his place among them.

"I think we've all earned a few moments' rest," Bonhert began. "Lord knows we've been pushing hard, harder than we thought possible. Let me take this opportunity to remind you of the end toward which all our labor is bent." When he had every eye and ear, he continued: "Last night this message came in from the captain of the *Quo Vadis*. Most of my communications with the ship are administrative details, but this message is meant for *you*, the future crew of the great ship. Ladies and gentlemen, I give you Captain Nicholas Kitcher."

A holo sprang to life at Bonhert's side. Before them stood a florid-complected man with great muttonchop sideburns sweeping onto a broad face. He wore an impressive gold and black jacket adorned with brocade along the shoulders and lapels. Mitya guessed him for a very hale seventy-five years. Crew had heard of this Captain Kitcher, but no one had seen his image except Bonhert and his close advisors until now. The comparison with the Captain he stood next to was inescapable. Kitcher was an old man, tending to fat. Bonhert was in young middle age, all muscle and drive.

"Station Lithia," Kitcher began. "We are about to meet at last, and I do look forward to our . . . reunion, one might say. Our paths took divergent courses many generations ago, but we come from a common mother, and I count you as my fellow Terrans." He had been standing, but now sat down in a chair. Around him was a small cabin, sparsely decorated except for a fine model replica behind him of what Mitya took to be the *Quo Vadis*. The ship was, as they had heard, enormous, much larger than earlier ships of the type. Three biome spheres bulged from its profound horizontal planes. Mitya tried to listen to Kitcher, but his eyes were fixed on the replica—its bright cabin windows, the polished metal skin, the complex yet unified body of the vast starship. He shivered. In this powerful construct people lived with the highest technology ever achieved by humanity. He thought its wonders would take him the rest of his life to fathom. Like many in the dome that day, Mitya began to fall in love with the *Quo Vadis*.

". . . a little tour of our ship home," Captain Kitcher was saying. The view switched to the forest biome, with its lake, and to the grassland and agricultural biomes. Then there was a grand corridor where crew in black and gold uniforms milled for shopping and passed by on their unknowable errands. Storefronts pulsed with lights, strobing the faces of crew with flickering expressions that Mitya took for joy. In other views they saw a stupefying control room, where crew, Captain Kitcher said, interfaced with the smart ship through their body nets, using subvocal voice commands. Everyone wore the black and gold, handsome and, Mitya thought, masculine colors that he would wear someday when he had earned a fine position—perhaps even on the bridge. . . . And then they saw a sparkling mess hall, empty and gleaming, vid emporiums with single- and double-seat sense environments, an infirmary of dizzying complexity, and finally a common crew cabin—not as big as Mitya had fantasized, but neat and cozy, complete with its portal to the stars, but oddly curtained with a bit of floral cloth. That would be the first change Mitya would make, were it his cabin: The portal would be bare to the stars.

The last stop was the propulsion plant, an enormous industrial hold filled with massive machinery and banks of controls at two levels. In the darker upper regions, Mitya noted, the crew did not wear black and gold, but common civilian clothes, perhaps signifying their more menial tasks. Then Captain Kitcher was thanking "Station Lithia," as he called it, for its assistance with the raw ores they would process onboard. He ended with a warning to orthong monitoring this transmission that the mission was a friendly one to rescue human survivors, but that if a threat presented itself, the *Quo Vadis* had powerful weapons at its disposal and would mount an aggressive defense. Kitcher ended by saying "Good luck to us all," as though luck had anything to do with their destiny, as though the *Quo Vadis* needed luck, with its power and brilliance.

As the holo snapped from view, spontaneous clapping broke out as tired faces grew animated, and even Bonhert's enemies set aside their resentments to revel in their good fortune. But nearby, Mitya heard Tsamchoe mutter to someone, "A ship that big, seems like they had room for everyone on Station. A ship that big could've tucked in four hundred, easy. Stingy, our *fellow Terrans*." As Mitya pondered this remark, he caught sight of Stepan, who slowly shook his head. *Keep your nose out of crew grumbling, Mitya,* he'd told him. *You're Bonhert's man now. Act like it.*

Mitya stood in Bonhert's quarters, reporting as he'd been told. It was very late, with the science team still watching the modeling runs, while the rest of the crew had dimmed the main lights and begun settling down to sleep. Bonhert was sitting in the semidark, his data screen the only illumination. A small glass of amber liquid sat next to the Captain's elbow.

"Sit down, Mitya."

He sat on the edge of the Captain's bunk, keeping his expression pleasant. It was hard to remember how he was supposed to be. He guessed he made a lousy spy if it took so much concentration, but despite this he produced what he hoped was an eager attitude. *Act like the Captain's your hero. It's what he expects.*

"Tell me again, Mitya, exactly what crew said about Lieutenant Cody."

Mitya repeated what he'd said before, trying to

evade Bonhert's probes with *I don't know* and *Probably it's nothing*. By the expression on Bonhert's face, he wasn't improving the man's mood. The Captain's head and shoulders were backlit by the data screen, making him a cutout silhouette, his face a dark well. But his voice conveyed much.

"*Sneaking* in. What constitutes sneaking? She came in; she has business in that room. . . ." He took a sip of his drink, savoring it. "Val Cody has enemies, same as me. Maybe *exactly* the same as me. Could be people are saying things to drive a wedge between us."

He wasn't looking at Mitya, and Mitya squirmed, not knowing why he was there, and fearing suddenly, that Bonhert knew he was lying.

But the Captain raised his glass at Mitya. "Sorry I can't offer you some, lad. You're young to be taking up drinking." He sighed, and in the pause that followed, Mitya felt he should say something, so he offered:

"I'm sorry if your friend's done something wrong, Captain." Then, at the snap of Bonhert's gaze, he added, "It's not fair. After everything you've done for us."

Bonhert snorted. "I've done my best, Mitya." After tossing off the rest of his drink, he said, "We both know how harsh it is to be isolated." He nodded thoughtfully.

"Yes, sir." It was a bad feeling, to be cut off. But damn if he was going to feel sympathy for this man. "I'm sure Lieutenant Cody would never do something against you. She's been a lieutenant a long time; she's used to taking orders." That was a line Stepan had suggested.

Bonhert was pouring another drink from a bottle at his feet. "And maybe she chafes at taking orders, eh, Mitya?"

The conversation had now gone beyond Mitya's level of comfort. As he struggled to compose an answer, Bonhert waved the subject away.

"We won't settle this tonight. Most problems, I find, are happy to sleep over and greet you in the morning."

"Sometimes they look worse at night," Mitya said, repeating something his mother had often said, and shocking himself that he was saying these very words to Station Captain, trying to comfort—and not comfort—him, a thing that would have been an inconceivable intimacy six weeks ago.

"Night terrors, eh? Well, we have many worse problems than anything Val Cody can dream up. We've still got ash clogging the vents, the modeling work that everything depends on, and then there's Captain Kitcher to worry about. It never ends, Mitya. If you ever fancy leadership, think twice."

"Captain Kitcher?"

Bonhert rose from his seat, stretching his massive arms. "Oh, you were no doubt impressed with our visiting captain and his gold brocade, were you not?"

"Well . . ."

The Captain waved away the response and began pacing, swinging his arms slowly as though warming up to hit something. "He may look like a high-and-mighty starship captain, but never forget, the man's a politician first. He manages the ship, yes, but most important, Mitya, he manages people. And now he's trying to manage us."

"Manage us, sir?"

Bonhert glanced at Mitya suddenly, as though he'd forgotten he was there. "Yes, manage us! He's short on resources, so we negotiate for every last benefit. He's giving us nothing, Mitya; we're paying for this mission of mercy. And even then we won't end up with much!"

Bonhert laughed at what Mitya's expression must have conveyed. "Oh, it looks like a great ship, doesn't it? And it is, it is! By our standards, Mitya, they do have great opportunities. But they've been mismanaged, squandered. Kitcher is weak; he's tried to democratize everything to avoid the hard decisions. It's no way to lead. In short, Mitya, *Quo Vadis* is in trouble."

Mitya's heart sank. "Trouble?"

In a spurt of energy, Bonhert strode to his data station and punched in a command. "Look here, if you don't believe me." More scenes of the ship interior, but this time crowded with people. People winding their way through crowds of shipmates, people sleeping in corridors, balancing trays of food on their knees, eating on the floor. Where had all these people come from? Where were the sparkling great rooms, the tidy compartments? People dressed in assorted clothes, dingy and ill-kept, squads of children running wild, and cabins crowded with makeshift beds and piles of belongings. A view of the agricultural biome showed that its fields were little more than garden patches among shanties and tents.

Mitya felt sick.

"This is the worst of it, these scenes. I'm sure Kitcher picked the worst to show me, to lower my expectations, to justify his damned quota."

"What we saw this afternoon . . ." Mitya tried to reconcile the two images.

"He cleaned it up a bit, didn't he? No sense alarming our people. But between Kitcher and me, we've gotten past the bullshit." He called for the screen to darken, and slumped into his chair again.

"Is the ship full, then?"

"No, it's not full! They've shut down an entire biome because of malfunctions and deterioration. If that had been Station, by the Lord, we would have bloody well fixed it! But they've got factions and feuding, and nothing gets done." His voice lowered. "Things will change when we get there, Mitya. They need new blood, and by God they're going to get it."

Bonhert sipped his drink, watching Mitya. "How'd you like to have your own quarters on the ship, Mitya?"

His own quarters? But he'd *assumed* he'd have his own room, dreamed of it, decorated it. . . . Now he saw how naive he'd been. "Yes, sir," he whispered. "I'd like that."

"Those who serve well will be rewarded. And the rewards will be very great, Mitya, very great. If you stand by me, you shall have your cabin." He grinned, a broad and unsettling smile. "And wear the gold and black of *Quo Vadis,* eh?"

Before Mitya could formulate a response, a knock came at the door.

Bonhert blanked the computer screen as Lieutenant Roarke entered. His face was flushed with late-night euphoria. "Captain," Roarke said. "We hit home. Ground zero."

Bonhert rose. "How many?"

"Two. Two of the moles made it. Smack down to mid-mantle, sir." He wiped strands of hair off his forehead. "Blew it to kingdom come. Lithia went up like an insect in fire."

The Captain stood immobile, except that Mitya noticed he was nodding very slowly, as though the surface of the man was stirred by an unseen current. "Well done, Lieutenant," he said softly. Roarke, exhausted and elated, smiled and left the Captain and Mitya to savor the news.

Bonhert glanced at the dark screen, where he might have seen the *Quo Vadis* still.

"Gold and black, my boy," he said. "We're on our way."

11

1

Day forty. Dooley shooed the guards out of the room. "Leave us, leave us, leave us!" He shook his head as the Somas departed. "They're afraid this office isn't suitable for you, because you'll arm yourselves with stones or something. You won't, will you?"

Reeve, Loon, and Spar stood in a cluster, taking in their new joint quarters, a perk Brecca had finally managed after three days. Tables and shelves were littered with computer components, dust-covered office equipment, stray clipboards, and shards of broken coffee cups. The entire far wall had caved in, thrusting into the office a huge fist of rock and rubble, making the room a dusty hybrid of geology and architecture.

"Because if you cause any trouble here, they'll calm you down with injections that'll make you so drowsy you won't be able to enjoy your transformation at all, and probably won't remember a thing about it. Then what will you have to tell your grandchildren?" Dooley's thin face rippled with a worry tic. "I went out on a limb for you, getting you together. So promise you'll be good."

"We promise," growled Spar, unconsciously reaching to rest his hand on his empty sword hilt.

Dooley faced Spar. "You called me names the other day. That wasn't nice."

"I got just two lives left, boyo." Spar strutted into the ruined storeroom, kicking at the shelving and raising clouds of dust. "That means I don't have time to wait till you finish talkin'."

A worry frown dipped into Dooley's forehead as Loon began sorting through the rocks at the slumped wall. "You can't get out that way—it's a rock slide that goes back thirty feet. It plugged up the whole western wing of the Lab two hundred years ago. We get tremors now and then, but that was a big one." Ignoring him, Loon had picked up a fist-sized stone and was licking it. Dooley watched her dubiously. "You sure she's not a defective genome?"

Reeve patted Dooley on the back. "Don't worry about her, Dooley. She and I, we're . . . base pairs. That's all you have to know."

"You're what?" came from Spar.

"I knew it!" Dooley's eyes crinkled in pleasure. "Mind your Qs and As and Brecca will do your codes and arrange the match! You see, you can be happy here. I know you're apprehensive; it's only natural. There was one time—this was even before Gregor arrived—this one inturn . . ."

He trailed off as Spar advanced on him. "Boyo. There somethin' important you're forgettin'."

"There is?"

"You got business elsewhere."

"I do?"

Spar stood close enough to force the shorter man to look straight up at him. "And you're late."

Dooley retreated, glancing from Spar to Reeve to Spar again. He rapped on the door for the guards. "I'll be back later, when you're feeling more like talking." As Spar walked slowly toward Dooley, the guards opened the door, giving Dooley his exit. "I'll bring some food—would you like that?"

"No." Spar continued to advance, shoving him firmly in the chest and shutting the door on him.

He turned toward Reeve, shaking his head. "He's more of a damn fool than you are." Spar walked over to Loon and crouched next to her. "How you feelin'?" Loon smiled at him and went back to examining rocks. Taking the discarded padded jacket that Dooley had provided her, Spar draped it around her shoulders.

Reeve and Spar surveyed their cell. The lighted walls flickered now and then, as though wincing in pain from the earthy intrusion.

Spar turned to face Reeve. "I like these Somafools even less than I liked the rats. And that's sayin' something."

Reeve nodded glumly. Slumping to the floor, he braced his back against the shelving. Dust hung in the air, and he coughed, deprived now of the breather. His list of failures was growing long. Here in the bowels of the earth, among the spectacular failures of the Mercury Clave itself, his ineptitude was confirmed. Or perhaps it was the doom foretold by the Whale Clave woman, whose curses still haunted him. . . .

"You know what this doodad is?" Spar held up a spindly length of flexible pipe.

"Looks like part of a computer screen frame."

Spar nodded. "Make a good fishin' pole." He continued his rummaging, inspecting with disdain the spare parts of technology from the last five hundred years.

Reeve was indescribably weary. After his session with Brecca, he'd hardly slept. The Somaformers had come that night and taken blood samples from everyone else, but long after that Reeve had lain awake, his mind grasping at stray thoughts, trying to knit them together. At least, he was with his friends again. He beckoned for Loon to join him.

She wiped her hands on her shirt and came to sit

next to him, placing her jacket over his knees. It was cold in here, evidence of the failure in some areas of the Labs' heating system. He put his arm around her, and she nestled into his side.

"They mean to make us like them," Reeve said. "To change our bodies."

"No," Loon said with authority.

"We'll still be who we are," Reeve said. "I'll still love you." It sounded feeble, even to himself.

"No," she said. "I am my body."

"We're more than that. Aren't we?"

She shook her head. As with so many subjects, Loon seemed certain of her opinion, certain in ways that were closed to him but that lent her a confident dignity.

Spar was standing next to the shelves, noting Reeve's arm around Loon's shoulders. For now he said nothing, but held up a cube bristling with wires, turning a quizzical look on Reeve.

"It's a coil projector."

Spar snorted in contempt at yet another useless scrap of big tech, and tossed it onto the shelf. He continued pawing through the doodads, muttering, "We been losin' most of our fights lately, Reeve. You notice that?"

"I noticed." Reeve thought for a moment. "We kicked ass with those Mudders in the rainstorm that time, though."

He heard Spar's quiet laugh. "We whupped 'em, all right. Made me glad I didn't slit your throat like I wanted to at first." He came over to join Reeve and Loon. "So, Stationer, how we gonna whup these critters?"

Reeve looked at Spar. It was bravado he saw, but it heartened him.

Drawing in the dust at his feet, Spar said, "From what I seen so far, here's where we are, and here's the outer caves. Bet those caves lead to the surface."

Reeve traced in the layout of the great atrium and what he'd seen of Brecca's wing. "Maybe there's a diagram of the place we could get our hands on."

"Yeah, and maybe Lithia will crack open the cliff and spit us out of here." Spar grinned his crooked grin at Reeve. "You're too sour for her to stomach more 'n a few days."

Reeve tossed back, good-naturedly, "You're no great prize yourself."

They sat quietly a long while, Spar picking at his teeth with his tongue and staring beyond Reeve's shoulder. At last he said, "Don't know I'm gonna let 'em stick me with any more needles, boy."

"It's better than dying, my friend." Wasn't it? If it came to that, Reeve mused, wouldn't they choose to live, as many unwilling Somaformers had chosen before them? Reeve watched as Spar's face hardened.

"That's for Mam to say."

As these dark words sank in, Spar put a hand on his shoulder. "Could be we'll climb out of this hole yet. We bamboozled the rats, didn't we?"

Reeve closed his eyes. He should have died in the shuttle crash if he was going to be stopped here, in this rocky cell. He should never have met Loon and Spar if it was for nothing. Could they come all this way and still fail?

"There's something I've got to do," he heard himself say.

He hadn't known he was going to say it, but he knew it was right and past time for them to know. It was hard to look them in the face, to say what his people had in mind, but he pushed aside the shame of it and, beginning with his last coldwalk on Station, told them everything. Gabriel Bonhert. The ship coming. What he had to do. Spar and Loon watched him in dreadful silence. He felt their eyes on him, painfully, but he plunged on, sparing nothing. It was their world. They deserved to know.

Spar looked at Reeve sideways, in that old, suspicious way. "Ain't nobody can blow up a world."

"I wish that were true. But it's not."

Spar shook his head. "This what happens when you give crazy folks big tech."

It was hardest of all to look at Loon. When he forced himself to face her, she nodded at him solemnly. "You will go. To stop him."

They sat then for a long while, as Spar muttered. He kept shaking his head, saying, "Ain't nobody can do a thing like that."

Reeve felt ashamed. After all, it was his people that had brought this doom on the world. He wondered again about what blame he shared, and whether, as Kalid said, betrayal spread its stain over many people and years.

After a time Dooley came with food, as promised. Then, seeing their mood and failing to engage anyone in conversation, he left. No one touched the food.

"Reeve." Spar's voice was gravelly and low. "Remember how you said you got no clave?" At Reeve's nod, Spar continued: "Well, I been thinkin', that's no good. Specially now, things bein' as bad as they are. It ain't a good way to die, without a clave."

"No." Reeve thought of Station, and wondered if it had ever been his clave, truly. All those years of coldwalks, watching the great churning globe below, he'd felt the pull of the planet claiming him. Maybe it was what was wrong with him from the beginning. No clave.

"He needs a clave," Loon pronounced.

"I know that," Spar said. "So I figure he might as well have mine." Spar avoided Reeve's look while he continued: "Stillwater ain't a bad clave. Had its great warriors, its share of claver glory. It ain't the biggest or the grandest clave, but it might do if a man wasn't too picky."

Reeve couldn't speak for a moment.

"You can think about it, if you want. You always think 'bout stuff a good bit."

"I don't need to think about this one, Spar. I'd be honored."

Spar grinned. "Well, I don't know 'bout *honored*— you ain't seen our little clave. It's about as pretty as a warthog's hind quarters, and folks there think a soup ladle's big enough tech for them. But it's got its qualities. Might do in a pinch."

Loon got up on her knees and hugged Spar. He returned the hug stiffly, saying, "Now don't get all ripped up—this ain't nothin' but what's right. Only thing is, the adoption ceremony don't go right without some decent food. Back at the Stillwater, we'd roast a deer. A wild pig wouldn't go bad, either."

"Well . . ." Reeve looked at the meal pouches Dooley had brought.

Spar grimaced. "Might have to do."

Loon shook her head. "No Mercury food."

Spar sighed deeply. "Well, you ready for this thing, Reeve-boy?"

Loon put her hand on Reeve's arm, urging him up. "Do it now. Before."

Before they change us. Before I'm not Loon anymore was what she said, and didn't.

They got to their feet and followed Spar over to the blasted wall, with its rubble of rocks and sand.

"Looks more like home than the mess over there." Spar shook his head. "Times like this a man could use a good sword. Somethin' about swearing on a sword that helps things take real good."

He positioned Reeve in front of him. Their tread had kicked up a small cloud of dust that flickered bright and dark in the faltering wall lights. "Reeve Calder," Spar said. "You got no clave, that right?"

"I have no clave."

"Now that you are among us and seen our faults and the limits of our larder, are you for throwin' in your lot with us, and stickin' around till the end, whenever that might be?"

Till the end. Yes, he'd known all the way from the swamp that he would stay until the end. "Yes, I am." His voice was a whisper.

"And you'll stand by any of Stillwater Clave against any other clave, and count any Stillwater life as your life, and share all with all?"

"I will."

"And whatever the Lady wills, you will accept, for the sake of her watching over our clave?"

"I will accept." He felt Loon's hand in his. "Whatever the Lady wills."

Spar nodded slowly. "So then, if you're for stickin' with us, say who your clave is, so all can hear."

"My clave is Stillwater Clave. And it always has been." His eyes met Spar's.

"Well then." Spar's voice came in a low whisper. "Count yourself a Stillwater, Reeve."

Loon stood between them, her hand stretched out. A small mound of soil was in her palm. The two men each took a pinch of it. When Reeve put it on his tongue, it turned to a rich mud, part saliva and part soil.

Spar embraced Reeve, clapping him on the back, while Loon spun around in three quick twirls, a startling show of coordination. The expression on her face was luminous. She grabbed Reeve's hand and spun him around with her until the room swirled and they both got dizzy and sank to their knees, breathless.

Spar nodded, saying, "Man's got to have a clave."

2

Salidifor sat across from her, his chair surrounding him on three sides and overhead. Nerys found these chairs disconcerting, as though they would swallow her up, but she sensed that Salidifor found them comforting. His arms rested on indentations in his chair. She was coming to know the ridges in his face and thought she might be able to identify Salidifor in a group of orthong even without the gray line running down the side of his face. It would probably be easier to distinguish the females, since their arms, with their feint gray streakings, were exposed by the sleeveless tunics; but Nerys had seldom seen a weaver except for glimpses in the outfold.

This evening Salidifor served barley soaked in an aromatic herbed sauce. A sprinkling of raisins, plump from stewing, dotted the mixture. Nerys nodded in appreciation, but didn't pick up her fork.

<What is lacking?> Salidifor asked, in his way of indulging her questions.

Little by little Salidifor had grown to tolerate her wish for language instruction. Usually, Nerys kept the subject mundane, so that Salidifor wouldn't take offense and cut off the lesson. Thus they discussed Nerys' berm, how the women organized themselves, the room in which Salidifor and Nerys met, its construction and amenities, and, of course, food. He took interest in her meal preferences, but was less willing to discuss how it was prepared. When a translucent tip of claw would peek out from the creature's great paw, Nerys would dig into her meal and compliment him on the taste, or suggest improvements.

Progress was slow at first, with Salidifor spelling the meanings of signs, using the common language. The women had explained to her that the orthong could read the common language, but that they refused to allow the women to communicate with their lords in writing. What discourse took place would be on orthong terms, in sign. Nevertheless, as Nerys' vocabulary soared, she edged into more complicated, conceptual topics. But it was lengthy and frustrating to say even something as simple as *I would rather learn than eat.*

<Among my people, it is . . . not respectful to eat in front of someone,> she said. It was a line of questioning she had avoided until now, but she felt emboldened today. Her collarbone, not broken after all, had stopped hurting so much, and the memory of orthong temper was dimmer now.

<All the human women do so.>

<Yes. But orthong . . . do not take any meal for themselves.>

Salidifor's eyes gleamed emerald green. <What is lacking?>

<To know how you eat.>

He sat back in his chair, and the hood retracted slightly, as though he might need more breathing room on this one.

She asked if he understood her sentence, and he raised his chin: Yes. Still, he said nothing.

Nerys ate in silence for a while, afraid she had gone too far.

Then he said, <We do not eat.>

<What instead?>

A claw slipped out on his right hand, and slid back. She quickly picked up her fork, but to her surprise he answered, <It is a hard concept for one who speaks poorly.>

<To be content, I want to learn.>

Talking with Salidifor had become a battle of silences. Whoever remained silent longest could force the other to answer—or to eat. This time, Nerys won. Salidifor answered: <Sometimes it is called deep walking.> The freewomen suspected that orthong drew in nourishment with their feet, since they had been observed to take water that way. Nerys leaned forward in excitement. He continued: <You have a word for the world?>

<For Lithia?>

<For the small parts of the world?>

<Plants?>

<Smaller.>

<Cells?> There were smaller things, yes. What were they. . . . Molecules, atoms, she thought.

They had no shared vocabulary here. Eventually, they settled on molecules. That, then, was what orthong ate. Chemicals, at the molecular level. But Salidifor corrected her each time she said *Eat,* looking to the side, his gesture for *No.* It was knowing, not eating. It was deep knowing.

This, then, was a glimpse of how the orthong saw their world. When Salidifor said the females *knew* the outfold, Nerys caught a glimmer of meaning. They knew it at the level of the very small. Chemically. Her heart raced as she considered what she might be guessing about the orthong, what Salidifor might be allowing her to learn. She found herself thinking, in the way of the freewomen, that Salidifor in some small way was coming around, skirting the edge of a friendly regard.

She watched his face for clues. The folded ridges of his skin, which at first had seemed to immobilize his face, in fact moved in subtle permutations as he watched her or signed. It might be surface twitches, or emotion, or habits of concentration. But she was beginning to deduce that his expressions did convey things like surprise and displeasure and thoughtfulness—if she was not projecting her expectations upon him.

Her barley stew was now utterly cold, but still she picked at it to prolong their conversation. The light dimmed in the translucent ceiling as night came on, prompting the wall sconces to glow, though from what energy source, she didn't know.

To her surprise, Salidifor took the initiative to say something. <The human woman Pila made a sound without words.>

Nerys considered this. <What is lacking?> When had Salidifor observed Pila? It was not Salidifor's custom to visit her at her berm, although he had once, at the beginning. He could have seen Pila then.

<What was this sound?> he persisted.

Among all the questions Salidifor had ever asked her, this one was different. It was the only one that he had initiated out of his own curiosity. But now she was afraid she couldn't understand the question.

They sat in silence, with Salidifor apparently unable to describe the sound. Then Nerys had it. Pila sometimes sang songs to her fetus.

Nerys hummed, mimicking Pila.

He raised his chin.

<It is singing.> She spelled out this new word.

<What is singing?>

It was Nerys' turn to sit wordlessly now. How to explain a song to someone without a mouth? Finally she said, <It is deep feeling.> Then Nerys sang for Salidifor. It was a tune from an old ballad that she hummed, filling the earthen room with a sound she herself had not heard for a very long time.

Salidifor sat unmoving for a long while. Then he made a sign that always brought an attendant to remove Nerys' tray. As Nerys turned to watch the orthong depart, she saw an orthong child peeking in from the room's perimeter. It was about four feet high, one of Salidifor's older—or at least taller—children. It was, like all children, purest white. The child saw her observe it, and moved behind a protuberance in the wall.

When she turned back to the table she stared at the spot where her food had been. <I have a . . . deep feeling . . . for my lost child,> she said. It was nothing she planned to say, nothing she ever thought she *would* say, not to an orthong. He held her gaze a very long time, until a lump arose in her throat. <She died,> Nerys said.

He was signing something. It took her a moment to look up.

<. . . important children,> he was saying.

<Repeat, please.>

<Now you will have important children.>

<Important children?>

<Of your lord.> When she finally registered his meaning, it felt as though he had slapped her.

After a moment she repeated, <Of my lord. Children of my lord.>

<Yes.>

But of course they would not be her children. Not only would they not be of her own body, she would never see them or have any relation to them whatsoever. And this great hulking beast assumed that the role of breeder was meaningful to her, more meaningful in fact than her actual child. This insight seeped into her like oil into sand. She considered whether he had deliberately humiliated her, or only casually disregarded her. *Coming around,* indeed!

She didn't dare to lift her hands from her lap. Clenching them hard, she waited wordlessly until he at last excused her, then managed to walk in a self-contained manner through the lumpy progression of compartments into the outer room and down the steps. From the corner of her eyes she caught the movement of several orthong pups as they skittered into the shadows to avoid her.

As she stumbled in a fury back through the outfold, a deep knowing clicked into place. *They despise us.* Never mind the phony suitor crap. *They despise us.*

3

Three Somaformers the size of buffalo shuffled up the stairs behind Reeve and Gregor. One, with an impenetrable mass of brown curls covering his face and neck, looked like he *was* a buffalo, or a Somaform version of one. The other two sported the Somaformers' usual close-cropped heads.

They passed another landing on the staircase, trudging ever upward, their way illumined by the glowing walls themselves. Reeve stopped to catch his breath a moment.

"You're out of shape, Stationer." Gregor had stopped to wait for him. In his spotless white lab coat, his fuzz of red hair gave his scalp a neon cast.

"Where are we going?" Taking a deep breath, Reeve started up again.

"No lung capacity." He shook his head at Reeve. "We've made lungs our specialty," he said, rendering it as a five-syllable word. "Most of us could run up and down this flight several times without collapsing." Gregor continued the climb. "And we're going to the Contact Place."

"Tells me a lot." Of all the Somaformers he'd met, Gregor was the most annoying. He had a calm, superior attitude that needed serious correcting. But the presence of the three buffalo encouraged a certain deference.

"Even a generation ago," Gregor said, "the elevators still worked, or one bank of them did. But the elevators have been discredited. It's a waste of technology, to expend effort on creature comforts that tend to weaken the form."

The soft, plodding voice reminded Reeve of some of his Station teachers, who spoke only to hear their own ideas. For such types, communication was beside the point.

"But I notice you have the comfort of filtered air," Reeve said.

The sounds of their steps rang on the grated treads. Here in this shaft of a thousand stairs were no doors or vents, no visible means of escape. But Reeve scanned everything, as he had been doing for days, struggling to make sense of the layout of the place. It had clearly been built with defense in mind.

"We have teams that volunteer to live in the caves—

without air filtration. One group had subjects that lived to be forty."

"Imagine that."

Gregor turned around to address his buffalo. "You see how he mocks us? Tell me, Stationer, how long were your lives on the space station?"

"One hundred years. Then people made room for others."

"So you lived roughly three times as long as the average enclaver. And perhaps twenty percent longer than we do, in the Pool. All that technology used for your own benefit. Did you ever pity those you abandoned?"

"Of course we did. Did *you* ever think that someone had to occupy the Station, and it couldn't be nineteen million colonists?"

Gregor paused to regard his prisoner. His eyes were burnished silver in the hall light, and in them, Reeve saw his own image, so tiny he couldn't swear it was really him and not just some bearded stranger. "You mistake me, Calder, if you think I resent Station for that. I'm just wondering how you justified cutting yourself off from humanity."

"We always meant to come back."

Gregor's eyes flicked in the direction of the guards, then peered intently at Reeve. "Did you now?"

"Well, I'm here, aren't I?"

"Yes, you've come back. Exactly my point." Gregor looked with satisfaction at the guards, then turned and resumed the climb.

They came to the last landing, where padded jackets of various sizes hung on pegs.

"Access outside. Protein scaffolding," Gregor said, apparently using a password. A section of the wall scraped aside, revealing a small door with a simple bar across it. Sliding the bar off, one of the guards opened the door, ushering in a cold, briny wind. They donned the jackets and walked out onto a narrow ridge of stone set into a sheer wall of rock.

It was snowing. Or raining ash. Looking up, Reeve saw that ash from the eruption still hung in the upper atmosphere after a week. A wan sun bleached out a section of the shadowed sky. On the ledge where they stood, a black slurry of mud made for slippery footing, and Reeve hugged the hillside lest he slip down the fifteen-foot embankment. A depression in the surrounding rock formed a semicircle, in the middle of which stood a man possessing a normal-looking form. He wore thickly padded clothes, and by his feet lay a satchel and several large stones.

When he heard the others above him, he turned in alarm. Where his mouth should have been was an elongated proboscis. His forehead bulged outward in two mounds of flesh or bone.

"We have high hopes for this one," Gregor said. "Notice the trunklike nose? Without a mouth, he uses that to ingest liquids."

Great, soft flakes of dirty snow blew against Reeve's face, crusting his eyelashes.

Gregor noticed him looking at the sky. "That's from Mount Kosai. Olympus Archipelago. A fairly large eruption, even for Kosai. Thousands will die from the particulates, those with advanced indigo, mostly. Those that don't come here for help."

"You help them like you helped this fellow?" Reeve looked down at the waiting Somaformer.

"If they're lucky. Jamey volunteered to test himself at the Contact Place. He has a chance to find acceptance. By the orthong."

Reeve turned a startled look on the man. "You interact with the orthong?"

"Surprised?"

"I thought the orthong only took females."

Gregor's face was bone white in the light of day—a function of living underground, or a function of genetic choice, perhaps. "Well, yes. That's why all the emissaries are male. So we know that if the orthong take one of them, it's not because they're female."

"So he's some kind of sacrifice to the orthong?"

"Don't be lurid. We hope the orthong will adopt him. If they do, we'll know we're on the right track, that one of us has found acceptance." He gazed serenely at Reeve and nodded once, as though Reeve had finally grasped the essence of the thing.

He hadn't.

"The orthong bring us our penance." His face lit up with a rapturous smile. "They are the instruments of Deity to cleanse humanity and transform it." He shook his head in bewilderment at Reeve. "You've been afraid of them, demonized them, haven't you? So ignorant. Your information about the orthong is based on superstition and prejudice." He gazed out at the surrounding cliffs. "The orthong, you see, are the instruments of the Reversion. They are sweeping out the abomination of the Terran overlay, and teaching us to move up to the next stage."

"*That's* superstition," Reeve said. "The Reversion started long before orthong arrived here."

"Yes, of course. But we believe the orthong seeded the Reversion from a great distance, sending catalyst ships in advance of their colonization."

"A tidy belief, Gregor. To blame geology on the aliens."

"We don't blame them. We thank them. They are far, far more advanced than mere humans. But we hope to live in peace with them someday. Between the orthong and the Somaformers, your terraform plans are doomed, Reeve Calder."

"My plans?"

"Your associates at the Rift are the main thrust, I'm sure. We tracked the shuttles coming in. We were waiting for you. It was foretold."

"Gregor, do you have any idea what you sound like?"

Gregor turned the two tiny mirrors of his eyes around to reflect Reeve. "You're about to tell me? A man whose life is in my hands has a quibble with my scientific position?" His voice was very soft, out of hearing of the guards. "Careful. Brecca may have made promises to you, but, believe me, they're not worth the junk jewelry she decks herself out in. Terraforming is a projection of our fear of change," Gregor continued, returning to his calm demeanor. "We try to shape the world to us, ignorant of the blessing in conforming to the world. So perverse. It defies understanding."

"And you learned this from the orthong?"

Gregor shrugged. "No. The orthong don't speak with us—yet. They come for our xenoliths. We mine them from a kimberlite pipe accessed through the east lab wing, a very rich source." He nodded at the large stones beside the man standing in the Contact Place. "The rocks come from three or four hundred miles down. We were blessed with being near a deep magma pipe. We just dig into it from the side, and take out our offerings. The xenoliths have come up so fast—sometimes in seconds—they don't melt or respond to pressure changes. They're perfect representatives of the deep planet. In a way, they're like alien visitors." He raised his eyebrows to emphasize the significance of this tidbit. "We don't know why the orthong like the xenoliths. All we do know is that they come for them, regularly. Afterward, we remove the rejected man from the gene pool."

Reeve had a pretty good idea what that might mean.

"When one of them is finally accepted, we'll pursue his genome to its logical conclusion. We will produce the transgenic survival race. Fit to live on Lithia as it is becoming."

Reeve looked at this deluded, white-coated fool,

hoping for a level of genetic engineering thousands of years beyond the Somaformers' outdated equipment and theories. "The Lord of Worlds is certainly lucky to have you here helping evolution along."

Gregor almost smiled. "I didn't expect you to understand." The fellow below sat down cross-legged and gazed out, away from the observers. His head and shoulders were covered with a layer of dirty snow, like mold from a petri dish. Gazing outward, he seemed to wait for the aliens to find in him some beauty or utility, to justify his being.

"You will follow this man, after your transformation," Gregor said to Reeve. "We'll have to chain you to a post, which is crude, but you're not a believer, after all. As for your comrades at the Rift—we don't worry about them for now. The First Scientists foretold that Stationers would come back again to inaugurate the second terraforming. The second abomination. We don't have the army to stop you yet. But we're getting bigger every year, as the starving flock to us. Even the . . . jinn that arrived with you, even they have elected to join us."

At Reeve's skeptical look, Gregor shook his head. "We offer more than Atlantis Clave ever could. So we grow. Before your people can do much damage, we'll swarm northward and absorb them into the Pool." Gregor cocked his head at Reeve and appeared to scrutinize his face. "Actually, I don't blame you. You're the product of your upbringing. But the Somaformers will demand your offering, and I try to give them what they want."

"Rumor has it they want *you* out of the gene pool."

Gregor looked at him a few beats. "I don't like you, Calder. That's a problem. I always try to be dispassionate in my gengineering. I'm going to have to work hard at forgiving you before you die."

"Better men than you have tried that. You should stick with genetic tinkering."

A flicker of color washed into Gregor's eyes, a slate-gray solidity that seemed to bring rational sight to the vacant irises. But, looking up, Reeve saw that it was the sky being reflected, and that the sky was darkening by the moment as thunderheads collected overhead, laden with black flakes of stone.

4

Spar's face was a scowling nightmare mask, thrust into Reeve's sleepy view.

"Wake up, lad. We got trouble."

Reeve propped himself up on his elbows, blinking against the light. It was the middle of the night, and he'd been sleeping his first real sleep in days. "What?" he managed, while his brain struggled to get firing.

"She's gone. Mam's gone."

The words slapped him full awake. Scrambling to his feet, Reeve said, "What do you mean gone?"

Spar regarded him darkly. "What do you *s'pose* I mean?"

Reeve paced through the room, conducting a fruitless search. He stopped in front of the rubble wall.

"She ain't no mole," Spar's voice came. "They came and took her."

Reeve fought off panic. "No. We would have heard them."

Spar kicked the remains of the food tray. It sailed up into the air and clattered against the shelving. "The freaks drugged us. You were sleepin' harder than a dead man."

A fumbling sound at the door snatched their attention. The scratching continued until the door began to open a crack and a shaven head peaked inside. Spar grabbed the man by the neck and hoisted him into the room. Dooley was trapped, bug-eyed, in Spar's iron embrace.

Reeve peered out into the hallway. It was dim and deserted.

"Where is she, you vermin?" Spar demanded.

"Reeve! Make him let go of me!"

"Why should I?" Reeve advanced on him. "You took her. And we were base pairs!"

Dooley shook his head frantically. "No, only Brecca can decide pairs, and that's only if . . ." Spar's grip around his neck tightened. "She wants to see you," Dooley's voice squealed out.

"Where is she?" Spar growled.

"In her quarters. Hurry. We have to hurry."

"What quarters? Make sense, or I'll snap your worthless neck!"

"Brecca's room. She sent for you, but we have to hurry or . . ."

Reeve held Dooley's chin in his hand, forcing him to look at him. "Pay attention, Dooley. My friend here is Spar of Stillwater Clave. Children have nightmares about what he does when he's upset. He's *real* upset right now. Now where is Loon?"

"The girl? I don't know! She's gone?" The look on his face was so horrified that Reeve was inclined to believe him.

Dooley sputtered: "He'll kill you all, Gregor will! You don't know what he's like. You want to stay in the gene pool, don't you?"

Reeve looked at Spar. "Let's get out of here."

"Shall I break his neck?"

"No. I think Dooley will help us. Will you, Dooley?"

Dooley gaped at Reeve. "Come to Brecca's?"

Without answering, they dragged Dooley into the hallway and tried to get their bearings. A long, dusky corridor stretched in both directions. A whir of fans sounded like birds beating their wings nearby.

"Where are we, Dooley?" Reeve asked, gripping the man's elbow.

"You can't escape—everything is guarded and secure—and you promised you wouldn't, that you'd be good." He was whispering, craning his neck to look down both ends of the hall. He tugged Reeve to the right. "Come this way, and hurry!"

Spar shrugged and they set off, Dooley pulling on Reeve like a man demented. "Brecca's in a fury; she'll have me discredited if I make a mess of this!" One of the walls was caved in along this section, forcing them to pick their way through stones and rubble. Dooley scrambled over debris and started to run, Reeve and Spar racing with him.

They came to a junction of two corridors where a section had slumped, and Dooley pointed to a crawl space halfway up the wall. "In here."

"Dooley," Reeve said, putting his hand on the man's shoulder. "Tell me how we get out of here. Just give me a hint. No one will ever know it was you. We'll go see Brecca. Then we'll just disappear. I have a mission, Dooley. I have—an act of devotion to perform. There's a great evil loose in the world, Dooley, and right now you have to decide whether to trust me."

Dooley looked at him in consternation. "I have to decide?"

A noise of a door opening sent Reeve and Spar scrambling into the hole, Dooley following.

They flattened themselves in the stony tunnel and waited. A muffled sound from the hallway gradually faded and left them in silence.

"Straight ahead," Dooley whispered.

They began crawling through a rocky tube that plunged into blackness.

"What is this place?" Reeve asked as he felt his way forward.

"These are the hiding tubes; the whole hillside is full of them."

Reeve stopped and managed to turn around. He could hear Spar's breathing next to him, and Dooley's fluted breath an arm's length away.

"Well?" Reeve said. "Have you decided?"

After a long pause, Spar prodded. "Don't go silent on us now, boyo."

An anxious sigh from Dooley. "I don't decide things."

"Yes you do."

"I'm not important! My sequence won't go into the gene line!"

"Dooley, think about what you're saying, just think! Is it all about evolution? What about love and friendship? Does your fancy Gregor know more about those things than you do?"

"No." Dooley squeaked in surprise. "Is that the shortest sentence I ever said?"

"Let me just break his neck," Spar growled.

"I don't know how to get out of here—I'm not important enough to know something like that." He began pushing them to continue. "Now hurry, before Gregor finds us."

They scrambled on for fifteen or twenty minutes, until their knees and hands were ripped. Once they had to pick their way across a jumble of bones, including a human skull, long rotted to bone.

Spar's comment was: "A ghost hole. This tunnel's the granddaddy ghost hole."

"A few people have deserted the Pool," Dooley said, "but I think this is as far as they get. Most people think the tubes lead out of here, but they don't, not really. They're just for hiding, if the Labs were ever invaded. If you try to escape, this is what your fate will be."

Spar grumbled, "You sure you ain't mixin' up your fate and mine?"

"Shhh." Dooley had stopped. "This way." He turned into a side tunnel, Reeve and Spar close behind him. "We're here."

"And a fine spot it is, too." Spar coughed at the cloud of dust their passing had raised. "This where your Brecca is?"

A flash of light was his answer. Then it was pitch black again. Dooley had disappeared. In another moment, Brecca's face appeared in front of them, surrounded by a halo of light.

"Nice of you to drop in, boys." She smiled, a big, pasted-on grin. Then her face collapsed into a snarl. "Now get the hell in here."

Reeve felt himself yanked forward, and he toppled out of the tube and through a hole in Brecca's wall. As he sat stunned for a moment on the floor, he saw Brecca hoist Spar through and then drop a wall hanging back over the hole.

The three men were sprawled on the floor staring up at a woman dressed in an enormous brocaded nightgown with gray hair cascading around her shoulders. She took a huge drag on a cigarette and blew out the smoke viciously, contemplating them like a crocodile its next meal.

Spar muttered, "Am I dead, or do I just wish I was?"

"And who is this delightful gentleman?" Brecca said in a sprightly yet menacing manner.

"He insisted on coming, Ministrator," Dooley squeaked.

She cocked her head and peered more closely at Spar. "He did, did he?" Brecca turned her gaze on Dooley, who reflexively scrambled backward. "And where is the girl?"

Dooley shaped a word with his mouth, but nothing came out. Brecca smiled an awful smile and nodded her encouragement.

"Gone," Dooley managed to whisper.

"*Gone?*" Brecca trumpeted.

"Shhhh," Dooley said, then flinched at the expression on her face. "You said we had to be quiet."

She bowed her head. "Well, so I did. Thank you so *much* for reminding me, Dooley." She turned sweetly to the other two men. "Good staff are the backbone of my organization, as you can see." She stubbed the cig-

arette out into a dish with a downward twist that deci-
mated the butt. "Dooley, kindly take the thin
gentleman here into my office. Make sure the outside
door is locked." She turned to Spar. "That's for your
protection. There's a mad priest out in these hallways
who will murder you on sight. In my present mood, I
don't much care if he does." She smiled perkily. "Off
you go."

Dooley scrambled to his feet and tugged on Spar's
arm until Spar reluctantly followed.

"I'll be OK, Spar," Reeve said.

"You about as OK as a fly with the legs torn off,
boy," Spar said on his way into the next room.

When the door clicked shut, Brecca turned to face
Reeve. They were obviously in her bedroom. A large
canopied bed occupied the center of the room, its covers rumpled.

"Dooley tells me you're in love with this girl, is that
right?"

"Yes."

"Then if you want me to save her, tell me where
she is."

"They drugged us. When we woke up, she was
gone."

She swore. "Damn Gregor to fourteen hells! He got
to her first, the slimy, rat-faced pedant!" She began
pacing in front of him. "And Mr. Calder here, he just
threw his sweetie's life away, by not telling Brecca all
he knew. *Not telling me.*" She swung around to glare at
him. "Did you think I was going to dissect her?"

"Tell you what?"

She shook her head, her ashen hair rippling about
her shoulders. "No, no, no. You're *way* beyond that
maneuver. *I know* about her. I have her genetic analysis. So, you see, I know more about her than you will
ever know about her, and your little dumb act is a
dead-ass waste of time."

"I don't know about her. *She* doesn't even know who she is. Brecca, tell me. Please."

Brecca stared at him, her anger deflating and her plump face losing its high color. "Oh shit, oh dear. This is a worse mess than even I could have planned, and that's saying something." Then, "Turn around," she said. When he hesitated, she said with elaborate patience: "I'm going to get dressed, young man."

He obeyed on the instant.

Behind him, amid rustling of yards of cloth, Brecca said: "Your Loon has been modified, Mr. Calder. The techs ran the analysis well into the night. One of them managed to alert me before Gregor killed them. Now only he and I know the truth. And Loon."

She forced him to ask, but he wasn't all that sure he wanted to know. "What is the truth?"

Her voice was muffled as she slipped something over her head: "She isn't human."

Reeve turned around to stare at Brecca in consternation.

She was patting her robes into place. "She looks human, that's the remarkable thing. No creative morphology on the outside. Robust health. But her alimentary track, her lungs, her skin—her *chemistry*— someone has altered her. Rather grandly." She swiftly wrapped her hair up on her head, securing it with pins, then draped several ropes of necklaces around her neck and clipped on earrings the size of her fists. "Damnedest sequence I've ever seen, and hands down the best. Gee." Here she screwed her mouth into an ironic pout. "I don't know whether to celebrate or shoot myself." She charged toward the door. "Let's go."

Reeve stood very still. "Not human?"

Brecca sighed hugely. "Oh please, don't get queasy on me. It's all a continuum, hon. The genetic overlap between humans and cows is ninety percent, for example. The genetic distance between you and Loon is probably less than that."

"That's supposed to be reassuring?" He found himself wanting to throttle her.

"Her codes are . . . extraordinary."

"You don't know anything for sure!" Reeve blurted. "You call yourself a scientist, and you didn't even notice when your research lab turned into a torture chamber!" He was in her face, but she hadn't backed up.

"I'm *so* glad you got that off your chest," Brecca said in her mock-friendly patter. "Feel better now, do we?"

He felt sick, actually. "Brecca . . . what *is* she?"

"Let's decide that after we find out if she's still alive, what do you say?"

Reeve followed her out of the bedroom, his mind stumbling, but disciplined enough to ask: "Why does Gregor want to hurt her?"

Spar snapped to attention and followed them as Brecca swept through the outer office to the lab corridor. "Because, my dears, when our work succeeds—or someone succeeds in our place—Gregor's unemployed. Fallen from high priest to just a ginger-haired obsessive with pasty eyes. If he can't justify the big doomsday religion anymore, we're left with just the science. *Not* his strong point."

Hurrying to keep up with Brecca, Reeve said to her, "If we find Loon, help us get out of here. It's the right thing, Brecca. You know it."

Her laugh came out as a snort. "Oh, to be so certain about *right*. What about our future on this delightful planet, young man? If she's got mutations for survival, wouldn't it be nice to share the information with the human race?"

They were bursting out of the double doors from her wing of the Labs. "You've got a blood sample, Brecca. That's all you need."

A crowd was gathering in the great atrium.

"I've got her genetic road map. I don't yet know what her journey is. That's in the whole person; ergo, I need a longitudinal study. She stays here." She fixed him with beady eyes. "We *all* stay here."

5

Loon backed up. The priest was very agitated, stepping forward with every step she took backward, his silver eyes stuck into his sockets like chunks of ice. She feared him, but not because of his eyes. It was the needle she feared. If that was how the change began.

"Where is the lab?" the priest asked again.

He'd said the word before: *lab*. He used many words, but never said much.

"Where are you from?"

This she would answer. "Stoneroot Clave."

He shook his head. "We know Stoneroot Clave. You're not from there." His voice was quiet, but his eyes carried his unhappiness.

Though the priest spoke the truth, she would never admit it to him.

"I'll give you chemicals. Maybe they won't make you talk, but they could make you sick. I could make all kinds of drug mistakes with you."

It made her sick already, to think of something trickling through her body, cutting channels, eroding. Her body was all she had. All these years she had followed what her body said. Altered, she would be like this priest—mad, unknowing.

"Outside," she said, looking at the door.

"Outside?" He frowned. "What's outside?"

She outwaited him.

Finally he said, "You're saying it was *this* lab that worked on you?"

"Outside."

He took her by the elbow and escorted her from the

room onto the long deck that looked down on the floor below.

"Show me," the priest said. The very large guards were outside, waiting.

She looked around for Spar. Spar who had stood with her all these months with his sword. Spar who was always here. But he was not here now. And Reeve was not. Reeve who said he loved her. They had slept, slept, as she'd screamed and fought. Tears collected heavily around her eyes. She gauged her jump.

"There," she pointed, arm stretched out down the row of doors. The priest looked that way.

In the next instant, she covered the distance to the low railing and jumped onto it, balancing on its narrow beam.

The priest turned and made a move toward her.

She stepped along the rail, avoiding him, and he froze, holding his hands out to stop the guards from approaching.

Beneath her, so very far down, people stopped to gape up at her. She could barely see them in the dim light, in the nighttime this place made for itself. She wasn't sure why she had jumped onto the rail. It wasn't an improvement. The priest could push her off.

"I guess I never find out where you come from then, do I?" Gregor said, placidly enough. "Before you jump, I'd just like to know: Are there more like you?"

When she'd had to confront a claver on the plains or a wolf in the Stoneroots, she'd always known what to do. She could run, she could sling rocks, she could outthink or at least outwait all the enemies she'd ever known—until now. But here in this place of metal walls and floors, she was weak from hunger and her thoughts moved sluggishly.

The priest lunged.

She jumped.

The square pictures hung from the ceiling by cords. She leapt for the nearest one and clung to its sharp side as it swung wildly. Hoisting herself up by her arms, she clambered onto the top rail. Her swing veered close to the rail, and then away. The movement exhilarated her, like the times she had swung on rope swings so long ago.

The guards were jabbing at her with a long pole. Pulling herself to a standing position, Loon rocked back and forth on her perch until the arc of the swing brought her close enough to the next hanging frame. She leapt onto it. For good measure, she jumped to another frame.

More people stared up from below as the hall filled with Somaformers. The priest was calling to her, but she ignored him, shutting out everything except the decision before her: whether to die or not. In the framed picture below her, a woman's eyes seemed to look up at Loon. The old woman had an interesting face, with nose and mouth combining into an odd mixture, but in her eyes dwelled the calm regard of someone who had known life and lived well. She wondered if this woman had had a lover, and the thought gave her pause. What was that like, to have a lover take you in his arms and give himself to you, as Dante had loved Isis, as her father had loved her mother, as Reeve had loved the slave girl? She pressed her cheek against the metal chain holding up her perch. She tasted it with her tongue, flooding her mouth with sharp, cold violet flavors. Closing her eyes to savor the tastes, she heard a voice speak her name: "Loon."

6

Reeve elbowed his way past the thickening crowd until he could see Loon more clearly.

"Loon!" he called again.

At his side, Brecca said: "We can lower those placards to the floor."

"No," Spar said. "She'll jump before she'll let you glom onto her."

"Oh, damn and double damn," Brecca said. "They've got guns."

Reeve looked up to where Gregor was directing his guards to aim at Loon.

Wheeling around, Brecca stormed up the broad staircase and raised her arms, addressing the crowd. "Beloved! That poor creature up there has special knowledge for the glory of the Labs!"

From across the atrium, Gregor's voice came: "Brothers and sisters of the Pool! Brecca has a story to tell you, of the journey she made, all in secret, six years ago!"

Brecca's voice carried effortlessly: "That's between us, my colleague. And it always has been."

The gathered Somaformers looked in confusion from ministrator to priest and back again.

"Perhaps it's time to share it," Gregor shouted.

Reeve's eyes were fixed on Loon, and hers on his. In all the commotion, he didn't think she could hear him, but he called up, "I love you. I love you."

Meanwhile, Brecca's expression was stormy behind her bright smile. "My beloved!" She raised her arms to encompass the crowd. "Let us gently bring the placards down, and"—here she looked pointedly at Gregor—"my colleague and I will jointly decide the genetic destiny of this suppliant called Loon."

"Brecca, Brecca," the throng chanted. Brecca smiled benevolently on them.

Gregor made no move to call off his guards, who were still aiming at Loon.

"Swing!" Reeve called up to her. "Swing!"

Loon began to dip her body, first to one side, then to the other.

From the mezzanine, rifles followed her, a target now on the move. There was nothing Reeve could do to protect her except urge her to swing, and he waved to her, shouting, "Higher, higher!"

She swooped wildly, following an ever-wider arc.

The rifles lowered. Defeated for now, Gregor made his way around the mezzanine to join Brecca on the stairway. Together, making a show of unity, they watched as the placard was lowered.

Loon clung to her perch all the way down, watching the ceiling recede as though it had been some hoped-for destination. Within a few feet of the floor, she jumped off. Given a broad circle of space by the confused Somaformers, Loon waited, looking small and vulnerable despite the feat she had just accomplished. She searched the crowd, looking for something. For him. Reeve stepped forward, holding out his hand to her, and she walked forward to join him.

7

Someone was shaking Nerys as she lay in her bed.

"Wake up! Nerys!"

She opened her eyes to find Haval, wild-eyed and disheveled. It was dark, by the skylight.

Nerys raised up on one elbow. "What's wrong?"

"Pila," Haval said. "She's run off." Haval practically dragged Nerys to a sitting position. "And Salidifor's here, waiting." She nodded at the corridor outside.

Nerys had been sleeping deeply and now struggled for coherence. Pila had run off—but couldn't she leave if she wished? The young woman had given birth two days ago to her pup, and had come back to the berm, subdued and withdrawn. Nerys had tried to draw her out, and wrote off the flat reaction to convalescence.

Haval was pushing her toward the door.

"Let me at least get dressed."

"Salidifor's waiting."

"So let him wait." She pulled on her drawstring long pants. "Tell me what happened."

Haval threw her arms wide. "She took the pup! She ran off and took the pup—the Lord only knows how she got ahold of it!"

Nerys stopped, one foot in one pants leg. "Took the pup?"

"They're tracking her, but Salidifor wants you to intercede. So she won't harm the pup." She grabbed Nerys by her arm. "Talk some sense into her, Nerys— she likes you, she'll listen to you. This has never happened before. It could get bad."

Nerys hurried outside and down the berm steps to join Salidifor. A thinning of the darkness showed that dawn was near.

She noted Salidifor's glare. <She won't hurt the pup, Salidifor. She . . . has affection for it.>

<You will make sure she does not inflict harm.>He headed out of the courtyard directly into the outfold.

<Was that a *Please*?> she signed behind his back.

Proceeding her, Salidifor cleared away the nighttime cobwebs and dew from the rubbery growths of the forest. Nerys, like all the women, stayed on the paths, partly because they were the quickest routes, and partly out of a sense that they were not welcome in the pathless interior spaces. Now, in the midst of a great section of lavender stalks as high as her knees, Nerys quickly became disoriented. So much of the place looked the same, with its unnatural uniformity, until a change of color announced a new set of growths. The purple columns glowed slightly, adding some light to the journey.

<What will happen when we find them?> Nerys asked.

Salidifor's face took on a pale lavender cast from the forest growths. <You must tell what the madwoman will do.>

<She's not mad. She's . . . distressed. She is confused about what it means to birth this pup; she thinks she is like a mother.>

To her surprise, Salidifor answered, <She *is* like a mother.>

<Well then, she is visiting her pup.>

<She will not visit.>

Nerys let her blank stare convey the stupidity of his comment. As they continued, they crossed into a bright yellow mass of shoulder-high polyps. Buds studded their sides. They waded across a small stream, and Nerys noticed that the water carved the yellow growths at the bottom, sculpting them like a sandbank. On the other side, an object caught her attention. Protruding from the side of a yellow polyp was what looked like a sleeve, as though a coat had been consumed by the polyp. Then she saw that the growths in this area were full of discarded clothing, partially subsumed by the vegetative matter.

Letting this go for now, Nerys pressed her point about Pila: <This *mother* has emotions, Salidifor. We're emotional beings, not vegetables like your forest.> Here she waved at the outfold.

Salidifor spoke as they hurried on, side by side. <This we know. You have emotions. You must be content.>

<Yes. But why?> When he was mute on this issue, she pressed on: <So we'll stay?>

<You stay because of food. But you must be content for the pups.>

This was an odd idea, since the women weren't allowed so much as a single touch of their issue.

A few birdcalls threaded down from a huge wall of moss-green pillars some twenty yards away. Salidifor turned for a moment toward this deeper forest and paused, scanning for something.

As he tramped on through the purple grass, she ran to catch up with him, fired suddenly by an idea. <But the pups *notice*, don't they? Inside us. It's not good for them if we're upset.>

<No,> Salidifor signed. <It is not.>

Nerys laughed. Her merriment echoed off the flat wall of green they were approaching.

The sound stopped Salidifor in his tracks. He looked at her with what seemed some alarm.

Facing him, Nerys grinned. <Don't worry. That was laughter. A sound we make when something is funny.>

Salidifor knew the concept *funny*. Or knew it as much as he could. They had spent a couple hours one afternoon trying to define it. They had finally left it at: a sudden sensation of simple happiness over a surprise. Which drained it of every ounce of amusement, but seemed the best they could do. Outright laughter, however, he had apparently never heard, not this close up.

<What is the surprise?> Salidifor asked.

Nerys answered: <That some of the human women think you actually *care* about them.> She signed the word *care* twice for emphasis.

<We do care.>

Nerys snorted. <No, Salidifor, you don't. Trust me on this one.>

<You are difficult to understand,> he waved at her.

<Not really. You just never tried.>

Salidifor ducked into the stand of green pillars. Nerys paused before following him. She was trembling with anger. The women had always known that if they went to the orthong they would be breeders; if your scruples didn't allow it, you stayed in your clave. So maybe she was developing scruples. Or maybe it was the subtle manipulation that rancored. The orthong had raised expectations of emotional succor and intimacy, and the self-styled *freewomen* were falling for it like fools.

A soft shuffling noise caught her attention. A garment was wriggling loose of its polyp. It dangled for a moment by a tendril, and then a perfect orthong long coat fell to the forest floor. The polyp sagged as though it had given its all.

Nerys plunged into the looming green wall of the outfold. The taller growths bled off the progress of the dawn, burying her in mossy dimness. An overwhelming smell of sweet spices assaulted her. Here the columnar growths spiked two hundred feet to a tangled top notch. The sides of the trees were covered in small crystals that shed into piles at the bases.

Salidifor waved her forward, and she joined him at the edge of a clearing dominated by a tall rock outcropping. Here a dozen orthong had tracked Pila to her hiding place, a thirty-foot-high monolith where she stood holding a wrapped bundle as she would have a human baby.

Salidifor turned to Nerys, his face crumpled into a furrow that she took for extraordinary displeasure. <She will not give over the pup,> he said. <Communicate with her.>

Pila's lord approached them. <She has stolen my . . .> Nerys struggled to interpret, but he spoke in a different dialect, using his whole upper body in a robust and flowing movement very different from the hand-signing.

<Tell her she can visit,> Nerys signed to him.

<Visit?> The lord signed this word twice, in consternation.

<Yes, visit the pup. It won't hurt the pup, and it will make her content.> Nerys looked up at Pila, but the woman didn't take any note of the gathering below her. She just stood staring into the outfold.

The two orthong were talking. It was a new language, one she couldn't understand. Salidifor interpreted. The gist of it was that no, she must never visit.

At last Nerys called up to Pila, "Sweet one, listen to me. You don't want to harm that baby. You know you don't. Let me come up and we'll talk." Pila said nothing, and Nerys began to climb. She lost sight of Pila as she grappled with the rock in finding a route to the top, but after a few minutes she hauled herself onto the narrow summit where Pila now crouched down, clasping the bundle close to her body.

"My baby," she said.

"Can I see?"

A look of suspicion crossed Pila's face, but she drew aside the blanket. The infant's face was traced over with a network of many lines, the apparent precursor of the more familiar skin ridges. Its eyes were wide open, the color of spring buds of green.

"His father misses him, and we must give him back, Pila."

She shook her head.

"There are ten strong orthong males down there. They will take the babe, and they will punish us all. Give me the babe, Pila."

Tears came to the young woman's eyes, and Nerys moved to embrace her. As the woman wept, Nerys held her and rocked her until the forest grew bright. Light cascaded from the tall canopy, sparkling from the sides of the crusted trees.

Nerys took the pup. She extended her hand to Pila, and they walked to the edge, where Nerys negotiated her way down the first drop. When she found a place with surer footing, she turned back to see that Pila had not followed. "Pila?"

From out of sight, Pila responded, "I'm not coming."

The pup stirred in Nerys' arms. To her surprise, it struggled to a position of looking over her shoulder. She had assumed it was as helpless as a human newborn.

"What do you mean, you're not coming?" This question was answered with silence.

"Come down, hon. I'll help you get through this. You will get through this, I promise."

"Did *you*?"

"Did I what?"

"Get over your babe?"

The question bored into her. *Anar*. Nerys' eyes blurred to the green and gold of the outfold, seeing only washes of colors, like the love and grief within her. What could she answer? "I got through it," she said. "Not over it." As the pup wriggled in her arms, she decided to climb down and deliver it safely to the orthong before returning for Pila. Carefully finding her footholds, she made her way down. Pila's lord met her, snatching the bundle from her arms. Then, to her alarm, he passed the pup to another orthong and started scaling the rock with a ferocious burst of speed.

Before she had time to think, Nerys was scrambling after him. Her fingers were raw from clawing at the rock, but she pulled herself at last to the top. In front of her, the orthong lord was standing over Pila. Blood streamed from her neck.

"No! Pila!" Nerys rushed to her side, oblivious to the orthong towering above. Blood spurted from the severed artery, and from her windpipe; her last lungful of air frothed out in a red foam. A convulsion rocked her body. With equanimity, the lord swept past Nerys and descended, having dealt out his punishment to Pila.

"Salidifor!" Nerys shouted, hearing her wail rush into the outfold. Though she pressed her hand against Pila's wound, blood surged between her fingers. "Pila," she whispered, "Pila . . ." But Pila had lost consciousness. From below came the scraping noises of Salidifor's ascent, and then he was standing atop the outcropping, watching as she pleaded with her eyes. Moving forward at last, he crouched at her side. Then he did something rare: He touched Pila. His large paw covered her entire neck, and he held it firmly.

<Save her,> Nerys said to him, but he was intent on Pila's wound. The three of them remained motionless for a long while, Nerys wondering if Salidifor's touch might bring a miraculous healing. But even orthong

healing had limits. When Salidifor finally stood, Nerys knew Pila was gone. The savagery of her death, and its loneliness here on this rock, caused Nerys to shiver. She looked up at Salidifor. She couldn't read his expression, but she wouldn't have been greatly surprised if it had been indifference. His eyes, with their deep green, might have been glass marbles, for all that the creature saw.

One thing especially he didn't see, and that was Nerys' new advantage. If having content women was important, how content would the women be to learn that the orthong had had no mercy on Pila? How content would they be to learn that the orthong had slit her throat like a sacrificial goat?

As Salidifor turned to go, Nerys said something, and he stopped to face her. She did not bother with sign. "You understand our speech, don't you?"

He towered over her, watching her impassively, his right hand painted in blood.

"You heard me call out, and you heard your name. You understand our speech." Rolling past Salidifor's silence, she said: "But it's beneath you to allow human speech, so you require us to sign, as a show of submission. At the berm, they'll be interested in that. And your murder of Pila here today." She kneeled down and covered Pila's face and chest with her jacket. "Among my people, it's customary to cover the face of one who has died." She gazed up at him. "But it is not our custom to take a life for such a small crime. So you can see the trouble you're in."

Salidifor signed, <This should not have happened.> He was not bothering to deny that he understood her speech—a small victory, Nerys thought, but not enough. Not by a long shot.

"You're damn right this shouldn't have happened." Then she jumped to the core of it. "*I am not content, Salidifor*. And maybe a bunch of us aren't going to be anymore." As they faced each other in silence, it occurred to her that she might be the next one to be slaughtered. She threatened the orthong charade with their breeders. Salidifor, or one of the others, could easily kill her for that.

But he merely signed, <Do not tell them.> He looked at her with what might have been worry, and at that moment Nerys decided that perhaps, after all, she might someday witness Salidifor *coming around.* "I won't tell them," she said. "But I want something in return.

"I want you to teach me your language—your real language, not this baby talk we use with each other. I want to learn. I want to learn about you, Salidifor— what you do, what you think about. What the outfold is, and how it makes clothes. What your women do, and where you come from. You can decide for yourself if you want to treat the others like barnyard animals, seeing to their health and *contentment* so you get your pups. But you don't treat me that way anymore, not when we're alone. That stuff's over now."

His claws were out, all of them.

But this was her moment; she had to finish. "It's a trade, Salidifor. You don't have much to lose by it. And then I would be content." She hoped her *contentment* still mattered to him. Out of the corner of her eyes she watched his hands, where the stilettos rose from the white flesh.

He signed, <Why do you want these things?>

Why indeed? She gave the only answer she knew. "I'm curious."

They stood looking at one another. Then he said, <We will explore this word *Curious,*> sign-spelling the new word as best he could.

"Yes, as a start," Nerys said. "Then you agree?"

His chin rose in a surly *Yes.*

Nodding, she said: "I'll tell the women that Pila took her own life. And how upset her lord is that she died." She fixed him with a damning stare. "Make sure he tells the women he's sorry about Pila." With elaborate patience, she added: "Among my people, we say *I'm sorry* when someone dies."

Maybe they could start their lessons with some basics on manners.

12

1

Day fifty. An otter cut a V through the glassy water, a silent arrow heading for the middle of the lake. Reeve watched the simulation as he sat, arms around knees, in Brecca's special room. Behind him, on the opposite wall, the sunset was lingering on the tops of the snow-laden mountain peaks.

Except for the otter and a blue heron, folded into flight mode and skimming near the far shore, Reeve was alone. Spar and Loon were somewhere else in this underworld place, sequestered for the further uses of the Somafools, as Spar called them. As spiders collected and stored food, the Somaformers collected and stored genetic material, and the bearers of such: people. It was not enough, Brecca had said, to have the genes; one must look at what they wrought. But when she and her Labs had studied Loon for a year or a decade or a lifetime, Reeve mused, they still wouldn't know the real Loon, the Loon who swam in the cold Inland Sea like a seal, or scaled the distilling towers in the Jupiter Dome, or searched the cliffs from the deck of the *Cleopatra,* wild-eyed upon hearing her name.

He would have cried if he could remember how.

But he had forgotten, except for the body memory of tears swelling his throat like a water balloon, and swallowing them back. He hadn't cried for the Station, that blooming flower of light, fueled by plutonium and flesh. He hadn't cried for Cyrus, unsure if he had the right to cry for a man who'd wished for a different son. Or for Marie, alone now in an alien land. But he wished he could let the tears come for Loon.

Dry-eyed, he picked at the food they'd left for him as dusk settled over the mountain escarpment and the pine forest below it hardened into night.

"This is my escape room," Brecca had told him. She'd smirked at Gregor, who had stood nearby, holding Loon in his grip. "Gregor tells me this is as far as I'm ever going to get from the Labs. So, if you hunger for the open air—and I *do*—this is the consolation prize." Her face had looked haggard as she'd inhaled her cigarette. "I've spent twenty-five years embellishing the place. What do you think?"

"It stinks," Reeve had answered.

She'd shrugged. "It's *so* lonely at the top. You see, Gregor, why we have to stick together. We're the only ones who can stand us." Then Brecca had turned back. "Spar begins his transformation tomorrow, Reeve. I expect you to be nice to him while he adjusts to his new self. And as a token of my goodwill, we'll give you and Loon some private time." At Gregor's frown, she'd responded. "You really have no clue how to win friends and influence people, do you, Greggy?" And they'd slammed the door, with a series of daunting locks.

In the ceiling of the room, in the last of the daylight, a hawk fell like a stone, colliding with a hapless bird. Feathers and bits of bloodied flesh erupted in the moment of contact, a detailed display on which Brecca must have lavished great attention. Perhaps Brecca saw in herself this hawk stooping daily to shatter Gregor the Successor. Or vice versa.

Dead tired, but dreading to sleep, Reeve stared at the walls as the forest sank into jade shadows and the lake became onyx.

The door opened. Loon stood there with her escort, one of Gregor's buffalo. He touched her softly on the back, urging her forward, as though she were a Ming vase and not just another miserable gene sequence. But, of course, she *was* a priceless vase to them. They would keep her, no doubt, in exquisite storage.

He went to her, and they held each other, fiercely, until she suddenly ducked away. Above, a squadron of bats swooped over the lake.

"It's pictures," Reeve said.

Loon was at the wall, touching it. Her fingertips glowed when she made contact.

"Like home," she said, looking up at the mountain peaks behind Reeve.

"The Stoneroots," he said.

Loon moved along the wall, probing, as though there might be a door into this visual world, this vision that gave and took away at the same time. Reeve watched her, glad simply to be with her. When she finally turned to face him, they were enveloped in deep evening dusk.

He held out his hand, and she came to him. The room had Brecca-sized chairs, and they sat together in one. As a fog moved in across the lake, it brought an impression of chill with it, impelling them into each other's arms for warmth. The soft splash of a fish joined a substrata of cricket noises. It was illusion that they sat beside this lake, illusion that they were safe, but they were battered enough that it made no difference. Eventually, Loon slept, her head against his shoulder.

He didn't want to think about how she was . . . different. But Brecca's words came back to him: *She's altered . . . rather grandly.* Tightening his arm around her shoulder, he felt regular bone and muscle—muscle that let her pole a raft and climb every available vertical object despite the fact that her only nourishment came from the soil. There were no secret binges with human food. She was altered. Altered.

And yet . . . in the fog engulfing the room's walls, he saw her as she was that day, drenched from the swim, flipping herself effortlessly onto the raft, the sun firing her hair and bronzing her body, proving she was no child. . . . *No creative morphology on the outside.* Water dripped from her body unto the raft. For a split second he told himself to look away, but then his ruder instincts took over, and he stared.

Loon moved in his arms, and her eyes opened suddenly. She lifted her chin, moving her nose along the side of his cheek, inhaling him. The touch of her face against his was as soft as an insect's wing, yet it was all he felt in his whole body. When her tongue touched his face, he didn't dare move. He felt the slide of her tongue like a low throb of electric current, and he was instantly aroused.

He reminded himself that Loon tasted many things, and that this might be just a casual taste of her friend Reeve. Her tongue darted out in short, staccato probes. . . .

"Loon," he whispered. He turned his face toward her so she would have to kiss him or move away. He waited for a moment, and when she inhaled the very breath from his mouth, he kissed her, so lightly, so gently, she could at any moment just tilt her head away, and never guess his urgency.

Then she did pull back, gazing at him. "This?" she asked, resting two fingers on her lips.

He looked at her, trying to figure it out.

At last she said, "Like Dante's girl?"

Dante's girl. Did she think *that*? That he would use her like a slave? "No, Loon!"

The fog fused with the night, soaking up all the

light, and every sound. "But you taste like it," she whispered.

"Like what?"

"Like you want me." She slipped one of her fingers into his mouth.

Her flesh was deeply fragrant, and he was breathless with her taste, the startling intrusion of her finger in his mouth. This tasting went on for some time, the tactile sensation of his tongue on her finger nearly doubling him over with longing, and then he was kissing her lips, more harshly than he meant to. By the time he got control again he would have eased off, but she had climbed on top of him in the chair and was straddling his waist, bending over him, and their mouths were joined. In another minute she had emerged from her clothes. It was then that he remembered to tell her, "I love you, Loon," because he would have her know she was no whore of Dante's.

She answered: "I love you, Reeve. Taste me."

They slid to the floor, and he did. Into the deeper night of the forest he learned that, however strange she might be, and whatever her cells might know that his didn't, they could know each other in every human way. The realization would have hit him with profound relief if he hadn't been so intent on his pleasure and hers.

2

Loon trailed a hand up Reeve's bare back, following the line of his backbone. The solidity of his flesh anchored her after the intoxication of his tastes. It was a kind of drunkenness, this lovemaking; she never knew what she would do next, or what he would. And it was also like a storm that, once approaching, must pass through. Reeve had stormed her senses, making her feel wondrous but helpless, and she would have held back something, some layer of herself, except that she thought this might be her only chance to be loved in her real body. And she wanted, just once, to be loved this way.

It was very deep sharing with a man who, until a few weeks ago, had been a zerter, and a sickly one at that. But he was not helpless now. He was tanned and hardened, and had grown a proper beard. And he had a thing to do, to save Lithia from big-tech madness, a goal that might be as hopeless as her own. He was a man out of place, but he dared to go on anyway. She felt a bond to him because of that, and because of tasting him and finding him even richer than the good soil.

For this reason, she wanted to tell him, to share with him everything else.

"Reeve." Her hand left his back, and he slowly curled up into a sitting position.

He was waiting for her to speak, and she tried, but nothing came out.

Slowly, they dressed as a sliver of moon rose over the mountains. When they had settled in to watch the lake catch the silver light, she said: "My people."

Reeve took her hands in his, waiting. He trusted her to tell him, believing there was nothing she wouldn't give him now. And it was true.

"I found out." Then she told her story in the order she knew it best.

"In Dante's prison," she began. "The orthong."

He urged her on. "Pimarinun," he said.

She nodded. "I killed him."

This was where her story began, in a strange knot of events that twisted back from Atlantis Clave to the Stoneroots, from the dungeon to a deep fissure of rock filling with snow, drowning its occupant.

That day in the awful prison beneath Atlantis, she had reached up and touched the orthong on the face. And tasted home. Late that night she went back, folding open the doors in the floor and closing them over her head. Even in that perfect darkness, she could see the heat of the beings in each cell, shimmering in yellows and oranges, especially near the heart. She crept past these doomed creatures, and they slept on, until she reached the orthong cage.

He was waiting for her, standing there, long arms folded around the metal bars. Compared with the other prisoners, Pimarinun looked dim, radiating blue and lavender.

They stared at each other, and she found herself afraid to approach him, now that they were alone. But finally her curiosity drove her forward, and slowly she raised her fingers to his arm and touched him. At the tips of his fingers translucent slivers slid out of their sheaths, and receded. If Dante thought he had taken the claws, she'd reflected, he might have a rude surprise someday.

The orthong skin was suffused with a deep well of dark, tawny sustenance. No longer merely a tincture hidden among others, this taste was vivid, aromatic and heady. It overwhelmed. Too pungent. She drew back.

He also pulled back his arms. Then he signed: <What are you?>

Even in the dark he must have seen her answer: <I don't know.>

<Touch me.>

His hand rested on her palm for a very long while.

It was then he struck the bargain, and when she agreed, he told her the story that he had to trade.

When he was finished, she understood why no one could tell her before, and why her father had died with her secret. She had thought herself human, like Spar, like Reeve—and she was, but she was also orthong. Or that was how she interpreted the story Pimarinun told her, halting and confused, using the slow and clumsy language that orthong shared with humans.

Among the orthong a story was passed, but never

openly, of Tulonerat, chief of all the orthong. She was very old, having long been in the stage of retreat from the world. But among the orthong, transition from one ruler to the next was always difficult, and its uncertainties were put off for as long as possible. So it fell to Tulonerat the duty of traveling to the place scouts thought suitable for habitation, now that orthong numbers were sufficient to establish a new outfold. In her dotage, she fondly brought along on the journey a favorite in-between, Divor. Such immature ones, no longer children but not yet adults, never left the keeping of stern orthong masters, whose responsibility it was to teach them deep knowing before they killed someone or damaged the outfold. But Tulonerat would have her way, and the party traveled through the Stoneroots eastward to the deciduous forests beyond.

Whether the journey was successful or not, Pimarinun did not say, but he told of the return journey, where Loon's story began. The in-between child was, as they so often were, willful in the extreme, and would taste everything she came upon, until the party was several weeks delayed. But still Tulonerat indulged Divor. By this time Tulonerat was spending her days in contemplation, and they carried her in a covered chair, air travel not being suitable for a journey of this import, and ever distasteful to females under any circumstances. Thus it was that the snowstorm came upon them, high in the mountains, with blasting winds, and in the midst of this, Divor disappeared. Frantic, Tulonerat sent her servants into the storm to search, but everything had the taste of snow, and her soldiers were blind to Divor's trail.

She was found, eventually, not by Tulonerat but by two humans returning from a trading mission, who were also surprised in the open by the storm. These two, a man and a woman, found Divor wedged deeply in the cleft of a split rock. Because she had spent a long time pushing snow away from her upper body so that she would not be buried, by the time they found her she was weak. Fatefully, the humans lowered a rope. Divor had little strength left to hold on, but she fastened it about her upper body, and after several hours they managed to tug and haul her to safety. They fashioned a lean-to and tried to nurse her terrible injuries, and during this time she lashed out in pain and rage and, delirious, did great damage to the woman who nursed her.

The orthong search party heard the howls of rage of the human man. When they found Divor, bloodied and weak, their claws came out. As they moved to kill the humans, Divor prevented them, urging them to make fair payment for her rescue. Shamed by the child's good judgment of the trading obligation, the orthong worked the woman's wounds. It was then they realized that she was pregnant, and that her issue was even now undergoing terrible damage from the molecular changes unleashed by Divor's claws.

Those who repeated this tale held that healing the woman's outer injuries would have been sufficient, and that the fetus should have been left to abort. But the orthong party did not wish such an ill omen on this venture, and brought the human couple to Tulonerat for judgment.

Tulonerat had made herself comfortable in a cave they had found and, in deep trance, had little motive to travel anytime soon. So, though it was hardly worth her concern and effort, she decided to heal the woman and her embryo. Learning all this entailed of human chemistry, she became fascinated and finally obsessed with discovering the many subtle points of human proteins and genes. All this unfolded because Tulonerat's skills were profound, and she could, by pressing her hand on the woman's torso, discern the smallest details of her chemistry, and alter them.

Even so, it took days. She asked the human woman what special thing she wanted for her daughter, and the answer was *a long life*. Tulonerat would have also made the child beautiful, to save her from the disfiguring human features so repulsive to the orthong, but the mother made a great fuss over this suggestion, and Tulonerat acquiesced. Then she formed the embryo to live and thrive in ways humans could not in what Lithia was becoming, and these ways were similar and not similar to those of the orthong, who were well adapted, but not yet perfectly. She set this limit: that the changes were for the child only—not for the mother, and not for any future issue of the child. So it was a child for a child, a fair compensation in Tulonerat's mind, however much it was a scandalous one among her party.

And then, growing bored at last, Tulonerat called for her chair, and the orthong party left, thankful to be rid of any further obligation and eager to get Tulonerat back to the outfold, where her whims and casual regard for the practical world would do the least damage.

Pimarinun never said Loon was the child Tulonerat changed. Nor could he describe the mother and the father in any way that she recognized. But she knew. She had seen the terrible scars on her mother's chest, milky lines wandering from neck to navel. Even without her mother's scars, however, Loon would have known that she shared with Pimarinun some primal vein of being.

And then he had asked her to kill him. He showed her where to strike him, after convincing her that he could not, in good honor, kill himself either directly or indirectly, by starvation. He thanked her for delivering him from the degradation of Dante's keeping.

It was a long while before she could bring herself to kill so magnificent a creature. But finally she found among the rubble of the underground prison a rock large enough. Then she waited for Pimarinun to back up against the cage, his head between two of the bars, his bare neck bent forward slightly.

When it was done, she wept, her hand resting on his body until all the colors had fled. As she sat there, she thought of her foolish hope that there was a home for her, people like her. There were no other people like her. And of the ones most like her, she had just killed her first acquaintance. Shortly before dawn she crept back to the upper dome and washed off Pimarinun's blood.

Now, in Brecca's strange room, she turned to Reeve. "I have no place," she said.

He held her fiercely then, as though the strength of his arms could make it all better. And for that moment, it did.

3

Brecca was wrong, Reeve thought. She'd said that Loon wasn't human. But Loon *was* human . . . with orthong mixed in; and if he loved her, it was for all that she was, not just part of her. Not just the easy parts. Her revelation made not the slightest difference in how he felt about her. With relief, he abandoned himself to another exploration of her body, and she responded, as eager for him as the first time.

Finally they rested, and Loon slept. As tired as he was, something kept him from following her into oblivion. Wrapping himself around her, he considered the possibilities embodied in this woman sleeping in his arms.

Loon was adapted by the orthong to survive. If the orthong could do that much, then they might know how to manipulate true germ line cells. The orthong— not the Somaformers—were the true gene engineers of the world. And if they were—Reeve concentrated so hard that he seemed frozen in place—Lord of Worlds, it was a small, dim hope, but wasn't it at least possible that the orthong could help them, that somewhere in all of this was an answer?

It was a very long while before sleep came to him.

They awoke to an explosion of rock and dust on one side of the room. The lake had erupted, and a monster loomed out of its depths, barking and coughing.

"You two better put some clothes on—it's cold in here, and your knees will get all scraped up. But you have to hurry." Another cough, and a flurry of waving arms urged them forward.

"Dooley?" Reeve struggled into his pants, peering through a suspension of dust. Dooley was peering from a gaping hole in the wall.

"Yes. Hurry up." He reached out a hand to help Loon into the tunnel. He looked at Reeve, and smiled a crooked, loopy smile. "I've decided," he said.

4

Mitya stared at the data field as it scrolled interior heat readings, functions of depth and speed of the mole. With heat and pressure modeled, they could forecast the sloughing of the mole's housing, the deterioration of the propulsion unit, and the timing of the blast.

Cross-checking the modeling runs had kept Mitya busy for days. He'd won the post after spotting a minor data slug that no one else had caught. After Lieutenant Roarke finished his rampage about the science team's needing a thirteen-year-old to check its math, Mitya was assigned to the cross-check full-time. It was tedious work, though the quantum computer was as powerful as anything Mitya had ever been allowed to touch. Normally its sheer capacity would have thrilled him—even at this small node where he worked a parallel processor—but his heart wasn't in it.

He kept thinking about the population of the *Quo Vadis* . . . separated into the uniformed and the barefoot: the crew with spit and polish, and the majority packed together like lab rats and eating in the corridors. The bulkheads were dented and peeling, hatchways missing and covered with curtains. It was nothing like he'd imagined. Nothing like the glorious flagship that it must once have been, hundreds of years ago . . .

Mitya stopped the scrolling numbers; his mind hadn't registered what he was seeing for the last five minutes. He didn't bloody care about the numbers or what the crew had jokingly come to call the dismantling project.

One by one his dreams were crumbling away. Since his parents had died with Station nothing remained but fake people and fake hope. He'd been eager at first to give his loyalty to *something*. The Captain could have had it, or Stepan, or the terraform project, or the great starship. But each had fallen apart in sequence, sinking in lies, falling away from him until he was left with empty hands, empty heart. In fact, he'd begun to despise the geo cannon and all it stood for. The planet might be harsh, and it might even kill them, eventually. But it was in some way their fate. Here is where they were. It was solid ground. They were still alive. Didn't that count for *anything*?

Lieutenant Cody hovered for a moment behind his left shoulder. "Trouble?" she asked.

Mitya came to with a start. He poked the tab, starting the data run again. "No, sir, just resting my eyes."

Cody was dogging him lately, eyes cross and voice tight. She couldn't know he'd been talking to Bonhert—not unless Bonhert told her, and Mitya knew the man told as little to as few as possible. But she didn't like the apparent friendship between him and the Captain, and it galled her to think she couldn't do as she liked with a mere youngster. Meanwhile, Mitya thought it a stroke of luck about the data slug, since it lent unexpected credulity to the tale that when honest crew slept, someone—maybe Cody—prowled the clean room.

"You can take a break when the adults do," she said,

embedding her little barb as she turned to other duties.

Mitya smirked, his expression hidden from her. She couldn't know anything. She was just exercising her canines.

A dull series of thuds from outside the dome just had time to register on Mitya's awareness when behind him a shout roused the entire room.

"Gunfire! Someone's shooting out there! Stations!"

The room emptied so fast Mitya was left sitting in his chair, staring at the door. *Orthong* was his first thought. Excitement, mixed with dread, spiked his nerves. He bolted to the door to see the main room in an uproar: Stepan was headed through the air lock with a knot of armed crew, people were dashing for weapons, and Tsamchoe was shouting orders, while Bonhert strode toward the air lock, gun drawn—he wasn't a coward, Mitya noted.

No one had ever said what Mitya should do in an emergency, but it was obvious: stay out of the way—a skill he had honed to a fine art.

From outside the dome came muffled shouts. Mitya wondered if the orthong would bomb the dome or try to overwhelm its defenses with sheer numbers. He imagined pulse after pulse of white-hided invaders, chests bristling with weapons strapped within easy reach, armature cuffs slinging lobs of plasma fire. . . .

A commotion at the air lock drew every eye and trained gun. But: "Coming through. Man wounded" was the cry from beyond the door. Then it slammed aside and a crew member backed in, carrying someone feet-first into the dome.

As crew gathered around, Stepan said, "We're under control. This claver came in with one of ours. Stand aside and let Lieutenant Hess have a look."

Medic-trained, Lieutenant Hess took charge as Mitya sidled into the crowd around the wounded man.

Someone brought a med kit, and while Hess worked, crew pressed forward to watch.

When Mitya finally worked his way close enough for a good view, he was astonished at what he saw: a giant of a man, and very pale, with a bluish tint in his hair. Across from him, he saw Oran openly gaping at the creature. Oran caught his eye and made a face at the odd fellow lying bleeding at their feet.

The man's shirt was soaked red. Hess split it down to the claver's waist and pressed a white pad onto the wound. Hess was talking, saying, "We're going to help you, stay calm now. . . ." He administered an injection and the claver's eyes opened wide.

Mitya saw that what he'd taken for blue hair was actually a blue pattern on the man's skull, under a short brush of hair. The claver was staring up at the ceiling and saying something. Lieutenant Hess responded with a reassuring murmur, while behind them the air lock was opening again. Bonhert walked through, in the company of several officers.

"Home, home," Mitya thought he heard the claver say.

Then Bonhert was talking to Lieutenant Tsamchoe: "They thought he was chasing her; he's big as an ox and she was running like hell. . . . Sergeant Dias brought him down."

Staring straight at the ceiling, the wounded man spoke again, this time saying clearly, "Dome home."

Then, to Mitya's amazement, Marie Dussault stepped forward. Marie, killed in the Station disaster—Marie was here with a giant claver! She stood looking down on the man.

"Medea," the dying man said, his voice oddly deep and resonant for one in his condition. "Now we will live forever? In the dome home?"

Hess looked up at Captain Bonhert and slowly shook his head.

Marie stepped closer. "Live?" she asked. Her mouth

hardened. "Like those women of the Whale Clave? Like the youngster you threw from the distilling tower?"

His face went slack as he murmured, "Isis, I am dying."

"Yeth," Marie lisped at him. "But thanks for the ride home."

Lieutenant Hess frowned at her sarcasm and pleaded with his eyes for the Captain to silence her.

"He's a murderer," Marie said to the crowd. "A petty king who liked to throw defenseless women off seventy-five-foot drops. Don't waste your drugs."

Bonhert took her by the arm and they disappeared in the direction of his quarters for a debriefing with Cody and the others.

When Mitya looked back to the claver, Hess was closing the dead man's eyes.

Rumors and conjecture were all they had for the rest of the day, but it was enough to keep everyone talking. Mitya found excuses to leave his station at the processor and mingle with crew in the main dome, where he figured the best gossip would be. He refused to let himself hope his parents had been in the other shuttle; told himself, over and over, No, they're dead. No last-minute reprieve. No more phony hopes. Dead.

But a knot of crew with more optimism refused to work and stood outside of Bonhert's quarters, where he and his chiefs were holed up with Marie Dussault. Everyone hoped for word of a loved one, friend or relative, but they turned away disappointed when Bonhert came out to announce that along with Marie, only one other survived, and perhaps not for long: Reeve Calder. For a few minutes Mitya hated Reeve Calder and Marie Dussault, hated their good fortune, when it might have been . . . might have been . . . And then, to his surprise and relief, he let it go. He was no worse off than he was a few hours ago: in a bloody awful mess made not one whit worse by the arrival of the woman and the blue-headed claver.

That evening the crew gathered to hear Marie Dussault recount her adventures, a seven-week-long odyssey that held Mitya enthralled. She began with waking up on the crashed shuttle in the midst of a forbidding place called a swamp.

A swamp. Mitya's imagination grabbed hold of Marie's words, spinning them into a vid. He saw the great trees with their feet in brackish, black water, the nets of moss, the darting hordes of gnats, and—far in the distance—the screams of the savages come to claim the booty of ship and crew. . . .

And that was the least of her tale, followed as it was by the pursuit of the savages across the Forever Plains; then her hooking up with two oddball clavers, an addled fellow and a grimy girl; and finally being captured by pirates and imprisoned in the old Jupiter Dome. Marie described the hideous jinn, and their bloodthirsty leader who called himself Dante. Mitya was horrified and fascinated by the vision of the ruined dome with bodies hanging outside and children being hurled from the towering vats of the terraform plant.

By subterfuge Marie had persuaded the leader to take her and Reeve Calder to the Rift to rejoin the Stationers, a journey on a great river through canyon lands with birds swooping over the deck of the three-masted sailing ship. Then Reeve had been lost when enemy clavers swarmed the ship late one night, and Marie, alone and bereft of Reeve, whom she loved like a son, had sailed on in the company of pirates, who'd threatened to kill her if she should fail in her promise to persuade "King Gabriel" to make the Jupiter Dome whole once more.

When the time had come for Marie to leave the ship and head overland to the camp, she persuaded Dante that King Gabriel might take alarm at an armed force approaching and that therefore he should accompany her personally—and alone—to the great meeting between kings. There Dante could explain the extent of his realm and all the benefits of trade between their two people, and describe how the holds of his ship were bursting with rich presents. So Dante and Marie set out on foot, leaving the jinn to guard the ship and wait for their return, when they would bring along with them King Gabriel's finest engineers, for whom fixing the "dome home" would be as easy as turning on a flashlight. She told of how their long hike through the toxic red lands of the Rift made Dante sick, despite the breathers they used, and how, in a rage, he threatened to kill her for the suffering they endured. And how finally she had fled from him and how, with Dante gaining on her and fearing for her life, she'd called out her name to Frank Dias, who, when he saw the claver stumble into the clearing, shot him, and nearly killed Marie as well, for by then she was dressed in rags and looked nothing like the old Marie, a close associate of Cyrus Calder in the life before.

When she had finished, a long silence fell over everyone as each listener thought of all Marie had endured and all she had been privileged to see. Finally someone ventured, "You are a lucky woman, Marie. To survive the crash and such a journey."

She smiled a thin, mirthless smile. "It should have been Reeve Calder sitting here telling this tale. I wish it had been." She looked down at her hands. "I am an old woman."

"A good night's sleep fixes most things, Marie," someone said softly.

"Sleep fixes nothing. You're a fool to think so."

As someone helped her to the showers, the crowd watched her leave, the rousing tale soured by the ending. But for Mitya nothing could spoil the wonder of it all, and he went to his pallet thinking of how he would have faced the dangers of that journey, and if he would have done so half as bravely as Marie Dussault.

"Extra guards tonight," he heard Lieutenant Tsamchoe say, and a squad of crew hefted their rifles and filed out of the air lock to guard against jinn.

5

Dooley skittered along like a rabbit in his burrow. "Hurry, hurry, hurry," he urged. The lamp hanging around his neck swung wildly, making the tunnel walls appear to pulsate as though they were crawling through the gut of a gigantic—and never-ending—snake.

"A man wasn't meant to run on his knees," grumbled Spar.

"If Gregor catches us, you won't *have* any knees," quipped Dooley, "and if you don't think Gregor is coming after us, you don't know him very well. As soon as they find the hole in the wall, they'll be after us. And after he makes me clean up the mess, he'll bust me back to ranks and make my life miserable, which he's really good at—if being good at misery makes any sense."

"Young nitwit," Spar muttered.

They had been on the move for an hour, with Loon following Spar and Reeve bringing up the rear. Reeve's hands were already bleeding, torn by sharp rocks and by a splinter of bone from a previous tourist of the grand tunnels. But in spite of the discomfort, from the moment Dooley's head had emerged out of the misty lake, Reeve had been filled with exaltation. The tide had turned. Somaforming in the Mercury Clave was not to be their doom, not if these tunnels led upward to daylight.

Loon stopped in front of him. "Bleeding?"

He didn't think she could see his bloody hands in the semidark, but he held them up to her. "Yes, a little.

You?" He was starting to speak like her, he noted: the short phrases, speaking exactly what he felt, no room for embellishment—or pretense. She answered him by touching his face with her hands, dry and dusty, and not torn. In many ways she was tougher than he was, and he loved that toughness, her natural relation to the wilderness and its rigors. And now, as Reeve knew, her relation to the new, reverted Lithia.

Dooley had taken a turn into a side tunnel, one in a series of tributaries that led ever upward. As he turned the corner, it threw Reeve's portion of the maze into sheer blackness. He stumbled into Loon. He patted her leg by way of apology and crawled on, thinking of the shape of her calf, her legs, strong and muscular and wrapped tightly around him. . . .

Up ahead came the sound of swearing.

When Reeve and Loon joined the other two, Spar was cursing Dooley, and then suddenly he was lunging for him, so that Loon had to insert herself between them to save Dooley from a blow to the face.

"You son of a jackass!" Spar barked, reaching past Loon to plant a swipe at Dooley's head.

"What?" Reeve asked.

"What? What?" Spar growled. "It goes *down*, that's what. The tunnel is headed *down* again, and nitwit here, he don't know where he's goin'!"

Dooley had pressed as far as he could into the dirt of the tunnel wall, whimpering.

Reeve sidled next to him. "Dooley, where are we headed? Is down the way to go?"

"I . . . don't know. I *told* you I don't know."

"We thought you did."

"Well, I don't. I was just hurrying to get away from Gregor. He'll be after us, him and his thugs. Then we'll be in for it!"

A snort from Spar punctuated a longish pause, and Reeve whispered, "We thought you knew."

"Turn off the light," Spar said. "Save the juice or we'll be worse than lost—we'll be lost in the dark."

Dooley obeyed, plunging them into absolute black for a few minutes, each with their own thoughts. A spindle of dread poked at Reeve as he considered the unpleasant possibilities.

"All Brecca said was *Go north,*" Dooley said, "and when we first set out from the room I knew which way north was, but then we got all turned around and everything, so I . . ."

"So you just kept crawlin' to the middle of nowhere!" Spar finished for him. "I'd throttle you now, 'cept I owe you our lives, stinkin' little that they're worth."

"*Brecca* is behind this?" Reeve asked.

"Yes, Brecca—who did you think? She said to get you two and slice you out of the Pool. She said Loon is her own genetic destiny, and no one should tamper with her, not even the ministrator herself. So then I came and got you, but I brought along your friend— that was the part I decided, to bring your friend so you wouldn't be separated. Now I wish I hadn't."

"Dooley," Spar said.

For a moment Reeve thought Spar was going to apologize. But he said: "What was that Brecca said 'bout north?"

"She said we should go north, just north, and the tubes would feed outside."

Reeve slumped against the wall, knees drawn up to his chin in the confining space. "What good does *north* do us? We're blind as moles."

"No we ain't," Spar said. "Not blind at all, long as we got Mam."

"You know the way out, Loon?" Reeve asked.

"No, she don't know the way out—how could she know?" Spar snapped. "What she knows is *north.*"

"Turn north, then," Loon said.

"We're not going north?"

"No."

In the profound silence that followed, Spar said: "All the way down from the Stoneroots, she kept us on course for the Inland Sea. Straight as an arrow flies. Mam knows which direction is which, and she don't need no little gadgets. She just knows."

The sound of scuffling, and Reeve felt his legs stepped on. Loon was crawling past him, heading back the way they'd come.

Dooley snapped on the light to watch Loon scuttle away.

"How does she know?" Reeve asked.

"By the taste," Spar said, heading out after Mam.

Dooley was pulling on Reeve's foot. "Here's the lamp. The leader should wear it."

"I don't think she needs it, Dooley." But he took it for himself, strapping it around his neck and lighting the way for the three of them, trying to keep pace with Loon, now far ahead in the tunnel.

Reeve wasn't sure if Loon could get them out of their maze, and if she could, *how* she could. It didn't seem likely she could taste direction, but it might have something to do with magnetism, he reasoned, and if she could sense that, they might have a chance—that is, if the rock they were traveling through had not cooled at a time when the planet's magnetism had reversed, as it had occasionally in its geologic past. But their choices were slim to none. He followed Spar, trusting in Loon's good sense and her extraordinary body.

Side vents gushed cool air at them from time to time, announcing alternative corridors that sometimes led steeply upward. But Loon never paused, taking a route that soon was impossible to remember, sometimes plunging downward and once involving their digging out a collapsed section—requiring the group to pass rocks along, one to the other, before crawling on.

After several hours they agreed to rest. They

switched off the light and lay exhausted in the sensory-deprivation chamber of their dirt prison. Loon crept into Reeve's arms and seemed to rest, while Dooley's unnaturally amplified breathing filled their ears.

Reeve must have dozed. He awoke to Loon's voice. "Many people," she said.

Trying to wake up, Reeve repeated: "People?"

Loon was scuttling down the tube.

The three men followed her, catching her excitement. Reeve could smell a change—a freshening of the air, infused with oxygen. He gulped it in with conscious gasps. His eyes started to work again as he made out the contours of the labyrinth, and then a searing hole in the dusky world appeared up ahead. Reeve slumped against the shaft for a minute, staving off a ferocious headache, letting his eyes adjust.

"By the Lady," came Spar's whispered voice.

And then Loon's throaty, triumphant voice: "The sun is back."

Indeed, when Reeve slithered forward to join them at the egress hole, the first thing he saw was the sun, a startling gold disk commanding a blue sky cleansed of ash. The four of them gaped at the world.

"I *thought* I had one life left," Spar said, smiling, "less I can't count no more."

They looked out on a narrow canyon filled with a ragtag mass of people, many huddled around campfires and others sitting and chanting.

"Curry, curry," the chant came from far below them.

"We gone crazy or what?" Spar muttered.

"Mercury," Dooley said. "They're chanting for Mercury Clave, because they're hoping to be let in. This happens every time there's an eruption—people line up to get in." He tittered, his old enthusiasm returning. "Not like you folks, so eager to get *out*!"

A movement outside, and they craned their necks to look along the flank of the cliff. Below them, Brecca had emerged onto a rock shelf to view her new batch of volunteers. The crowd stirred below her, and the chanting intensified.

Dooley nodded his head at the clear sky. "Volcano's settled down for now, wherever it was. But these folks came a long way, looks like, and now they want their chance at inturning." He looked around at each of his traveling companions. "Guess I'll go help them get adjusted. It's not easy, transforming, but lots of times I can help people get into the spirit of it."

"Dooley," Reeve said. "Don't you want to come with us?"

Dooley's eyes were round with true surprise. "With you? You're inviting me along with you?"

Reeve caught Spar's vivid body language, but he nodded at the young man who'd risked so much for them.

Dooley smiled a small, worried smile. "Thank you all. I am deeply touched, because most people don't want me around. Just Lillie, and we're base pairs, so I guess she's used to me." He looked out of the hole, shaking his head. "No, I hope you don't mind, but I'm staying with Brecca. See, out in the world . . . well, you're doomed, you know? I wish it could be different. But Lithia doesn't think much of humans."

Spar nodded, muttering, "First right thing I ever heard you say."

Below them, the crowd surged forward for processing into the Pool.

———————————————— 6 ————————————————

Nerys looked up into the brilliant outfold. A light snow powdered the growths, catching glints of late-afternoon sun. She pulled her hide jacket more snugly around her and searched the upper reaches for any sign of movement.

Here in this glade, a stone's throw from the path, a

series of lavender, velvety humps spread out like umbrellas embedded in the soil. It was Nerys' custom to sit on one, legs drawn up to wait for her visitor. She patted her belly, feeling the answering kick from the pup growing inside her. She wasn't like Pila—the fetus elicited no maternal feelings. But neither did it bring revulsion or shame. This was her choice. She was neither slave nor whore; she was a trader, had traded this use of her body for several things she wanted, among them knowledge, status, and respect.

True, Salidifor could still gall her. When he'd taken her for impregnation, she'd asked how the body managed not to reject the foreign egg. It was then she learned that Salidifor had been altering her with chemicals in her food for many weeks. Not that she would have objected, this being a necessary thing, but she hated that he had done so without even mentioning it. She allowed her anger to show, and Salidifor did not chastise her for the display.

Little by little she taught Salidifor to notice her and know her, to alter his behavior accordingly, even if only in small ways. Small things were a victory, and she savored them even while dreaming of larger breakthroughs.

The canopy shook for a moment. Nerys rose, peering at the vibrating bridge above her. She arched upward pressing her hands into the small of her back as she had seen her mother do when heavy with child. Even though Nerys was only two weeks into bearing, with only a small protruding belly, the stretch seemed right—as long as she never forgot that this issue was not a baby, but a product of her gestation. A pup, nothing more.

The other pup had not yet come. But she would, Nerys felt sure.

It was forbidden, of course, for her to have converse with Pila's pup. The breeding stock weren't supposed to interact with the precious orthong pups, or the precious orthong females, or any other interesting aspect of orthong society. Salidifor had made a great point about how she must stay away from the pups. That caused her curiosity to deepen, a thing Salidifor might have anticipated if he'd been paying closer attention.

Meanwhile Salidifor, true to their bargain, taught her some things about the orthong: that weavers raised female pups and the lords raised male pups, in the orthong way of imprinting sexual roles, chemically and behaviorally. The weavers were the supreme manipulators of the outfold, natural biochemists, pursuing both the physical needs of the habitation's residents and pure knowledge of molecular processes. What the weavers could do with depth and relative ease, the lords could also undertake, but more crudely. The lords pursued political arts, trade, war, and teaching of the in-between, young orthong coming into their chemical knowing.

Males were the apparent lords of the outfold, except that the high chief was a female, one whom Nerys understood to be very old and never seen by humans. She was in what Salidifor termed *end cycle*, which meant she took little interest in outside affairs. When someone of her rank moved to the final stage of the weaver life pattern, she would pursue what Salidifor could only describe as *very deep knowing*. At this point she would never speak again, and soon die. The chief's name was Tulonerat.

The weavers gained prestige from molecular manipulation, each according to her talents, whether in humble tasks like building clothes or growing homes, or in the planetary studies of Lithia, or—highest of all—in the outfolding of progeny. But despite these abilities, the weavers had failed to bear many pups on Lithia, causing their settlement's survival to be in doubt until the human breeders had helped to build up the orthong population. The alternative of nonsentient crèches had been rejected in favor of the emotional-chemical makeup of the human host mothers. But, as Nerys knew, the human women *were* in fact considered by the orthong merely crèches. Animal-like crèches. And human men were lower than beasts.

A movement in the canopy caught her attention. Vikal was here.

The pup stood on the narrow bridge high in the outfold, a small, upright figure, effortlessly balanced upon the swaying footpath. Half-hidden by a bulge from an adjacent tree, she peered shyly down on Nerys.

Nerys bent her knees deeply and swept her knuckles along the ground in the way of an afternoon greeting. Vikal raised her arms and bent forward, her wrists bent backward in a way that Nerys could not replicate, but had learned to read from Salidifor: *You bring pleasure to the afternoon*.

Nerys repeated the movement as best she could. And she *did* feel pleasure—a forbidden pleasure to be sure, for there might be hell to pay for interacting with the pup. Yet the pup had sought her out after the first week, sometimes appearing for only a few minutes in the high outfold, darting out to watch Nerys and then disappearing. But each day the pup had grown stronger and had spoken as her instinct bade her, without knowing what she should and shouldn't say. This glade had become their meeting place, and now Vikal often stayed for an hour or more, and they—well, they *danced* together.

Vikal, the pup said her name was, a short name that Nerys thought might take on added syllables as the pup grew older. Vikal's communication was childlike, talking of what she saw in the outfold—the colors, the tastes—and expressing simple curiosity about Nerys and why she looked strange, and smelled different. And from the body speech that Salidifor was teaching her, Nerys followed along in clumsy and halting expression. Here was a simple sharing free of the endless orthong rules of conduct. It was a relief to talk without trying to win or to defend herself.

Vikal scooped snow from a polyp towering next to the ribbonway. In her hands the scoop melted and Nerys ran to let the water fall on her, laughing at its icy slap on her skin. When Nerys looked up to share the moment with Vikal, the pup had vanished. A noise in the outfold drew Nerys' attention, and there stood Galen.

"What are you doing?" Galen asked.

Nerys wiped the water from her face and turned to face the woman. Galen was not her friend. Ever since they had arrived together at the outfold, Galen seemed to think they had a special relationship. But Nerys avoided the plodding woman, taking up friendships instead with Pila and Odel.

She shrugged. "I was dancing."

Galen's eyes flicked up at the high outfold. "I know what you were doing. We've seen you with the pup."

Nerys' face reddened. They'd been spying on her. She wouldn't have put it past Mave, Himirinan's woman, who seemed to take on her lord's disdain of Nerys, but now Galen was reproaching her for a harmless pastime.

"It's *not* harmless," Galen said in answer to Nerys. "We're not supposed to be around the youngsters—you know that. Look what happened to Pila."

Nerys bit her tongue. What had really happened to Pila was something Galen would never know.

Galen followed as Nerys shouldered past her and headed toward the path. "You could endanger all of us! What do you think Salidifor would do if he knew what you were up to? Or Himirinan, for that matter?"

Nerys swung around. "And who's going to tell them?"

"That's not the point!"

"Isn't it? Aren't you just terrified of breaking the

rules, so terrified you could even betray one of your own people?"

Galen stormed after Nerys, raising her voice louder than was prudent, given the subject matter. "My own people? What about you? You don't care about what the freewomen have built here. We have a kind of peace with the orthong. We're comfortable and live long lives. All they ask is for us to follow a few simple rules."

On the edge of the compound Nerys stopped. "Simple rules like pretending we aren't cattle? Like pretending that we have relationships with our lords? Like never seeing a female orthong, much less ever talking with one, and never touching one of their babes? I don't think that's *simple*, Galen. That's really troubling and profound, but I don't expect you to understand."

"*I* understand." Haval had joined them, followed by a group of her followers. "You want to change the balance of power. You want to achieve distinction. You're ambitious, Nerys. And you're going to fall a long way."

Mave nodded darkly. "I just hope you're not going to take us all down with you."

Haval, Galen, and Mave stood before her, frowning and hostile. A number of other women put down their afternoon chores and joined the group, eyeing Nerys coldly. Odel wound her way into the group, smiling encouragement at Nerys, her white hair lending some authority to her presence. Nerys managed to swallow the sharp retort she had planned, and took a deep breath instead. "It doesn't have to be this way. We could learn something about these people."

"Oh, it's *people* now, is it?" This from Galen.

Nerys looked at her and smiled at the woman's contradictions. "Whatever they are, it's clear we share a place with them. This forest. This planet. We do bear their young. Aren't you curious about them?"

"We know a lot about them—we've been studying them longer than you have," Haval said.

"With *sign language*. You talk to them in a dumbed-down slang. Because you don't need to talk, and neither do they, except to say, *How would you like your venison steak?* And, *Are you content?* You know why they want you content?" Nerys stopped herself. She'd promised Salidifor.

Haval knitted her brows. "Why?"

"Just so you'll stay," muttered Nerys.

"They know we'll stay. They don't have to be solicitous. Most of us would stay for the food alone. It's no small thing, if you don't remember the old days."

"I remember the old days," Nerys snapped back. "I remember being able to sit in on councils and having the respect of my neighbors and going begging to no one."

Mave put her hands on her hips. "If it was so great, why don't you go back?"

Nerys advanced on Mave. "If it comes to that, I think *you'll* be the one to move on."

"Stop, stop," implored Haval. She held up her hands, trying to silence the group. But tempers were high, and people had things they'd been dying to say to Nerys for a long time. They said some of them now. Comments about her arrogance as Salidifor's freewoman, her troublemaking attitude, her condescension toward the other women.

Nerys stood stock-still, hearing them out. Then, when their voices subsided, she said, "Did you know their leader is female? That only weavers tend the outfold because they're masters at it, and can build and change the inner essence of matter? Did you know that they've been traveling for thousands of years, and had come to their last ounce of strength when they found Lithia? And now their women need help to bear the young while they chemically adjust to this world?"

Mave and Galen sneered at this, but some of the others looked at Nerys wonderingly.

"How do you know these things?" Odel asked.

Nerys turned toward her. "I'm learning to dance. That's how."

Odel made to answer, but glanced at something beyond Nerys' shoulder.

Turning, Nerys saw Salidifor standing at the edge of the compound.

A murmur went up from the group. In a rare gesture for one of his rank, Salidifor held a small tray with what appeared to be a meal.

The group parted to allow Nerys to approach him. <My lord,> she signed.

She led the way to the tea room of the berm, the place most fitting for Salidifor, where he spread her meal before her at the central table. There were strips of smoked duck mixed with vegetable-like nodules that tasted like zucchini and corn. There was applesauce topped with cinnamon and honey.

<Your favorites,> he said.

Nerys had to keep from smirking. She was bearing his pup. Now it was especially important for her to be content, and for a moment she did feel pleased. Then she chided herself. *Slippery slope, Nerys. Slippery slope. Pretty soon you'll get a crush on him.* She shook her head, smiling.

Salidifor's face creased in confusion.

<It's nothing,> she said. <Thanks for the nice meal.>

He watched her dig into the applesauce. Out of the corner of her eye, she could see the other women going about their business in the courtyard, trying not to stare. Let them stare, she thought. Let them see how little danger I am to them, when my Lord Salidifor brings me smoked duck.

Salidifor signed, <How are you feeling?>

<Wonderful. How about you?>

He paused, no doubt processing another crazy human question. At last he said, <I have looked forward to coming here today. Now I am here.>

He threw in a body movement that lent sincerity to his statement, and a little wistfulness. It stunned her. She put down the spoon.

<You have a question?>

<No. You surprised me, that's all.>

His chin went up, acknowledging. He had known it would surprise her.

Confused, Nerys bent to her meal, telling herself that Salidifor was just up to the old contentment game. In the midst of this, the compound stirred with the arrival of another visitor. It wasn't until he mounted the steps to the tea room that Nerys realized it was Himirinan, come to visit Mave, no doubt.

Himirinan paused while he and Salidifor exchanged brief acknowledgments.

When Nerys pointedly kept her seat, a murmur of disapproval came from the women in the courtyard. She should rise in token of respect. Instead she turned to Salidifor. <Could I have a piece of duck?>

Slowly, Salidifor reached down to her plate and selected a choice morsel. He fed it to her. From the courtyard, many whispers greeted this outrageous scene, while Mave scowled at Nerys' rudeness.

The duck was tender and soaked in herbed butter. <Thank you, my lord,> Nerys said to Salidifor, allowing herself to wonder which was more delicious, the food or the revenge.

13

1

Day sixty. A cold wind battered Reeve's face, a wind full of carbon dioxide, fatigue, and headaches. He and Spar trudged along the cliff tops, carpeted with tough, rust-red bubbles that made for slippery going and sometimes collapsed under their feet.

Loon had been gone for hours. Though she had fashioned a new sling, and ranged far in search of game, she often returned with nothing, not even an insect. But she ate, Reeve knew. And she had fuel to spare, racing along the cliffs, bounding from rock to rock, effortlessly covering six times his distance, unnaturally thriving where he and Spar sickened. Reeve swelled his chest, trying to find sustaining breath, but the air was hardly more nurturing than saltwater to a thirsty sailor. He gasped, wheezing like an old man.

"Don't go wobbly-kneed on me now, boy," Spar said, narrowing his eyes.

Reeve grinned in response, tearing his dry lips. After not eating for a day and a half, sustained only by water from the occasional stream, and without a breather, Reeve needed Spar's goading. Sympathy would kill him now; he needed to muster every hard instinct he'd ever learned just to continue. He found himself checking his fingernails, looking for blue traces, telling himself that as long as his nails were pink, he wasn't a walking dead man.

They'd argued about whether to head straight north over the plateau or continue on to the great valley. It was no doubt a shorter route to stay on the plateau; but a short route to death as well. Here there was little food, only the Lithiaform flora that claimed these lands in deepening hues of red, an index of Reeve's ability to breathe. It was an inverse relationship.

Nearby lay the Rift Valley, the goal of all their striving. But they would enter it at the middle tract of that vast sunken plain, whose northern reaches harbored the great plume. In that valley, Spar maintained, was the great city Rhea, where food might be found, though the habitation had been abandoned since the Dark Days, when clouds of ash had hounded enclavers from the valley forever. Water was less of an issue so far. Spar had devised an elaborate straining system to render stream water drinkable, but this also entailed waiting for the water to pass through the matted sieve and, cumulatively, hours of delay.

They had been heading west for days now, precious days, when eight weeks of their allotted ten had already passed. By his reckoning it was day sixty since landfall, since Grame Lauterbach had told his story and changed Reeve Calder's personal catastrophe into the world's. It was an ugly fact that when you desperately needed it, time clicked by at the same unrelenting pace as when you pared your nails or did any other trivial thing. There was no quarter given for human extremity, and the trudging of Reeve's feet marked off the indifferent seconds, minutes, and hours. Sometimes, covering the miles in a kind of trance, his father reproached him. *What are you going to do, Reeve?* Cyrus would ask, as he had so often over the years. Now, at twenty-four, Reeve finally had an answer: *I'm going*

*to walk up the valley of the shadow of death. Going to
stop Gabriel Bonhert once and for all, if I can. Or die
trying. Is that good enough, Cyrus?*

The only answer was the audible rush of the Tallstory River, frothing in the canyon below.

He could only hope that the river took Marie to the
confluence with the Gandhi, and then north, with her
ambiguous protectors. He could only hope that she
would forge on to the Stationer camp and find a way to
thwart Gabriel Bonhert's plans. Practical Marie, with
her quiet courage and survivor's instinct—she just
might get the job done. As for himself, thinking of the
long journey still ahead, he wondered what the valley
would be like, and whether it could sustain them for
another week. He cursed Brecca silently, for her foolish impulse to release them without any breathers.

He watched Spar leading the way over the rocky
terrain. Though his nails were flat and violet-hued,
though his lips sometimes looked black and blue, Spar
never faltered. He was better adapted than Reeve, and
perhaps more determined. Reeve knew what kept Spar
going, and envied his faith in Loon and that safe har-
bor he would help her find. Meanwhile Reeve was sustained by a different hope: that Loon was not the last
of her kind, but the first.

Loon had not told Spar Pimarinun's story, the story
of her parents and the old orthong chief. There had
hardly been leisure to talk. During the day she disappeared to hunt, and in the evening they struggled to
make temporary shelter and quickly fell asleep. Once,
around a small campfire they'd built to cook up a milli-
pede, Loon started to tell Spar that story. She said
outright that there were no others like her. But Spar
had become agitated, and wouldn't hear more. "That's
what we been doin' all these months," he said, "goin'
toward your people. . . . Without that, we got
nothin'. I may as well lay down an' die." He stared at
the campfire, sinking into a mood. " 'Bout time, any-

ways." Loon looked up at Reeve, and they said no more.

Now Spar led the way, head into the wind. With his beard and long staff, he looked like some prophet wandering in the wilderness. But he was ever a warrior-prophet, with one end of his staff fire-hardened and sharply pointed.

Now Spar was waiting for Reeve on a promontory, carpeted in muddy-brown polyps that Reeve recognized from the red wall in the Jupiter Dome. Spar stretched out a hand to heave him the last step onto the rise. When Reeve straightened from his climb, he saw that Loon stood a short distance away, perched on a ledge gazing out on a great vista.

The Rift Valley.

It was the largest thing Reeve had ever seen. No mere *rift*, or tear, it was a stupendous plain beside which the canyon of the Tallstory was only a gully. The Forever Plains might have been larger, but like deep space itself, the plains didn't seem so much vast as endless. This valley was bounded and defined by its matching escarpments—the one on which they stood, and the distant black cliffs of the western rim. Sprawling between lay the stupendous valley, in glistening red hues, as though the planet's surface had been ripped away, exposing the raw flesh of a new land.

A city commanded the juncture of the Tallstory and the Gandhi Rivers, a clave built close to the ground, and surrounded by a ruined wall. From a communal hub of buildings at the core, streets radiated outward. And clinging to the city, the signature colors of Lithia bled out in maroon and carnelian.

Across the Gandhi River arced half a bridge, with twisted girders suspended from its severed edge. If the Tallstory had been deep and fast-flowing, the Gandhi was wide and stately, flowing southward, mocking their need for progress north. Looking up-valley, the merest wisp of cloud teased the image of the fire spigots and the great plume to mind.

For many months the valley had held their hopes and fears. Now, it might bring them very much less than they desired, or very much worse, but they had earned the right to enter this place and claim their fortunes. Despite all that Lithia could throw in their path, they had arrived, following Loon and her imperatives. For a moment Reeve heard in his memory Spar's simple dictum: *Yonder, yonder by the soil.*

Reeve moved to Loon's side to share the moment with her, but Loon had more mundane things on her mind. She turned to him, holding out something, her face lit up with an impish grin.

Here was their dinner, dangling by its tail: a rat. Reeve's mouth watered.

The lava had not come this far in the Dark Days. The city lay structurally preserved, aside from the spectacular ruin of the bridge and collapsed portions of the defensive wall. Walking through narrow residential streets, they passed a bizarre tree—sprouted in the middle of the street—that looked like plates on a stick. The breeze wafted a pink pollen from it. Vines with heavy red fruit clung to the faces of buildings. But some dwellings still boasted decorative tiles set into adobe-like building materials. Reeve could imagine a matron coming to one of the doors, broom in hand, to peer at the strangers or sweep up the remains of a flowerpot, now all dust and shards where blooms should have been.

Inside, the dwellings were ransacked, reduced to piles of furniture, heaps of clothing, and broken mementos. Raiders had been here, perhaps those who traded with the jinn, bringing this booty to the Jupiter Dome on overladen rafts. It was a dreary sight, but for now nothing could sour the prospect of a night's sleep under cover. Reeve reached out to touch Loon's arm, hoping that Spar would grant them time alone together. She smiled at him and darted off, sorting through the chaos for preserved food and *Reeve's air*— her term for the breathers.

When he and Spar followed her to the inner courtyard of one of the homes, they found her standing very still. The garden was crowded with filament-like grass, topped with nodules that bowed the strands over. Loon pointed to movement in the grass.

There, amid the Lithian grass, a round object twitched on the ground. About the size of a large man's fist, the ball was pockmocked in a regular pattern. It lurched to the side a few inches, then pivoted back, rocking on the ground as though trying to dig a hole. Perhaps it was a robotic gardener, though if so it had done a miserable job the last few hundred years. They backed away, not liking the look of the thing.

When they retraced their steps to the street, they found dusk beginning to settle over the city, with steep shadows sucking the last of the warmth from the day. Just as they were standing at a street intersection hesitating about which direction to go, something struck Loon. She reeled, holding her neck, where a little blood was seeping. A ball hovered nearby, at neck level. It had bitten her.

Spar's stave knocked it against the building across the street, his reflexes as fast as ever. When Reeve determined that Loon was all right, he joined Spar at the wall to examine the downed sphere, which lay dented in the rubble of the street.

"Voider," Spar said. "I heard of these, yes, sir. City folk used 'em to keep out riffraff. You thought twice before you raided here." He winked at Reeve. "One of these up and takes a chunk out of you, if it don't like you."

Loon wiped off the blood and shrugged at them.

Spar probed his teeth for the last of the rat meal.

"Their poison don't mean much to Mam, I reckon. Or maybe it's gone wobbly over time."

"I think it followed us from the courtyard," Reeve said. "Suppose there's more of them?"

"With the luck we been havin' we best make ourselves scarce." Spar spat into the street.

They quickly made a choice for shelter, ducking into a two-story construct set back from the street and covered in front with a vine-choked portico.

Finding a room less in shambles than the others, they barricaded the door and lay down to rest. A separate room for privacy seemed an unlikely prospect under the circumstances, but Reeve hoped Loon might find a way to finagle privacy for herself, and then . . . Before Reeve had long to connive the matter, however, he found himself falling into an exhausted stupor. At the edge of consciousness, he could hear Loon rustling about, poking into corners of the room. Once she crouched nearby and whispered in his ear, "The good soil, Reeve. The good soil."

Later, he dreamed of her hand coming up to his lips, with a pinch of bright red loam. When he tasted it, it was an explosion of flavor, and it ran, laughing, into his veins. Then he looked at Loon as though for the first time and saw, under the shallow upper strata of her skin, a crisscrossing pattern of fault lines.

2

The sun was barely up, but Loon had been tracking the wolves for an hour. She knew they smelled her. As usual with wild animals, it was a smell they couldn't identify, and so far these two tolerated her at a distance. She wasn't sure what they found to hunt in the barren streets, and in truth they were threadbare specimens. If she could bring them both down with her sling, Spar and Reeve would feast today and pack extra for up-valley. She watched as the animals nosed into piles of rubbish, once fighting over an old shoe, or perhaps playing with it. Crouching down, she sampled the packed-down soil of the street. Just a tiny bit, but it was a sheer and deep pleasure.

This, *this* was what it felt like to eat the good soil, to let its pure extracts truly feed her for the first time. She resisted the urge to run through the patterned streets and scale the nearest climbable thing. *Run,* her body said. *Jump!* It would be fun to sprint until she dropped, to spend the energy saved up in her muscles. She wasn't sure that energy was an entirely good thing. Her legs sometimes felt like they didn't belong to her: She wanted to run when she knew she must creep, to leap when she must crouch. Patience, patience.

The thought of Reeve and their night together filled her with happiness. She replayed his tastes in memory, marveling at the complexity of him, the foreign world of his body . . . then her mind raced ahead to the next task. She would find Reeve's air for him, so he could swallow the tube and keep indigo from claiming him. He was young to be coughing. But he was—had *been*—a zerter, and was weak like all zerters because of living in the sky tube, with no good soil to sustain him.

She had allowed her attention to drift. What was this? One of the wolves was down, lying in the street. She crouched behind a wall and watched. Ah. Here was a voider, hovering over the wolf, darting now and then at the other wolf; then, when it made a quick sprint away, the ball put on a burst of speed and hit the animal square on the flank, bouncing off it and rolling away, as though it had spent its last breath. The second wolf staggered away, down the street.

Loon tucked her sling into her belt and watched for a few minutes to see if the voider would rise again. When it did not, she began looking for something to drag at least one wolf home on. This search took her

into a small side street where she found a length of
tarp that would serve for the animals, one at a time.

When she emerged back on the street of wolves, the
creatures were not alone. A large, egg-shaped thing
floated in the air above the first wolf. If this was a
voider, it was surely a powerful one, as big as a beef
calf. It slowly settled onto the ground, and a flap
opened in its side. From this hole dozens of voiders
emerged like a swarm of bees. Even more astonishing,
legs protruded from the egg and latched onto the wolf,
dragging it inside the belly. Then the egg rose, hovering as though smelling her. Loon hid under her tarp,
curled up like a turtle. Perhaps it was looking for the
body of the other wolf. Or perhaps it was looking for
her. She could hear the whine of its motors as it
passed by. *Oh please, Lady Over All,* she thought, *let
me not be food for the wolf-eater.*

She had wondered if the Lady would listen to such
as her, a creature neither this nor that. She wondered
if, instead of the Lady that Spar had taught her to love,
the orthong god was now hers. Or no god at all. Finally
she gave up praying and cautiously peeked from under
the tarp.

The great egg was just disappearing down a side
street, trailing smoke with the unmistakable smell of
burning flesh and hair. The smaller voiders followed it
like ducklings after their mother.

The downed voider still lay immobile across the
street. Loon doubted the ball could fell her, but she
didn't want it to call its mother. After many minutes
Loon worked up the courage to set off in search of the
second wolf, hoping she could get to it before the egg
did.

3

Reeve had finally broken into the house information
net. Its one functioning node was in the kitchen,

where a screen resolved into a barely readable image above a sinkful of broken crockery. The voice interface wouldn't talk back to him, but it would present visual data, including, at the moment, a simple map of the city.

Spar peered over Reeve's shoulder. "Ask it 'bout them body snatchers," he suggested.

"No," Loon said, shivering at the thought.

Though slow and at times faltering, the kitchen screen divulged that the voiders were extensions of the urban police system. It seemed to Reeve that they had now degraded to random killing. From the wall around the city Reeve deduced that the townspeople had for a time held out against marauding clavers. If this were true, the cremation machines might have been busy in the old days.

Reeve's jaw ached after gorging on boiled wolf, chewing the stringy meat until he could eat no more. The three of them had cut the remaining carcass into strips and packed it into satchels they'd found in the house, along with the best warm clothes they could find and other provisions for the journey north. The task now was to discover the most direct route out of the city to minimize contact with the voiders and any other aggressive defenses the Rheans might have devised.

A coughing fit seized Reeve for a moment, doubling him over. When he pulled his hand away from his mouth, there was blood on it.

Spar looked at the blood and pursed his mouth. "You usin' up your lives too fast, Reeve."

"It's not my lungs," Reeve said. "Teeth." He pulled back his gums and pressed on his teeth, where his bleeding gums were showing evidence of scurvy.

Spar smiled a halfhearted smile, showing his own teeth problems, which were either worn, missing, or blackened. "Well, all you need is a couple good ones," he said.

Loon examined the blood on Reeve's hand, wiping it onto the sleeve of her shirt. Then, looking past Reeve at the kitchen screen, she frowned and pointed. As Reeve turned to follow her gesture, Loon asked, "This?" She was pointing to a schematic line that seemed to bisect the screen from one corner to the other. A written caption at one end of the line read: LAKE VISHNU.

Reeve hadn't noticed it before. "Information," he said to the computer. "Lake Vishnu."

The screen coalesced into an image of a green line departing from the city and connecting to a large, narrow lake. Calling up more information, Reeve's pulse spiked at the next screen of information: a travel timetable.

"There's a train or transportation system of some kind connecting to a Lake Vishnu . . ."

"Yep," Spar said, "I heard of that."

"What, the train?"

"Nope, the lake." His chin worked back and forth a moment as he thought hard. He glanced up at Reeve. "It's south of Rhea, that lake."

Reeve nodded slowly. Then he turned back to the node. "Information: map of city." At the display he pointed at the green line heading in the opposite direction out of the city. The next display showed it connecting to the Grendel Hot Springs.

Then he called for a map of the Rift Valley.

The hot springs were north of Rhea, straight up-valley, within ten or twenty miles of their destination, though no antique train would be running. He called for the schedule anyway. The screen showed no fixed schedule, but a demand-responsive personal rapid transport system on a horizontal elevator. The crude computer was dutifully providing 150-year-old information.

It displayed: CAR AVAILABLE.

Spar spoke for Reeve when he said, "Broke, most likely."

The two of them stared at the screen for a few moments. They weren't finding stores of preserved food so far in Rhea. The streets were patrolled by venomous flying tennis balls, whose "Shoot Now, Ask Questions Later" policy could get them incinerated. Time was wasting away. They had to head north in any case.

When Reeve and Spar finally decided to investigate the transport line, they found that Loon had already shouldered her pack.

4

Nerys and her escorts were winding their way down the paths of the outfold, keeping an easy pace in consideration of Nerys' pregnancy.

When Salidifor had shown up at the women's compound with four other hulking male orthong, Nerys thought her punishment for her rudeness to Himirinan had arrived. From their smirks it was plain the other women thought so too. But Salidifor was friendly enough, and said she must come with him, instructing her to clean up and wear her best clothes. The orthong waited patiently while she did so.

While she was dressing, Haval came to her cubicle. "Nerys, they're taking you to see someone important." The expression on her face flickered from bewilderment to incredulity and back again.

"Who?" Nerys turned a handle to release water into her basin from the water tubes and washed her face.

"They won't say exactly, but I think this is the chief we've never seen." She shook her head. "Salidifor says she is . . . curious about you."

Nerys wiped off her face and straightened her hair. "Well, I'm curious about her, too."

"Nerys! She could be dangerous. You don't know what to say, how to act."

A grin met Haval's worries. "Only one way to find out."

Now, with the orthong escorts preceding them, Nerys walked at Salidifor's side, watching as he instructed her on the protocols.

She was to bow to the chief, and not look directly into her eyes. She was to accept all offers of food graciously—no putting down of spoons, Salidifor said pointedly. She would answer all questions, and demonstrate what she knew of their language. For this, apparently, was the thing that had come to the chief's attention, and she wished to see for herself if Nerys had gained some fluency. More Salidifor could not say, since he was merely reporting what others had told him. It had been several years since he had personally seen the chief.

Tulonerat was very old, he said, and generally did not interfere with the routine affairs of the habitation, much less any matter involving the breeder women. It had astonished the lords that she wished to see Nerys, and that she had asked to see her without consultation with Salidifor, and without a proper briefing. Moreover, Nerys was to see her in her own berm—a most inappropriate intrusion, Tulonerat's attendants had made clear.

<This is not necessarily a good thing,> Salidifor finally admitted.

<Try not to worry,> Nerys said, thrilled at the prospect of her interview.

Salidifor looked sideways at her, which was comment enough.

<I'll be good.> She used sign, so as not to embarrass Salidifor in front of the other orthong. If an orthong's knowing human language gave too much respect to a breeder woman, now was not the time to challenge the notion.

<Yes,> he said. <That would be well.>

When they entered a great clearing in front of a

rather larger-than-average bermed dwelling, they paused for a moment while Salidifor tucked a lock of Nerys' stray hair behind her ear, a gesture so human-like Nerys had to smile. It was clear she was on display in some way, and that Salidifor wished for her to do well. But it was not lost on the orthong escorts that Salidifor had touched her. They turned away, affecting nonchalance. Salidifor must be nervous indeed, she thought, to have committed this lapse of orthong good taste.

They entered the berm, led by orthong attendants, who herded them down its gnarled hallways, making clear she was to touch nothing. At length Nerys emerged through a door into an expansive outdoor room, very like a walled courtyard—except that it was sunken perhaps twenty feet into the ground. The grounds as well as the surrounding walls were covered with the growths of the outfold, but in very small dimension, and with great diversity. Nerys recognized a few of the forms—but in fact, as she looked more closely she saw that many of the growths were highly unusual, with patterned and blended colors, surprising given the orthong propensity for blocks of uniform coloring. Sun streamed into the garden, and under its hot gaze, the outfold seem to throb.

A great many orthong stood about, most in the sleeveless tunics typical of the females. And it was clear whom they attended upon.

Nerys bowed to the individual half-sitting, half-lying on a long chair that, like so much of the orthong furniture, might just as easily have been grown as built. Tulonerat was small, not much larger than Nerys herself, and she was silver-gray, except for the palms of her hands. She wore a sleeveless tunic without embellishment, as though at her age she was beyond vanity, or that at her level display was unnecessary.

The center of the garden was paved in flat hexagonal stones. The six directions of each hexagon allowed for expression of subtle emotional states, as Nerys had learned, but as yet she used the hexagons clumsily. She felt Salidifor's hand on her back, and his soft push, propelling her forward.

Tulonerat watched her from the pinpricks of her barely open eyes. Then she closed them.

Respectfully, Nerys waited for Tulonerat to say something. And waited. As the minutes passed, Nerys grew exceedingly uncomfortable. She turned around to query Salidifor with her eyes, and he made a nearly imperceptible chin movement: *No*. Nerys turned back and waited.

Next to Tulonerat, one orthong—female by her clothing—stood close by the high chief, watching Nerys with glittering eyes. Nerys struggled to keep her gaze down when in fact she wished to see everything possible. Time seemed stuck. The orthong attendants seemed capable of enduring this boredom with equanimity, and did not communicate with each other or move from their set positions near Tulonerat.

After perhaps fifteen minutes, when Nerys thought she could bear no more, the old orthong finally opened her eyes and signed, <Sing for me, human woman.>

This was a disappointing beginning, prepared as Nerys was to show off her dance language. <What would you have me sing?> Nerys spoke in her best orthong, but managed a misstep due to nervousness.

<Sing,> Tulonerat repeated.

Nerys was never the best of singers, but she produced a tune of her clave, in human song:

From these waters you left without warning,
I will miss you if you don't miss me,
But return to my arms by the morning,
And I'll love you again by the sea.

She had time to think how strange it was to sing a Whale Clave song in the garden of an orthong chief.

<What is the meaning?> Tulonerat asked.

<The song is about a woman whose lover has gone on a journey at sea, and she misses him.>

Tulonerat was fingering a white and yellow, bulbous plant by her side, a stalk with a coil of patterned blue and purple around it. Then she signed: <Why did she give permission for him to leave?>

Nerys took a step forward and danced, <She never would have let him go, but he did not love her enough to care what she wanted. But she loves him nevertheless.>

<A foolish individual.>

<Which? The male or the female?>

This question caused a stir among Tulonerat's attendants. It was likely rude for her to ask questions, and Nerys resolved to be more careful.

The old orthong watched Nerys for a long moment. <Tell me of the sea. I have never seen the sea.>

Nerys hesitated for a moment, planning her moves. Then she danced, using left-side and right-side high movements, dipping movements—all as Salidifor had shown her. <I lived by the sea. The sea was how we traveled and how we ate. The sea brought its weather to us, and threw its treasures on the beach.> She was proud of how she'd learned to combine hand sign with dance, a complex grammar of great flexibility. She went on, <The sea stretched very far eastward and could be beautiful when it was not stormy. In the days of my parents, there were still whales in the sea.>

<What is a whale?>

Here, Nerys waxed more eloquent, daring to use the hexagons, facing to the right, using forceful, active verbs to describe a whale in motion. Everyone watched her closely now, even those attendants that had been rudely looking elsewhere while she danced. As she continued, she felt the whale's presence, and her arms took on its fleshly power. When she was finished, Nerys thought that for the first time she had managed to amaze an orthong—in fact, a roomful of them. She glanced at Salidifor to see if he approved, and she thought from his demeanor that he was pleased, though he remained quiet as stone.

Tulonerat now turned to the plant at her side, and did not bother to look at Nerys as she signed, <This is a pup's tale.>

Taken aback, Nerys found that she couldn't help but correct such an impression. <No, such creatures did exist. They came from my ancestors' world, Earth.>

<Where is Earth?>

Nerys hesitated. Where indeed? <Far away in space, many stars away.>

<You have airships, then, that travel star to star?>

<My ancestors had them.> With some shame she said, <We do not have the memory of how to make them now.>

<A pup's tale, these star planes,> Tulonerat said.

To Nerys' great annoyance, Tulonerat closed her eyes again.

Anger flickered in Nerys' chest. She pushed it back down, but it flared up again. She would not be dismissed after having performed for this old hag, and she would not leave unanswered the accusation that she made up stories.

Nerys found herself saying, <We arrived here and found the world a dreary place.> The attendants stirred, but Nerys didn't care. <We changed the world, and made it as we wished, full of animals from Earth— including whales. Many of the animals still on Lithia are animals that were carried on the starship as eggs and brought to life by my ancestors.> She moved full around to the hexagon in back of her and, swiveling upon it, said with sadness, <When the eruptions started, the planet changed and many of us died. Learning and knowledge died.> She considered trying the movement for anger, but prudence won out. She finished by saying, <But it is *not* a pup's tale.> She sensed that she had danced very well. When a claw or two flashed, however, she knew she had gone too far.

Many of the orthong now stood watching Tulonerat, who seemed oblivious of any insult, closing her eyes once more. But Salidifor came forward and took Nerys firmly by the arm. His look, she thought, was a little angry. Then he stopped, looking past her, and slowly turned her around to face the court.

Tulonerat's closest attendant stood in front of the chief. The attendant said, <Step forward, human woman.>

As Nerys did so, the attendant walked around her, observing her carefully. At this, the other orthong turned away. This was to be a private conversation.

The attendant stood in front of her now, at a little distance, saying, <Do you have math?>

Nerys looked back at Salidifor, who had turned away. She had to answer as best she could, and not stray from protocol this time. But if this was her only chance to speak to these chiefs, how much should protocol matter? As they said in the clave, corn ripens only once. <I have a little knowledge of numbers. But my people knew numbers better once.>

<The women of your berm do not have math.>

<True, they have not *much* math.>

<Do you know the world?>

Here was that word, *know*. It held special meaning for orthong. <I know the world poorly, but seek to know more, to know better. But I cannot know the world as the orthong do.>

<You do not know the world,> the orthong concluded.

<I have no deep knowing. It is not the human way.> Then she took a risk. <I have regret that you never met my ancestors who knew in the human way. Then you could believe that our knowing is as strong as yours, but different.> It was hard to judge this orthong's reaction when Nerys was so intent on the form of the

dance. But when she finished she found the female watching her with stony eyes. <The breeders of your berm do not speak as you do,> the orthong said.

<Some of them care more about food than learning. But some are curious to learn.>

<They do not dance.>

<They are afraid to offend.>

<The breeders fear us?>

Nerys felt a moment of astonishment, that the orthong could be unaware of this basic fact. <You control the food. You control us. We have become meek because of this.>

<You say that you do not know because of us?>

Nerys recognized the signs of exasperation. <We cannot blame the orthong for what we have become. But we cannot thank the orthong either. To live without knowing may not be worth it.> She was shocked to hear herself say that. She hadn't known she felt it until she shaped the words.

<You are not content?>

The old orthong query. Her new answer was: <It is a hard question. A deep question. I do not complain.>

The orthong stood immobile a long time. Behind her, Tulonerat had closed her eyes and appeared to have fallen asleep. The garden pressed down on Nerys, and her face felt hot with exhaustion. After a time, she saw that an attendant had come forward with a small tray. On it was a morsel of food. It looked like a small sweet cake.

Her arm hung at her side like a pipe. She knew the polite thing to do, but somehow her arm wouldn't move. She was becoming orthong, she thought, for movement to have such meaning. Nerys longed to turn around to Salidifor, but he was, she knew, facing away. *Give me permission not to eat this,* she would have asked him, *let me say I'm not hungry.* But it was her own decision to make—when to be polite, when to offend. It was a privilege she savored for a few moments.

Then, with great effort, her arm obeyed her mind and her hand reached out for the cake, and she picked it up and took a bite.

Salidifor fairly dragged her back through the outfold.

<That was a disaster,> he told her.

They were alone now, so Nerys spoke out loud: "I ate the damn cake." It had not gone especially well, but they had taunted her, called her a liar. Why was she taking the blame?

<Yes. You ate. We might both be dead now if you hadn't.>

"Your Tulonerat is rude. Her assistant was better, but she thinks we're dumb."

<That assistant is Tulonerat's successor. Divoranon is very powerful, and doesn't fall asleep in the middle of conversations. You were in great danger, talking freely.> He stopped his pell-mell plunge down the path, and turned to face her. <Tell me everything that was said.>

Nerys related the exchange between herself and Divoranon. When she had finished, Salidifor seemed somewhat calmer.

<That was not poorly handled.>

"Thank you, I guess."

Salidifor stared into the outfold, contemplating. Then he said, <Divoranon was intrigued by you. She questioned you to explore your capacity, and determine why you seem different from the other breeder women.> Nerys winced at the pejorative term, and Salidifor amended it to *freewomen*. He repeated: <That was not poorly handled. You showed some discretion.>

"Surprised?"

He looked down at her for a long moment. <Nerys. Not much that you do surprises me anymore.>

For some reason, she found herself smiling.

But Salidifor was serious, still standing there in the path, gazing into the outfold.

"What is it, Salidifor? Is it not well for Divoranon to learn more about humans?"

They resumed their walk down the path. <It may be, or may not be. If Divoranon comes to think that you are *knowing* creatures, what will happen?>

"What *will* happen?"

After a moment he said, <Things will change.>

The way he said it, with a strong undertone of unease, discouraged any flip response from Nerys. They continued down the path without talk.

14

1

Day sixty-one. The only sound of their vehicle was the hissing of wind outside as they sped up-valley. Reeve sat on the floor, leaning against the wall, hungry for oxygen, sapped of energy. The inside of the transport car was stripped of seats but, oddly, the controls were in perfect condition, and the elevator rails had functioned so far without a lapse.

Spar stood by a window, infused by a new eagerness, his eyes squinting against the afternoon sun. From the moment they'd entered the personal rapid transport car and discovered it worked, Spar was like a kid on a circus ride. He laughed and hooted when they gathered speed out of the station, and seemed to take it as a great turn in their fortunes.

A cough shook Reeve's chest, a bad, dry cough that sounded like the squawk of an angry bird. Loon winced as he leaned into the spasm. She took his hands in hers, patting them absently, staring past him out the windows, as though she would rather be running up-valley than riding.

"We're 'bout there, Reeve," Spar said. "I can feel it." He nodded for a moment, looking out at the red wash of scenery. In the lee side of rocks and on lower levels of the platform trees, a dusting of snow took refuge from the sun, throwing the vermilions and red-browns into high relief. "Bound to be our people out there somewheres. Bound to be." Sometimes he called Loon's people *our people,* a simple mixing of what was Loon's and what was Spar's.

Loon and Reeve exchanged miserable glances. If she thought to bring up Pimarinun's story now, Spar wasn't helping her any.

"Who else fixed this here railroad? Tell me that?" Spar laughed quietly, as if to confirm his opinion. "Somebody been tinkering with it, yes sir, and it got to be somebody who likes it here in the bloodlands."

Spar had a point. It was hard to believe the transport car could function after hundreds of years of rust and vandalism. And it was a saving thing, since Reeve didn't know if he could make it up-valley very far on his own legs, in this meager air.

Spar gazed back out the window, muttering: "That's where we'll find 'em, I figure. At the end of the line."

Reeve's thoughts turned to his fellow Stationers, and where exactly their camp might be. From what he remembered of the Station plans for the reterraforming expedition, they were to set up camp on the valley rim, using shuttles to and from the main valley lava vents. If their shuttles were damaged in the Station breakup, though, they might have been forced to camp in the valley. Reeve hoped their shuttles worked, since sighting a shuttle flight path would be his best chance to zero in on Bonhert's camp.

And once there, he would stop them—if not by persuasion, then by whatever means it took. He didn't know if he had murder in him, but figured that most people did, even those without half the reasons he had. Oddly, it wasn't revenge and colder thoughts that gave him his courage—it was an upwelling of hope, the hope he'd glimpsed since that night in Brecca's escape room, the hope to find a place, a home on Lithia. So love, he figured, drove him to do what he must do, and though it didn't make it any easier, he felt more at ease with himself, with the man he had become.

He knew the choice was harsh: to become like Loon, in all her strangeness. To one who loved her, it was not so great a jump, but Stationers might react like her own Stoneroot Clave and drive her out. Even if they didn't, though, there was no guarantee on the orthong side of things. Far from it.

All humans had ever traded with the orthong were women and rocks. Now he would see if they would bargain for something new: information. If they meant to make Lithia their home, what might they pay to know of Gabriel Bonhert's plans?

Another fit of coughing came over him, scraping his throat as if he'd swallowed pins.

Spar handed him the water pouch and urged him to drink. "That's right," he said, nodding as Reeve managed to stifle his cough long enough to swallow. "Couple more days, after we whup that Station Captain, we got to get you out of here. Maybe go back to Stillwater, eh? I walk back into that clave, folks'll call me a liar for sayin' I been to the sea and the Rift. That I been on a pirate ship and to a clave of monsters. That I got snatched from a bad orthong death by a princess of the stony world." He grinned with relish. "You gotta come with me, Reeve, to tell 'em Spar's no liar."

"No man's ever going to call Spar a liar if I'm around," Reeve said, and fiercely meant it.

Spar slapped himself on the knee. "Yeah, you a scrappy fellow all right. You gonna do OK in the world, Reeve. It took all my teachin', but you gonna do OK."

They stood on the train platform. The tracks ended at a deserted landing overgrown with ropy red weeds.

Spar pursed his lips, searching. If he expected a welcoming party, he didn't admit it, but a sense of anticlimax gripped them. Ominously, Spar coughed. For the first time, Reeve thought about how limited Spar's days were, like any claver's. Like his own days.

Loon quietly took Spar's hand, gripping it. Reeve thought she might tell Spar who she was, freeing him of his myth. But her words were fewer than ever, as though she had started to run out of them. Yet even in their predicament, Reeve could still look at her and find her lovely. She had submitted to Spar's fussy insistence that she use some of their drinking water to wash up. Her slicked-back hair made her look fresh and honed down: no frills, just the essential new human.

In the distance stood a rambling three-story building that still bore itself upright, though hugged by brown moss until it looked like an animal, the eyes of its windows glowering down on them. It clearly had once been a grand place—with the look of a hotel, Reeve thought, if he was any judge of such things. A stream of cloudy water had cut a gorge down the slope from the ruined building, spiking the air with its sulfur fumes.

They hiked in silence up to the building, turning to note its commanding view over the Rift Valley, with the Gandhi River a flash of silver in the distance.

Spar looked up at the overgrown palace, frowning. "Ain't nobody in *there* worth talkin' to," he declared.

"Might be some supplies we could use, though," Reeve said.

Spar chewed on his cheek a moment. "You go ahead, then. I'll check out what else we got." His voice still held hope that there *was* something else. He turned to go, then looked back to see if Loon was following, but she was disappearing into a tall stand of platform trees, her sling drawn in the expectation of a kill. Spar wandered off, leaving Reeve alone.

A cold breeze was sweeping down the Rift Valley. It bore a swarm of tiny pods across the hillock before him, what Reeve took for seeds, however out of season. Lithia was in control here, no mistake. He gazed up-valley, judging they still had a long walk—no more than fifteen miles, he hoped, but it might be twenty or twenty-five. And as for time, well, he had given up keeping track of the days. Somewhere between the Mercury Clave and Rhea, he had just lost track. They would press on, that was all. Some decisions were simple. He would press on if Lithia let him breathe.

Except for the rush of the stream, it was quiet. No Terran thing lived here to chitter in the bushes or scold them from a tall tree. Reeve tied his jacket closer around him against the chill, turning up his collar to keep out the breeze. He could have lain down on the steps of the great building and fallen asleep, he was that tired. For a moment he looked about for a place to sit out of the wind. But then his curiosity fueled him, and he turned toward the mossy building and climbed up the stone stairs onto the great covered porch.

The late-afternoon sun poured into the hallway through the collapsed door, inviting Reeve in. He entered the outer skin of the place, noting that its mossy fur was actually a thatch of small, tough spikes. Inside, the foyer was stripped of furniture, but nothing could hide the good bones of the place, its gracious shape, with curving staircase and arched doorways. Light poured in from many windows, throwing blocks of sunlight onto marble floors. From the walls hung tatters of paper, its former decorative covering eaten away by time and acid winds. But for all its sense of ruin, Reeve felt the elegance it must once have known.

He explored the first floor, its dining room, kitchen, and rooms of unknown purpose, filled with remnants of chairs, picture frames, and computer screens. In one corner lay a great pile of cloth-bound books, their soft materials slumping into a gooey clay.

Upstairs, past the fine carved railing and the defaced paintings, Reeve found a broad hallway lined with many doors, and choosing one, he opened it to explore one of the guest chambers. A huge bed commanded the room, with a ragged canopy overhead. With its chairs and sofa and broken but fine tables, Reeve thought it a room fit for a station captain, and felt a pang of envy for people who might have come here and experienced this luxury.

He opened a door into the bathroom. A beetle as large as his foot raced on many legs for the shelter of the sunken bathtub. From the scrape and rustle of the tub, Reeve didn't need a closer look to figure the creature had joined many others there. He closed the door, suddenly less enamored of the ruined place.

A shout from outside. At the window in three strides, Reeve leaned forward to search the grounds in back of the hotel, quickly spotting a group of four orthong at the edge of an encroaching woods. Heart racing, he saw worse: Spar lay on the ground, and Loon was racing toward him.

Jamming out into the hallway and down the staircase, Reeve emerged onto the porch, nearly doubled over from the exertion. He spat out a wad of bloody sputum and forced himself into a run along the front of the hotel, then around the side. Nearing the back of the hotel, he stopped himself in time to reconnoiter before racing to meet and perhaps startle the orthong. As he cautiously stepped forward, he saw that the orthong had begun to advance on Loon and Spar. Hoping to distract them, Reeve walked out into plain view. The orthong turned to him, one of them pointing an arm straight at him, cuff winking a cutting light. But Loon stood up and interjected herself between Reeve and the orthong. As the creatures hesitated, Reeve quickly covered the distance to her side.

Spar was on the ground clutching his arm. Blood pumped, soaking his sleeve. His wooden staff lay at his side, and he gripped it now, trying to rise into a sitting position.

Reeve stood by Loon as the orthong slowly advanced. They were all well over seven feet tall, and to Reeve's eye looked identical, except that the leader had streaks of silver reaching up from its collar onto its head. It wore the same long coat as the first orthong he'd met. The black material glistened in the sun like a flake of obsidian. One orthong was in the lead, and the others stopped some fifteen yards off while this individual stepped forward, not overtly threatening. Perhaps the creatures realized Loon was female, changing the nature of this encounter.

"See to Spar," Loon said, not looking at him.

Reeve realized that she meant to handle this encounter on her own and was relegating him to the background. With a stab of worry, he thought she would give herself to these creatures to protect him and Spar. And worse, that perhaps giving herself to them was what she desired to do in any case. Kneeling close to Spar, he saw that his friend's forearm was seared from orthong gunfire, but not badly. He moved forward to press the palm of his hand flat against Spar's wound.

"Spar is . . . ?" Loon asked, whispering.

"He's OK. Burned, but OK," Reeve said. It was Loon, facing off with the orthong, who was in the most immediate danger. Would they see her as a woman who might defect to them, or would they see her as something else, something very much more unsavory?

Loon kept looking down at Spar, staring at his bloodied arm. The lead orthong was turning back to its companions. When it came back it had something in its hand. Reeve couldn't see it, but he figured it for the one gift that meant nothing to Loon: food.

Then Loon set in motion a fateful chain of events. When the creature reached out with the morsel of food, Loon spat into its hand.

The next things happened so fast, and so slow, that Reeve was helpless to either prevent them or ever forget them.

The orthong raised a claw-studded hand as though to strike her. Beside him, Reeve felt Spar surge, bounding to his feet, his hand sweeping out for his staff as the orthong leader swirled to face him. With the point of his staff aimed at the orthong's middle, Spar launched himself forward. Somewhere, as though from very far off, Reeve heard Loon's startled cry, and then the orthong's great arm came down on the staff, shattering it and spinning Spar off balance. The orthong delivered a heavy blow to Spar's head, then turned to face Reeve, who had risen and was staggering forward—too late—to restrain Spar.

Loon came between the orthong and Reeve, and for a moment all was silent. Reeve crouched by Spar, who lay crumpled on his side. He pulled him gently onto his back to better see the wound on the side of his head. Blood, brilliantly red, welled from his temple and pooled in the socket of his eye before spilling down his cheek.

Holding Spar in his arms, he watched as the orthong turned to Loon, seeming to regard her more closely. She stood frozen in place, whispering, "Spar? Spar?"

Reeve whispered back: "Don't anger them. Stay very still."

The leader brought its great hand forward and touched Loon on her cheek. She stood rigidly, allowing this, still repeating, "Spar?" The creature touched her hair, pinching a strand as though it were some great oddity.

Meanwhile Spar's blood collected in Reeve's lap—a mortal wound, perhaps. Reeve was too stunned to think, but Lord of Worlds, the wound was bad, swelling massively. Reeve wiped the blood from Spar's eyes, cradling his head as he lay drifting toward unconsciousness.

Reeve watched the orthong, expecting another blow. But then, abruptly, the orthong leader turned and walked away from Loon, striding toward the others. After a brief exchange in sign, the three other orthong stared at Loon. Then the orthong moved off, disappearing as a group in the high brush.

They were gone. But Spar lay in Reeve's arms, one side of his head ruptured. "Spar . . . ," Reeve whispered. "Spar . . ." He wasn't sure that Spar heard him. Loon was beside him, making a small moan deep in her throat, her eyes frantic. "We're here with you," Reeve said, "me and Mam."

Loon laid her head gently down on Spar's chest, circling her arms around him.

Blood flowed copiously, though Reeve held his jacket against the ruptured temple. But surely Spar would rally . . . he had been strong and hale only a moment before.

Spar tried to speak, a hoarse rasp. Then Reeve heard: "Mam . . ."

"She's right here," Reeve said as Loon lifted her head and touched Spar's lips with her finger.

Spar whispered, "Guess we . . . scared off . . . those thongs, eh?"

Reeve mustered a voice: "Yeah. We showed them."

Spar laughed a little, a silent shudder that sent a trickle of blood from his mouth. Then he shut his eyes.

"Come back," Loon said. For a moment Reeve thought she might have that much magic, or that Spar might believe that she did, making it true. She bent over him, encircling his chest again with her arms as though barring the way for him to leave.

Reeve looked to the woods to be sure the orthong had not changed their minds and returned. There was no sign of them. When he looked back at Spar, his friend was still dying. Reeve prayed. It had been a very long time, but he prayed.

After a time Spar opened his eyes again, saying, very faintly: "Had eight lives, see? . . . All of 'em . . . good."

Loon glanced at Reeve. Her eyes were clearer than his own. Perhaps she had no way to cry, or knew enough to wait.

Spar's arms curled in toward his body, as though defending against further harm. Reeve stroked Spar's forehead, lightly, the merest touch to let him know they were near. And after a moment, when he could speak clearly, he said, "Give me your blessing, Spar . . . so I can keep going." He didn't know why he needed this.

But Spar seemed to understand. "You keep on, boyo," Spar said. "For Lithia. She got all the strength you need. You lay yourself down . . . every night in her lap, and rise up in the morning. By the Lady."

Spar began to shake and Loon took off her jacket, spreading it over his chest. After several minutes of labored breathing he struggled to say something, and Loon crouched low over him.

"Mam . . ."

She pressed her hands onto his face, as if to say, *Here I am, here I am. . . .*

"Mam," came his voice, no more than a slight breeze: "Give me leave . . . to go."

Loon paused as though considering whether she could or not. But then she bent down and whispered in his ear: "Beloved Spar. You go now. Yes. In peace."

And then, as the cold shade of the great hotel crept over them, they waited with him. After several minutes, his chest stopped moving, and they sat there still. But Spar was gone.

When he knew he wouldn't disturb Spar's passing, Reeve broke down and wept without shame. He thought of Station, and all its medical tech, and how it could have saved him. And how here, in this place, he could do nothing except hold his friend while he died. He was still holding him. At last he laid Spar's body out on the ground, drawing the jacket over his face. Loon removed the jacket, and would not move from her place beside him.

She sat with Spar's body through the night, not letting Reeve bury him. Finally, Reeve slept there by her side. When he awoke the next morning, she was digging the grave, and when she was finished they laid Spar in it, covering him with the good soil.

2

Vikal was back, and Nerys was glad. Here was one being in the whole world who genuinely seemed pleased to see her. It gave her a keen pleasure, and a stab of guilt, too, thinking of Pila and how much she would have wished to have this contact for herself.

The pup stood in the crook of a bifurcated outfold tree. <Hello,> Vikal said.

<Hello, Vikal. How are you today?>

<I have floaters.>

Vikal liked the small pods that, when cracked open, let out an armada of floating motes. She used a sign to designate these pods, and in her mind Nerys called them floaters. Vikal now cracked one open and waved her hand through the resulting cloud.

Nerys laughed and clapped, and Vikal imitated the clapping.

<Where did you find them?> Nerys asked.

Vikal made her way onto the ribbonway and danced, <In the outfold of my mother.>

It was uncommon for Vikal to refer to her mother, and Nerys jumped on the opportunity. <Do you see your mother very much?> She had so many questions about female orthong. What exactly was their relationship with their offspring? Did they feel affection? Did they have relationships with the males, and of what sort? What were their lives like, and why were they so isolated from outside activity?

<My mother teaches me,> Vikal was answering.

<What did you learn today?>

<A new path I can deep walk in the outfold. What did your mother teach you today?>

Nerys paused to think. <Humans who are all grown up have no mothers anymore.>

Vikal had set the bridge to rocking back and forth, and sat, legs dangling from the edge, making Nerys nervous she might fall. <Does your mother ever see Salidifor?> Nerys asked.

The pup was now sitting, making it harder for her to answer, but she signed, <No.>

<Why?>

<They do not share a bond.>

<What is a bond?> Nerys asked.

<Nerys and Vikal have a bond.>

Nerys stood looking up at the pup, Vikal's brilliant white coat catching flashes of sunlight as the bridge rocked in and out of the light. They had a bond. It startled and thrilled her. Then she heard a noise behind her and whirled. To her chagrin, three orthong stood at the edge of the clearing. Worse, one of them was Hamirinan.

At a rustle in the upper story, Nerys glanced there to find that Vikal had vanished. But it was too late— Hamirinan had seen them together. She was certain he wouldn't be pleased.

As he strode toward her, she knew she guessed right. In an instant, Hamirinan grabbed hold of her hair and yanked it so hard she thought her neck would snap. She fell to her knees, gasping. One of the other orthong came forward and, surprisingly, helped her to her feet. The second orthong looked eye to eye with Hamirinan, and Hamirinan deliberately and slowly pushed him aside. Grabbing Nerys again by the hair, he propelled her out of the small glade and finally onto the path, where he began walking with such long strides that Nerys had to scramble to keep from having her head ripped off.

She despised Hamirinan, but she also feared him. He was huge, and when a creature that large got angry—as Hamirinan often seemed—his movements could be terrifying. The other orthong did not hinder him from his rough treatment this time, and Nerys began to fear he meant some bodily harm to her.

<I want Salidifor,> she managed to sign.

Hamirinan spun around to face her, releasing her hair and pointing at her face with a very long extended claw. The message was not in sign, but its meaning was clear: *Shut up or I will cut you.*

When they burst into the women's compound, the women were dumbfounded. Hamirinan still had Nerys by the hair and now propelled her forward into the middle of the yard. Women were backing away in alarm.

Haval emerged onto the steps from the berm and stood, frozen. Meanwhile Hamirinan pushed Nerys to her knees and released her hair, while, behind him, the other three orthong stood like pillars of salt.

<Bring me this breeder's belongings,> he told Haval.

Her eyes flicked at Galen, who fled into the berm to do Hamirinan's bidding.

No one moved. Kneeling beside Hamirinan, Nerys saw that his claws were fully extruded. They were translucent, with tiny yellow cracks lacing through them. Nerys wondered if he dared use them on her, pregnant as she was. The other orthong standing here wouldn't let him maul her, she told herself. One of them had actually touched her, helping her rise to her feet back in the clearing. No, they would certainly protect her. But who had ever seen an orthong in a rage?

Might all custom be set aside in deference to the rampage of an orthong lord?

"Nerys, what happened?" Odel stood nearby, and whispered this.

Hamirinan turned to look at her, and Odel raised her chin in defiance. Nerys whispered, "Don't interfere, Odel; what happened is my fault."

But Odel glared at Hamirinan, a very dangerous thing to do. The freewomen had judged that the orthong respected Odel for her age, and therefore treated her with courtesy. Nerys, however, knew that the orthong merely wished to prove to the women that when old, they would be cared for, so that they would be content on that score. Odel must not press too far, Nerys thought.

Now Haval plucked up her courage and moved down the stairs. <What has the freewoman done to offend, my lord?>

Hamirinan told Nerys, <Turn around.> She did so, facing the outfold. Nerys realized they were communicating, but pointedly, without her. After several minutes, one of the orthong signed her to turn back.

Galen emerged from the house carrying a small stack of items, all that Nerys called her own in this place. For a moment she thought she was to be banished, packed off into the wilderness.

<Set it down here,> Hamirinan ordered.

When Galen had done so, Hamirinan took up the mug that Salidifor had given Nerys and dropped it to the ground, cracking off the handle. Then he lifted her few garments, and one at a time, methodically rent them into strips with his claws. The ripping noise was the only sound in the clearing.

Nerys was not surprised when he ordered her to undress. He would be as mean as possible and still get credit with the women for his restraint in not striking her.

As she stripped she handed him her items of clothing rather than letting them fall to the ground. This forced him to interact somewhat with her and gave her some semblance of dignity. If he noticed this, he affected not to, but calmly tore each item to shreds. While he did this, she stood, her belly protruding enough to shame him, she hoped. But she did not look him in the eyes. She knew enough to keep her life. Perhaps he wished to goad her into some act of punishable rudeness, but she denied him this.

When her clothes were a pile of rags on the ground, Hamirinan ordered her to bring his breeder Mave some tea. Nerys went into the berm and prepared the tea, feeling dazed but defiant. Then she brought a small pot and a mug to Mave where, at Hamirinan's order, she sat in the middle of the yard. When Nerys approached her she saw that the woman was trembling, and for a brief moment she forgot her anger and felt pity for Mave and for all these women, forced to accept the orthong charity and to suffer their outrages. If Mave had showed the slightest satisfaction with this situation, Nerys might have lost her composure and dropped the teapot, perhaps in the woman's lap. Ever afterward, she credited Mave for the grace to be terrified. She poured the tea, and Mave accepted the cup, rigidly holding it, unable to drink.

When Nerys looked up again the orthong were disappearing down the path into the outfold. It was over.

Odel was placing a cloak around Nerys' shoulders. At that moment, her belly contracted sharply, and she bent over in surprise. And then it happened again. The pup was stirring inside her, distressed by her distress. If she believed she had weathered this event without emotion, she wasn't fooling the babe within her. With a sudden horror, Nerys thought she might miscarry. But she knew she mustn't lose this pup; then Hamirinan's anger might not stop with tearing clothes. Her pregnancy was her best protection, and her best link to Salidifor.

Salidifor. He was higher in rank than Hamirinan. She had a moment to hope for revenge before another contraction swept her and the women rushed to help her inside and to her bed.

"Salidifor," she gasped. "Send for Salidifor."

Waves of nausea coursed through her for the next few hours. The women brought teas and blankets and held her hands, genuinely kind. Odel rubbed her feet and murmured reassuringly.

"Salidifor," Nerys whispered over and over. If he would come, he would set everything to rights.

Finally Haval knelt by her side and answered her. "We've sent for him, Nerys. But we can't find him. He'll come, I'm sure."

The pup kicked violently.

Exactly my reaction, Nerys thought miserably.

3

The valley lay before them, its vastness dwarfing their progress. Reeve set a goal each day of reaching a certain distant hill, a side canyon, or a copse of trees, but often by the time they made camp, their goal was still far off. He couldn't judge distance on this wide plain of wind-whipped trees and stubby grasses. They were like Spar's ants—toiling on, calling their inches good progress. In the back of Reeve's mind he heard Spar's voice: *That's right, you just like ants, boy, don't be thinkin' you something more. . . .*

But Reeve and Loon didn't speak of Spar. Loon had all but given up on speech, and there was no breath left in Reeve, anyway. He gasped for each lungful of air, yet with every inhalation he sickened himself more. Coughing, fatigue, and headaches were constant, but the worst of it was a ballooning mental confusion that made even simple tasks challenging. One of the simple tasks was to avoid low-lying areas, ghost holes of carbon dioxide or chlorine. Loon charted their course to avoid gullies and depressions, and Reeve never left her side. She had become his eyes, his caretaker. Loon's own sustenance was the primal soil that she nibbled and against which she sometimes firmly pressed the palms of her hands.

Every night as they huddled together in front of a smoldering fire, he thought he might not wake to another day. But Loon was dragging him onward, building them nests to sleep in at night, and bearing his weight by day as they walked with one of his arms wrapped over her shoulders. She filtered his water and ground his food between two rocks to feed him as his gums turned clayey like the soil beneath his feet and he could no longer chew.

He had feared for Loon after Spar's death. She had given up everything for Spar . . . spurned the advances of the orthong when she might have gone with them, indulging in a moment of anger that sealed her fortunes for the worse. Sometimes she wept openly for Spar, and Reeve hoped it gave her some release. Her tears were a reassurance to him of all they still shared, despite his debilitation and her vitality, separate sentences handed down by the valley itself.

But for Reeve, Spar's death hit harder than he could have expected. He had died so suddenly. One moment he was just going to look around the grounds at the hotel, the next he lay dying. It was the way the world killed clavers. It reached out through disease or violence and snatched people up in ways that he had seldom seen on Station. It was the way they would learn to die once more, if humans stayed on Lithia. They would live with the elements and bow to their demands, and maybe people would become tougher and deeper because of it. For now, all Reeve knew was that the two clavers he met on the Forever Plains were the best people he'd ever known. Better than he'd been when he first looked up to find a dirty girl and a scrawny warrior bent over him as he lay in the grass.

He hoped Spar summed it up right when he said, *You gonna do OK in the world, Reeve. It took all my teachin', but you gonna do OK.* He held on to those words.

And so he and Loon plodded along, always heading north, the days slipping by, the air growing colder and more foul, and Loon's silences deepening.

The night of the fifth day, Reeve was too weak to eat. He lay on his back covered with the two blankets they carried in their packs, and watched shooting stars tracing their final seconds in the sky. Each breath was a desperate gasp that brought him little more than a ragged throat. Chlorine was the worst of it, he knew, even at these low levels. As they approached the deep plume vents it would get worse, far worse—if he lasted that long. But if he was dying, he was too exhausted to care. In fact, it seemed a very good thing to shut his eyes and be done with it. But someone had to go on. He tugged on Loon's arm to get her attention, and she moved close to him.

"Go to them, Loon. Tomorrow, climb out of the valley and find their camp. The orthong camp. Tell them about Bonhert. Stop him." He was having great difficulty sorting it all out. Telling the orthong was a betrayal of his own people. Except now he had a new clave . . . didn't he?

Beside the fire, her face remained impassive. He wasn't sure she was listening.

"I can't go on, Loon. My body . . . is all used up." He managed to pull on her sleeve until he brought her closer, but all he saw was the firelight reflected in her eyes.

They huddled together in silence then as a frigid wind pulled the last heat from his body. He wanted to say, *I love you, Loon, forever.* He hoped he did say it, but he was sinking into sleep or death, and his time had run out.

He dreamed he was suited up for a coldwalk. He

could hear his breathing amplified in his helmet. The white Station hull stretched out endlessly before him as he pulled himself from one handhold to the next. *Hurry, hurry. Something bad going to happen, but what is it?* He crossed into the shade of the radar banks and then back into the blinding, glacial light of the sun. Up ahead was a man, suited up, BONHERT, G. written on his arm. He was going to kill Reeve. Bonhert stood there, waiting, knife flashing. *Hurry, before the bad thing happens.* Reeve was running out of air. He labored to breathe. What had Kalid said about killing a man with his bare hands? *Calm the fire, become dispassionate. He will show you his weakness.*

They were standing close now, facing each other. Kalid handed Reeve a knife, saying, *A short blade with a long handle will give you leverage to thrust deep.* As his hand rose up, Reeve saw his face reflected in the other's face plate. In that moment's hesitation, Reeve saw that his tether was cut, and then felt a sickening shove, and he floated free, falling a few feet away from Station. Brit Nunally's voice from Station ops came through the earpiece: *That's an unauthorized walk out there, Calder. That's your last walk.* And he began to fall. The long, slow fall to Lithia. His stomach registered the slipping away. It was all so slow, it would take a long, long time to hit bottom. He saw Station receding from him . . . and he saw Tina Valejo tumbling head over heels, cut adrift as well, but falling upward, to the stars.

That dream came back a few more times over the next few nights, and a dream of lying on a travois, being dragged along a flat plain filled with shiny black plants. Loon was pulling him, passing the same tree hundreds of times, passing the Station, lying in a heap of rubble. He glimpsed his father, busily huddled over star maps. Marie waved to him, calling out, *Try not to hate him!* When he looked again, they were gone.

Sometimes the sky was black, and sometimes it was white, but the platform trees kept passing by.

In and out of dreams, he was sure he saw Marie's face. Once she said, "Come back to us, Reeve. Come back." And there was the face of someone he once knew . . . a skinny teenager who kept giving him sips of water. Above him, the struts of a dome soared into the sky.

It was noisy. People everywhere, shouting, talking, hammering. His head felt like it had been used for a soccer ball. He opened his eyes a slit and saw the kid named Mitya. Yes, Mitya, vaguely remembered from Station days.

Mitya leaned in closer. "I figured you were feeling better. Want some water?"

Reeve tried to gauge whether he was dreaming or not. After a moment or two he decided not. He was at the dome. Somehow, he was finally here. "Drink," he heard himself say. His voice seemed deeper, like it belonged to someone else. He could breathe. He felt the gaps in his mouth where he'd lost teeth, but he felt like he might live. When he'd finished the cup of water Mitya gave him, he asked for Loon.

Mitya shrugged. "She likes it outside. Everybody thinks she's weird. Can't she talk?"

They were close to the dome wall, surrounded by crates on two sides. Out the makeshift doorway, Reeve could see crew intent on errands. He recognized Lieutenant Tsamchoe, Koichi . . .

He got himself into a sitting position, his stocking feet steadying him. "Boots," he said.

Mitya retrieved them from the corner and helped Reeve into them.

"How long have I been out of it?"

"The girl dragged you in here two days ago. She must be pretty strong to do something like that. . . ."

Mitya began to lace his boots for him, and Reeve let him.

"What's the date?" he asked the boy. When Mitya told him, his heart sank. He had two days left. "The ship . . . when does it arrive?"

Mitya's face slumped. "Six days, they're saying."

Reeve nodded. The ship was late. A small reprieve, but sorely needed.

Perhaps anxious to change the subject, Mitya cocked his head toward the dome wall. "What was it like . . . out there?"

"Hard to breathe," Reeve answered. "Cold. Dangerous." As Mitya waited for more, Reeve added: "Beautiful."

"You saw a river? You floated on a real river?"

It seemed like a hundred years ago, that he'd sailed on the Tallstory River with Kalid and Dante and Spar. "Yes," Reeve said. "That was the beautiful part." Sitting up wasn't bad. In fact, it was pretty damn fine after what felt like a month of lying flat on his back.

"And the dangerous part?"

"That would be the Somaformers and the claver raids and"—the next he threw in to get a reaction—"the pirates."

Mitya nodded eagerly. "One of those pirates died. Right here. One of the guards shot him."

Thinking in alarm of Kalid, Reeve asked, "Which one?"

"You know their names?"

"Yes. Which one?"

From behind Mitya, someone said, "Dante." Marie stepped into view. "It was Dante who died." She knelt down by his side, taking his hand. "Reeve," she said.

He looked into her face, tough and lined, framed by hair like fine wire. "You made it," he said.

She grinned. "*You* made it."

He gripped her hand, speechless for a moment.

"I see the Mercury Clave didn't turn you into a

monster," she said. "How'd you get free? Loon won't say a thing."

Reeve looked past her to Mitya. "We'll talk more later, OK?"

When Mitya had gone, Reeve said, "Marie, God, Marie." As she squeezed his hand, he said, "I thought I was a dead man. Several times."

"I'm very glad you're not."

He waited until no one was nearby, and then said: "Marie . . . the cannon . . ."

She turned grim. "They're building it. It's here. Beyond that wall." She gestured over her shoulder.

Reeve waited. "And Bonhert? Where do things stand, Marie?"

She pursed her lips. "It's complicated. This can wait."

"No, tell me. Where do things stand?" He watched her for a few moments in an odd silence. "Marie?"

"Reeve, it's not that easy to describe. So much has happened."

"Well?" He hoped they were good things, but by her manner he figured they weren't. "Will anyone listen to us?" When she remained silent, he prompted, "What about Bonhert? Is he vulnerable?"

Now he was becoming impatient. "Lord of Worlds, Marie, where do things stand?"

A shadow in the doorway. And Gabriel Bonhert was standing there. Marie turned to see him, and stood up. As Bonhert came forward he put his arm around Marie's shoulder. "How's our invalid?" he said, in a deep, bass voice.

An arm around her shoulder. It stayed there.

Reeve didn't answer Bonhert, but stared at Marie. She raised her chin a little, staring back. In the long silence that followed, Reeve's mind cranked hard: She was pretending to be loyal to Bonhert . . . was cozying up to him. But the arm stayed around her shoulders somewhat too long.

Then her expression hardened. And he knew he was wrong. Bonhert had subverted her. They were . . . lovers. Yes, somehow that was clear. Bonhert had come in here to stake his claim on Marie, to say, *She's with me*. Reeve closed his eyes, wondering if he was still suffering from low oxygen, hoping he was. When he opened his eyes again, nothing had changed.

Finally, Marie said, "I'm sorry, Reeve."

Reeve smiled and nodded, affecting casualness. "Sorry . . ." A vent of anger was gathering energy in his core.

"Yes."

"Well then, if you're *sorry* . . ." He said *sorry* with all the venom at his disposal. Then he slammed to his feet. "You two are together, then?"

Bonhert laughed softly. "She's a little old for you, Reeve, after all."

He would have rushed at Bonhert, but the man was built square and strong, and Reeve was still weak. "You're a bastard, a murdering bastard." His voice was getting loud, and people were stopping nearby to watch the scene.

The affability left Bonhert's face. "You can say that once, since you're a sick man, Reeve." He smiled flat, like a turtle. "Once."

"Let's go to your quarters," Marie told Bonhert. Then she snapped at Reeve, "For privacy. And keep your mouth shut until we get there, for godsakes."

They walked out into the main dome, passing crew, who nodded at Reeve, smiling. Somebody shouted, "Reeve! Welcome home." But the three continued grimly toward a room at the back of the dome.

When Bonhert had shut the door, Reeve stalked to the end of the room and then spun around and pinned Marie with his stare. "What did he offer you, Marie? A role as Mrs. Captain? A stateroom on the big ship? A chance to screw the Captain?" He paced in the confines of the small room. "How long did it take? A day?

Two? How long did it take to forget everybody who died on Station that day?"

Marie had the grace to be ashamed. Her face slumped, making her look very old. "I wanted to tell you. . . . I couldn't. You had your opinions, Reeve, you had your loyalties. We had to get through our journey. We might have died. I didn't . . . I couldn't . . . tell you."

"Couldn't tell me what?" He looked at her in consternation. Then, in the quiet that followed, he pieced it together. He whispered, "You couldn't tell me that you've always been with this bastard?"

Bonhert burst forward, grabbed Reeve by the front of his shirt, and cuffed him hard on the side of the head.

Reeve reeled under the blow, but kept his feet.

"Give me a reason to shoot you," Bonhert said. "Give me a real good reason." He stood firmly planted in front of Reeve, his hand resting on his holstered pistol. Marie pulled on Bonhert's arm and he relented, walking over to his chair, where he sat, glowering.

Marie made as though to touch him, but Reeve recoiled. "How long, Marie? All those years with my father? You were with Bonhert all those years? Spying on him, on his work? How do you live with yourself?"

Her eyes snapped up to challenge him for the first time. "So I'm a traitor? Anyone who doesn't agree with you is a traitor?"

"You didn't betray my father?"

"Your father," she spat back. "Your father never knew me. . . ."

"Apparently not!"

"No, he never knew me. He treated me like a lackey. I did his grunt work for twelve years, Reeve, and in all that time he never knew me, never asked me how I was, what I thought."

"So you got him back, is that right?"

"Hear me out, goddamn it!" She ran her hands

through her hair for a moment, then continued: "He thought we could build a starship. He planned for the big retrofit. To gradually consume the Station to make the big ship . . . And all the while, there was no planet. No planet, Reeve. We had no destination. Cyrus Calder just said we'd find one. As though we could leave here on an act of faith!"

"And faith, as we all know, is something you were born without."

She waved him off. "Yes, maybe. And so what? I made my judgment. I judged that your father was a pathetic egomaniac who couldn't see beyond his obsessions. He gave a lot of folks a wild-eyed, dreamy hope that we could survive in space and find a good home. He split us down the middle, diverting us from the terraforming project. . . ."

"A project you never gave a damn for, either of you!"

Over in his chair, Bonhert rolled his eyes.

"Oh, yes we did!" Marie cried. "We cared, because we had to! There was nothing else, no other hope!" She looked over at Bonhert, who frowned at her shrill voice. She softened her tone: "We had our doubts, but we worked on the nanotech solution for terraforming. It wasn't going well. People doubted it was working, and they sabotaged our efforts, and sowed doubt among our science team. It was hell, Reeve. You didn't know—you were a child, and shielded from all that."

Reeve said, "So then, when the big ship called, you dropped terraforming like a hot bolt."

She hurled at him, "Yes! You bet we did."

"All of a sudden you had a revelation of faith, isn't that fine? That the new ship would find a home in space . . . and prove my father right."

"Your father wasn't right about anything in his whole life." Her face had turned ugly, and Reeve had the feeling he didn't want to hear any more from her. And was going to anyway.

"He was wrong to think we could build a ship," she

continued. "That was a pipe dream. He was wrong to think we could find a new planet with our limited technology. We could have wandered for a thousand years and not found anything . . . gradually slipping into decay and death. You talk of faith as though it's a good thing. It's not. Your father was a man of faith, Reeve. And look where it got him."

Reeve turned to Gabriel Bonhert. "Yes. An ugly death, blown apart along with Station. Brought to us by our own Captain. A man who wanted to be sure there was no one left behind who could tell the big ship the truth. The truth about what you planned to do."

Bonhert shook his head pityingly. "You got that one wrong, boy."

"No, I don't think I do. I saw you, Gabriel. That day outside Station. I was *out there*, see? I saw you push Tina Valejo off. Was she getting in the way of your setting those charges on the hull? Or was she just someone you needed to get rid of?" Reeve had advanced on Bonhert and now stood looking down at him.

"Wrong person, Reeve," Bonhert said softly. Then he looked beyond Reeve's shoulder to some point behind him.

When Reeve turned, he saw a terrible look on Marie's face.

Later, he thought that it was then that he lost the impulse to kill. He had been ready to kill Bonhert, but in the next moment, he was paralyzed. "Marie?"

Her chin came up defiantly. "Anyone could have done it," she said. "We were *all* thinking of it. But nobody else had the guts to do it." She looked bitterly at Bonhert.

After an awful pause, Bonhert spoke up: "So Marie here, she just took it on herself to get rid of Station. She's an unsentimental woman, our Marie."

"As for Tina," Marie said, "she agreed with me. She

was going to help. Then at the last minute, she got cold feet. Happens to the best of us, cold feet." Marie threw a vicious look at Bonhert.

"Tina was one of you. . . ." Reeve felt the revelations coming like a succession of blows. "But I saw Bonhert's name on the suit. . . ."

She nodded. "Only way I could work outside, in full view of the monitors. I pulled rank, using Gabriel's suit. It earned me a minute or two extra before Station ops got curious. It was enough." She sneered at Reeve's expression. "Neither of you has the guts to do what's needed when the chips are down. Neither of you." She wandered over and sat on the edge of Bonhert's cot, looking a little lost. "But I'll tell you this, Reeve, for all that you think I'm a monster. I loved you. I did it for you as much as for me."

"Don't you dare talk to me about *love*. Don't." He wanted to say more, wanted to strike out, but he stood immobile, trembling.

She went on: "Your father cast you adrift all your childhood, and I tried to help you grow up. I was the only mother you ever had. You don't have to like it, but I was. You can hate me now—I don't expect any better. But I always loved you."

"Shut up!" He charged forward and then stopped as Bonhert rose.

Bonhert was smiling. "Just give me an excuse. Any excuse."

He wanted to have at it with this man. But Bonhert was armed, and in his full strength. And he still had his job, the job he'd come to do.

He backed off. In a hoarse, small voice he said: "Why can't you people just leave? Leave on the big ship. Why do you have to kill everything that stays behind? The ship is coming. So go!"

Bonhert snorted. "I don't have time for this. . . ."

"Let him finish this, goddamn it," Marie snapped. "You owe this to me."

A huge sigh from Bonhert. "Reeve, Reeve. Yes, the ship is coming. But they're *interested* in Lithia. You know what that means? They haven't yet found a home. It's been hundreds of years they've been wandering. So maybe Lithia looks pretty good to them. And they have new technology. They're talking of reterraforming."

"Then let them try! Maybe it could work."

Bonhert shook his head and smirked at Marie. "A chip off the old block. A wishful thinker, just like your father."

"Don't you mention my father." He said it quietly enough, but murder bubbled inside him again.

Bonhert held up his hands in mock defense. "All right, all right. But understand this. Nothing can terraform this planet. It's reverting. Even if they have powerful new technologies, it will take hundreds of years, if ever, for this world to come around. Generations! That means a miserable, grubbing existence for you and your children and your grandchildren. Is that what you want?"

Reeve spoke softly. "That's hardly the point, is it? The point is what *you* want. You want to escape, and you'll take the whole planet apart to do it."

"It *will* happen," Bonhert said. "You can't stop this, Reeve. It's bigger, much bigger than you. Everyone in this dome is working for the same thing, and there's nothing you can say that will change their minds. And no way you're getting anywhere near that cannon."

Reeve considered telling him about Loon. But instead, he made for the door.

"Come with us, Reeve," Marie said, her voice thin and carping. "Lithia is lost to us, one way or another."

He looked at her like she was an insect grown large. "You're the one who's lost." He threw open the door and strode out.

Marie was after him in an instant, following him out into the dome. "Please, Reeve . . ."

He plunged toward the center of the dome, shaking off her attempts to restrain him. "Think of me when you press the button," he hissed at her. "It *will* be you, won't it—the one with guts—who blows us to hell and gone? Think of me then, *Mother*."

As he made his way to the center of the main room, he saw Loon standing there, as though she'd been waiting for him. She turned to face him, and his heart surged with relief.

"Stand by me, Loon," he whispered, as though she needed to be asked. He stood there gazing at the Stationers, nodding at friends and acquaintances, trying not to think of what they had done, but only of Lithia, only of the future. Gradually, people left off what they were doing and gathered around.

"Stationers," he said. It was time to say what he'd come here to say.

More people set aside their work and wandered over to stand in clumps, people he knew: Mitya, Val Cody, Liam Roarke, Gudrun, Tenzin Tsamchoe, Koichi . . .

Meanwhile, Bonhert had emerged from his room and, seeing this, Marie hurried to him, placing her hands on his chest, stopping him from barging forward. They argued in fierce whispers, Bonhert never taking his eyes off Reeve. Marie was arguing for him, it seemed clear, though he couldn't thank her for it.

"Stationers," he said again, pumping up his voice to reach everyone. "I've come a thousand miles to say this. So hear me out." He took Loon's hand for strength, and her grip was adamantine. "I know what you hope for. It's what we've all hoped and prayed for for five hundred years. To live. I know that you think you don't have any choice but to ruin this planet and force the ship to travel on, taking you with it.

"Some of you, though, may not like the idea of huddling in a big metal ship for the rest of your lives, hoping for a new world . . . a new world that this ship obviously hasn't yet found, in all its searching. Maybe if there was some other choice, you'd take it."

Val Cody's face knotted into wariness. People shifted, but stayed. Bonhert shook off Marie's restraints and pushed his way forward, closer to Reeve.

"OK, I'm bringing you that choice. So far it's only an idea, but maybe it's one worth working for. An idea about staying here, and . . . getting used to this place."

Stepan, standing toward the front, shook his head. "Walk around in space suits? No thanks."

Reeve put his hand on Loon's shoulder. "This woman doesn't need a space suit. She doesn't need a dome, or a breather. She's adapted. To Lithia."

A murmur at that, a wave of skepticism through the crowd. Bonhert looked at Loon, his eyes loaded.

It was time for Loon to be known; though it brought her to the attention of new enemies, it was time. Reeve told them, then, the story of Loon and her parents, and how the orthong had altered the fetus to survive. It wasn't salvation for those in this dome, he said. But if they were willing to change, it might be salvation for their descendants.

They looked at her then. All eyes were on her, but instead of curiosity or hope, the undisguised look on their faces was disgust.

Reeve pushed onward, growing desperate. "She's strong. She thrives in what Lithia is becoming. She's the new breed of people, our hope for a future, a real future."

"She's retarded!" someone shouted.

"Can't even talk," Stepan mumbled.

Reeve turned to Loon. "Tell them, Loon. Tell them what it's like—to be free, and healthy. To live here."

Loon hesitated. She looked out at the faces of the Stationers. The pause grew very long, and finally into a profound and disturbing silence. She said nothing.

"Loon!" Reeve whispered. "Tell them, something!"

But still she was quiet.

"Loon . . . please."

A few people turned and walked off, Stepan and Val and Koichi and Gudrun . . . and then a few more.

She looked up at him, and her eyes looked trapped in her face. She opened her mouth, but nothing came out.

"Pathetic," someone murmured. And then the crowd was dispersing, and finally they were alone, only Marie and Bonhert standing by. Marie stared at the floor as though embarrassed for him. She hadn't believed a word of it. Shaking his head, Bonhert took her by the arm and led her away, back to his quarters.

It must have been several minutes, but at last Reeve looked up and saw Mitya standing in front of him. He held two heavy jackets, and handed them to Reeve and Loon.

"You have to go now," he said. "Leave, while they still let you. OK?"

Reeve was too stunned to move. But he took the jacket, staring at it. He had thought they might listen, and perhaps they would have. But Loon's voice was gone. Perhaps, on that long trek up-valley, she had traded her voice for orthong strength, or alone with an unconscious man, she had at last forgotten the way of speech.

Mitya handed him a canteen of water. "We don't have any food to spare. Koichi wouldn't let me pack you any food. I'm sorry."

Then Reeve took Loon by the hand and trudged to the air lock. Mitya walked with them, as Reeve's former friends and companions on Station turned away from him, ignoring him for their more pressing duties.

"Do you think the orthong would? Help us?" Mitya asked.

Reeve whispered, in a daze: "Worth a try. Better than living cooped up in a metal cage." He'd never thought of a ship, or the old Station, as a cage. But somehow, over the last few weeks under the open sky, his thinking had changed.

He turned to go, but Mitya said: "Reeve? Is she retarded?"

Reeve turned back to him. "No," he said quietly. "She's the smartest and best of us."

They passed through the air lock and walked into the foggy clearing around the dome. It was evening, and a neon-purple sunset washed the horizon, bringing a Lithian tint to Loon's face. As they walked to the perimeter wires the guards let them pass, and they walked away from the dome, heading east this time, breaking pattern with all their previous days.

They were several miles away before Reeve slipped his hands into his jacket pockets and discovered a liberal stash of breathers that Mitya had collected for them.

3

IRON
WINDS

15

Day seventy. They had entered a great forest of blackened trees that sucked up the daylight, permitting only twilight by day and utter blackness by night. Since leaving the dome two days before, Reeve and Loon had wound through the deeply folded hills, surrounded by conifer trees clasped tightly by a new Lithiaform bark. Slick and hard, the black skin shone with ruby highlights. At first Reeve thought that these were Lithian trees, but soon it became obvious that the black growths were Lithian coverings of Terran trees. They adhered to the trunks, shoring the dead trees upright. Occasionally the black skin of the trees glistened in a stray bounce of light, bringing random slashes of sunlight to the forest without relieving its deep shadows.

As they moved away from the Rift Valley, chlorine concentrations dropped and breathing became easier, aided by young Mitya's gift of the breathers. Reeve was still weak from their ordeal in the valley, but gradually regained some strength, nourished by regular meals of roasted millipedes.

The forest was a silent world. Devoid as it was of birds or mammals, only the wind and the sound of their own footfalls kept them company. Loon did not speak, but had begun communicating with him in sign, a system he understood only poorly. He thought her refusal to speak might be a delayed reaction to grief, but even so, it hurt to have her far from him even as she walked by his side. He had his own grief as well, both for Spar and now Marie, that bitter and sad loss. He'd turned to Loon for comfort, for solidarity, and she was as faithful, as dependable as ever, but her heart seemed scoured of the love they had briefly known.

As they journeyed deeper into the transformed landscape, the very light of day seemed distorted, twisting known shapes into parodies of themselves, even as the people Reeve had once known were now growing unrecognizable.

They stopped to rest in a gully. When Reeve leaned his back against an ebony tree, it shifted behind him, a deep crack issuing from underneath the glossy surface. Reeve stood and gave it a kick with his boot. Slowly the twenty-foot sapling toppled over, split off a few inches from the base. The interior was deeply grooved, filled with spongy wood, from which mite-sized insects streamed forth.

Loon was filtering water that she carried in a canteen from a nearby stream. Her skin was by now deeply tanned from their journey, bringing her pale hair into high relief; it seemed the only source of light in all the forest. He reached out his hand and touched her arm. To his surprise, she left off her work and turned to him.

"Loon. I miss you."

She looked at him for a long moment, then crept into his arms, wrapping her arms around his waist.

"Where have you gone?" he heard himself ask. His voice sounded scrappy to his ears, an odd intrusion into this alien forest.

"I'm here," she whispered.

After days of silence, her voice came as a sharp relief. "But I'm afraid you're not here. Not really." He held her as though she were the last thing left.

She pulled back and faced him, putting her hand lightly on his face, trying to reassure him. A smile crept across her face, hesitant at first, then sweet and deep.

"Loon . . ." He wanted to say, *Do you still love me?* But he couldn't bear to hear the answer. He gazed at her. She was, had always been, part orthong. Could there be love between two such different creatures as the two of them? As the volcanic soils served up Lithia's deep nurturance, she moved toward her true self in a kind of somatic drift. Her body knew the way and could take along no passengers, no bystanders. Tears started from his eyes. "Are you leaving now?" he whispered to her.

<Not yet,> she answered.

He stared into the forest, at the snatches of glinting sun that for a moment appeared to be the language of the forest, its undecipherable sign. He closed his eyes against the pain and despair, and finally slept.

Loon woke him late in the afternoon. She was packed, ready to go on.

"Loon," Reeve began. "Loon. You must find an orthong. Persuade him to listen to us."

She looked solemnly at him, frowning a little.

"They'll kill me if I approach them," he said. "You go first. Tell them enough to get them worried. Ask them to listen to me. If they won't, then it's up to you. It'll be in your hands."

She nodded.

"Go, Loon. I'll wait here." He hated to send her on, alone. But it was true—their first approach to the orthong would go better without him.

She stood there, looking forlorn. For a moment he thought she might be reluctant to leave him; he wanted to believe that. "You have to go, Loon. For me and Spar. For what we started. Finish it." Again, she nodded. Reeve stood up, brushing the dust from himself. He wanted to embrace her, to say good-bye like lovers do.

But then she quietly turned and walked away, dragging his heart behind her. Deep in the trees, she turned around, and he could just see what looked like: <Wait for me.>

<Yes,> he replied, and then she disappeared into the shimmering blackness.

2

Wait for me, she told him. She wanted him to wait, and help her explain the crazy Sky Clave actions to the orthong. But as she looked at him, standing there on the edge of the clearing, she doubted he would last long. He was thin and pale. His flat skin was so thin it glowed blood pink and had a strange oily smell. His arms were mere strands of flesh. When she looked into his face, she saw a hundred expressions chase one another, as though he could hold no thought longer than an instant. His smell exuded fear and anxiety that did not lessen when he looked at her. So when he said that he loved her, this was another thought that he could not long hold.

Her heart raced with a surge of energy. She began a measured lope through the trees, feeling her legs reach for the ground, race up hillsides. It was a relief to run, to let out the damped-down energy that coiled in every cell of her body. At all costs she wanted to avoid eating. She could run all day on a pinch of soil, and indulging in more brought her headaches and visions. Inflamed by the sun, shimmering colors patterned the world, revealing their taste by color, and beckoning her to feast. But no. She ran on.

In the back of her mind a small voice warned her she was losing her mind. The children of the clave gathered around her, taunting, *Loony, loony.* They had been right, perhaps. But it didn't matter. She was her body now, more than ever, and her body didn't want to think or remember. It sang, *This is my hill, the up flank, the down flank, the veins of rock and the layers of soil, and this is my dance!*

She ran until finally she paused, gasping for air. Her legs had collapsed under her. When she looked up, the world became convoluted with color and smell. She was blind. Globs of light moved through the trees, eclipsing trunks and bushes. The globs revealed their own rhythmic colors, grew larger.

Stood next to her. Offered her food.

Orthong had found her. They offered her dried strips of beef, smelling of blood. There were eleven of them, the one in front the leader. She rose to face them, but had to look very far up at them.

Bringing herself under better control, she told them: <I do not eat this food. But I live, from Tulonerat's gift.> Then she knelt down and took a pinch of soil, placing it on her tongue and summoning the saliva to swallow it.

Standing immobile, the leader stared at her. Then, slowly, he reached out his great paw of a hand and touched her on the forehead, resting his rough fingertips there.

As he did so, he flooded her senses. It had terrified her, the few times she had been touched by an orthong. First by Pimarinun in Dante's prison. Then by the orthong who killed Spar. It had sent a shot of poison through her, she thought at the time. But this time, it came as a fragrant stream, complex and urgent, with an undertone of sexual arousal. At once, his fingers left her face and an expression flitted over his face, unreadable.

She burned with embarrassment. He could read her, she was certain.

Finally he signed, <Turn around.>

She obeyed, conscious of movement behind her, which she finally deciphered as the orthong robustly communicating. At last the orthong walked to her side and said, <We have nothing for you.>

It took her a moment to realize they were preparing to leave.

<I have something for you,> she responded. She repeated *you* twice, for emphasis.

He looked her over, noting perhaps that she carried no rocks to trade, and in fact carried nothing at all. The others were beginning to turn away. She signed, mustering her limited ability: <The humans. They will destroy the orthong. But one human will help you. I have this knowledge for you, so you can live.>

The leader watched her for a long moment. His heat patterns were pronounced on his white skin, great swirls like storms. <The humans die,> he said.

<Yes. But they also kill. Will Tulonerat wish to know the danger?>

<What is the danger?>

<My friend Reeve will tell you. He comes from the human clave of the sky wheel.> She pointed upward.

The leader's hide glowed with a yellow heat pattern. <Where is this human?>

Loon hesitated. This could not be given away lightly. <What will you trade to know this?>

<What will make you content?>

<You do not kill him. You bring him to Tulonerat.>

<No.>

<The humans will destroy this world. They will do so in just a few days. Will Tulonerat wish to know this?>

He stared at her, green eyes seeming to tunnel through her. <Turn around,> he signed.

After a very long while, the orthong came back, saying, <This human will speak to me and then he may leave here, but if this human speaks to one of impor-

tance, he may die.> He gazed at her as though waiting for her to respond. <It is a choice you will make.>

Loon shook her head. <*He* will. Reeve will make the choice.>

He seemed to think long and hard on that, and she thought she detected a current of annoyance in him. She had heard that in trading with the orthong you do not push too hard, that sometimes they would rather kill you than bargain for long. If they would not listen to Reeve, then she must tell them the story of the humans, and their machines and their plans. But what she knew of these things was very little, and she doubted she could make them understand.

The forest grew toward dusk, bringing out the patterns of the tree lichens, pulsing with their throbbing life. Finally the orthong leader gestured to the rest of his group, and they set out, following Loon as she retraced her steps.

3

At dawn they began removing a section of the dome. A team pulled away a segment defined by four structural ribs, making way for the geo cannon and superstructure components, which were then loaded piece by piece into the shuttles.

As the first segment came away, a rare blue sky peeked through. The constant clouds had disappeared, presenting a show of vibrant blue through the missing section, as though they had been held all these weeks within an egg and were now pecking their way out to the world. The sight made Mitya a little sick, because it was so beautiful and hopeless.

The *Quo Vadis* was approaching, just a few days away.

And all was ready, or as ready as things were likely to get. Under the strict supervision of Roarke and Cody, the components were carried from the clean room, some pieces requiring a half dozen strong crew to bear them to the shuttles. Though the carbon nanotube material of the moles was relatively lightweight, other pieces were steel and carbon matrix and brought the shuttles to their weight limits before they were full. Each shuttle load carried heavily armed crew, even though the only trouble they'd seen so far had been *inside* the dome. As Mitya watched, the first shuttle lifted off, hovering for a moment over the site as though reluctant to leave the brood nest unattended, then swept out over the valley.

Everyone was in high spirits. The *Quo Vadis* was heading in. Their ride home. Or their home itself, possibly. Some of the crew admitted they'd doubted the ship would actually come. The *Quo Vadis* crew were strangers with little reason to care for the Lithian colonists; anything might divert them from a rescue mission, and the lure of the uranium ore might, in the end, not be enough. Now the *Quo Vadis* was making good its promise, coming to take on ore and passengers.

After watching one of the shuttles take off, Oran wandered over to Mitya's side. "Guess you won't be Captain's boy anymore once we're on the big ship. Different captain." He smirked. "Different rules."

"OK by me." Mitya didn't want to think about living on the big ship. From what he'd seen, it was going to be a rude surprise to most.

Oran looked up at the clear sky. "Too bad we got the sun out today. The mist gave us some cover. Now we really got to watch for the thongs." He patted the gun in his belt webbing.

The plateau where they stood stretched to the east as far as Mitya could see. In the opposite direction behind the dome, the valley lay in perfect focus, an amazing expanse of land bisected by the distant Gandhi River. It was overwhelming—both the size of it all, and the plans to destroy it. Mitya kept thinking of

Reeve Calder and the claims he'd made for the silent girl named Loon. And whether it was true or not, whether it was possible or not, Mitya would have cast aside these shuttles and their cargo in an instant for just the chance to make it true.

The image kept sliding into his mind, of how he might wander away when no one was looking. He wouldn't live long once the moles hit home, so there was no escape. But he also knew he couldn't go to that ship. Sometime in the last few days, he had come to that conclusion without even thinking about it. He just realized, in the middle of doing other things, that he wasn't going.

"Do you ever wonder if we should look into . . . what Reeve Calder said?" he asked Oran.

Oran looked surprised. "What did Reeve say?"

"You know. About that girl. About how we could learn to breathe here."

"You're crazy." Oran snorted. "Reeve's gone native. I hope he enjoys the fireworks."

There wasn't any point in talking to Oran. He went along with things. They all did. Maybe he and Oran had been halfway to being friends once, but that was a long time ago, when Mitya was a child. Now, he figured, if he was going to die—and decide about it— maybe that made him a man. He almost blurted out the truth about the *Quo Vadis*. Almost told Oran he'd be one of those ragged, barefooted grunts that passed for crew. Oran would be sleeping in the corridors and grubbing for food, and jostling side by side with hundreds of other gunk-heads. And if he thought he'd wear a black uniform with gold buttons, then he was more of a child than Mitya was.

Tenzin Tsamchoe walked by. Mitya wanted to grab him by the arm. Wanted to say, *Look at what we're giving up. A chance to live a real life. Blue sky. Solid ground beneath our feet. That ship up there—it's dark, cramped and ugly. It's a lousy trade. Doesn't anybody care?*

But he said nothing.

The second shuttle rose from the clearing in a blast of fire and dust. Soon the first one would be back, and they'd stuff it full of equipment and crew. The whole thing was a clockwork machine, oiled and running, unstoppable.

Mitya began to think about how he would slip away, when the time came.

4

For two days Nerys lay in her bed fighting with herself to stay calm. To *become* calm. But as she lay immobile, her anger grew against Hamirinan, and her resentment against Salidifor, who was still absent. To save her pregnancy, she knew she must try to relax—the one thing she did miserably.

To her surprise, the women were bringing her food. Haval told her that an orthong—*not* Salidifor— brought packs of food twice a day for Nerys, but would not enter the berm, a gesture the women took for concern over the unborn pup, and also a reflection of Nerys' ostracism. Haval, Mave, and Odel were her rotating attendants, and other women came in to visit, as though her loss of face had made her finally acceptable. Nerys chafed against this conditional regard, but was also grateful for the company and the relief from the boredom.

At times she gazed out her window into the yellow polyp thicket, and beyond to patches of sky, a mere blue lace when viewed from the bottom of the outfold. Perhaps Vikal would find her. Through the square of her window she watched for flashes of white, but she saw no orthong, young or grown.

After two days, her womb quieted, the pup settling back in. With relief Nerys rose from her bed, dressed in clothes borrowed from Odel, and emerged into the tea room. A dozen faces looked up in astonishment.

"Not dead yet, am I?" Nerys asked.

Haval rose. "If you want something, I'll fetch it."

"Thanks, no. You've all done enough for me. I have some business to take care of."

Odel blocked her way. "Think twice, Nerys. Where are you going?"

Nerys locked gazes with the older woman. "I'm going to find Salidifor."

Odel sighed. "I don't think he wants to see you."

The pup stirred inside her, reflecting her anger. Nerys took a deep breath and said, "If he doesn't, then I'll leave. But I have to know."

Gently brushing past Odel, Nerys descended the stairs and quickly crossed the courtyard before the others could gang up on her and counsel caution. She *would* be cautious; even Salidifor admitted that she could handle some things with discretion. Somewhere in the outfold a lone bird sang. Whatever the orthong had engineered into the growths, the terran birds loved it, making Nerys wonder if some of the seeds were edible by humans. But that, no doubt, was another taboo. As she made her way to Salidifor's berm, a movement in the outfold caught her eye. She stopped to watch more carefully, and in the distance she could just make out an orthong—no, two orthong walking there. They were weavers, by their sleeveless tunics. As Nerys peered into the deep outfold, she saw that there were dozens of weavers making their way through the forest, all traveling in the same general direction. If they glimpsed her where she stood on the path, she likely registered in their minds like a squirrel in the woods, of minimal interest.

As she approached Salidifor's berm, her chest constricted with excitement. This place had become a great pleasure to her, an oasis of the deepest satisfaction, a place of learning. She'd started to cross the courtyard when an orthong she didn't recognize emerged from the front entryway and bade her stop.

Through a brief exchange, she learned that Salidifor didn't dwell here anymore. He didn't know where Salidifor had gone. She started to back away in response to his orders to leave. Behind him, Nerys saw another orthong emerge from the entryway.

Hamirinan.

She stared at him as the other orthong continued to herd her away. So. Hamirinan had taken Salidifor's place. For an instant she worried that *he* would become her lord. But of course, that would be too great an honor. And if such an offer was made, she would have to tell him where he could put it.

She plunged back down the path, a trickle of acid etching into her stomach walls. The pup struck out, and she patted her bulging middle. "Don't worry," she whispered. "Don't worry." But she was talking more to herself at that moment, as her mind raced to imagine what had happened to Salidifor. She stopped on the path as a deep chill enveloped her. She wished she'd worn a warmer shirt.

Rubbing her bare arms, she was standing on the path trying to figure out her next move when she noticed a weaver watching her from the edge of the outfold. She was alone. Slowly, Nerys turned to face her. Nerys greeted her in the most gracious style she knew. The female regarded her stoically, and kept glancing at Nerys' belly.

Then Nerys found herself dancing on the narrow path. She apologized for her boldness in speaking unbidden. She asked about Salidifor. She spun, executing a turn, and when she looked again, the female was gone.

<Thanks anyway,> Nerys signed, adding a tinge of irony to her movement.

It was too much to hope that the females would be any more trusting than the males. Or perhaps trust was too fine a point. The female had simply disregarded her. It was tiresome in the extreme, that orthong tendency.

But soon another opportunity arose. The outfold was full of orthong females this morning. Nerys cast about for a better introduction, thinking it might be well to offer a gift, or more to the orthong point, a trade item. It struck her as odd that she had absolutely nothing to give—not even some small, worthless thing. Only the clothes on her back, and these the female orthong had given *her*, indirectly at least, as a product of the outfold. No, it must be something from Nerys herself. When she finally realized that she did have something, she raced back to the berm for the tool she'd need. She had no idea if the orthong would consider it a trade item of value—rather doubted it, in fact—but it was a chance.

Back on the path once more after raiding the tea room, Nerys used the small knife to cut off her single thick braid of hair. It took a few moments to saw through it using one of the dull blades the women used for cutting the yarn on their weaving projects. When she had finished, the two-foot rope of hair lay in her hands like a glistening snake. She tied a piece of yarn around the loose end to preserve the braid, and stepped just off the path.

At first nothing moved in the outfold, and Nerys worried that her opportunity was lost, but at last a couple of females emerged from a stand of yellow columnar growths. When they saw her, they altered their course to avoid her. But when a second group became visible in the distance, Nerys waved her arms, luring a group of three closer to inspect her.

They looked at her belly, but ignored her attempt to communicate. In another moment they turned to go, but one of them stayed behind. She was, as was evident from the amount of silver streaking, very old, and like the others, she wore a sleeveless tunic of shimmering black. Salidifor had told her the black covering was a chemical wrap designed to conduct heat away from the skin, heat generated by the intense chemical processes of their metabolism. The weavers had less need than the males for dispersing body heat and thus went sleeveless, a convention both useful and culturally imbued.

When the orthong paused in front of her, Nerys swung into action. Laying the braid on the floor of the outfold, she danced her best, using subtle flourishes to describe her great need to speak with Salidifor, explaining that he was her lord, and would be waiting to hear from her. She had no hexagons to guide her, and hoped she didn't mistake her directions. Then she picked up the braid and offered it to the female. When the orthong made no move to accept it, Nerys laid it on the ground and waited.

The old female raised her arms to speak. <How many of you are there?>

Nerys tried to understand the question. <There are twenty-two breeders in my compound. But there are other compounds.>

<How many worlds do you . . .> Nerys could not quite see the last word.

<Say again, please.>

<How many worlds do you eat?>

Nerys swallowed hard, trying to figure out what to say. <I don't understand,> she finally admitted.

The orthong looked toward the others, who had now disappeared into the outfold. She bent down and picked up the braid, closing her eyes as she fingered it. This continued for a long time, and Nerys waited with a newfound patience. The creature kneaded the braid with the fingers of her right hand, her eyes unfocused. At last, the braid slipped through her fingers and fell to the ground.

The weaver locked a newly interested gaze on Nerys. <Who is the pup you bear?>

Nerys' heart sank as she realized that here was another question she couldn't answer. <It is the pup of Salidifor.> She hoped that was enough.

<Do you not know its outfolding?>

<No.> Whatever *outfolding* meant.

<You do not know the pup,> the orthong concluded.

<No. But I wish I did.>

<It is not necessary,> the old orthong said.

Nerys swallowed her annoyance. <Maybe not. But it is necessary to find Salidifor.>

To Nerys' dismay, the female turned to go. As she began walking off, she raised one arm and pointed halfheartedly in the direction of the deeper outfold. That was Nerys' answer.

It was all the answer she needed. She began threading her way into the forest.

The exchange left her feeling sour. Why was she always discontent? The other women managed to find their happiness, such as it was. But Nerys would always push and push, sometimes not satisfied until something broke: a rule, or a relationship. Sometimes things were no better because of it, and sometimes they were worse; as now, with Salidifor in disgrace and she roaming the outfold, pregnant and ignored.

And her daughter . . . No, she wouldn't think of her now. But indeed, she would. Anar died, the thought came, because . . . because her mother wasn't satisfied with their clave, and decided that life would be better among the orthong.

And her mother was wrong.

Stopping on the path, she stared into the trees. Anar, Anar. A sob rose up into her throat. *You died, Anar, not because of Reeve Calder, but because your mother didn't know how to be content.*

She plunged on through a glen of lavender stalks, velvet to the touch, hating the brush of them against her body, the fruity smells, the cloying colors. It would have been so restful to look upon green trees and proper leaves and grasses. In truth, she missed them so badly she felt ill. But everything she looked at was despicably orthong, reminding her that this awful place was her chosen clave, and yet she was more outcast here than she'd ever been before.

When at last she found Salidifor, a light snow had begun to fall, and she no longer cared why he had abandoned her.

Fifteen paces from where she stood was a lean-to, under which the ground had been dug away to a depth of several feet. Salidifor was inside, stacking rocks in the back of the den. He turned when he caught wind of her. He stood there with his hands at his side, inexpressive, waiting.

She wanted to hurt him, so she said: "One of your females told me you were here. It cost me my hair, but she told me."

He turned away from her, but this orthong tactic wasn't going to work. He could hear her, she well knew. And *would* hear her.

"So how long are you going to sulk in the woods?"

He made no move to speak.

Nerys walked closer, noting that his berm had almost nothing in it, just a neat stack of rocks and a rough blanket. She thought for a moment that he had fallen very low, and felt a pang of regret amidst her anger. "I've been sick for days and I've spent all day looking for you. You could answer me." The snow was melting in her hair and on her shoulders, making her shiver.

He bent down and took up his blanket. Then he stepped out of the berm and approached her, putting the blanket around her shoulders. She bit back tears.

"Salidifor," she said, not knowing what to say. Then, surprising herself, she burst out: "I'm sorry."

He looked down on her with eyes gone opaque, reflecting snow. <Have you no respect for my teaching?>

"Ordering and commanding aren't the same as

teaching. Humans are hard to confine the way you like to."

<I have failed to teach you. To think that once I was proud of what you could do!>

Nerys winced inwardly. "Like a pet dog! Run, jump, lie down!" But the orthong did not understand the concept of pets. It was useless to try to talk to someone who had no common references. They had tried over many weeks to communicate, and they had failed badly.

"Salidifor, I didn't touch Vikal. I never touched the pup. After that day with Pila."

<Vikal? You know her name?>

"Is that forbidden too?"

He made a gesture of exasperation. Turning, he led her into the berm and out of the falling snow. They sat together on the floor, which was covered with soft outer husks from a lavender thicket.

In this cold and barren place, she didn't have the heart to be angry. "Let's not fight," she said.

He looked at her sharply. <You would lose a fight.>

She smiled. "I meant, let's not speak harshly."

<I agree.> He reached in his pocket and retrieved a length of honey-colored rope she had first eaten when Bitamalar guided her and Galen to the outfold. <You should eat something.> He urged a morsel on her and she took it, savoring its nutlike taste.

He pulled some of the leaves around her feet and calves in an effort to keep her warm.

Then, as he gazed out on the haze of snow outside the hut, he said: <You understand a warrior? Your men are warriors sometimes.> He made an orthong shrug. <Not very *good* warriors . . .>

She smiled, indulging him.

<I am one of these, Nerys, a warrior. My bond fathers were all warriors, even between the worlds. I was a warrior for all the decades we have been here, until just eight years ago, when I was elevated to Tulonerat's service. I have lost Tulonerat's service now. Maybe it is for the best. Now I will go kill humans on the plains, which I am very good at.>

"And all because I spoke to a pup?"

<Nerys! It is not just a pup. It is the pup that bonded to you when you took her from Pila! When Hamirinan saw the pup dance with you, he knew there was a bond. It was not the dancing that mattered so much. It was what it signified.> He looked over at her. <This is why I told you not to have contact with the pup.>

Nerys was abashed. It was not just a simple rule she had broken—she had revealed important information to her enemy. "How bad is it, then?"

He looked back out. <Bad enough.>

"How can Tulonerat elevate that creature Hamirinan?"

<Hamirinan is a brave warrior and a trusted advisor. He has made no grave errors. His bonds extend widely, and he is sought by everyone, and many females as well. It is true he does not like you. But he believes you are not constructive.>

It was bitter indeed to think that Hamirinan might be right. And bitter as well to think that Salidifor liked Hamirinan. She considered telling him what Hamirinan had done to her that day in the compound. But he had enough troubles without hearing hers.

"Are you really leaving, Salidifor?"

He brought his chin up, *Yes.*

"I will miss you."

He turned to look at her, with an expression she couldn't decipher. She waited for what he might say, but his stillness went on and on.

"I will miss you," she repeated. Then she reached out and touched his arm, a thing she had never done before.

His skin flinched slightly under her fingers, then became exceptionally warm. His hand came around her wrist, and she could feel a slightly extruded claw dent her skin. If she thought he might allow the intimacy of a touch, she could see how wrong she was. He looked at her with a new expression, and she suddenly feared him. He lifted her hand off his arm, in a slow, measured movement.

"Salidifor . . ."

He rose to his feet. He paced away, then turned in a swift movement to face her. <Do you know why you are told never to touch an orthong?> He signed in a clipped, rapid fashion—very angrily.

She shook her head.

<Because to touch, except in combat, suggests a bond. Can *establish* a bond. Do you wish to bond with me, Nerys?> Sarcasm, there.

Perhaps she did—would that be so bad? She was so unutterably sick of the orthong and all their rules and not knowing the rules. Not *liking* the rules. "I am lonely. I do have feelings; I thought perhaps you had some for me."

<Do you wish to ruin me among orthong and you among humans?>

It was a question he did not expect her to answer, but it filled her with confusion. Was her affection for Salidifor a thing of ruin?

<Do you wish to destroy yet more? I am done with you. Done with you!>

She couldn't prevent an angry, flip response: "Can't you just say no?"

He moved toward her in one gigantic step, grabbing her by the upper arm, pulling her toward him, and lifting her onto her toes. The thin strand of gray that pierced the side of his face seemed to flare, and his skin exuded a spicy smell. Her pulse raced as he fixed her with a brackish-green stare. Finally he glanced away, looking down at his hand clutching her arm. He was hurting her. Gradually, he released the hold. His claws were all extruded, but he had managed to grab her without puncturing her skin.

She remembered to breathe again as Salidifor paced away to the far corner.

<Now everything is changing,> he said. <Nothing holds together. That should please you, Nerys.> He turned from her and leapt out of the berm. She followed him. A white sunlight had dispelled the snowstorm, sending tendrils of pain into her eyes from the glare.

He watched her for a long moment. <Your people have proved Tulonerat a fool. A ship between stars has come, circling above us, and it is human, showing that you did not lie. You will learn how much of a victory it is to make a fool of a queen, and you will learn from better teachers than I.>

Though she was sick at heart for his scorn, she found room to be curious. "A ship? A spaceship?"

He ignored the question. <Now all the warriors will be needed. Fewer administrators, more fighters. That is a world I know well.>

He looked at her with what she thought was great sadness. <Leave me now. I do not see you anymore.>

The words were like a full set of claws hitting her skin. She wished he had cut her physically rather than this way. She waited for a long while. Though he had turned away from her, she could have spoken to him, could have said, *It's all my fault. Forgive me.* But she wanted him to turn to face her, to give her permission to speak.

He didn't turn around. The snow melted around his great feet, and still he didn't move.

According him a last measure of respect, she kept her silence, turning back into the outfold, biting her tongue so hard she tasted her own blood. But keeping silent.

16

1

Day seventy-two. Reeve and his escort emerged from the onyx forest, stepping onto a ledge of rock overlooking a broad valley. Reeve squinted as a sheet of sunlight peeled away the gloom that had shrouded them for days. For a moment the utterly clear air, its pale blue buffed to a high sheen and throbbing with light, distracted him from another wonder below: the orthong forest. They had arrived.

Below them, a lavender wall enclosed a seemingly endless biome of jumbled colors. It was impossible to judge its height or extent, nor could any feature or building be seen, other than the demarcations created by abrupt changes of color. No orthong milled about in that valley, except, presumably, within the depths of this habitation.

Loon stood beside Reeve, her face wiped clean of any expression. He'd given up trying to communicate with her. A narrow tube had been secured around her waist, and an orthong held the other end of the tether. Responding to the commands of the reins, she accompanied the group passively enough, but with the aura of an animal ready to bolt. He suspected that they had

drugged her in some way, but why, he couldn't guess.
Nor could he protest.

He thought that once they entered the orthong
habitat he was unlikely to come out. The lead orthong
had made clear that his demand to speak to someone
of importance was dangerous. But he'd been in more
or less constant danger ever since he set foot on
Lithia, and the orthong could not be any worse. If he
had wondered at Spar's harsh life and his keen satisfaction in it, he thought maybe now he understood.
Death was on every side. So you just kept going forward, grateful for each of your eight lives. He hoped to
die with Spar's grace, with the grace to say it had all
been good.

They climbed down the side of the ravine, a descent
over crumbling clay soils and talus slopes scoured of
Lithian growth. The breeze brought a sharp new smell
that he took for the smell of the orthong forest, sweet
and harsh at the same time. As they walked closer to
the biome itself, Reeve could see that the purple wall
was not uniform, but composed of huge plates that in
places appeared to be the remnants of bubbles. In a
constant play of light, the wall seemed to change, knit-
ting up here, expanding there. As he watched he became convinced that the thing was altering even as he
watched it, becoming more solid, as though to say, *Do
not enter.* In fact, they didn't enter, but stopped some
twenty yards from the wall and waited while one of the
orthong went into a fissure that Reeve hadn't noticed
before.

He sat with Loon, holding her, feeling the heat of
her flushed skin. She was alert, but only to what she
saw inside her bright and semiliquid eyes. If he'd
hoped for help from Loon in translating, that hope was
fast receding. Now that they weren't moving, his body
sagged with weariness. The stray thought came that
here was a young Stationer who had once longed for

adventure and who was now surrounded by eight tall aliens and who, even so, might just fall asleep.

Finally a stir among his orthong escort caught his attention as a new fissure appeared in the lavender wall. Out of this rent emerged several orthong, with one leading the way toward Reeve's group. This individual, wearing the typical long-sleeve coat, had a slight streak of silver flushing its neck and bore the demeanor of a leader.

He—or she—signed to Reeve, but he couldn't make out the meaning. Turning to Loon, Reeve tried to rouse her so that she could interpret, but although she stood, her attention wavered. His heart sank with the realization that she was not going to help with this. But he gathered his concentration and signed: <I speak only a little.>

<Where will the humans fall?> the orthong seemed to say.

<Do you wish to trade?> Reeve responded.

<Do you wish to live?>

"Tell them," he heard Loon whisper.

He turned on her. "I *can't*. Wake up, for the Lord's sake!" His harsh tone seemed to penetrate for a moment, but then she looked away, vacantly.

He tried his sign again: <The humans will kill all. I will help you. Do you wish to trade?>

The orthong responded, but again, Reeve could not follow the flash of his hands. After a time, one of the other orthong came forward, and instructed him to turn around so that his back was to the group. Gently, they turned Loon to face away as well. His skin crawled as he feared some blow from behind.

They stood thus for a very long time. An hour or more passed. Behind him he could occasionally hear the orthong moving around in some way. At last an orthong came to his side and bade him turn around.

When he did so, the woman called Nerys stood before him.

His shock could not have been more pronounced. Her hair was chopped short, and though she looked healthy, her eyes were haggard and her expression was as grim as those of the orthong creatures around her.

When she looked at Reeve, her face registered her own amazement, followed quickly by a narrowing of her eyes. "You," she said.

He realized with dismay that this woman had been brought as a translator—perhaps his final piece of ill fortune.

Her glance quickly took in Loon. "I hear you've come for a favor of us." Her tone conveyed the likelihood of a favor being granted. And her reference to *us*—she and the orthong—was not lost on Reeve.

"Nerys. I bring a pice of news that's bad for all of us. Can you communicate with them?"

Her smile was awful. "It's hard to believe you bring bad news, Reeve Calder."

Stepping carefully, he said, "I've lived with your curse long enough, Nerys. You know that Dante killed your daughter, not me."

"But you helped, didn't you?"

"If I'd chosen her, it wouldn't have helped! She would have died quickly in the wilderness on her own."

"She died quickly anyway, didn't she? She died in an instant!" In the next moment she stepped forward and hit him on the side of his face, a strong blow. He took that blow, though he could have blocked it.

"You chose," she said hoarsely.

"By the Lord of Worlds, Nerys! They forced me to choose. Try to forgive me."

At her fierce stare, he braced for another blow, but instead, her face sagged. She took a very deep breath and looked past Reeve, past his shoulders to the wall of the valley.

They stood silently a very long while as the orthong looked on with an eerie patience. Finally she said, "If you've come to tell the orthong about the spaceship, they already know that piece of bad news."

"No," he said. "It's a lot worse than that."

Nerys looked up as the orthong chief signed to her. Looking back to Reeve, she said, "This orthong lord is called Hamirinan. Don't get crosswise with him. Now tell me your news. A summary, quickly."

Reeve told his tale. He told of the ship that might stay, and the faction of humans that wanted to be sure they didn't. He told of Loon, and how she was altered, and how she lived and thrived, although the orthong had drugged her into stupidity. He described the trade that he proposed: human lives for orthong.

Nerys stared at him all through his tale, murmuring once, "Everything is changing, as he said." She looked back at the orthong called Hamirinan, whose expression was a curdled maze of white. The creatures almost had faces; a ripple of skin could be mistaken for a human emotion registering there—could be *mistaken*, Reeve reminded himself.

When he had finished, she said, "If you're lying, we'll all be punished. You'll die, and many more. Is that what you want?"

"What I want is the same as you. To live. This is a chance for us all to live."

She watched him, fiercely. Then, she turned to Hamirinan and moved before him, in what looked like a slow, measured dance. He realized she was speaking to Hamirinan, but it was not like any sign he had ever seen.

The dance was short. Nerys glanced back at Reeve, saying, "I told him that for a matter of such importance, this breeder woman craved the instruction of Lord Salidifor."

"Lord who?"

"The one who taught me to speak, and much else."

Hamirinan was advancing on Nerys. She stepped backward as though she expected a blow. As the great creature towered over her, she did an astonishing thing: She started to remove her clothes. Her jacket dropped to the ground. She began unbuttoning her shirt.

Hamirinan signed, <Stop,> and she obeyed.

With fewer clothes on, Nerys looked as though she might be pregnant. The whole scene was bizarre in the extreme. But Reeve knew enough to remain silent just now.

Hamirinan and Nerys faced off. She said, <I . . . the teaching of my lord.>

It seemed to Reeve that she was afraid of this Hamirinan, that she spoke with elaborate deference. Perhaps, he reflected, it was required by the orthong, as the conquerors. Hamirinan watched her closely, then gestured to one of his attendants, who dashed off and disappeared into a narrow gap in the front wall of the habitat.

"What's going on, Nerys?"

She ignored this question. "If you're lying, I'll kill you with my own hands."

He held her eyes with his own. "I'm not lying. I wish to the Lord above I was."

She nodded. "Then perhaps you bring Salidifor's redemption."

His expression begged her for explanation, but she merely smiled. "Only tell the truth. I'll interpret. We'll then be bound together by your words. Don't dishonor me here. I have enough of that already."

"I swear, Nerys."

She snorted. "Why do I listen to you?" She turned her back to him and stood impassively, like the orthong. After a moment he heard her whisper to him, "No matter what happens, avoid looking at an orthong directly. Never touch one. And do exactly as I say."

After a long wait, a crack appeared in the lavender wall and an orthong emerged from the habitat to join them.

"This is my Lord Salidifor," she said in a low voice. "You will obey him in everything, you understand?"

Nerys approached the orthong and engaged him in a flurry of hand sign. Suddenly the creature strode over to Loon. In alarm, Reeve moved to her side.

"Stay away, Calder," Nerys warned.

He stopped in mid-stride, and watched as Salidifor reached out to touch Loon on the neck. The creature's great paw remained there for some time. When he withdrew his hand, Reeve didn't know whether he had satisfied himself of Loon's validity or not; but he suspected that Loon's chemistry spoke in some way to the orthong.

Salidifor then approached Reeve, signing, <You . . . > Reeve gave up trying to follow him.

Nerys said, "Your people are destroyers of worlds?"

Reeve answered Salidifor: "To my shame, my people will destroy this one."

Nerys interpreted Salidifor's hand sign: "Why would our chief listen to such creatures?"

Reeve spoke, taking care not to look Salidifor in the eyes. "You only have to stop them. That's not much risk. If you succeed, you'll live."

"And if," Nerys said, watching Salidifor's sign language, "if we succeed, you will ask a very magnificent favor. To surround us with many generations of shame-filled humans."

"Do not make the mistake of thinking all humans alike," Reeve said.

The side of Nerys' mouth moved into a half smile, and she interpreted this to Salidifor, her eyes pointedly downcast. It was odd to see this bold woman taking on an attitude of slavish deference; but he suspected the woman had been well broken to their service.

Salidifor gazed at Reeve for a very long while, as though he might discern truth just by standing still and watching. Turning to the other leader, Salidifor exchanged a brief flurry of sign, after which the one called Hamirinan gathered his escort around him and strode away.

Nerys' eyes shone with a great intensity. "Yes," she whispered, and "Let's see if Tulonerat falls asleep *this* time."

Reeve moved to put his arm around Loon. He had no idea what was going on, except that he was on his way, it would appear, to unburden himself of the message he had traveled so far to deliver. "It must be soon, Nerys. We have to hurry," he said.

She turned an incredulous look on him. "The only time I ever saw an orthong move fast was to kill something. I suggest you cultivate patience." She turned back to Salidifor, but the great orthong remained silent, treating her, Reeve thought, with not much more respect than the other leader had done.

"We should go *now*, Nerys, if our efforts are going to count."

Without looking at him she said, "They won't let you into the outfold. The females won't allow it. I don't think they have much tolerance for the enemy being inside, infecting their forest."

Beside Reeve, Loon stirred, but her eyes were still vacant.

"Why have they drugged her?" Reeve asked Nerys.

Nerys shrugged. "She's sick. She mustn't eat anything for a while."

They stood thus in the brilliant sun, watching the lavender wall for whatever would come next. Some eight of the orthong escort still remained, and they stood perfectly immobile, as though their lives had been devoted to silent waiting.

When it began it was almost unnoticeable. A shimmering of the wall, which might have been a play of light. Then it became pronounced, as a puckering of a ten-foot-wide section slowly lifted the front face of the outfold, as Nerys called it. The wall over the last hour had been solidifying, with each declivity and crack slowly filling in as though the entire front had been heating up and melting into one unit. Now, a pattern was emerging. The rumpled edges formed a cowl, in the center of which a hole appeared. The cowl crept forward—rapidly, by orthong standards—producing a tunnel with twists and folds. From it wafted a breeze filled with a piquant smell. After the tube had extended to a distance of about twenty feet the forward edge began darkening to blue and then black. It was done growing.

Something appeared in the depths of this great tentacle, a human figure. No, an orthong. The creature, slightly smaller than any Reeve had seen before, moved into sight at the end of the tube, surrounded by many other orthong, creatures draped in black sleeveless garments, solemnly gazing out at Loon, it seemed. Their numbers stretched to the limits of his sight.

"Tulonerat," Nerys said softly.

Salidifor appeared to have understood her, for he signed something briefly, and Nerys whispered to herself, "No. It's Divoranon."

"I know that name. . . ." Reeve searched his memory.

Nerys nodded. "She was once called Divor, before her adulthood came to her. Didn't you say that Loon's parents saved one called Divor?"

"Yes."

Nerys nodded. "Well then. Divoranon is important now." She watched the tube with its pale assembly of watchers. "When my lord commands you, tell your story, Reeve."

He prayed for eloquence.

Then Salidifor turned to him and made a sign gesture: <Speak.>

Reeve spoke.

2

Nerys translated on the hexagonal floor of the tube just at the opening, where she could see Calder on the outside and Divoranon on the inside. As a deep, moonless night fell over the valley, the only light was the glow of the tube itself as a network of veins surged with a frazzled light. Nerys danced past exhaustion. Once, Divoranon graciously offered her food to keep her energy up. Then the questioning continued again, punctuated by Divoranon's long absences as she retreated into the tube, where the other females crowded around her. Then she would emerge again with more questions.

At one point, Calder was disciplined by an orthong, receiving a modest cuff that sent the Stationer flat on his back. This occurred when they took Loon into the outfold. Calder was protective of the hybrid creature, though he could surely have no claim on her. According to Salidifor, Loon had *lost confidence,* an expression related to her inability to manipulate her chemical intake, the most basic level of molecular *knowing.* Sickness was virtually unknown among the orthong and was considered a form of neurosis when it did occur. Loon, however, was an anomaly: an adolescent, yet an adult. In any case, they had taken her away.

Now Nerys stood on the borderland between human and orthong. She was the intercessor between this despised zerter and her ambiguous masters. But at the interface lay power. With her demeanor and her interpretation she controlled what both learned and some of what both might conclude. She made Calder sound more intelligent than he was, while reinforcing her theme that humans could learn and were eager to do so. At the same time, her scrupulous protocol and patience displayed, she hoped, her new constructive approach.

The thrill of having such power infused her muscles with unflagging energy. Here was the nexus of all her struggles. She was indispensable to the orthong, and they relied on her unquestioned language skills. The new ship and the weapon of planetary destruction now proved that humans had *math*, if not peaceful intentions. Whether they would concede that humans had real intelligence, given their propensity for foolishness, she didn't know. At the very least humans must be acknowledged as formidable foes.

As interpreter, all this information was hers to manipulate. Most important, she built up Salidifor in front of Divoranon, turning to Salidifor for clarification, reinforcing his position and demonstrating her loyalty. And behind it all, with delicate nuance, she demonstrated her remorse to Salidifor.

See, I have learned after all. From a master.

And in turn, as they waited for Divoranon, Salidifor gradually relented. He stepped closer to her, giving her guidance in how to explain things to Divoranon. And during one of Divoranon's absences, he told her that Tulonerat had entered end cycle, giving over all leadership to Divoranon. As Nerys waited, not probing for more but letting him reveal at his own pace, he added details: that Tulonerat had shown not the slightest interest in the arrival of the human ship, and that her aides, growing frantic, had waited by her side for three days, refusing sustenance, until at last she looked at them and said, *I will not speak again.* By this they knew she was deep in quantum structures, and that all that she learned from now on she must never reveal. When she said *I will not speak again,* they rushed to find Divoranon, leaving Tulonerat in the sunken courtyard, surrounded by her incomparable constructs—some of such exquisite design they were complete mysteries to everyone but Tulonerat. But even these held no interest for her any longer. She was in the deepest world, and she would not emerge again.

Salidifor explained that the outfold was morphing into a protective bunker. Its outer shell was now a shield. Inside, defensive and offensive tropisms made passage by nonorthong impossible. This was why Calder could not enter, nor any new breeder women who might be unmodified and therefore classified as nonorthong by the outfold.

Divoranon had been gone a long time. Calder was fairly stomping with impatience, but Nerys could have stood there all night. This was her night, her victory, no matter what happened.

Salidifor left for a time, returning with a tray of food, small biscuits filled with fruit. She ate, eyes downcast.

<You can look at me, Nerys.>

She glanced at his face, believing that she saw in it a kind of warm regard. He was close enough that they might talk in simple sign without being seen by others.

<Things are changing, Salidifor.>

His head tilted slightly. *Yes.* <I was foolish to think it would always be as it was.>

She didn't think him foolish, but was grateful that he was willing to take some blame . . . and admit it to her. <There are so many things I didn't know,> she said. <I was not a good student. I'm very smart, but I can be stupid too. It's typical of humans.>

She thought he might say it was typical of orthong too. But it wouldn't be like him to assign flaws to other orthong.

<You rise, Nerys.>

<Do you say so?>

He held eye contact, a gesture of intimacy. <I say so.>

She could barely see him in the dull glow of the tube, but she thought he looked tenderly at her. The impulse to touch him passed, reluctantly—that wasn't his way, with her at least, and some things she couldn't have. Still, she filed the notion away for later reexamination. There were many things that Salidifor had told her were impossible that hadn't been so very difficult, when one put one's mind to it. . . .

The night moved on toward dawn, and still they waited together, sometimes watching Calder as he paced, pitying his restless, energy-wasting movements. He would learn soon enough that, when it was time to wait, one remained still.

She ventured a thought: <If touching causes a bond, why is it that orthong have sometimes touched me? For example, Hamirinan has . . . been rough with me.>

<We can shield ourselves. But if you touch, you may catch us off guard.>

<In the shelter yesterday . . . did I . . . catch you off guard?>

A commotion from within the canal registered at the corner of her eye. A crowd of orthong attendants approached down the tube. If Divoranon was among them, Nerys couldn't differentiate her. But someone was at the forefront. That individual stepped forward.

Her hair had fallen out except in blond wisps around her ears. She stood tall and alert, dressed in a brown tunic, setting her apart from the black garb of the others.

Close to Nerys' side, Reeve Calder whispered: "Loon."

Loon gazed directly at him, with eyes of deepest green.

<We will trade,> she signed.

3

"Mitya! Mitya!" they called. He hunkered down behind a jumble of boulders so they couldn't see him. They were loading the last shuttle, preparing to abandon the dome.

Let them call. There was really no one he would

miss from the whole bunch of them. They were a squabbling, grubbing, miserable bunch, down to the last crew member, and they could have their *Quo Vadis* and their long ride to nowhere. He carried a rock in his heart as big as the one he hid behind. They would blow everything to pieces. It didn't take a genius to realize that was a great crime, or that every one of them was afraid to die but not to kill. They had sabotaged the Station, and now Lithia. He never wanted to see their faces again.

And he wouldn't, he realized with a pang.

He had managed to slip away in the confusion of the final loading. He just took that little walk beyond the defensive wires, and then crawled through the scrub until he made it to his hideaway. There wasn't a lot of cover out here, but he figured they wouldn't look for him very hard. The last few days had been a frenzy of activity; protocols slipped and tempers flared as Bonhert carped on the schedule. The ship was in orbit, and they didn't want any surface visits from that quarter, oh no. They'd plant the moles in a hurry and ferry up to the ship in time to watch the whole thing come apart under their feet. Looking for a thirteen-year-old runaway wouldn't be a big priority.

As he watched from behind the rock, he saw a figure emerge from the dome and stand there, looking around. It was Captain Bonhert. It surprised Mitya to hear him call his name. That he would be on Bonhert's mind at a time like this seemed unlikely. But there he stood, the last man out, the last man onboard the shuttle. Maybe done for effect, the heroic effect. Mitya could imagine that once onboard the big ship, Captain Kitcher could kiss his gold braid good-bye. The thought of the hapless old fart welcoming Bonhert onboard made Mitya smile and shake his head. If Kitcher thought he had his share of factions and plotting now, wait until he met Gabriel Bonhert.

"Mitya!" Bonhert bellowed. "Last chance! The black and the gold, my boy."

Mitya felt a pang for that old dream. And the Captain that had almost been his hero. He turned around with his back against the sheltering rock and put his head on his scrunched-up knees. He was scared to death. But he'd be damned if he would move an inch.

When he heard the shuttle rumble, his stomach felt those engines in their very walls. But then he just kept thinking of that little can of humanity dragging itself among the stars, and he held his ground. And when the shuttle rose into the air, he stood up and watched it sweep away over the dome, and he heard the thought in his mind, *Go with the Lord*, because they were going to need it, and he didn't want to die hating them.

After another minute the sound of the shuttle was gone, and an utter silence descended. It was the worst moment of Mitya's life. Not once had he ever experienced total quiet. Certainly not on Station, and not in the crowded dome. There were always the sounds of people talking, or murmuring in their sleep, the clang of construction, the hum of machinery, and the sighing of vents. Now there was no way to contain the silence, and in that vast domain everything rushed past him, fled out of him. He thought, *If I sit down, I won't get up again.*

So he started walking back to the dome.

As he got closer he saw that things littered the ground everywhere: cast-off pieces of hardware, broken sections of dome, empty food packets, a clipboard, a used-up breather, a discarded jacket. They had left the place a mess.

Moving through the gap in the side of the dome, he plunged into a murky interior. It felt like a tomb, and gave him a little shiver. With relief he found that the lights still worked; he flipped the switch back on. But under the glare of the light tubes, the place seemed emptier than ever. The canisters were gone; the geo cannon was gone.

He walked aimlessly around, kicking at piles of junk, looking for anything of interest. In the galley he found the remains of breakfast. He sat on the floor spooning cereal into his mouth and staring at the door, expecting at any moment for Koichi or someone else to come in and begin ordering him around. Their ghosts were here, hurrying to and fro, pushing to meet schedule, jostling against each other's agendas, and sometimes taking time to grouse at Mitya for not standing up straight enough or not saying the right thing. Somewhere under his skin, his body filled with tears, but he kept eating.

After he'd made himself sick on porridge, he wandered out into the main dome and watched as a school of flying insects swarmed in the curtain of light falling through the gap. He was thirsty. Over at the old water gauges he checked on whether the filtration system had been shut off. It had been, so he flicked it back on.

Then he saw someone lying on the other side of the water vat.

Mitya hurried over, his pulse kicking up a storm. It was Stepan. Blood welled from the center of his chest.

"Shot, Mitya, shot . . . ," Stepan rasped.

Trembling, Mitya pulled aside Stepan's clothes to look at the wound. Just to the right of center, a round hole seeped bright red.

"I'll be right back," Mitya said to him. He rushed to the first-aid stowage bin, where to his relief, everything was still fully stocked. Grabbing an emergency kit, he ran back to Stepan, wondering if he'd be there, if he'd really seen his uncle lying in a spill of blood.

He had. Mitya took out the diagnostic scanner, remembered how to turn it on, and ran it over the wound, his hands trembling.

"Give me a pain patch, Mitya . . . ," Stepan

gasped, sending an extra spurt of blood out of the wound as he spoke.

Mitya fumbled for the right patch, ripped open two of them, and pressed them onto the back of Stepan's hand. Then, picking up the diagnostic assembly again, he tried to make sense of the readout.

"It says, 'Bullet wound, right lung, resulting in secondary hemopneumothorax and secondary respiratory depression.' And then it says, 'Apply occlusive dressing.'"

"Guess you better do what it says, boy." Stepan closed his eyes, relaxing into the medication.

Mitya knew little more than how to apply a bandage, but did the best he could.

"Get the whole thing covered real good," Stepan whispered, sweat beading up on his face. "Keep the air from pushing inside and collapsing my other lung."

His trachea was bulging over to one side, which the diagnostic said was caused by blood pushing up from the chest. It was calling for intravenous solutions to get the blood pressure stabilized, but that was far beyond the med kit and Mitya's skill. Bright red bubbles appeared at the edges of Stepan's mouth. Mitya knew then he was going to die.

He covered Stepan with blankets where he lay, tucking a small pillow beneath his head.

"Mitya . . ."

"What happened?"

Stepan managed to say, between short gasps for air, "Needed my spot, you see?"

Mitya held Stepan's hand, grateful for the company, even in this awful circumstance. For a moment he wondered where the gun was that had shot Stepan. Perhaps several guns had been left behind, and could be used to give things a quick end. But he didn't think he could kill Stepan, or himself.

Stepan was talking again: "It was Gabriel that shot me. Left me for dead, boy. Guess I'm not . . . yet."

"The *Captain* shot you?" Mitya was still capable of being shocked, even now, as bad as things were.

Stepan struggled to swallow or to talk. It looked like he was strangling. "Don't act surprised," he said. "You know the man."

Mitya wasn't sure what to say, so he whispered, "It shouldn't end this way; it wasn't supposed to."

Stepan nodded. "No . . . wasn't supposed to. But, Mitya, make sure they give you my place." He grimaced. "Hurts, boy. Give me another patch."

The diagnostic warned against this, calling instead for oxygen but Mitya ignored it. He didn't have oxygen, but he *did* have pain meds.

Finally Stepan closed his eyes, breathing noisily. Mitya couldn't follow the diagnostic's directions. It kept giving him more and more information, all of it bad. Stepan's right lung was shattered, and now the blood in the cavity was pressing against the other lung, plus blood was trickling into the good lung from the right lung. Pretty soon Stepan wouldn't be able to breathe.

But saving his life was useless anyway. After all, they had only a few hours left in any case.

Mitya sat beside Stepan there on the floor of the dome, staring at a swarm of gnats catching a slice of sunlight from the gap in the wall. After a while Stepan lost consciousness. Helpless to give his uncle any aid, Mitya slipped away to walk and steady his nerves. His hands were shaking and as cold as Stepan's.

His footsteps echoed in the main dome. Fleeing this ghostly accompaniment, he entered the clean room. Walking down the line of computers, he fired each of them up in turn, until they pulsed and whined, lending their quantum life to the old workroom. He left them on and went in to Bonhert's quarters. Though curious about the man's things, he couldn't bring himself to rummage through the drawers.

He switched on Bonhert's computer and accessed

the geo simulations for a while. Then he called up the *Quo Vadis* transmission and watched as Captain Kitcher did his grand tour of the ship, then searched and found the real tour of the ship, the tour of the rat warrens.

He swiveled the chair around and stared at the room. The impulse came to lie down on Bonhert's bunk and sleep, but he couldn't sleep, not with Stepan dying. Pushing himself out of the luxury chair, Mitya went back to the clean room and its pulsing monitors.

Standing amid the cast-offs of the great expedition to end the world, Mitya thought again about the scenes he'd just reviewed: the *Quo Vadis*; those ship corridors crawling with humanity; the tatters of their clothes. The offer to take on a hundred survivors. Stepan's words, *You can have my place.* . . .

He turned around and walked slowly back into Bonhert's room.

Peering into Bonhert's list of files, he whispered: *What place, Captain?*

One by one he called up the files. Eavesdropped on the filed conversations between Bonhert and Kitcher. The negotiations for this privilege and that concession. All friendly on the surface, they danced around each other, evaded, manipulated.

Then Mitya went hunting for the rest of the files.

Bonhert was not a careless man. He'd left his files, but some were deeply protected. The Captain hadn't counted on anyone having the time to pierce the locks. Mitya had that time—checking on Stepan from time to time, but otherwise solely concentrated on the buried files, the ones Bonhert had deemed inexpedient for others to see.

At last Mitya emerged from Bonhert's quarters. He walked over to Stepan and sat down next to him. He realized at once that his uncle was dead. Mitya pulled up the blanket to cover Stepan's face. In the press of things, it was more than he could bear. He heard himself crying. He'd never heard himself cry out loud, not since he was little, and the sound surprised him. It echoed strangely in the dome. He sat for a time, feeling like the big stone he'd been carrying inside had moved downstream.

He stood up then, looking down at his uncle's body. "There weren't a hundred slots," he told him. "There were ten." He stared at the lump under the blanket. "You killed Station for the sake of ten people." He started to walk away, and then turned around again. "And I don't want *your spot*, Uncle."

As he strode into the center of the main dome, he scattered a phalanx of armored insects that had begun marching into the place. Foraging for a backpack, he found many to choose from, and stuffed one with enough canteens and snacks to fuel his long hike.

If he could get there in time, those forty crew members might like to start planning which *ten* of them were going to live. They might not come up with the same list as Bonhert.

As he emerged from the dome he took a big breath, tainted, despite his breather, by sulfur. Hitching his pack more comfortably on his shoulders, he set out toward the valley rim. One thing he didn't have to worry about, at least.

He knew the way to the vent.

4

Loon had begun to know the outfold. It towered over her, hugged her from the sides, sprang into the soles of her feet. Even without touching it, she cried from joy, from relief. Scents could arouse her to powerful sexual spikes that receded quickly, leaving her breathless. Within the plants of the outfold, infrared currents beguiled her. There were no auditory names for the constituents of the outfold, and the true names could not be translated. The name for the tallest growths was

< . . . , > the movement. To translate meant one must find a human common language equivalent.

But, delightfully, there *were* names for the orthong. Golanifer had a name. It was beautiful to hear. Humans desired to hear names, or they could not relate to individual orthong, and the breeders had to relate, so orthong condescended to assign themselves auditory names, which they spelled in sign, and humans pronounced.

Golanifer was Loon's friend, if *friend* could describe the feeling she had for this orthong. She suspected it could not. There was an orthong concept for what she felt. . . . Human concepts, orthong concepts—she moved back and forth in her viewpoint, wanting to drop the human but not entirely able.

Loon reached out to touch the blue coils clustered on the ground like barrel hoops. The colors sequenced through azure to turquoise to glistening purple. An orthong hand clutched suddenly at her wrist, stopping her. She looked into Golanifer's reproachful eyes.

She knew she mustn't touch things without permission. But it was a great temptation to finger the blue coils seething with light, and receive their bestowal of hot energy.

<No touching,> Golanifer chided yet again.

Loon drew back her hand. She wished very much not to offend her teacher. Golanifer was old, with shoulders covered by a silver-skinned mantle. Loon had never been in the presence of such a wondrous being. She could smell Golanifer's unique essence, and it made her giddy.

They had been walking for hours. Everywhere, weavers stopped their work and came up to them, watching Loon out of slitted eyes, and then gradually asked questions, touching her on the arms. Having trouble understanding that Loon had no memories from the womb, they asked questions that she couldn't answer. When they wanted answers about humans,

Loon sometimes forgot what a human would do and say. But they were very patient with her, except for some who hung back—those who Golanifer said were unreceptive to the mixing of human and orthong, and must be given time to adjust to Divoranon's decree.

The outer and inner colors of the outfold, along with their scents, played on Loon's emotions, making it difficult to attend to the weavers' questions. Golanifer was a steadying influence, taking Loon's emotional surges in stride, calming her confusion and some of her delight with matter-of-fact explanations. Loon could sense the condescension, but it didn't matter. Loon was half mad, and knew it.

The habitat was very active just now, changing by the hour. Weavers could be seen everywhere, touching the growths of the outfold, cupping their palms along stalks, fingering the surfaces of their creations. They had hardened many square miles of the perimeter outfold and transformed others into poison zones. Even though the habitat was not in immediate danger of attack, the weavers instinctively altered the outfold for defense.

Loon and Golanifer passed breeder berms where human women crowded into courtyards and peered fearfully at the masses of weavers. There were many thousands of breeder women in the habitat, Golanifer said, as though discussing a herd of goats. Human women were easy to come by, and had flocked to the habitat over the decades. None were ever turned away lest other breeders be discouraged from coming. So they took all: young, old, infirm.

At first some of the infirm died. The orthong had no concept for *doctor*. If an orthong grew sick, as had sometimes happened in their history, an older weaver might try to assist the individual. But since sickness was usually the first sign of complete breakdown, an irreparable loss of confidence, the individual soon died. So when the orthong observed humans becoming sick with some regularity, they had much to learn about healing at the human cellular level. The orthong were surprised at how well humans responded to such ministrations, and that the breeders had no concept for the inherent shame of illness.

By the time Golanifer was called upon to heal Loon, the orthong knew much about human makeup. Still, Loon was a great challenge. She had been poisoned by her indiscriminate feasting on the soils near the Rift Valley, and was neither human nor orthong. They had to find an experienced and willing weaver to deal with her. Golanifer was a good choice, a proponent of mixing human and orthong to expand what she called genetic diversity. She was doing a fine job with Loon, except for one misstep: She didn't prevent Loon from forming a bond with her.

A touch upon Loon's arm. Golanifer nodded at the berm. Salidifor's berm. They had arrived.

Loon felt a lurch of alarm. Golanifer was leaving.

<I will be back for you,> the weaver said.

<Stay, please.> Loon looked uneasily at the broad courtyard. Salidifor stood at the head of the berm stairs. He was an important individual. She bowed to him, as protocol dictated a human woman should and a weaver shouldn't. Standing next to him was a short creature with skinny appendages. A tangle of black tendrils was embedded on the top of her head. Loon could smell her oily scent: not very interesting.

<Stay, Golanifer,> she said again.

Golanifer looked with some distaste at the creature standing beside Salidifor. <Divoranon has allowed the human woman to speak to you alone. I will not be far away.>

Divoranon was the highest among the orthong. Everything she said had to be properly outfolded. On Divoranon's command, Loon was to speak to the outfold weavers, as many as she could. Loon was to let herself be touched by all. She was to be on her best behavior so that the weavers would form a good impression of her, hybrid that she was. Now she was to respond to the human woman, despite the fact that she was not of interest and so much else *was*! However, if Golanifer would be pleased, Loon would do her best.

The human woman approached. She wanted to be known as Nerys.

Loon concentrated. She had known this one called Nerys once. Long ago they were together in a small, dark spot, smelling of urine and fear. Some Stationers were there, prisoners like her. And, ah . . . Spar. Tears sprouted. The orthong had killed him. She had spit on them. Now she loved them. She sank down on one knee, her head filled to bursting. Golanifer was at her side. After a long time, Loon was able to stand again.

<Close down the scents,> Golanifer advised her. <Later, when you are stronger, you can remember these things.>

Loon tried the *closing off* that Golanifer was trying to teach her. It was miserably hard. Meanwhile Nerys stood there, and had begun voicing something.

<Sign, please,> Loon said, to slow the woman down.

<How are you feeling?> Nerys asked.

She *would* start with a hard one. <Fine.>

<How are the orthong treating you?>

<They are my people.>

Nerys nodded. <What are they doing with you?>

Loon looked into the outfold, but Golanifer had disappeared.

Nerys was speaking again. <Loon, help me to understand. There is so much I don't know. Salidifor teaches me, but from an orthong viewpoint. Divoranon wants me to learn fast, so I can be a good translator. You can help me.>

Loon was having some trouble keeping up with Nerys. She was surprisingly fluent.

<Slow down,> she signed.

Nerys repeated her speech.

Loon relented. The sooner Nerys was satisfied, the sooner Golanifer would come back for her. <What do you want to know?>

Nerys smiled, showing odd, white teeth. It was disturbing to see a hole in her face in just that spot.

<Tell me about the female orthong, for starters. I know little about them.>

<The weavers command the outfold; the whole habitat and everyone in it is in service to Divoranon. Women like you must obey them.>

Nerys' mouth hardened for a moment. <I know that much. Tell me something I don't know.>

She was halfway to disliking this person. But Golanifer would soon return and they would stroll through the outfold once more. Loon would give her something challenging to think about: <There are very few orthong. The fewer there are, the harder it is for them to have normal pups. Lithia is harsh to them. That is why they live in the outfold, and why they use human wombs most of the time, because they are weakened. All their efforts are toward survival.> She regarded Nerys' pregnancy. <You are fulfilling a need, bearing that pup.>

Nerys got one of her funny looks, that stiffening of her face that made her look like she had eaten bad soil. <Yes, so I've been told.>

<Some weavers argue that mixing orthong with human, sexually, would be useful although distasteful. There would be more outfolding to work with, to strengthen the race.>

Nerys asked: <If the orthong can create such a one as yourself, why can't they fix their females?>

<That is a rude question.>

<Don't get too orthong on me, Loon. You're not one of them, as much as you might like to be.>

Loon stared her down. This was becoming tedious. But she answered: <They told me the humans are of very diverse gen-etic makeup. There was much to work with in my case, less so in themselves.>

<Will they alter themselves?>

<Some orthong think the time has come, because the orthong are a dying race. They do not wish to take chances. They intend to suppress much of the outfolding of human characteristics, so that orthong remain orthong.>

Nerys smirked. <No doubt.>

Loon definitely did not like her attitude. <You do not understand the orthong.>

<You'd be surprised how much I understand.>

<I am tired,> Loon said, searching the outfold for Golanifer.

<First tell me, what is it like to be part orthong? What will it be like for our children?>

Loon considered how to answer. <It is a very deep feeling. We cannot hide from ourselves or others unless we shield ourselves. Our bonds are . . . very strong. To preserve our dignity, we have many rules of conduct and relation to others. I am just learning them. It is not easy. But the world is beautiful, and we smell and taste it. We are of the soil, but must learn restraint, and not eat foolishly. It is hard to talk. Mostly, we don't.>

<Why have you lost your hair?>

Loon put her hand to her head. She'd forgotten. Golanifer said it might grow back; Loon hoped it wouldn't. Then she spotted Golanifer. The sunlight fell through the tall outfold onto the orthong's arms, where her silver streaks gleamed. Nerys was saying something, but Loon could only watch as Golanifer approached. She ran a few paces toward the orthong.

In response to Nerys, Golanifer said, <Perhaps I came too soon. Do you require further instruction?>

<No, let her go,> Nerys said. <Why is she so dependent on you?>

<Unfortunately, she has contracted a bond with me. She couldn't stop herself. We will work on this.>

<A bond between human and orthong makes one crazy?> Nerys asked.

Golanifer didn't answer, but turned and guided Loon toward the edge of the compound.

Nerys followed them a few paces. <Does it? Make one unbalanced?>

Golanifer stopped and stared at Nerys and her forwardness. Then she took Loon by the arm and led her into the outfold.

This Nerys was a pest, and Loon was glad to be rid of her. Back in the beloved outfold, her eyes were drenched in an explosion of color, as the outfold, now streaming with afternoon sun, created morphing patterns on every surface. Loon stopped in her tracks, unable to see the path for the twisting displays of heat and color.

<Only a little farther,> Golanifer said. <We will rest in the underlay.> Loon felt Golanifer's hand firmly grasping her upper arm.

They came to a portal in the hillside. It arched high overhead, and a warm current issued from the opening. At once Loon felt the visual and olfactory relief. She covered her face for a moment, to get her bearings. The smell of good, brown soil both calmed and aroused her. She found herself on her knees, scraping at the packed soil of the floor with her fingernails.

Golanifer crouched beside her.

When Loon looked into the orthong's face, she could only weep. <What is the matter with me? The smell of things, the color of things. I'm drowning. . . .>

<It will soften, as you learn to eat more wisely.>

\<When will I be wise?\>

\<Do you trust my instruction?\>

\<Yes.\>

In Golanifer's dark eyes sparks of light blinked on and off, like fireflies near a campfire. \<I say you will grow past this difficulty to great power.\>

Loon was glad to see this comment, but she could take little hope from it, numb as she was. \<Is your god the Lord of Worlds or the Lady of the World?\>

Golanifer made her smile-look. \<Yes.\>

\<Am I orthong or human?\>

Golanifer raised her chin: *Yes.*

And so, not knowing anything but trusting in everything, Loon followed Golanifer into one of the great caverns where they created their hardcasts. Loon was so tired she barely regarded the airships that the weavers were outshaping. Their ships would carry the strike force into the Rift Valley. But Loon had little interest in such things. Weavers did not like to fly. Loon decided she did not like to fly.

As Golanifer led her through the cavern, many weavers crowded around, touching her. These females were attracted to outshaping, since their skills were not conducive to the more complex outfolding in the forest. Loon felt their hands on her arms, her temples, the back of her neck. They shielded themselves, she noted.

Golanifer led her to a small room in back, deep in the soothing tunnels of the cavern. There she lay down on a bed, and Golanifer put her hand on Loon's face, asking her if she would sleep now.

Loon responded, \<Yes, please.\> And in the next moment she passed into a state of blessed unknowing.

17

1

Day seventy-four. They were packed into the airship so tight Reeve could barely move. At least twenty-five orthong warriors were crowded into this airship alone, making him feel decidedly uneasy. The vibration of the deck plates beneath his feet and an occasional turn of the craft were his only sensations of movement in the silent ship. He hadn't even had a moment to inspect the craft from the outside to guess at its propulsion system before he was herded onboard with this cadre of orthong.

He couldn't determine if Salidifor was present. This orthong lord was in charge of the operation, and Reeve desperately needed to talk to him. Salidifor—with help from Nerys—had questioned Reeve extensively about the Stationers and their defenses. But for his own part, Salidifor would reveal little, promise little. There would be lives lost—Reeve had resigned himself to that—but they must take prisoners, Reeve had pleaded. When Nerys translated that, Salidifor hadn't answered. At Reeve's protests, Nerys only shrugged, saying as she had before that the orthong did what they pleased.

The orthong giant next to him shifted uncomfort-ably away from Reeve after a veering of the craft tipped them ever so slightly together. Reeve shared the fellow's reluctance to touch, but here they were cheek by jowl, with not much room for personal niceties.

He had a sinking feeling that he was being exploited by the orthong, that they had no intention of honoring any agreements. The whole thing was out of control, heading toward what Reeve feared was disaster. Nerys put great store in Salidifor, trusting him. But Reeve didn't even trust Nerys. He didn't entirely trust that Nerys' translations were without prejudice. Or that she would speak favorably for the Stationers in any way. But then, why would she? Reeve himself had given them over for slaughter.

They had arrived. The craft touched down so lightly he only realized they had landed when the side of the ship clanged open.

As the orthong poured out, Reeve followed, noting that the warriors simply hopped down the ten-foot drop to the ground and were already loping away. He swung himself down and hurried to catch up, keeping a watch for Nerys. Vapors boiled around them, making it impossible to judge their position, but he spotted Nerys and forced his way through knots of orthong to her side.

"Nerys," he said, taking her by the elbow and forc-ing her to look at him, "I don't want a bloodbath. We just need to prevent them, not massacre them."

She regarded him with irritation, one hand resting on her belly. It seemed to Reeve that her pregnancy had advanced greatly even in the two days he had been in her company.

"You've told him that," Reeve said, hoping it was true. "Impress it on him."

"I have," she said. Around her, in eerie silence, the orthong were clustering in groups and handing out weapons.

Reeve searched her face. Surely she wouldn't take out some perverse revenge on the Stationers. But once she had made clear that she hated "zerters," and now she had them in the palm of her hand.

"Where is the dome?" he asked her.

"Up on the ridge." Noting his expression, she said: "We flew over it. It was abandoned. We're in the valley."

It didn't need saying where the Stationers were now. Reeve felt the news in his chest, pushing his breath back into his body. No wonder the orthong had mobilized so fast.

A warrior approached them, and by his aspect of authority, it was Lord Salidifor.

Reeve signed to him, <Do not kill unless you have to.>

Tufts of mists clung to Salidifor and drifted away in an intermittent breeze. The orthong regarded him with that maddening immobility.

<Do you carry a gun?> Reeve thought the creature said.

"Will you kill a Stationer if you must?" Nerys translated, loosely enough.

He hesitated, but knew his answer. <Yes,> he signed to the lord.

Salidifor handed him a gun as tall as Reeve himself. He had three minutes to learn how it worked before the entire company was racing over the cooled black lava flows of the valley floor, into a mist so thick the only thing Reeve could see before him was Nerys' dark hair.

2

Mitya crouched, staring into a small pool surrounded by orange oxidized rock. Stained jade green from the iron chloride suffusing the water, his reflection was a face trapped in a poison world. Pulling his mind back to the task at hand, Mitya stood and glanced once more at what he'd hidden among the rocks. He had rigged everything the best he could, given that there was no time to indulge his urge to check and double-check. He could hear the occasional shouts from the camp, signaling the final adjustments to the cableway over the vent.

It was time. A microearthquake rumbled beneath his feet, synchronized with his own trembling. He would march into camp, make his excuses, then wait for the right moment and tell them everything. They might just stare at him, or kill him outright. He couldn't stop trembling. Finally he walked toward the voices.

Theo, guarding the perimeter, almost shot him. But Mitya called out his name in time, and the man let him through. Mitya ignored his questions and walked straight into the middle of the makeshift camp.

Liam Roarke saw him first.

"Mitya, by the Lord!" Roarke cocked his head. "Where the hell have you been?"

Jess and Gudrun stopped at their tasks and stared, as did several others.

"Tenzin!" Roarke shouted. "Look who dragged himself in!"

Tenzin Tsamchoe was up a small embankment of rock, at the base of the nearest cable tower. He looked down and waved.

But Mitya's arrival was only a minor turbulence in this scene, with crew hauling materials from crates and hastening in all directions under the shouted orders of Val Cody. In the near distance stood Captain Bonhert, intent on his handheld display. Everyone had a gun at the hip, and most of the crew were on perimeter duty, watching for the orthong raid they had expected all this time. Mitya wondered which ones were the chosen ten. He didn't doubt that Roarke and Cody were among them.

"Where the hell were you?" Roarke asked him.

"Fell asleep," Mitya said, hoping the questions would go no further.

"Nearly slept to death then," Roarke said, shaking his head. Moving on to other tasks, he left Mitya peering at the cableway, judging its readiness.

Through the belching steam and gases of the roaring vent, Mitya noted that both towers were in place and cables suspended between them, with the giant truck ready at the far tower but resting on the ground prior to being hoisted into place. Crew were muscling the geo cannon into the truck with the help of a great winch. This activity was obscured by the intervening vent and its bilious outpourings. But it was clear they were closing in on their goal.

One problem Mitya had not foreseen was the noise. Besides the rumblings of magma under their feet, the roar of the vent itself was formidable. It would mean people would have to stop running around and pay attention in order to hear what they had to.

He would have to make them pay attention, thereby blowing his cover.

From the vent, occasional lava fountains spewed small shards of quickly frozen basalt that fell in a crystal rain, prickling his face. When Mitya swallowed it felt like his trachea was shredding. He stood straight, gathering his courage. Any moment they could have the truck up and running on the cable.

Captain Bonhert was standing with Marie, turning around as she pointed out Mitya. The Captain's face flushed with pleasure, and he came striding over.

Mitya knew that Bonhert would read him like a book.

It was time to speak up.

3

Stumbling on the irregular terrain, Reeve picked himself up and ran on. The orthong, with their long strides, had left him behind. In truth he could barely keep up with Nerys, so weakened he still was. But the sheer panic of their late arrival kept him going, feeding adrenaline to limbs that hurt in every joint.

He saw shapes in the fog, spindly trees that looked like crucified men, rock outcroppings in the shape of hulking insects. Once, he thought he saw Spar, sword drawn, parrying an orthong.

Reeve heard Spar say: *You see a group of thong, boy, kiss your behind good-bye.*

I know, Spar, I know. But I have to trust them, you see?

Don't see nothin', boy, but a young fellow gettin' led around by the nose. Spar shook his head. *Least you got yourself a good sword. Maybe you ain't forgot everythin' I taught you.*

No, I'll never forget, Spar, never.

When he looked again, there was nothing.

He ran on.

In the distance, he heard a noise. A giant's voice, spreading through the mist.

4

The expression on Bonhert's face as he strode forward was one of genuine pleasure mixed with confusion. Mitya knew the Captain didn't like ambiguity. So he went for clarity.

Mitya screamed. He screamed as loud as he knew how, a wild, long animal wail that he didn't know he was capable of. He took off running as he screamed, stopping everyone dead in their tracks. He bounded up the blackened humps of lava that had domed around the vent until he judged he was far enough way from

Gabriel Bonhert to avoid his questions and the pistol in his belt webbing. It was hot up there, with his back to the river of magma flowing just a few feet away in its open pipe.

He stood on the heap of coiled and cooled lava and looked at the amazed crew, who had paused in their work, staring at him. Reaching into his pocket, Mitya brought out the little black signal pad he'd programmed, and punched in AUDIO, loud.

From two sides, where he'd hidden the amplifiers, came Bonhert's voice:

"*I tell you, this is hell, Kitcher.*"

Pause, static. "*. . . know that, know that, but we have our extreme circumstances as well . . .*"

"*Damn your extreme circumstances! Ten isn't enough—we have forty-two. How am I going to explain this?*"

Mitya's stomach felt like molten rock. The recording was hard to hear. And now Bonhert was shouting at Mitya, bounding toward him.

The recording went on: "*That's your own problem, Captain. Many of us didn't want to divert your way in the first place. I'm under constraints as bad as yours, never doubt it.*"

Static. Bonhert swore. "*Then if you're set on your number . . .*"

"*I'm sorry . . .*"

"*I say, if you're set on your number, then ten it is. Ten slots on your grand ship for eighty pounds of ore. I'll pull this off, Kitcher, but I don't know how.*"

Bonhert had reached Mitya's side. His look was purely murderous. "Turn it off. Now."

Kitcher's voice was booming out: "*If you're worried, we can cancel this here and now. . . .*"

"*I'm not worried. I'll handle my people.*"

"*See that you do. They still have their chance on the surface. Maybe they'll fare better than we. Only the Lord knows.*"

"The Lord has no hand in this devil's bargain, Kitcher."

Mitya brought the signal pad out of his pocket. As Bonhert reached for it, Mitya tossed it into the flow of magma.

"Ten. It's my final offer," the recording droned on.

"Yes, all right; done then."

"I presume you'll be one of the ten?"

Pause. *"Who's coming onboard is no concern of yours. I'll choose. That's all you have to know."* Static. *"And Kitcher: We won't speak of this again."*

"Understood."

It was the end of the recording. Bonhert looked as though he would blow Mitya's brains out. But instead the Captain turned to his people and held up his hands. He was preparing to speak, to spin this story, somehow. Mitya eased away from the man.

And then the recording began again: *"I tell you, this is hell, Kitcher."*

Bonhert slowly turned to Mitya, raised his pistol. The expression on his face had solidified into a profound sneer. The real face of the real Captain, at last.

There was nowhere to run. The recording went on. *". . . I'll pull this off, Kitcher, but I don't know how . . ."*

And then Oran, in a rage, was scrambling up to where Bonhert stood. Bonhert swung and shot him between the eyes.

Now every gun was trained on Bonhert. From somewhere, a lone shot. Bonhert took a wound in his leg. Then another in his pelvis, a hit that sent him sprawling backward. Another shot ricocheted off the rock. Bonhert was slumped along the line of the vent, unmoving. With a muffled *thunk*, the surface of the ground broke in two under his left shoulder, and his arm flopped into a red stream. Fire ripped over his jacket.

Then Tenzin Tsamchoe was pulling him away from

the vent, slapping out the flames with his own jacket. Bonhert lay inert. Then a moan came from the man's throat. He couldn't be alive—but he was, the exposed arm still smoking from the flame.

Now Val Cody was by his side. She drew her pistol and shot Bonhert in the side of the head.

The audio went on: "*I presume you'll be one of the ten?*"

"Turn it off, Mitya," Val Cody said. "You've made your point."

"Have I?" he shouted above the recording. "Were *you* one of the ten, Lieutenant?"

Tsamchoe said, "Gudrun, secure that cannon. No one goes near it."

Gudrun, who by chance was positioned on the other side of the vent, moved to cover the truck and its geo cannon cargo.

But Marie Dussault was there already, and warned Gudrun off with her gun. As Gudrun froze in place, Marie shouted, "How many of you want to help me?" She swept her gaze over the crowd. "I need nine friends." She moved closer to the truck and the controls. There at the second cableway tower, she was separated from most of the crew by the long line of the vent.

It was then that Mitya saw the ghosts emerging from thin air on every side of the camp.

5

Reeve heard a shot in the distance. Then two more, and another. He was surrounded by an absolute whiteout, but he ran toward the shots and the booming voices. Now he would have to kill crew, friends, kin. A spike of nausea ripped through him.

From the mists, a shape materialized: arms, legs, real face—a crew member. The long automatic swung up to point at Reeve, but Reeve was already shooting,

shooting. The man was down, chest smoking. Orthong everywhere, some firing from their cuffs, others shooting from their long guns. People screaming. No doubts about whose side those screams came from. . . .

Amidst this, amplified voices punctuated the mayhem: ". . . *the Lord has no hand . . . my final offer . . . one of the ten . . . we won't speak . . .*"

In the background, through tatters of fog, Reeve saw a tall construct, wires suspended to another column, bridging the vent. There. The geo cannon. He ran toward it, swinging his gun once to fire at Bertram Hess, who stood in his way.

Lord of Worlds, he had killed Hess. The screams of the wounded surged through him; he felt their passage through his gut. He had done this, brought death to the last of the Station. What had he become but a murderer like Bonhert, finishing the job Bonhert had started? Betrayed them all . . . and why?

The cannon, that was why. He ran for it.

He found her slumped by the far tower. Blood stained her shirt, but she crouched with gun drawn, as though she'd been waiting for him.

"Marie."

She licked her lips, panting, "Help me."

"I'll help you. Move away from the tower."

A grin brightened her face, showing the old Marie for a moment. "Too much to hope for. That you'd help me fire this damn thing."

He looked up to find that the truck was in position above the vent, the curtain of steam issuing past the suspended truck, obscuring the cannon that surely crouched there.

"Oh, Marie . . ." His voice came out like a moan. Her hand was on the control pad.

"No point firing the damn thing if you're just going to kill me afterward." She grinned. It was pain, he realized. One arm hung uselessly at her side.

He nodded. "Yes. There's no point. Because I *will* kill you if you do."

"Unless your soft heart would prevent you." She cocked her head. Was she taunting him?

"No, you'll die, Marie. I'll kill you, I swear I will."

"You got it stuck in your craw, don't you, that this place is worth saving?" She shook her head. "Lord above, for a fool." She winced, hand trembling on the panel. "Come with me, Reeve. The shuttle is just behind us. It's got enough canisters on board to buy our passage. Come with me."

"You killed my father."

She sighed, long and noisily. "Yes, I suppose I did." She shook her head slowly, as though the world were an infinitely weary thing. "Just remember one thing, Reeve: Once I fire the cannon"—she threw the switch—"killing me will only be a useless act of revenge."

The cannon fired.

It was the only noise in the world. Reeve was thrown to his knees . . . oh Lord, too late, too late . . . and then he was scrambling back up, and was rushing at her, sickened that he had hesitated. She reached up to fire the second mole, and he shot her, square in the chest.

Shaking violently, he swiveled to face any others who would approach the control panel. He pivoted to one side, then the other. But everything was still. The battle was over, the shouting had stopped, the blaring recording was silenced. Only the ground beneath his feet rumbled with a very slight tremor.

Then a blast from an orthong cuff fried the cable and the truck sagged closer to the vent, hanging, useless. Finally it dropped into the magma chamber, its remaining two moles deactivated, dissolving in the great rock furnace.

But one had fired.

He sat, stupefied, staring at the vent. His eyes registered the heat of the neon-red river.

6

Mitya found Reeve by Marie Dussault's body. He was staring straight ahead. The cableway system had been blasted apart, but too late. They had all heard the firing of the cannon. It would be five or six hours before they would know if the mole probed deeply enough to do the job. If it would tear apart the valley or the whole world. Or if it would fizzle and die in the long throat of the planet.

"Reeve," Mitya said. "They're killing everyone. Stop them."

Reeve staggered to his feet. "No, they can't. . . ."

"They're ripping people apart. . . ."

Mitya hurried after Reeve as they scrambled along the old lava flows and came to a halt atop a rock pile overlooking the camp. Orthong were bending over the human wounded, killing them with extruded claws. Reeve bellowed and began running down into camp. He was unarmed, but ran straight for an orthong about to slice a man's chest open. "Nooo!" he roared.

The orthong straightened and raised its arm to strike Reeve.

A woman Mitya had never seen before stepped forward, making some gestures, and the orthong stopped.

A small crowd gathered, while Reeve shouted, "You promised! Tell them, Nerys, it was our bargain!"

As the woman interpreted to the gathered orthong, they stared at her. Then the crowd parted as one of their number came forward. The woman and this orthong talked in sign for a moment. Then she told Reeve, "Salidifor says your people killed orthong. *That* is a trade, as well."

Reeve looked into the orthong's hideous face.

"You'll be remembered for how you handled this! The stories will live, and humans will hate you."

"It's a mercy. They're wounded," Nerys interpreted for Salidifor.

Again, Reeve spoke directly to the orthong leader: "No, that's not how humans think! Start thinking like a human!"

The woman smirked, and spoke in a lower voice: "That was the wrong thing to say, Calder."

Mitya noticed then that Val Cody was lying wounded nearby. He went to her side and wiped the matted hair away from her head wound. The creatures turned to watch him, and Mitya thought they would kill him now that he had drawn their attention. But the scene was utterly silent and still. Val Cody stirred, her face sheathed in pain.

Then the lead orthong said something in sign. Mitya didn't know what he said, but he figured it must have been in Reeve's favor, because gradually the rest of the orthong dispersed, leaving Mitya and Cody alone and leaving the other wounded where they lay.

Then Reeve and Tenzin Tsamchoe and the Stationers who survived began moving among their fallen friends, giving what help they could. The orthong watched impassively, neither helping nor hindering.

Beneath them all, the ground gently rumbled.

7

Reeve felt for a pulse, but Koichi was gone, dead of blood loss from a deep gash in his chest.

He added his name to the list of the dead: Koichi Hayenga, Oran Lowe, Liam Roarke, Bertram Hess, Gudrun Anderson, Eva Kingrey, Donald Cress, Mai Shinn, Rolf Tielsen, Gerry Brandt, Yoo Lee, Dava Freiberg. Gabriel Bonhert. And Marie Dussault. Others would be added over the next few hours.

But the list was longer than this, much longer. Cyrus Calder. Grame Lauterbach, Carlise O'Donnell, Kurt Falani, Lin Pao, Brit Nunally, Dana Hart, Geoff Lederhouser, Amee Ryan. And Tina Valejo, the most lost of all, frozen solid and by now perhaps acquired by a family of comets. . . .

Some of the dead Reeve had killed with his own hand. But he hadn't killed the man he came to kill. Yet Gabriel Bonhert was dead, and all his plans with him. If revenge was part of Reeve's compulsion, then he should feel satisfied that he had killed Marie Dussault. But all he felt for that grand moment was ashes in his mouth.

And in the back of everyone's mind was the fate of the one mole Marie had managed to launch, the device that could yet shatter all their lives. But for that, they could only wait.

In the hours since the battle, Tenzin Tsamchoe had taken charge while the orthong troop stood at the edges of the camp, leaving the humans to clean up as best they might. Tsamchoe was the only officer still on his feet, and Reeve thought him a good choice in any case to lead what was left of the Stationer expedition. Tsamchoe had at his side, acting as aide, young Mitya, one of the few people Tsamchoe completely trusted now, after all that had happened and all that had been revealed.

Reeve sat down next to Koichi's body and rested his head on his knees. When he looked up again, Nerys was standing there.

"It's over," she said.

"Is it?"

She sat down next to him, her face grimy but her eyes keen. "Yes. The mole failed. It's destroyed."

Reeve snapped alert. "How do you know?"

"Salidifor said."

"How does he know?"

She shrugged. "He said it failed in the first hour." Turning to face the great vent behind them, she said:

"It's probably spit back up in that flow of lava over there."

His chest rose, and he inhaled. And then again. "By the Lady," he said in a low voice. "So we're pardoned after all."

"What?"

"Pardoned. For our folly."

An indulgent smile flitted over her face. "A funny thing to say."

"Maybe. Depends on your perspective." He was scratching slowly at the ground with his right hand, forming five grooves in the slaggy loam. He thought of Loon, and missed her.

They sat for a long while amid the ruins of the camp, gazing at the stream of molten rock. It was recycling the stuff of the world, mixing upper and lower, the surface of things and the heart of things. After a time he asked Nerys: "Do you think that the world—the natural world—has a memory?"

She took a long drink from her canteen before answering. "No, not like us. But it carries the past forward somehow, doesn't it? I don't know if it gets as far as forgiveness."

Reeve nodded, staring into drifts of fog studded with glowing drops of sulfuric acid. "It remembers the old air and soil, I think. The spores and the seeds and the eggs, all those things that were buried. They're working their way to the surface. That's a kind of memory."

Nerys shrugged. "From that standpoint, it's the *only* kind." She handed him the canteen, and he took a long drink.

They sat gazing at the vent as though at an oracle within whose exhalations some meaning might be found.

After several minutes, Nerys spoke again: "I don't know how much it weighs on you. But I want you to know I don't blame you anymore. For picking me. If it matters."

He looked into her face and acknowledged, "It matters. I have enough death to answer for."

"Think of it as life," she said. "*I* do." She nodded at him, a kind of leave-taking. Then she walked off to join a lone orthong who stood on a low rise in the distance, waiting for her.

18

1

Day seventy-five. They buried them in the valley. Stationers who never expected to rest in the ground were lowered one by one into their graves. Reeve felt that when his time came, he would count it an honor to sleep in Lithia's bosom, a truer rest than the Station's ponics farm or Tina's endless drift.

He'd helped to dig the graves and to lower the dead. When it was Marie's turn, he bid her farewell with a cold heart. Some, like Kalid, might forgive betrayal. Reeve figured in his own case it would take time. He would grow toward it. For now, there was other work at hand: farewells, and then the claiming of his due from the orthong.

The farewells were short. The orthong airship waited, and there was not much to say. Tenzin Tsamchoe shook hands with him, and then Mitya did the same.

"Some still want to join the *Quo Vadis*," Tsamchoe said.

"Salidifor says he'll speak to the ship," Reeve replied. "I'm sorry. I don't think we're in on the discussion."

"I'm staying," Mitya piped in.

"Me, too," Reeve said. He smiled at the lad, and got a grin in return.

The other Stationers disdained to see him off. He walked toward the waiting ship, sorry for the gulf between his Station companions and him. He thought that might change in the days to come, when they were offered something in return for what they had lost. If Divoranon came through on her part of the bargain, then the next generation of humans on Lithia would live free of indigo and domes and breathers. They would be different from their parents, and this might create a division among them, but nothing came without a cost. The price he wouldn't pay was Loon's price—sterility. His people had to continue their line. Even altered, it was still a human line.

He had spent seventy days with that new human, with Loon. If he could love her so fiercely, he told himself, it must prove she was human, or so close that it made no difference. He'd seen her yearn for home and belonging, treasure her friendship with Spar, and accept and love a clumsy Stationer—even if it didn't last. It was more than enough to set his mind at ease, and to help him wish the *Quo Vadis* Godspeed in its search for a better place. To Reeve, there could be no better place.

But now he was eager to visit Divoranon and to see how much orthong understood the concept of keeping their word. It nagged at him, that betrayal might not be just the province of humans.

2

Nerys stood on the edge of the freewomen's compound. Bundles of crafts, disassembled weaving looms, and folded clothing lay stacked in the middle of the courtyard. Galen looked up from the bundle she was tying off and approached Nerys.

"Galen, Salidifor is uncomfortable about all this," Nerys said. She had explained things to the women a dozen times, yet they still insisted on packing.

Galen set her mouth firmly. "He said we could bring a few things."

"Yes, but this . . ." Here Nerys swept her gaze over the mound of belongings. "You won't need any of this. They'll make everything new once you arrive."

"They can't make *my weaving* for me."

Nerys sighed. It was a test of wills between the women's compound and the orthong. When they had been *her* tests, it was fun. But now the women were doing some testing on their own. The women were attached to their belongings. They had their favorite clothes and their craft work. Naturally, they wanted to bring these things with them. It was just that the orthong could not grasp the concept of traveling with belongings. They thought it bizarre in the extreme to carry things from one place to the other, especially over long distances. Some of the female orthong thought the women might be suffering a major loss of confidence. Salidifor was impatient. *All right, tell them they may bring a few things,* he'd said to her. It was the least of his concerns, but he expected her to fix it.

"Galen, each of you may bring one thing. Decide. And get rid of that stack of stuff. It upsets the females to see it there."

"Oh, blast the females," came the response.

But Haval and Odel had come up to them. Haval laid her hand on Galen's shoulder. "No, she's right. Tell the others to make their choices." Galen made a face, but wandered off to organize the packing.

Odel looked into the upper outfold. "I see that pup follows you everywhere." Her wrinkled face crinkled further with her smile.

Nerys shrugged. "I know it's dangerous, but I can't stop her." Vikal disappeared behind a bulbous growth when she saw the humans regard her.

"Finally met your match, Nerys?" Haval watched her with a wry smirk.

"Perhaps. Children will be children."

Odel raised an eyebrow. "Oh, it's *children* now, is it?"

"I'm tired of the distinctions."

"You never could stand them, Nerys, and you know it." Haval spoke with some affection. The Lord only knew why Haval liked her, after all the trouble she had caused. But it was Haval and Odel who were the most enthusiastic about the instruction the orthong were promising. It was a point Nerys had negotiated with Divoranon, that the freewomen could have access to learning from their orthong lords. Though *lord* was a word the women still used, Nerys planned to come up with a new term as soon as she had time to think about such minor matters.

"Will you be ready to leave in the morning?" Nerys asked Haval.

Haval nodded wryly at the pile of belongings. "We'll be ready." She looked around at the outfold, which even here was beginning to look discolored and rangy. "Things are changing," she said.

Odel regarded Haval with a squinting stare. "The only ones who think things don't change are the young." She turned thoughtful for a moment and then said to Nerys, "It seems the whole outfold is . . . hardening. Why can't they just fix it?"

"I honestly don't know. They've lost interest in the place. But they seem very excited about the new location." Nerys turned to go. "I'll see you soon, my friends. But it might be a little while."

Odel raised her eyebrow again.

"I'm going to ask Salidifor if I can go with him."

"Oh, Lord," Haval responded. She shook her head. "Can't you just wait with us at the new temporary camp and join him in the spring?"

"No."

She backed up before they started in with their cautions. "*One thing* apiece, Haval. Everybody brings one thing."

Haval nodded. "And you, Nerys. Make sure you bring some patience."

"I *am* patient," Nerys said. "Look how long I've waited already."

When she entered Salidifor's inner room, she saw that he had an elaborate meal laid out for her. She approached the familiar grouping of chairs and low table, greeting Salidifor in sign. He sat in his hooded chair. <Your favorites,> he said.

It was true. Venison steak and small, round potatoes smothered in butter. Baby carrots and broccoli. Blackberry compote.

She eyed him with mock suspicion. "What's the special occasion?" She sat and bent low over her plate to inhale the aroma. The smells weren't exactly right, but the tastes were almost perfect.

<No special thing. Except it may be some time before you will have another excellent meal.>

They would all be on the move in just a few more hours. Nerys wasn't sure what the human women would be given to eat, but she didn't plan on being choosy.

Salidifor was bound by airship for the lands east of the Stoneroots to prepare for the orthong immigration to their new habitat. The new outfold would be at exactly the same latitude as the old one, for reasons only the orthong could know, and would in fact be the location old Tulonerat had picked out on her journey seventeen years ago. The female orthong, the human women, and a contingent of orthong warriors would make camp in the foothills and then follow on foot in the spring, when the Stoneroot passes were open again.

The venison was medium rare as she liked it, but barely warm. Orthong could not be persuaded of the wisdom of ingesting warm food. It seemed to repel them, so Nerys had learned to eat cold food—and relish it.

"Shall we be talking to Captain Kitcher again tonight?" Nerys had served as translator between Salidifor and the *Quo Vadis,* in the underlay chamber. It had been great fun to see the old walrus puff and frown at Salidifor's terms; but in the end Kitcher capitulated. He was tired of the intrigue and machinations. He was too old to captain a big ship, Nerys concluded, and certainly no match for Salidifor.

<No. I am done with this person.>

Nerys doubted that. Salidifor had conveyed Divoranon's decrees to the *Quo Vadis* regarding fuel and the transfer of passengers. The *Quo Vadis* could have all the fuel it wished, but it must leave and not return. It was to take onboard all former Stationers who still desired to go, and it was to allow any ship passengers who wished to come to Lithia; as it happened, many did wish it, despite the uncertain future. Kitcher was loath to head back out again, and bargained hard for one with so little bargaining power. In the end, though, he was at Salidifor's mercy, believing the orthong's threats to destroy the ship. Whether the orthong were capable of this or not was apparently not to be put to the test.

Nothing was kept from Captain Kitcher. The story of Bonhert and his schemes to destroy Lithia was met with a long silence. Finally, Kitcher had said, "Aye, that would have done us in, to have a man like that among us. I had an inkling he was that sort."

"Next time listen to your intuition," Nerys offered.

"I have a desire to see your orthong on the viewer," the captain said. Up to then, he had seen only Nerys.

She persuaded Salidifor. The captain was an old man, and might be given a small favor.

When Kitcher saw Salidifor step forward, he narrowed his eyes and frankly stared. Then he nodded. "Thank you." He looked off to one side, where, no doubt, his advisors were still experiencing the shock of the orthong's appearance. "We have all wondered what other creatures the worlds hold," he said. He shook his head back and forth. He seemed lost, and for a moment Nerys pitied him, though she could not guess his thoughts.

That was yesterday. Tonight, apparently, they would have to themselves. Outside, the light slipped from the outfold, and the room grew deep shadows. Nerys toyed with her steak and then put down her fork.

Salidifor immediately became watchful.

She gazed absently at her food. "Do you think, Salidifor, that I might be of some use to you at the new habitat?"

<No.>

Nerys paused a respectful beat. It was an unequivocal answer . . . as far as it went.

He continued: <You shouldn't leave Vikal that suddenly. Because of the unfortunate bond.>

"I can visit Vikal, by airship. Her mother doesn't want me around much anyway."

<How do you know what Vikal's mother wants?>

"Loon told me."

He made a gesture of impatience, as though to say, *There you go again, nosing around in things you shouldn't.*

Leaving the topic of the pup, Nerys pressed on: "You may have need to communicate with clavers, or even Reeve, should he prove successful in his venture. I could help translate."

<We do well enough in sign.>

"Yes, of course. But for some conversations you need subtlety. When sign can't convey certain nuances."

The color drained from his eyes in the darkening

room. <You will stay with the women, Nerys. They have need of your translations as well.>

She sighed. "Maybe I'm not thinking of what others need."

<Now you are speaking the truth.>

She looked down at her plate, watching the butter congeal. "There is the matter of the bond I feel toward you."

<Nerys . . .>

She held up her hand. "I know, I know. There isn't any bond. And if there were it would be a terrible idea. I've already got one orthong bond and everyone is unhappy over *that* one." She looked up at him. "Did I miss anything?"

<You understand. But you do not know.>

"Oh, by the Lord of All Worlds! I'm getting to know orthong homilies. Please, spare me." She stormed up from the table and paced, dancing out her frustration. <Salidifor. You took me on as a student. Humans feel loyalty and affection toward teachers. You and I came to know each other and trust each other despite great differences. Among humans, that creates a bond. It's not a bad thing to have one around you who would do anything for you, and who would rather die than shame you. And I'm not like the others, Salidifor. I have a desperate need to know how things *are*. I want to learn everything. The humans know little right now, and what they do know is all big tech, and I want to . . . I want to . . . know *you*. You and your people.> She looked at him directly, challenging him. <I think you want to know me, too.>

After a very long time she sat down again. There was no hurrying his response. Finally he said. <If I take you with me, Divoranon's enemies will use this against me. They will say I cannot represent orthong properly with you at my side.>

"I won't be at your side, then. I'll stay in the background."

He stared at her, and she had the grace to look away. Offering to stay in the background, she realized, might be more than she should promise. But she pushed on. "Divoranon will have enemies one way or the other. But she has many more supporters, including Golanifer. Loon is making a great impression among the weavers."

She watched him as he watched her. And then she had it, the whole dance. "Salidifor . . . this isn't about Divoranon, is it?"

At length he signed, <No.>

Nerys stared at her food. A small current of cold air ran up her arm, causing her to shiver. She thought back to the lean-to in the deep outfold where she'd found Salidifor that day in the snow. His hand had come around her upper arm, clenching it tight . . . and he hadn't shielded himself. He'd thought he was an outcast, soon to leave for wide-ranging duties far from the outfold, far from Nerys. And he'd been curious. Whatever his motives, he had . . . bonded with her, at some level where such a thing was possible between orthong and human.

They sat in the deep-bermed room as night came on. They left the lights off, the darkness matching the silence between them.

"Do we share a bond, Salidifor?"

His chin rose, in a gesture so minute, it was only by long practice that she recognized it as a *Yes*. After several moments, she spoke very softly: "We could learn together, Salidifor. Learn what this means. And how to lead others down a good way when it happens again. As it will."

<That would be well.>

His face seemed to hold a trace of amusement, or perhaps it was affection. She hoped to learn the difference someday.

<Would you be content to come with me, Nerys?>

She regarded him with fondness, catching herself

before she said, *Say please.* He had already said it, in his own way.

<Yes,> she gestured, with a gradual rise of her chin. Then she picked up her fork and began on her dinner, chewing slowly, and enjoying every morsel.

3

Loon's attention was distracted by the way the outer wall of the outfold lay sagging in places, creating rents through which the morning sun poured its cold yellow light. The outfold seemed to be turning sere with the onset of winter. But Loon knew it was the whole place collapsing under the strain of the hardening. For days, ever since the orthong had won the battle against Gabriel Bonhert, Loon expected that the outfold would spring back to its former glory. But it had not.

Golanifer stood beside her, along with young Mitya, who had been among them for a day and a half.

"Can I come back sometime?" he asked.

It was time for Mitya to leave. He had to return to the human habitat, the odd half bubble where they'd built their machine of destruction. Loon wondered if they would survive the winter so far north, but Mitya said they had plenty of supplies from the great ship, meaning primarily that they had food to ingest. Loon was grateful she need never watch that ritual again, of creatures pushing chunks of vegetative and animal matter into their faces.

"Can I?"

Mitya was saying something again. He seemed to be asking if he could return to the outfold.

Loon interpreted: <He wonders if he can come back.>

Golanifer turned to Mitya. <We will see,> she answered.

Loon doubted they would let Mitya come back: the weavers had studied him long enough. But for his act of volunteering to come to the outfold, Golanifer might allow him some small favor in return. Perhaps it would be a visit, given that this human seemed to like everything he saw and showed not the slightest fear of being around the orthong. They were reluctant to allow adult males into the outfold, but since they had to closely study some male in order to finish the human outfolding task, the weavers had been delighted that it was an adolescent who'd volunteered.

"We will see," Loon interpreted, and he seemed content with this answer. Loon took pity on him as he stood there, a boy who had lost both his parents, and who had shown courage and resourcefulness at the great battle. "Learn to sign," she told him. "Learn to speak for yourself."

"I'll be ready." He turned to Golanifer and said, "It was nice getting to know you."

Loon would have found this a humorous remark if she were human.

They had wound their way deeper into the outfold when they heard the soft *whoosh* of the airship passing over them, but Loon had already forgotten about the boy. It made her sad to look on the ruins of the outfold. Hour by hour the forest was cracking apart, drying up and paling from its former glorious colorations. Many of the growths had turned gray, and if any color remained it was only in the occasional seam or fold. The stalks cracked under their feet as they walked south toward the meeting place.

Some of the raiment bushes were split down the middle, revealing half-formed garments with yokes, hems, and sleeves sagging from their templates. These aborted forms filled Loon with a slight uneasiness, and she reached for Golanifer's hand. Golanifer allowed this contact, and they proceeded through the forest, avoiding the taller growths, which at any moment might topple and crush an unwary traveler. Admiring Golanifer's placidity and confidence, Loon watched as the orthong strode gracefully among the ruins of the forest. Golanifer did not grieve over the forest, and Loon decided not to grieve, either, but to her dismay tears welled in her eyes anyway. Whether it was the outfold, or Golanifer's grace, or the coming winter, or nothing whatsoever, she couldn't tell. Golanifer squeezed her hand. They continued on.

Loon noticed a wrong smell. Golanifer pointed to a long, low mound. On closer inspection it looked like a mole's burrowing, or like a wave of soil, frozen in place as it crested. Covered with a pulsating foam, it sparkled here and there with neon colors.

They followed the line of the mound until they approached a patch of unnaturally bright forest. Loon stared at this foreign-looking grove. It was an area of melted and asymmetrical shapes, some elongated as though pulled and stretched, others interlocking like off-kilter spiderwebs. Loon's impulse was to touch and investigate, but Golanifer warned her away, peering deep into the fantastical realm, where colors skimmed along wires and threads as though carrying messages.

She turned to Loon. <This is her doing.>

Loon nodded. <Does she yet live?>

<She must. This all will die with her, and soon, no doubt.> Golanifer began backing away. <We shouldn't be here.>

Loon looked at the ruins, the transformation of a once-grand berm, where Tulonerat still sat in her courtyard, knowing more and more about less and less. As they watched, a web fell of its own weight, and the glittering waves of soil lapped up the remains. Loon shivered, and they moved past this region. Already a hardened perimeter was forming around Tulonerat's abode, and would soon fence in her creations. Maybe this was the reason the females were so eager to leave the outfold, Loon thought. But Golanifer did not seem willing to discuss it, and so they left the deforming region behind and hurried onward.

When they reached the meeting place, Reeve was waiting there, a small sack at his feet as he peered into the outfold from the open valley.

He looked startled to see them, so clearly he hadn't picked up their scent as they had picked up his. Very thin and oddly pink-colored, Reeve looked sick, but his smell was similar to Mitya's, and Mitya claimed to be well. Reeve's face was covered with a black growth, and he wore many layers of clothes against the cold.

Loon stepped to the edge of the outfold and placed her hand on a bleached remnant of a tree to steady herself. She looked back at Golanifer, who gave her a gesture of encouragement.

She took a step forward, away from the outfold and into the direct sun.

Reeve drew closer, saying something.

4

He had almost given up hope that she would come. When she appeared at the edge of the outfold, Reeve hesitated to move, as though the merest step toward her would send her fleeing into the forest. She looked gaunt and wide-eyed. She was completely bald. The orthong attendant stood just in back of her, and Reeve wondered if she was free to come and go, or if they restrained her.

Loon stepped forward.

He hadn't planned what he would say. Out came the simple truth: "I was afraid you wouldn't come."

She looked in back of her at the orthong guard, as though for permission to speak. Sign language flashed between them. Then Loon faced Reeve again, saying something in sign.

The hell with this. Reeve strode up to her. "You know I don't speak that way. Lord above, Loon, look at me."

She nodded at him. "I remember you," she said.

He couldn't answer. Lord of Worlds, that it should come to this, all their journey and everything they had shared. Turning to face the valley for a moment, he steadied his nerves. He had come here to say good-bye, but good-bye wasn't enough, not nearly enough. Turning back to her, he said: "Sit with me, Loon." He took her by the elbow and drew her down onto the hard-packed soil. She was compliant, but wary. The irises of her eyes were green, and no lighter in the brilliant sun than they had been that night she'd announced the orthong decision to trade. It was as though nothing penetrated them, nothing got through except what she chose to notice, and that didn't seem to include him.

"I'm leaving now, Loon. I'm on foot, heading for the Gandhi River and the *Cleopatra*. Salidifor says I have safe passage through orthong lands, but I'll be avoiding the Stationers' dome. They have no love of me, those folks." He looked over at her to see if she was listening. She gazed out placidly at the valley, seeming to relax a little. "I heard you'll be traveling as well. Back to the east side of the Stoneroots, eventually . . . your home territory, Loon. Where you and Spar set out in the first place."

At Spar's name, Loon snapped her head around to stare at him.

"I hope you remember Spar," he said. "He'd want to know you were happy. Are you?" He looked up to the white shadow just inside the broken outfold. "Are you free to come and go?"

"Spar . . . ," she whispered.

"Yes, Spar. If you come across the Stillwater Clave, tell them about Spar. Perhaps there are others who loved him like we do." He looked at her and wouldn't release her until she acknowledged him.

To his surprise, she said: "I will tell them."

He smiled to hear her voice. "Yes." His own voice was husky, not up to the job.

"Loon," he said finally. "Are you happy? If you want me to leave you alone, you have to answer me. Because if they're messing with you, I'll have to do something about it."

Loon turned around to look at Golanifer.

"No, don't look over there," Reeve said. "You just answer me, face-to-face."

Loon gestured at the silver and gray wall of the forest. "This," she said, "is all my happiness." She smiled at Reeve, and turned him around to look at the outfold. "This."

From deep within the forest came a cracking sound, followed by a muted crash.

"Sloughing," she said, unperturbed.

It was what he wanted to hear, he supposed. But it lay on his chest like a heavy rock. Several minutes passed as he struggled for control, gazing at the valley with its burnt umber shrubs dotting black scrub grasses. He found himself asking the thing he'd promised himself he wouldn't: "Do you care for me, Loon? Tell me you don't, so I can be free of you."

When he looked back at her, he was stunned to find that tears were rolling down her face. It was the surest sign of her humanity, of the Loon he knew. She was still in there, somewhere.

She whispered: "Reeve, you go now. Yes."

Almost the very words she had said to Spar that awful last day. Reeve wondered if he was also dead in her eyes. But he decided to take it as a blessing instead. He opened his mouth to speak, but she put her hand on his lips to stop him. Whether by accident or design, she left a few crumbs of soil on his mouth.

Standing up, she began backing away toward the outfold. Reeve sprang to his feet, trembling, thinking he would just grab her and run with her down the valley. But she stepped into the forest, and by the time he reached the spot where she had stood, all he could see were the gray bones of the outfold and, here and there, motes of sun slanting in from the outside.

Where she had stood was a string sack, weighted down by four, large smooth stones.

His health was returning. The breathers helped, as did the decent food packed away in his backpack, and even the hike through the blackened forest and into the Rift Valley. He had turned down the offer of the airship. A long cold walk through the countryside was what his heart needed. Time enough to face Kalid and his jinn and make plans. For now, it was only solitude he wanted, and the simple challenges of setting up camp each evening and finding his way each day.

As was happening so often lately, Spar's voice found him, and gave him confidence: *You keep on, boyo. For Lithia. She got all the strength you need. You lay yourself down every night in her lap, and rise up in the morning. By the Lady.*

And that is what he did. The simple rhythms of waking and sleeping and walking under his own power were enough for him. His thoughts strayed to Loon now and then, but he'd known she was lost to him, known it since that day in the center of the dome when she'd gone mute. When, at the edge of the outfold, she'd given him leave to go, it was only the final measure of leave-taking. It hurt, but he would bear it.

His pack was very heavy with the extra weight of the geodes. They weren't ordinary geodes. Lining the cavity of each stone was a crystalline lattice which, the orthong assured him, they had coded with information. There were no instructions, but within the four round stones lay the folded secrets of the change. It was Divoranon's test: Humans must figure out the genetic instructions; if they could not, then the orthong disdained to help them. By Divoranon's standards she had fulfilled her side of the trade. Reeve had to admit it was more than he thought the orthong would do. But he suspected that decoding and following the genetic instructions wouldn't be the greatest challenge. Harder by far would be persuading people to undergo the changes. Without Loon by his side to show what a hybrid might be, few would wish to intermingle with things orthong.

But that was tomorrow's problem. For now, he allowed himself to explore the land and to hope for a future.

Sometimes at night, staring at his campfire, he thought back on the best times: building the raft on the beach with Spar; the first few days on the Inland Sea, poling westward, watching Loon swim like an otter; learning to fight from Kalid; standing at the rail of the *Cleopatra* with the Tallstory River splitting under the ship's prow . . . the one night that Loon and he shared in Brecca's escape room. The best times were all he remembered, or all he chose to remember.

And whether it was the Forever Plains, the rivers, the caves, or the great valley, the world itself shaped events. Lithia carried them on its iron winds, or thwarted them, or bounded them, or pardoned them, creating their lives as surely as their own wills, and with truer aim. When you looked at where the world took you, it was, as Spar said, a thing of awe. And if you had to ask what that was . . . *Well, then, you beyond help*.

After the ninth day, Reeve finally saw his goal in the distance.

The white sails of the ship caught the bright sunlight like mirrors. He stood on a low hill, gazing down the Rift Valley at the Gandhi River, a blue highway that could take them most of the way they had to go.

Reeve hoisted the pack onto his shoulders again and started down the hillside. After a few minutes, he could see people milling on the deck of the *Cleopatra*. He thought he could make out one of them, a dark man with his hair pulled back, who stood at the prow watching Reeve. In the distance, he heard the man shout, "Reeve Calder, by the Lord of Worlds!"

Reeve quickened his pace, eager, suddenly, for the company of a friend.

EPILOGUE

Reeve knew something was wrong when he and Kalid were able to scale the rock cliffs and enter the caves without challenge. They wound their way through the tunnel, finding the holding cells empty. Graffiti carved into the passageway wall proclaimed "Reform the Pool" and "Darwin's Revenge." Something had happened here, and Reeve feared the worst. Perhaps the Somaform defenses were not as fine as they thought.

Kalid ordered his jinn to spread out and secure the place. Leaving a group to guard their exit, Reeve and Kalid proceeded into the Labs, pushing their way through debris piled at the entrance.

Still illuminated by skylights, the great atrium was in shambles. The splintered railings of the mezzanines gaped open in places, while severed cables hung from the ceiling, pointing toward the smashed placards on the floor, with the twisted faces now deformed further amid the rubble.

Kalid pulled debris off a placard and stared at the grotesque visage depicted there. "Here is a face of nightmares," he said.

"One of these could have been me if I hadn't escaped," Reeve said.

"Yet you hold no blame for Mercury Clave?" Kalid kicked at the placard with his silver-toed boot, and it slid down the pile of junk to clatter on the floor.

"They were wrong about some things. Like everybody." Reeve shrugged. "We can't be too choosy about our allies if we want to survive."

Kalid flashed a grin at him. "You are either a great leader or a very bad one."

"Let me know when you figure out which." At a distant noise, Reeve glanced up to search the grand staircase and the mezzanines. Nothing. But the sound came again, like the bellow of an ox. Several jinn sprinted to the top of the stairs to pursue the noise.

A smile tugged at Reeve's mouth. "I think I recognize that sound," he said. "Come on." He hurried up the stairs after the others, then down the corridor.

As they strode through the outer apartments, Reeve heard cursing.

"Damn you to fourteen hells!"

He gestured Kalid and the others away from a door behind which a woman's imprecations thundered. He knocked on the door. Silence greeted this. He knocked again.

Finally, a voice roared: "Oh, come the hell in!"

Reeve opened the door. Brecca was sitting up in bed, still in her nightdress, her hair loosely braided, a great number of plates and dishes piled around her, as well as an enormous mound of books.

"Ministrator," Reeve said, in mock deference.

Brecca looked at him for several moments over her reading glasses, perched on the end of her nose. "I don't suppose," she said, "in all your travels you learned how to make a decent crème brûlée?" She waved off his attempt at an answer. "Surrounded by brutes. I'd give my left tit just to find somebody who knows what a crème brûlée *is*."

She swerved her attention sideways. "Take it *away*. All of it."

Dooley scampered forward and started stacking plates with remnants of meals onto a tray. He managed to stack the tray a foot high, and then couldn't lift the thing. He was dressed in white robes and wore Gregor's flat white hat with tassel. He nodded at Reeve. "I'm glad you came back. I could use some help, especially—"

Brecca trumpeted, "*Now!* Take it now." At his look of distress, she softened her tone and smiled a mockingly sweet smile. "Please, Dooley. That's a good lad."

Turning to catch the attention of a jinn standing just outside, Reeve signaled for him to remove the tray. Behind him, Kalid entered, bowing low to Brecca.

At the sight of the pirates, she pulled the bedcovers over her chest. "Are the unwashed masses invited into my bedroom? Have I sunk that far?"

Reeve pulled a chair close to the bed and leaned back into it. "Knock it off, Brecca. I came a thousand miles to talk to you. I've also been through a bit of trouble since I saw you last, so I'm in no mood for games."

She took off her reading glasses and rubbed her eyes in profound weariness. "So terribly sorry, dear boy, for all your *suffering*." She looked about her apartment, which was in disarray, with piles of clothes and books everywhere. "And what do you suppose it's been like here? Party's over, if you didn't notice."

"I noticed."

She repositioned her arm, which up until now Reeve hadn't realized was in a sling. "It's been a nightmare. Gregor tried a power play. He botched it, naturally, but not before my Somas went a bit nuts and ransacked the place. Poor Greggy just didn't understand that he couldn't pull me down without bringing the whole kit and caboodle down, too." She shook her head. "I managed to keep them out of my office. I guess they figured if they killed me in the doorway, they'd never be able to move my body. I jammed myself in and dared them to shoot." She smiled, an awful, yellow grin. "Worked like a charm."

"Where is everybody now?"

She closed her eyes and sank back into her pillows. "Gone. All gone. Most of them dead. Gregor forced some of them to jump from the cliffs. . . . It was ghastly. I would have pushed him off myself if he hadn't performed the final sacrifice." She opened her eyes, took one look at Dooley, and shook her head. "We're all that's left." She fixed Reeve with a commanding stare. "Make him take off that goofy hat, will you?"

Reeve sighed. "Dooley, what's with the high-priest routine?"

Dooley flicked the tassel out of his face, but it swung back. "Somebody has to be the Successor, don't they? I didn't want to be it, believe me, and I'm no good at it, which even—"

Brecca growled, "Never, *never* ask him a question."

"Take off the hat, Dooley. It upsets Brecca."

Dooley's eyes bugged out. "Take it off? But . . ."

Reeve gestured at a jinn, who swiped at the thing, sending it zinging across the room.

"Where's the girl?" Brecca asked. "I don't suppose it occurred to you to bring her along?"

"Loon is in the orthong forest."

Brecca sighed hugely. "So what do I get? Ruffians and fools." At *fools* she looked directly at Dooley.

Pressing on, Reeve said: "Loon sent you a present." Digging into his backpack, he pulled out a heavy geode and placed it on the bed next to her.

She narrowed her eyes and glanced from the stone to Reeve and back again. "OK, I give up. What is it?"

Reeve grinned at Kalid. "Should I give her the long story or the short one?"

"Just give me a damn cigarette for starters." Brecca

cradled her arm and made a small grunting noise, as though she was in some pain. "Dooley won't let me smoke," she said petulantly.

Dooley seemed startled to hear his name. "No, no, it's just that there aren't any, and I've looked everywhere, but she blames me just the same!"

"I could smoke *rat dung*, Dooley. But you don't have the brains God gave a cabbage. You could figure something out—"

She stopped in amazement as Kalid came forward with a pipe sporting a nine-inch stem. It was lit. He handed it over to her with a flourish. "Madame," he said.

Brecca took the pipe with a dainty hand. "At last, a man of breeding," she said, eyeing him with an appraising stare.

"I am your servant, Kalid."

"To be sure." She took a little toke, closing her eyes and murmuring, "And I'm your goddamned grateful Brecca."

After a few moments of quiet, with Brecca smoking and the jinn withdrawing to explore, Reeve said: "The orthong gave me the geode, Brecca."

Here she raised an eyebrow.

"It contains all the directions we need to survive. To become like Loon."

She looked at him with a dark stare. "And I should believe this because . . . ?"

"Because you don't have any other damn choice. You're washed up here." He allowed himself to smile with the genuine pleasure he was feeling. "Unless you want to team up with me."

She puffed away at the pipe, regarding him. Then she said, "I'll need test subjects. Tawdry as it is."

"That would be me," Reeve said.

Kalid added, "And me," bowing again.

Brecca sucked on her teeth and summoned a light for her pipe. A jinn jumped forward to oblige. "All righty," she said. "Let's take a look." She threw off her covers with her good hand and swung her feet over the side of the bed. "You boys might want to give me a moment to put myself together."

Kalid snapped his fingers, and one of the female jinn stayed behind. "Brecca's wish is your command," Kalid said, winking at the jinn.

"I like that young man," Brecca was saying as Reeve and Kalid closed the bedroom door behind them.

After a very long time Brecca finally emerged from her quarters, wearing a rather shopworn ensemble of robes, necklaces, and gaudy earrings. She shook her good hand, rattling the bracelets. "Feels like old times." Her face slumped resignedly. "*Very* old."

She led the way to her office, the others forming a ragtag procession behind her.

When the geode lay in front of her at her desk, Brecca turned it over and over, studying it for a way to open it. "As the holy representative of Deity in the world," she muttered, "I realize I'm supposed to know how to open the damn thing. . . ." Finally she looked up at Dooley with a menacing smile. "Would you care to try, Dooley?"

Dooley stepped forward and held the rock in trembling hands. It was clear that he was afraid to fail *or* to succeed. But within moments a crack appeared, allowing him to open the geode into two halves. He shrugged. "I'm good with puzzles. It's part of my transgenic plan, sort of."

"Well done, Dooley," Reeve said as the smaller man beamed.

Inside the geode, crystalline facets hugged the concave sides, flashing with glittering pinpricks of light.

"What is it?" Brecca asked, squinting at the interior.

"I don't know," Reeve said, "but there are three more stones just like this one."

"Well," she said brightly, "I do love a mystery." She smiled a pert smile at the men gathered around. "Keep me in tobacco, gentlemen, and I'll do science until I drop." She waved her fingers at Reeve impatiently. "Let's see the rest of them."

"There's just one catch," he said.

"I can't keep the pipe?" she said darkly.

"Keep the pipe, Brecca." He waited until he was sure he had her attention. "And keep your robes. We're going to need you to be the Holy Ministrator for a while longer."

She rolled her eyes, registering her disgust.

"Folks aren't going to accept transformation from the orthong. They hate the orthong. We're going to need . . . an intermediary."

"And the religion bit?"

"It could help." He eyed her pointedly, remembering the raid on his ship. "Without the proselytizing."

"That was Gregor's doing. Used a little too much persuasion."

"From now on, everybody makes their own choice."

She snorted. "Sweetened with a little pomp and circumstance."

"Just for a little while. Until we climb back into the scientific age."

"Could be a long climb." A profound sigh escaped her lips. "I'm too old for show business."

Reeve just smiled. "New show, Brecca."

"Well then," she said. "Let's get the show on the road." Reaching for an electronic probe, she began pecking at the interior of the geode, pushing up her glasses more firmly onto the bridge of her nose.

At her side, Reeve and Kalid bent closer to peer into the lighted stone maze.

ABOUT THE AUTHOR

KAY KENYON was raised in Duluth, Minnesota. She pursued a number of interests—radio announcing, TV-radio copywriting, acting, photographic modeling, and transportation planning—before turning seriously to writing. Her debut as a science fiction novelist was *The Seeds of Time* in 1997, followed by *Leap Point* in 1998. She lives near Seattle, Washington, with her family.

KAY KENYON

THE SEEDS OF TIME

____57681-X $5.99/$7.99 Canada

LEAP POINT

____57682-8 $5.99/$7.99 Canada

And now available

THE RIFT

____57682-8 $5.99/$7.99 Canada
